JF RYA
Echo
Ryan

D0977281

SA SEP 2015
OF Scot 15
MI 1/18

VE JAN 2018
SA Mar '20

Fifty years before the war to end all wars, a boy played hide-and-seek with his friends in a pear orchard bordered by a dark forest.

Mathilde, who was "it," sat on a boulder, buried her head against her knees, and began to count to one hundred.

The boy hurried away, determined to stay hidden longer than all the others, hoping to impress Mathilde. Her lilting voice intrigued him.

Even now as she counted, her words sounded singsong. ". . . thirty-six, thirty-seven, thirty-eight, thirty-nine . . ."

Although it was strictly forbidden, the boy ran into the forest to hide. Every few yards, he looked back to make sure he could still see the pear orchard behind him. When it was nothing more than a speck in his view, he sat against a tree trunk within a cluster of pines.

From far away, he heard Mathilde's faint call, "Here I come, ready or not." The boy smiled, thinking about the moment he would waltz back to home base, triumphant. He'd have to be patient, though, for it would take time for everyone to be rooted from their hiding spots.

He pulled a book from his waistband—one of the two things he had bought that very morning from a Gypsy for a pfennig. He ran his fingers over the title embossed in the leather cover:

THE THIRTEENTH HARMONICA OF OTTO MESSENGER

He had not been able to resist the purchase, especially with such a peculiar coincidence. The title held his given name, Otto.

He opened the book and began to read.

A Witch, a Kiss, a Prophecy

ONCE, LONG BEFORE ENCHANTMENT WAS *eclipsed by doubt, an anxious and desperate king awaited the birth of his first child.*

As it was written, the king's eldest would inherit the kingdom, but only if the child was a son. If the firstborn was a daughter, the monarchy would some-day pass to the king's younger brother, his most ardent rival.

Alas, the queen delivered a girl. But the king was devious. Moments after the birth, he whisked the infant away and ordered the loyal midwife to take it deep into the forest and leave it for the animals. He forbade the midwife to speak of it ever again. Then the king told the queen and his subjects that the baby had not survived the birth.

The kindhearted midwife hiked into the woods, knowing she could never abandon the child. As she pushed through brambles and climbed over logs, she sang lullabies to the wide-eyed infant. When she stopped singing, the baby wailed. Time and again, the midwife obliged, humming and crooning until she reached her destination, a tumbledown cottage that belonged to her cousin, a selfish and lazy witch.

"Won't you take this child?" begged the midwife. "You already have goats for milk. And someday she might sweep the hearth for you."

"I suppose," said the witch. "I will call her Eins."

The midwife thought it cruel to give the baby a number instead of a name. But she knew it was a far better fate than becoming breakfast for the bears. She kissed the small bundle and whispered the one gift she could bestow—a prophecy:

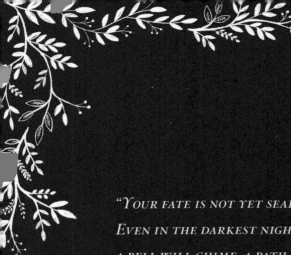

"Your fate is not yet sealed.

Even in the darkest night, a star will shine,

a bell will chime, a path will be revealed."

She spat at the ground to secure the fortune, left the child with the witch, and fled.

Within two years, the queen delivered another daughter. The king gave the same instructions to the midwife, who stole to the forest, singing all the while, for this baby, too, would be consoled only with song. At the cottage, the midwife beseeched the witch again. "Won't you take this child? Someday she might gather wood for you."

"I suppose," said the witch. "I will call her Zwei."

Another number for a name! It seemed a false start. But still, a far better fate than becoming lunch for the wolves. The midwife kissed the baby and whispered the prophecy again:

"Your fate is not yet sealed.
Even in the darkest night, a star will shine,
a bell will chime, a path will be revealed."

She spat at the ground to secure the fortune, left the child with the witch, and fled.

Two years passed and yet another baby girl was born. Three daughters, one after another! The king repeated the same deception. And the midwife dutifully traipsed into the forest, serenading all the while, for the infant's only solace, like her sisters', was a melody.

When the midwife reached the cottage, she implored the witch to keep this baby, too. "Someday she might stoke the fire for you."

"I suppose," said the witch. "I will call her Drei. Thus I can remember who was first, second, and third." She held up three fingers, ticking off one after the other. "Eins, Zwei, Drei."

Again, the midwife foresaw a bleak life ahead for the nameless child. Yet one far better than becoming dinner for the wild boar. And she would have her sisters for companions.

Eins and Zwei, who were already in service to the witch and toting small bundles of kindling, rushed to the midwife's side to meet their sister.

The midwife looked from the witch's hovel to the dirty, uncombed waifs, already cooing at the infant in her arms. She kissed the baby and whispered:

"YOUR FATE IS NOT YET SEALED.
EVEN IN THE DARKEST NIGHT, A STAR WILL SHINE,
A BELL WILL CHIME, A PATH WILL BE REVEALED."

She spat at the ground to secure the fortune, left the child with the witch, and fled.

At last, a month past a year later, the queen delivered a boy. The king happily proclaimed that his first child had been born—a son! Throughout the kingdom, church bells rang in celebration for the heir to the throne, who would one day be king.

OTTO LOOKED UP FROM THE BOOK.

He'd been so absorbed in the story that he'd forgotten the hide-and-seek game!

The forest had become cold and windy. The trees rustled and swayed. Otto shivered and looked toward the pear orchard, straining to hear his friends in the distance. Had he missed the call, *"Alle, alle auch sind frei,"* the signal for the ones who were still hiding to finally show themselves?

He stood to leave, tucking the book in his waistband. A sudden gust lifted his cap from his head. Otto spun around until he caught it. He peered between the trees, but he had lost sight of the pear orchard.

Otto wandered for hours.

He yelled, but the wind grew stronger and muffled his calls. His mind raced with all that he had heard about the woods: the dripstone caves inhabited by trolls, dangerous precipices that dropped

into witches' lairs, mud bogs that swallowed children in one giant slurp, not to mention the perils of bears, wolves, and wild boar!

He rushed from tree to tree, searching for the way out. In his panic, he tripped over a berm of twisted roots and fell. The world swirled.

Minutes or hours later—he wasn't sure—he sat up, touched his forehead, and felt a bump the size of an egg. Frightened, he covered his face with his hands and began to cry.

Between sobs, he heard a trio of voices. "This way. Come closer. We will help you."

Otto raised his head to see who spoke, but saw only the fluttering of shadows through the trees. Whimpering, he stood, taking hesitant steps until he came upon a procession of fir trees that formed an immense circle. He sidled between the trunks and found himself in a clearing.

Three young women dressed in tattered frocks

stood before him, the first a head taller than the second, who was a head taller than the third. They all talked at once. "At long last a visitor! Hello, boy. You poor thing. You must be weary. Oh, dear, you have hurt your head. Sit down and rest."

Slowly, Otto sat on a tree stump. "Who . . . who are you?"

"Do not be frightened. You are safe with us. I am Eins," said the tallest. "And these are my sisters, Zwei and Drei."

Otto pulled out the book and stared at it. "But you couldn't be. Those are the very characters from this story."

"It must be *our* story, then!" said Eins.

"Perchance, does it have a happily-ever-after?" asked Zwei, wringing her hands.

Drei pointed at the book. "Might you read to us so we may know our providence?"

The three sisters quickly sat in a huddle around him and leaned forward, their eyes eager.

Otto rubbed his brow, feeling light-headed. He looked at Eins, Zwei, and Drei, who seemed hungry for the telling. If the story was true, they had been torn from their mother's arms. What must it have been like to never know her? His heart ached at the idea of never seeing his own mother again.

"Please?" asked Zwei. "Perhaps we can help one another."

Otto thought it all strange, but he did feel safe within the tree circle. The sisters seemed harmless. And they appeared to be the only ones who might guide him out of the forest.

He turned back to the beginning of the book and read the first chapter again, this time out loud. He glanced up. Eins, Zwei, and Drei held one another's hands, their faces rapt.

Otto cleared his throat and continued.

A Secret, a Spell, a Final Deed

EINS, ZWEI, AND DREI GREW UP IN THE far-off cottage in the woods.

The witch told them they were foundlings, and reminded them every day of how grateful they should be for her generosity.

But it wasn't easy to be grateful.

The cottage was dank and ramshackle; the witch never replaced a thatch. She made the three sisters wear rags. And she did not love them. Heavens no! She was as indifferent to them as she was to a stone in a stream. But the witch found them useful because from dawn to dusk, they swept and toted and washed and cooked.

Imagine how spoiled the witch had become!

The sisters had two consolations in their lives of drudgery. The first was singing. They had three distinct voices: the first, that of birdsong; the second, a brook trickling over smooth stones; and the third, the yodel of the wind through hollow logs. When they sang, their voices blended so magically that the entire forest, from trolls to fairies, stopped to listen and marvel at their gifts. Even the witch recognized their talent, but at the same time she was jealous. When she ordered them about, she snidely called them names of musical instruments, her favorite being "my little piccolos."

The sisters' other solace was one another. Every night as they lay on their pallets of straw and looked at the night sky through the holes in the roof, Eins repeated the midwife's prophecy as if it were a prayer:

"YOUR FATE IS NOT YET SEALED.

EVEN IN THE DARKEST NIGHT, A STAR WILL SHINE,

A BELL WILL CHIME, A PATH WILL BE REVEALED."

Then each in turn they sang about the little birds that so easily took wing from the forest. For Eins, Zwei, and Drei had not given up the hope that they, too, might someday leave. They dreamed of a safe and cozy home and a family who loved them and called them by name.

The years passed. The king's brother, his rival, died young. All of the king's manipulations had been for naught, but still he did not make known the horrible secret of abandoning his three daughters in the forest. As his son came of age, the misguided king took ill and relinquished the throne. The kingdom hastened to prepare for the son's lavish coronation. But the king did not live to see it.

Every subject was invited to the festivities at the

castle and offered an audience with the newly crowned king. When it was the midwife's turn to approach the throne in the great hall, she realized there was no reason to keep silent any longer. She confided the story to the monarch and his mother, who were overcome with joy.

Without ado, the young king sent the midwife to find his sisters.

Once again, the midwife traveled deep into the forest to the cottage.

When Eins saw the midwife approaching, she ran to her and asked, "Have you brought us another sister?"

The midwife smiled. "Oh, child. I have brought you so much more."

Upon hearing the news of their family, Eins, Zwei, and Drei hugged one another and cried from happiness. The dreams they carried in their hearts had come true. They had a home! A family! And they were princesses!

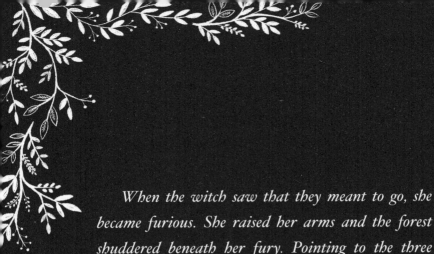

When the witch saw that they meant to go, she became furious. She raised her arms and the forest shuddered beneath her fury. Pointing to the three sisters, she yelled, "Ungratefuls! You would leave me after all I've done for you? After I saved your lives? Where would you be without me? Dead, that's where! If freedom is what you want, your choice comes with a price. See how you like my burden, my little piccolos."

The witch waved her arms and incanted:

"A MESSENGER BROUGHT YOU ABOUT.
ONE-AND-THE-SAME MUST BRING YOU OUT.
YOU MAY NOT LEAVE IN EARTHLY FORM.
YOUR SPIRITS TO A WOODWIND BORN.
YOU SAVE A SOUL FROM DEATH'S DARK DOOR,
OR HERE YOU'LL LANGUISH, EVERMORE."

In a rush of earsplitting wind, the witch, the midwife, the cottage, and every belonging from table to teacup swirled toward the clouds, disappearing into another time and place.

When the air quelled, Eins, Zwei, and Drei found themselves with only the clothes on their backs, confined in a large clearing of stones and stumps, surrounded by a circle of trees, in a world where the sun rose and set, yet time did not pass.

OTTO RAISED HIS EYES FROM THE BOOK'S PAGE, looking from sister to sister to sister.

Eins wiped a tear from her cheek. "It is all true."

"What happens to us next?" asked Zwei. "Oh, you must read on!"

"Do we reunite with our mother? Or meet our brother?" asked Drei.

Otto turned the page.

The leaves were blank.

He flipped through to the end of the book, but it was more of the same—parchment with no words. "It is unfinished," he said. "There is no middle or ending."

"Because we have not yet experienced anything after that page in the book," said Eins. "We've been here, bound forever as the witch's useless baubles."

"What does the spell mean?" asked Otto.

"She called us her 'little piccolos,'" said Zwei. "So, to make it more difficult to break the spell,

our spirits may be carried from the tree circle only inside a woodwind. By a messenger."

Otto looked at the sisters, now despondent. "If I could get home, *I* could help you," he offered.

"Do you have a woodwind?" asked Eins.

Zwei leaned closer. "A bassoon?"

"Or an oboe, perhaps?" asked Drei.

Otto shook his head. "I only brought one other thing." He began to unroll his sleeve, which had been folded to the elbow. "This morning, when I bought the book, the Gypsy insisted I take this, too, and did not ask for an extra pfennig."

He held up a harmonica.

The eyes of the three sisters brightened.

Eins gasped, "A mouth harp!"

Zwei stood and came closer. "If you will allow us to play it, we will help you find the way home."

Drei touched his arm. "But you must promise to pass along the mouth harp to another, when the time is right. For our journey to save a soul on the brink of death cannot begin until you do."

Eins nodded. "It is our only hope of ever escaping the spell."

"I promise," said Otto, for he wanted to go home. "But how will I know when, or to whom . . ."

The three sisters surrounded him and whispered, "You will know."

Otto handed the harmonica to Eins.

She played a short melody. Taking the instrument from her lips, she passed it to her sister.

Zwei played a different tune. As she performed, Otto heard both songs at the same time. Zwei passed the harmonica to Drei, who played yet another song.

"That isn't possible," said Otto. "I hear three melodies at once."

Satisfied and in harmony, the sisters said, "It is possible."

The sky had deepened. Night loomed.

Otto whispered, "How will I find my way? I'm afraid of the dark."

Eins stood tall and said:

"Your fate is not yet sealed.

Even in the darkest night, a star will shine,

a bell will chime, a path will be revealed."

Drei handed him the small instrument.

Otto whimpered, "But it's only a harmonica."

"Oh, it is much more!" said Eins. "When you play it, you breathe in and out, just as you would to keep your body alive. Have you ever considered that one person might play the mouth harp and pass along her strength and vision and knowledge?"

"So that the next musician who plays it might feel the same?" said Zwei. "It is true. When you play, you will *see* and find your way. You will have the fortitude to carry on."

Drei nodded. "And you will be forever joined to us, to all who have played the harp, and to all who *will* play it, by the silken thread of destiny."

Otto was overwhelmed by all of their strange suggestions. Forever joined by the silken thread of destiny? Their talking confounded him. His head ached, and he felt woozy. "I'm ever so tired. I want to go home."

"And so you will," said Eins.

"Slumber now," said Zwei.

"Sweet dreams," whispered Drei, her voice hypnotic.

He swooned and dropped to the pine needles.

When Otto woke, the sun blazed overhead.

He sat up and found himself in a thicket at the side of a narrow path. In his hand, he still clutched

the harmonica, but the book was nowhere to be found. Nor were Eins, Zwei, and Drei.

Had they kept the book, brought him to this spot, and left him?

Was the path the way home?

All day, he stumbled along the narrow trail, overgrown with wild geranium and thistle, until the sun disappeared behind the trees. The knot on his head throbbed. Darkness crept in. Weak and frightened, he began to give up hope, until he remembered the harmonica. He lifted it to his lips and played a simple tune.

The unusual tone of the instrument filled him with a peculiar and euphoric well-being. He felt . . . less alone. As he walked, he whispered:

"YOUR FATE IS NOT YET SEALED.

EVEN IN THE DARKEST NIGHT, A STAR WILL SHINE,

A BELL WILL CHIME, A PATH WILL BE REVEALED."

Overhead, the tree branches slowly parted. Stars shone down, lighting the way. He put one foot in front of the other. *Had* the sisters infused the harmonica with the strength to carry on? *Were* they with him, in spirit?

He thought he heard voices and stopped.

Was it Eins, Zwei, and Drei? Or wolves and bears and wild boar? Or just the forest playing tricks with his mind?

His heart raced.

Otto took a giant breath and blew hard into the harmonica. The chord pierced the night. The forest grew silent, as if the world stood still.

Otto heard voices again, calling . . . calling . . .

His name!

Someone was calling his name!

In the distance, he saw spots of light, bobbing like fireflies. He pushed forward, stumbling into the pear orchard, and found it crowded with towns-people, lanterns held high, combing the edge of the woods.

"Here! I'm here!" he yelled.

A song rang out. "He's found! He's found!"

Two men ran to him, clasped their arms together to make a sling, scooped him up, and carried him toward the others.

His father appeared and Otto collapsed into his arms. People cheered and children crowded around, patting him on the back. Mathilde was there, and her eyes filled at the sight of him. Otto was so shaken he could not talk. He could only bury his face in his father's chest and cry.

Later, at home, he whispered the entire story to his mother and father, beginning with the book and the harmonica he had bought from the Gypsy.

"Eins, Zwei, and Drei saved me. They guided me out of the forest."

His parents looked at each other and raised their eyebrows. "There now," said his mother. "There have been no Gypsies passing through our village of late. You must have found the harmonica in the forest, left by another mischievous child. And you were not gone overnight. You have only been missing since the morning. Rest now, for you have a bad bump on your head."

He fell asleep with the harmonica cradled in his hand.

After Otto recovered, he carried the harmonica wherever he went. He told his friends and anyone else who would listen about Eins, Zwei, and Drei. After several weeks, people became weary of the telling, and began to laugh and dismiss him.

Only Mathilde never tired of hearing the mysterious tale.

Concerned, his father sat him down. "People are beginning to think you are affected. You were lost and you saved yourself by signaling with that harmonica. That is all. I do not want to hear another word about a Gypsy, a book, imaginary sisters, or a magic harmonica!"

To please his parents, Otto kept the harmonica out of sight and never carried it from his house again. He stopped mentioning the three sisters and their story. Soon, life with his family went back to how it had been before he was lost in the forest.

But whenever he felt afraid, he secretly took the harmonica from its hiding spot, played a song, and escaped into its reverie, feeling the familiar sense of happiness and comfort, that peculiar and euphoric well-being. Each time, every detail of the story in the book and the events in the forest flooded back to him: the king's trickery, the mid-wife's journey, the witch's spell, his encounter with Eins, Zwei, and Drei, and his promise to them.

He never forgot that he'd been entrusted with their future. Or that the harmonica carried their deepest hopes—to be free, to be loved, and to belong somewhere beyond a tree circle—so that the rest of their story might someday be written.

He never forgot that their journey to save a soul at the moment of death would not begin until he sent the harmonica out into the world . . . when the time was right.

He was the messenger.

E C

A NOVEL BY

PAM

DECORATION

SCHOLASTI

H O

MUÑOZ RYAN

Y DINARA MIRTALIPOVA

RESS
NEW YORK

ONE

OCTOBER 1933

TROSSINGEN, BADEN-WÜRTTEMBERG

GERMANY

Brahms' Lullaby

music by Johannes Brahms

lyrics from *Des Knaben Wunderhorn*

5 5 6   5   5   6
Lul-la-by, and good night,

5   6   7 -7 -6 6
with pink ro-ses bed-ight,

-4   5 -5 -4 -4   5 -5
With lil-ies o'-er spr-ead,

-4 -5 -7 -6   6 -7 7
is my ba-by's wee b-ed.

4   4   7   -6   -5 6
Lay thee down now and rest,

5   4   -5   6 -6   6
may thy slum-ber be blessed!

4   4   7   -6   -5 6
Lay thee down now and rest,

5   4   -5   6 -4   4
may thy slum-ber be blessed!

I

In a town between the Black Forest and the Swabian Alps, Friedrich Schmidt stood on the threshold of his half-timbered house, pretending to be brave.

From his vantage, he looked across the rooftops of Trossingen toward the castle-like factory looming above the town. Within its walls, a smokestack rose higher than the tallest gable and puffed a white cloud, a beacon against the gray sky.

Father stood behind him in the doorway. "Son, you know the way. We've walked it hundreds of times. Remember, you have as much right to be on the street as the next person. Uncle Gunter will be waiting for you at the front gates."

Friedrich nodded and stood taller. "Don't worry, Father, I can do it." He *wanted* to believe his own words: that something as simple as walking to work by himself would be easy, that he wouldn't need Father's hawk-like presence, shielding him from the frightened, or steering him around the gawkers. Friedrich took a few steps toward the street, then turned to wave.

Father's hair billowed from his head in a gray halo, giving him a wild look. It suited him. He raised his hand in return and smiled at Friedrich, but it wasn't his usual jovial smile; it was halfhearted and worried. Were those tears in his eyes?

Friedrich went back and pulled him into a hug, inhaling his persistent smell of bow rosin and anise lozenges. "I'll be *fine*, Father. It's your first day of retirement and you should enjoy it. Will you join the pigeon feeders?"

Father laughed, holding Friedrich at arm's length. "Heavens no! Do I look like I'm ready for the park bench?"

Friedrich shook his head, happy he'd lightened the mood. "What will you do with your time? I hope you'll think about performing again." Long ago, Father had played cello for the Berlin Philharmonic. But he set aside that life when he married and had children, taking a more practical job at the factory. Shortly after Friedrich was born, Mother died and Father was left to raise him and his sister, Elisabeth, alone.

"I won't likely perform with an orchestra," said Father. "But don't you worry. I'll have plenty to keep me busy—my books, my cello students, concerts. And I intend to start a chamber music ensemble."

"Father, you have the energy of three men."

"That is a good thing, with your sister coming home today. Elisabeth will fill our house with directives, and I'll need stamina for that, to be sure. I intend to convince her to take up the piano again, so we can resume our Friday get-togethers, beginning tonight. I miss them."

Friedrich missed those evenings, too. For as long as he could remember, every Friday after dinner, Uncle Gunter, Father's younger brother, came for dessert and brought his accordion. Father played cello, Friedrich harmonica, though in truth, cello was his instrument, too. And Elisabeth played piano. Father and Elisabeth would argue about everything from the choice of songs to the order in which they were played. Friedrich had given up trying to determine whether Elisabeth and Father were opposites in nature or simply alike. Still, those were his happiest memories: the polkas, the folk songs, the spontaneous singing and laughing, even the bickering.

Now Elisabeth would be home from nursing school for three whole months! He couldn't wait for their late-night talks. Or passing a novel back and forth and taking turns reading it out loud. And their Sunday afternoon card games of Binokel around the kitchen table with Father and Uncle Gunter. The past year hadn't been the same without Elisabeth's mothering and bossing and cooking. His mouth watered just thinking about her cooking.

"Do you think she missed us as much as we missed her?" asked Friedrich.

Father smiled. "How could she not?" He pointed Friedrich toward the street and patted his back. "Have a good day at work, son. And don't forget to—"

"I know, Father. Look *up*."

2

When Friedrich was around the corner, he did the opposite.

He shoved his hands into his pockets, hunched his shoulders, and tilted his right cheek toward the ground. Father would never have tolerated this posture. But it made Friedrich feel less conspicuous, even if he was more vulnerable to things in his path. Besides, he often found a lost pfennig while looking down. Soon enough, he stumbled over a bundle of newspapers that had been tossed toward a storefront. He braced himself on the building and read the headline: PARLIAMENT PASSES LAW. Friedrich groaned. Another law for Father to criticize.

Since Friedrich didn't attend regular school, Father insisted they read the newspaper together every night as part of his studies. He could not count the times in recent months that Father had tossed the paper aside, disgusted with the new chancellor, Adolf

Hitler, and his Nazi Party. Father had been a member of the German Freethinkers League until a few months ago, when Hitler outlawed the organization.

Just last night, after reading yet another article, Father had paced the kitchen and ranted, "Is there no room in this country for more than one way of thinking? Hitler bullies the parliament to make laws on whims. Hitler takes away all civil rights and gives his storm troopers the freedom to question anyone for any reason. Hitler wants to cleanse the population for a pure German race!"

What did it all mean? What was a pure German race? Clear-skinned and perfect? Friedrich touched his face and felt his stomach tighten with worry, especially since he was neither.

He ran his fingers through his hair, which did him no service. It was thick, blond, and tightly curled. He could feel it frizzing in the damp air, just like Father's. No matter how long he let it grow, it stuck out instead of down. If only he had straight hair, he could let it drape across his cheek. But there was no hiding his blotchy birthmark. It was as if an imaginary line had been drawn down the middle of his face and neck. And on one side, his skin was like everyone else's, but on the other, a painter had dabbed shades of purple, red, and brown, turning his cheek into a mottled plum. He knew he looked horrid. How could he blame people for staring or being frightened?

At the next corner, he turned down the thoroughfare. When he reached the music conservatory, he could hear someone practicing the piano in an upper story. Beethoven's "Für Elise." For *this* he stopped and lifted his head, becoming lost in the music.

Unconsciously, his hand rose and bounced to the time of the song. Friedrich smiled as he pretended the musician was following his direction. He closed his eyes and imagined the notes sprinkling down and washing his face clean.

A car horn startled him.

He shoved his hands into his pockets, lowered his head, and resumed walking. He kicked at a rock in his path, feeling the familiar mix of hope and dread. His audition at the conservatory, for which he'd been preparing for as long as he had memory, was just after the New Year. What if he did not perform well? Yet, which would be worse? To be accepted or refused? A weight pressed on his heart. How could he want something and fear it so much at the same time?

He took a deep breath and kept walking. As he approached the school yard, he gave himself his usual lecture. *Don't look. Don't pay attention.* He tried to bolster himself with the things Father always said: *One foot in front of the other. Keep moving forward. Ignore the ignorant.* But without Father at his side, his heart pounded and his breathing quickened. He faltered and glanced up.

A group of boys huddled together on the steps, pointing at him, snickering and making faces in mock horror. He shaded his face with his hand, hung his head, and took longer strides, weaving around people, until he was running.

"Friedrich!"

He almost fell over Uncle Gunter.

"Good morning, nephew!" He put an arm around Friedrich's shoulder and drew him close.

Friedrich tried to catch his breath. "Good . . . morn . . . ing."

"Aren't you happy to see me? Because I am happy to see you. Come!" He guided Friedrich through the factory gates. "I'm moving over to your father's table today. We'll be side by side. Is that agreeable?" Uncle Gunter was his usual jovial self and it steadied Friedrich.

"Of course," he said. "It is what I'd hoped."

As he and Uncle Gunter crossed the cobblestone square, Friedrich could feel his heart and breathing calm. The towering buildings, the stone paths, and the arched passageways all meant safety. And the fat water tower—a stodgy obelisk standing sentry over the entire enclave—was his guardian in disguise.

Part of him wished he could stay and work at the factory forever.

The other part of him wished his life had taken a different course—that he'd been a boy who went to real school, had friends his own age and an ordinary, unremarkable face.

But Fate had stepped in his path. And when he was only eight years old, he became the youngest and smallest apprentice in the biggest harmonica factory in the world.

3

On that morning four years ago, Friedrich had followed Elisabeth into the primary play yard, as he had every other school day.

As usual, she steered him to a bench away from the others. He knew what he was supposed to do. Stay there and sit still.

But the night before, Father had taken him to the ballet to hear the orchestra. And the music had stayed with him as it always did—every movement, every refrain of Tchaikovsky's *Sleeping Beauty* still playing in his head, especially the waltz.

One, two, three. One, two, three. One, two, three . . .

Friedrich had hummed it all the way to school and no amount of shushing from Elisabeth could make him stop. While she checked his lunch and pulled his sweater tighter around him, he raised his arms, waving them to conduct an imaginary orchestra.

Elisabeth took both of his hands in hers. Eyes pleading, she said, "Friedrich, please. Don't make it more difficult for yourself. You already have enough problems."

"I hear music," he said.

"And I hear the names the others will call you if you continue to wave at the sky. Do you want the boys to throw rocks at you again?"

He shook his head and looked up at her. "'lisbeth, they call me Monster Boy."

"I know," she said, stroking his hair. "Don't listen to them. What do I always say?"

"They're not my family. And my family tells me the truth."

"That's right. And I say you are a talented musician. And someday you *will* be a conductor. But for now, you must only practice at home. Remember the trick I taught you?"

Friedrich nodded. "If I think I might wave my arms at school, stuff my hands under my legs and sit on them."

"Right," said Elisabeth. "Now, stay here until the teacher rings the bell. I have to go, or I'll be late for class." She kissed his cheek.

Friedrich watched her walk toward the secondary school, her blond curls bouncing behind her.

He tucked his hands beneath his legs. But the music from the concert pestered him until he couldn't resist any longer. He freed his hands and swished an imaginary baton. Closing his eyes, he escaped into the rhythmic waltz.

One, two, three. One, two, three. One, two, three . . .

He didn't realize he was creating a spectacle.

Or that all the children in the school yard were watching him.

He was so caught up in the music that he never heard the laughing or the taunting.

Or the boys running up behind him.

Until it was too late.

The next morning before the first bell, Father marched into the headmaster's office with Friedrich limping alongside him.

"I want you to see what your students did

to my son yesterday: a lip so swollen he can barely talk, a cut on his forehead that had to be stitched, and a broken wrist. He'll wear the sling for weeks."

The headmaster leaned back in his desk chair, his hands resting on his belly. "Mr. Schmidt, the incident was nothing more than boys being boys, a little playground bullying. Friedrich needs to toughen. Skirmishes are the best thing for him if he's to learn to defend himself. We try to keep an eye on these things, but given his disfigurement . . ."

Father's voice tightened. "It is only a *birthmark*."

"If you wish. But given this *imperfection*, and with all that waving of his hands at the sky . . ." He tilted his head at Father. "You must admit, it's odd. His strangeness bothers some of the others. Frightens them." The headmaster raised one eyebrow. "And he says he hears things."

Father's cheeks puffed and he looked as if he might explode. "He hears *music*. He's just a little boy pretending to conduct an orchestra! I've taken him to concerts since he was three, after which he can remember the entire score. Can any of your other students do the same? Do none of them ever pretend?"

The headmaster's smile tightened. "Of course. But the hand waving isn't the *only* issue. His teacher has complained that he finishes his mathematics long before the others and that he whispers to the person in the desk next to him."

Father looked at him and Friedrich nodded.

"Well, if he finishes before all the others," said Father, "perhaps the teacher could give him some extra work, or allow him to read. Wouldn't that occupy him and prevent him from talking to others?"

"I don't think you understand," said the headmaster, turning his gaze to Friedrich. "Can you tell us who sits in the desk next to you?"

With a fat lip, he could only mumble the name. "Hansel."

The headmaster turned to Father and smirked. "Mr. Schmidt, *no one* sits in the desk next to him. It is empty. So who, exactly, is this Hansel?"

Father knew. It was the same person Friedrich always pretended to talk to at home—the clever Hansel from the fairy tale "Hansel and Gretel," who, along with his sister, survived the witch and escaped from the dark and dangerous woods. Hansel, his friend, whose courage Friedrich wished he had.

"He has an imagination!" yelled Father.

"Your son is not usual and is quite possibly deficient," said the headmaster.

"You are right about one thing," said Father. "He is not usual. But look at his exam marks and you'll see he's not deficient. I'm not here to argue that point, though. I'm here to *tell* you that from now on, I will teach him. And at the end of the year, *you* will procure the exams and a teacher to administer them."

The headmaster's smile disappeared. "That is not acceptable."

Father pounded his fist on the headmaster's desk. "What your students did to my son is *not acceptable*! And I'm prepared to go to your superiors."

The headmaster tensed. He lifted a file from

his desk and opened it. "Well then, if that's how you wish to proceed, I see that his physician is Dr. Braun. I am sending him a letter, asking him to recommend the boy for psychiatric evaluation. I suspect there is more wrong with him than what we've discussed. There is a place for children like him. The Home for Unfortunates."

"That's an asylum!" said Father.

Friedrich clutched Father's side. Elisabeth had told him about such places—where they put lunatics and took away all their clothes except their undergarments. Could he really be sent there for conducting an imaginary orchestra and talking to a make-believe friend? His head throbbed.

Father's voice shook. "All this because he's not like the others? I am done being reasonable." He put an arm around Friedrich, ushering him from the office and down the hallway, now crowded with children.

Friedrich saw the stares and heard the remarks.

"Monster Boy is leaving . . . moron . . . belongs in a zoo . . ."

What was to become of him? Elisabeth went to school all day. Father worked at the factory. Would Father leave him home alone or put him away?

Outside, on the front steps, he caught Father's sleeve and tugged.

Father stopped and leaned down.

Friedrich cupped his hand over Father's ear and whispered, "Where will I go, Father, if I'm too dreadful for school?"

Father's eyes filled with tears. He kissed him on the forehead. "Don't worry. I will take care of this. Come. We must stop at the factory so I might . . . tell them why I did not come to work today."

Friedrich sat outside a windowed office while Father spoke to several white-coated supervisors. He couldn't hear what Father said, but he could see his animated gestures and his pleading expressions. Afterward, Father shook hands with each of the men. One blotted his eyes with a handkerchief.

The door opened and the supervisors filed out. The one with the handkerchief leaned down and put a hand on Friedrich's shoulder. "My name is Ernst. Your father is going to take you home to rest now. But starting tomorrow, *this* is where you will come. Welcome to the firm." He shook Friedrich's uninjured hand.

Friedrich didn't know what it meant. But he whispered, "Yes, sir."

As they walked home, Father explained. "I will oversee your schoolwork from now on. Every morning during the week, you will apprentice at the factory to learn about harmonica making. In the afternoons, you'll complete the assignments I give you at a table next to my workstation. And you'll continue your music lessons with me on weekends. Do you understand?"

Friedrich's wounds stung and his head ached. He didn't answer.

Father stopped and knelt in front of him. "Friedrich, do you understand? Where I go, you will go."

He looked at Father, unbelieving. He was not going to an asylum? Or back to school? He would no longer have to guess at the safest route to his classroom? Or dodge the food thrown at him at lunchtime? He would not have to determine which corner of the play yard would provide the most protection? He smiled, tears rolling down his cheeks.

Father carefully lifted Friedrich into his arms and carried him.

On the street, a car honked three times.

The rhythm of Tchaikovsky's waltz took hold again. Looking back across Father's shoulder, he lifted an imaginary baton with his good arm and conducted.

When the wind brushed his face, Friedrich felt a lightness—a weightlessness—as if, bit by bit, the dread and worry that always burdened him were taking flight.

Had Father not been holding him, he too might have floated away on the wind, like a dandelion's white-seeded parachutes.

4

The energy inside the factory was palpable.

Machinery clacked and wheezed. Wheels and cogs married. As Friedrich and Uncle Gunter entered the massive hall—part warehouse and part assembly-room floor—Friedrich listened to the comforting whir of saws interrupted by the staccato sound of metal being punched. Doors to the testing rooms opened and closed, and for the briefest moments, he heard the compressors sigh and hiss as air was pumped through the harmonicas, and notes slid up and down the scale. He searched for the giant A-frame ladder that migrated around the floor, and pictured himself standing on the top rung, two stories high, directing the percussive symphony.

At his worktable, he put on his apron and glanced at the paper tacked to the wall.

"What is that?" asked Uncle Gunter.

"New vocabulary words from Mrs. Steinweg," said Friedrich. "Every Friday she posts the words; the following Thursday she gives me an exam."

Mr. Karl from Accounting approached.

Friedrich reached into his pocket, pulled out his folded mathematics homework, smoothed it open, and handed it to him.

Mr. Karl smiled. "Stop by after lunch, Friedrich, and we'll review it." He waved and walked away.

On his heels, Anselm, a new young clerk, appeared with a box of harmonicas for Friedrich's table. "Mr. Eichmann from the third floor asked me to remind you to come to his office this afternoon to start reading *The Odyssey*. Must be nice to have private tutors, eh, Friedrich? And during work hours, too."

Friedrich avoided his eyes. What was Anselm's issue with him? They'd only exchanged a few pleasantries since he had started at the factory, but he seemed to enjoy goading Friedrich. "It's not during my work hours. I'm only paid for mornings."

"But Mr. Eichmann is paid all day. Quite the

disruption to his work when everyone should be rallying together for the good of Germany and the common man. Don't you agree?"

"I read to him *while* he works," said Friedrich. "And it's all been approved by the supervisors."

"Whatever you say, Friedrich," said Anselm. "You're some kind of favorite around here, aren't you? You know, the new Germany doesn't like favorites. We should all be of one mind and focus, for the fatherland, for Hitler's family, so we can be led out of darkness." He swaggered away, whistling.

Uncle Gunter stepped closer, keeping his voice low. "Ignore him. Let him talk, but keep your feelings to yourself. He's an arrogant Hitlerite. I don't care for this new young breed that worships Hitler like a god."

"Nor does Father," said Friedrich.

"As we all well know." Uncle Gunter smiled. "Anselm's right about one thing, nephew. You *are* a favorite. Apparently, Mr. Adler and Mr. Engel in Shipping have been arguing about which of them is the most suited to teach you Secondary History.

They have all adopted you, Friedrich. Don't let *any-one* make you feel bad about that." Uncle Gunter waved a finger at him and winked. "But don't ever forget your real family. Who taught you to ride a bicycle?"

"You."

"And to play the harmonica?"

"You."

"And who started the factory harmonica club on your behalf?"

Friedrich laughed. "I remember. You have nothing to worry about, Uncle." He watched him hang his tools above the next table, using a crate as a step stool. Uncle Gunter was shorter and much rounder than Father. "You're coming for dessert tonight, I hope?"

Uncle Gunter raised an eyebrow. "I wouldn't miss one of Elisabeth's strudels. How do you think my fingers got as plump as sausages?"

Friedrich turned to his work, smiling. His most recent job was to inspect each instrument for flaws. If the harmonica was in perfect order, he polished it and placed it into a slim cardboard box with a lid. He held one of the mouth harps in the palm of his hand and examined it.

How simple an instrument, yet with such capacity. He studied the shiny metal cover plates and the black-painted pear wood. He turned the harmonica over and ran his thumb across the symmetrical holes. What an improbable journey from pear tree to lumberyard to assembly-room floor to become something that could make music.

Every few hours a clerk came by to pick up Friedrich's harmonicas and off they went to be put into narrow cases of a dozen. The cases were packed in cartons, the cartons packed in crates, and the crates loaded onto a horse-drawn cart, which hauled them to an electric train. Then they were transferred to cars behind a steam engine, which chugged to the seaport of Bremerhaven, and off-loaded onto a cargo ship. This model—the Marine Band—was destined for a port in the United States of America.

Friedrich shined the harmonica in his hand and fitted it into its box, whispering his wish for happy travels: *"Gute Reise."*

His supervisor, Ernst, who was also one of the factory owners, approached with his hands in the pockets of the long white coat he wore over his suit when he was on the factory floor. "That is what I have always admired about the Schmidt family. You treat each mouth harp like a friend."

"Good morning, sir," said Friedrich.

"We hope this arrangement works for you, Friedrich." He nodded to Uncle Gunter. "Your uncle is one of the best craftsmen in the company. We thought it would make sense for you to be under his wing now that Martin has retired."

"Thank you," said Friedrich, picking up another harmonica.

"I wonder how long it will last." Ernst nodded toward the instrument.

"Sir?"

"The star. It looks like the Star of David. And with Hitler's appointment as chancellor, the anti-Jewish sentiment is growing. There is already talk of removing it. I hate to see it go."

Friedrich tilted the harmonica to get a clear

look at the company's emblem—two hands on either side of a circle around a six-pointed star.

He'd heard all the theories about the star: that the six points represented the original owner, Matthias Hohner, and his five sons; that the star was a replica of the ones carved on the church doors; that it was a leftover symbol from one of the harmonica companies Hohner had purchased over the years, like Messner or Weiss. Had one of them been Jewish? *Was* it a Star of David?

Ernst sighed. "But it will be better for business, I suppose, if it is no longer there. We can't risk offending customers, no matter where they are in the world. Everyone has an opinion about the Jews. And business being what it is . . ."

Uncle Gunter frowned. "Yes, it will probably be a casualty of politics, like so many things these days."

Ernst blushed.

Uncle Gunter reached out and put a hand on Ernst's arm. "Sir, please don't misunderstand. There are many who are grateful to you for what you have done. We need our jobs."

"Thank you." Ernst smiled politely. "Well then, Gunter, Friedrich . . . carry on."

After he left, Friedrich asked, "Were some people to lose their jobs?"

Uncle Gunter leaned closer and spoke in a whisper. "Ernst was visited by one of Hitler's officers. He was forced to officially join the Nazi Party if he wished the factory to stay in business. I've known him for years. He is not a Nazi."

"What would happen if he didn't join?" asked Friedrich.

"For openly opposing Hitler's politics? He'd be sent to Dachau. It's full of opponents of Hitler. They call it a 'work and reeducation camp.' But it's a hard-labor prison. There's a sign over the gate that says, *Work Will Set You Free*. It should say, *Work Will Set You Six Feet Under the Ground*. But what would you do if you were him?" Uncle Gunter turned to his table, shaking his head.

Friedrich resumed his work. What *would* he do? Would he become a Nazi, going against his own and his father's belief that there was more than one way of thinking in this world, in order to save the jobs of thousands of workers? Would he become a Nazi to avoid prison and possibly his own death? He'd never thought of such circumstances. Regret and guilt jabbed at him as he realized he would probably do exactly what Ernst had done.

As Friedrich inspected and polished any number of harmonicas, he became preoccupied with the stars emblazoned on the cover plates and their inevitable demise.

"Safe travels to you as well," he whispered.

5

"Won't you join me and the men?" asked Uncle Gunter when the lunch whistle blew.

Friedrich hurried to take off his apron and grab his lunch pail. "No, thanks, Uncle. I have lunch mates."

Uncle Gunter shook his head, waving him off. "Your father told me about them. Go on, then. But only if I might meet them someday. Or better yet, eat them for dinner."

Friedrich grinned and ran from the factory, knowing Uncle Gunter only teased. He skirted around buildings and across a large grassy field to the edge of a pond. Beyond, a dense wood loomed.

Friedrich slipped through the shrubbery to his favorite spot, where a felled tree lay on its side. He sat down and three red-necked grebes waddled out of the forest, rushing toward him. Friedrich tossed bits of bread to his greedy friends.

As he ate, a wind picked up. Dark clouds drifted overhead, obscuring the sun. The grebes' high-pitched quacking punctuated the air.

"Ladies, are you ready to be my audience? Please use your best concert manners," said Friedrich. The grebes ignored him, chirruping and pecking at the crumbs.

The pines rustled in a long, drawn-out *swoosh*. From the nearby lumberyard, he heard the pinging of a hammer on metal.

Quack, chirrup
swoosh, swoosh, swoosh
ping, ping, ping, ping, ping, ping, ping

Within the rhythms, Friedrich heard . . . Brahms' Lullaby. He hummed the melody. He picked up a stick, closed his eyes, and lifted his arms. He pictured the orchestra. His right hand kept the tempo with the baton. His left cued the instruments, bouncing on an invisible plane to bring in the strings, waving in the woodwinds, flicking his wrist to usher in the brass, pointing to the harp.

He opened his eyes and realized the music he heard was not only in his mind. Someone was playing a harmonica. The notes were clear, the composition complex. When he slowed the tempo, the music slowed, too. When he increased, it quickened.

A musician was following his direction! But from where?

He looked around. There was no one about. He dropped his arms, yet the music continued. The lilt was slow, resonant, and haunting. One moment the notes sounded as if they came from a flute. The next, a clarinet. In the low notes, he could hear the cello.

Friedrich had never heard playing like this before. He listened, mesmerized, his eyes and ears searching to determine the origin of the sound. They settled on an open window on the uppermost floor of the warehouse across the field. He sucked in his breath—*the graveyard.*

Friedrich had never been there. But he'd heard all the tales: *It's where machines go to die. Strange things happen in the shadows. There are glimmers and apparitions. Some people go up and never come down.*

Friedrich hesitated. But the song was so compelling, so curious. How frightening could it be? Besides, they were only rumors. He gathered his lunch, walked to the entrance, and left his pail on the threshold. Surely someone who made such music could not be a danger to him.

He opened the heavy door and stepped inside the foyer. The music came from far above. Slowly, he climbed the dim stairwell.

At the top floor, Friedrich pushed open a door and entered a cavernous room. Floor-to-ceiling arched windows ran down either side, but only a few needle-like gleams of light penetrated the years of grime on the glass, leaving the room in shadows.

Old machines, bulky figures of steel and iron, filled the space. On the ceiling, dozens of wheels had been suspended, and below them on the floor or attached to tables were their counterparts— all the elements of a once-elaborate pulley system. The leather belts, now disconnected and useless, dangled from the rafters like black snakes.

It's where machines go to die.

The music was louder now. But there was still no sign of a musician.

The stale, dusty air made Friedrich sneeze.

The music stopped.

"Hello?" he called. His word echoed. *Hello . . . ello.*

A mouse skittered across his path.

The refrain from the lullaby picked up again. It seemed to come from the far corner of the room. The music was so insistent that it pulled him forward. Tears sprang to his eyes. Who played so beautifully and with such passion?

He maneuvered around the deformed skeletons of machines. A large contraption covered with a dingy oilcloth blocked his view of the corner. He edged around it.

Again the music stopped.

He called out, "Please show yourself!"

Once more, he heard the lullaby.

He peered into the dimness at the spot where he was certain the song had originated.

No one was there.

Friedrich went to the window he had seen from the field. He was sure it had been open, but now it wasn't. The glass was dirty and opaque, like all the others. Spiderwebs draped the corners. The floor was covered with an undisturbed carpet of dust. No one had stood there for some time.

Glimmers and apparitions.

Was it a ghost he'd heard? Or someone playing a trick on him?

Friedrich turned and studied the immense space. The only way out was the way he had entered. No one could have slipped by him without notice.

He turned to the window again. A wooden, claw-footed desk sat in front of it. He leaned across it and rubbed at the grime on the glass, creating a porthole. He could see the felled tree where he'd eaten lunch and the grebes nearby. This *was* the right window. He tried the latch and, as he did, bumped the desk. Something rattled.

Friedrich opened the top drawer. Inside was a harmonica box. He picked it up and studied the lid.

MARINE BAND
MADE BY
M. HOHNER
GERMANY
No 1896

He opened it and removed the model that the company usually exported to the United States of America. The date on the box indicated the year it was introduced, but the coverplate looked newer, and the body older. Opposite the side with the blowholes, on the black painted edge, was a tiny red letter *M*.

Was this the instrument someone had been playing? If so . . . how?

He *had* heard music, hadn't he?

He felt a chill and shivered, his eyes darting from shadow to shadow.

The factory whistle droned. Friedrich jumped.

Strange things happen . . . Some people go up and never come down.

Quickly, he put the harmonica back into the box, slipped it into his chest pocket, and retraced his steps through the room. He scrambled down the stairs, tumbling the last few steps, until he burst out the door.

He had to bend over for a minute to catch his breath before grabbing his lunch pail and running back to his building.

"Nephew, what happened? You look pale as a ghost," said Uncle Gunter when Friedrich reached his table.

"I may have *heard* one," said Friedrich, putting on his apron and describing what had just happened.

"There's a logical explanation," said Uncle Gunter. "The sound of music is like water finding a path. It travels in many directions. It might have amplified sound coming from a different floor in the building."

Friedrich wasn't so sure. The music had felt so present, as if the harmonica *wanted* him to find it. "Do you suppose I could keep it?"

"I don't see why not. The company gives us several each year."

Friedrich stepped closer and pointed to the red *M*. "What do you make of this?"

Uncle Gunter studied it. "It looks like a crafts-man's mark. But it's not customary to do such a thing. It won't affect the sound. The instrument looks in good shape. Cover plate's been changed. There's no telling how long it was in the desk. Probably belonged to an employee from years ago. You'll want to clean and tune it." Uncle Gunter clapped him on the back. "Friedrich, my boy, you'll be a hero if the men find out you went to the grave-yard alone. Most of them wouldn't dare!"

As he walked home that evening, Friedrich pulled the harmonica from his pocket and lifted it to his lips.

He blew a few chords. Uncle Gunter was right. It was out of tune, but for now, Friedrich didn't mind. He played the first few notes of "Alle Vögel sind schon da," "All the Little Birds Are Back."

The harmonica had a rich, ethereal quality—the same alluring sound he'd heard earlier in the graveyard room. The more he played, the more the air around him seemed to pulse with energy. He felt protected by the cloak of the music, as if nothing could stand in his way. Was he just excited that Elisabeth was coming home and his family would be together again? Or was it something else?

He became so entranced by the tone of the harmonica, and the simple hypnotic song, that he'd passed the school yard before he remembered to feel anxious. He turned down his own block and realized he'd walked almost all the way home without hunching over. He didn't even mind that Mrs. von Gerber, their next-door neighbor, who always bothered him with gossip or home remedies for his birthmark, was out sweeping in front of her geranium boxes. Instead of avoiding her as usual, he called out, "Hello, Mrs. von Gerber!"

She stopped and stared in surprise. "Good evening, Friedrich . . ."

He waved and slipped the mysterious harmonica into his pocket.

With every step up the front walk, it seemed to thump against his chest, like a heartbeat.

Friedrich was embraced by the aroma of roasted meat and cinnamon and apples.

He grinned as he hung up his coat on the hall tree. Then he rubbed his hands together with anticipation.

The old cuckoo clock with its carved pinecone weights hugged the wall. The tiny door, framed in a wreath of linden-wood leaves and forest animals, opened. The cuckoo slid forward and chirped the hour.

"Too bad, old friend," said Friedrich. "You cannot enjoy our meal."

"In here," a voice called from the kitchen.

Friedrich found Father at the table and Elisabeth facing the stove, stirring something meaty with a wooden spoon. An apron was tied at her waist over a gray skirt and white blouse. Friedrich's eyes swept the small kitchen: the walnut hutch with his mother's collection of hand-painted saucers; the counter with the tin canisters sitting in descending order; the window with the green shutter; and Elisabeth, finally home!

He rushed up behind her, put his arms around her waist, and lifted her off the floor.

"Friedrich! Put me down!"

Father laughed.

Friedrich released her. "Did you miss me, 'lisbeth?"

She was almost eighteen, taller than Friedrich but not by much, with the same blue eyes as his and Father's. Her blond hair hung long and loose, and her dimpled cheeks were flushed pink from the warmth of the room. Fresh bread sat on a board on the table. Spaetzle rested in a pan. A strudel, dusted with sugar, cooled on the back of the stove.

Friedrich reached around to tug on her apron string. She dodged him, laughing, and threatened with the wooden spoon.

"Have you tried to scrub off a patient's birthmark with a shoe brush yet?" he asked.

She put her hands on her hips. "Will you never forget that?"

"I don't forget easily. Remember when we used to play hide-and-seek, and if you found me before I was safe, your reward was to bandage me like a mummy?"

Father nodded. "Even then, you were a nurse."

Last year, Elisabeth went to Stuttgart to live with their only relatives besides Uncle Gunter: Mother's cousin and his wife and their daughter, Margarethe, who was in nursing school, too. But now, Elisabeth's last three months of training would be in the local hospital with their family physician, Dr. Braun.

"It is good to have you home," said Friedrich, saluting. "I am ready to be ordered about."

Elisabeth pointed the spoon toward a chair. "Sit next to Father and I'll bring the spaetzle. Father, you start. Tell me all about your last days at work and your first days as a man of golden age."

At the kitchen table, Father talked about all the congratulations and good-natured kidding he'd taken during his last week of work, and the dinners and lunches to honor him. He talked about starting a small chamber ensemble of musicians. "Of course, it won't be as lively as our little performances in the parlor. I'm counting on hearing a polka on the piano later."

She looked at Friedrich and rolled her eyes. "What about you?"

"Father submitted my application to the conservatory."

"He will perform for the jury in January. I can tell he's apprehensive," said Father. "Talk to him, Elisabeth."

"Of course, you must. It's what you've always wanted," said Elisabeth. "What is your worry?"

Friedrich shrugged. Wasn't it clear what worried him?

"The jury is only eight people," said Father.

It was easy for Father to say. He wasn't the one who had to stand in front of strangers and pretend there was nothing wrong with his face and perform. And if he was accepted, what then? Would he be able to sit in a classroom with students he'd never met? Even if he could endure the furtive glances and downcast eyes, what would be the point anyway? How could he stand in front of an audience? Or dare to conduct *an entire orchestra?* The idea made his stomach churn.

"They will be lucky to have your talent," said Elisabeth. "And now, more than ever, Germany needs its *true* citizens to rise to their potential to be shining examples."

Father frowned. "Well, yes, that's one rationale, but—"

"And what of your work at the hospital?" Friedrich didn't want to talk about the conservatory. And he sensed an argument brewing between Father and Elisabeth.

"It's going well. I observed a reconstructive surgery the other day. On a small boy's lip. It was thrilling. I hope to work in pediatric surgery someday."

Friedrich noticed that she'd taken only a few bites of her food and had worried her napkin into a ball. "'lisbeth, what's wrong?"

She looked from Father to Friedrich. She set down her napkin, folded her hands in front of her plate, and took a deep breath. "Before Uncle gets here, there's something I have to tell you both. I hope you will understand . . ." She sat up straighter. "I've been reassigned to a Berlin hospital. I won't be staying in Trossingen or working with Dr. Braun."

"Berlin?" Father's eyes twitched with disappointment. "Why? It was all arranged that you'd be here."

"Yes, I know," said Elisabeth. "I only found out a few days ago. Dr. Braun has already been notified."

Friedrich stared into his plate, his heart sinking. There'd be no late-night talks, or passing a novel back and forth, or Sunday afternoons playing Binokel. He looked at Father, not knowing if he felt worse for himself or for him.

Father's face had wilted. "How long can you stay?"

"Only the weekend. I leave Monday morning on the earliest train."

"But we've seen so little of you." Father blinked back tears.

"I know this comes as a surprise, Father. And I'm sorry for that. But this position will be good for my career inside and outside the hospital."

"Can't you talk to someone and plead your case for Trossingen?" asked Friedrich.

"No. I . . . I *requested* to be reassigned."

For a few moments the only sound was the cuckoo clock ticking in the hall.

Father's face wrinkled with confusion. "Requested it?"

"Why?" asked Friedrich. Hadn't she wanted to be with them?

"So much has changed for me. Berlin is the center of many of my activities now. I should have told you the last time I was home, but there never seemed the right moment. You see, after I moved to Stuttgart, Margarethe and I joined . . . the League of German Girls."

Father's head snapped back as if he'd been slapped. "Elisabeth, you *cannot* be serious."

Friedrich choked on his spaetzle. "You're a Hitlerite?"

7

Was his sister sitting across from him at the dinner table or was it some other creature?

"Don't say *Hitlerite* with such disdain," said Elisabeth. "But, yes. The League is the girls' division of Hitler Youth. We advocate traditional German music, literature, and values."

"Instead of . . . ?" said Father.

"Well, nontraditional things. For instance, the harmonica, I am sorry to say, is not considered traditional and thought to be offensive."

"The harmonica?" said Friedrich, laughing.

"It's responsible for our livelihood, Elisabeth," said Father. "It's what enables you to go to school and live in Stuttgart with Margarethe. Let's not disparage an instrument that goes back to the ancient Chinese sheng."

"But, Father, even *you* don't play it."

"But I play," said Friedrich, pulling the harmonica

he'd found in the graveyard from his pocket and holding it up. "In the harmonica club."

"It's not the instrument itself," said Elisabeth. "It's the *type* of music people play on it. Unacceptable music."

"What do you mean?" asked Friedrich.

"I mean Negro music. Jazz. It's considered degenerate."

"Music does not have a race or a disposition!" said Father. "Every instrument has a voice that contributes. Music is a universal language. A universal religion of sorts. Certainly it's *my* religion. Music surpasses all distinctions between people."

"Some do not agree, Father. And we should follow the Nazi Party's guidelines. We should not listen to or play music by Jewish composers."

"Don't be ridiculous!" said Father.

The cuckoo clock warbled.

"Hush, cuckoo," muttered Friedrich. "Unless you wish to be mocked."

"Not at all!" said Elisabeth. "The Black Forest clocks are particular to German craftsmen. Hitler

86

advocates German pride, and we should endorse him. After all, he is our chancellor."

"But Hindenburg is *still* our president," said Father, slamming a palm on the table.

"Everyone says Hitler will be our president soon enough. He is the answer to our country's problems, Father. And the Nazi Party is the only acceptable political party in Germany now."

"Have you read his book, *Mein Kampf*?" asked Father.

Elisabeth looked directly at Father, steely-eyed. "Frankly, no. Intellectualism is frowned upon. Hitler is the leader of the workingman, of the common people, of true Germans. I am well versed in his hopes for the country, his ideology, and—"

"He wants a *pure* race," said Father. "He says all non-Germans are his enemies!"

Elisabeth looked at Father as if she pitied him. "Father, he is only trying to encourage national pride. The League is a wholesome organization for healthy girls of true German heritage."

"How do you prove that?" asked Father.

"Baptism records, health records, marriage

notices . . . Anyone can join if they can prove that there is no more than one-eighth of certain non-German ancestries in their bloodline. It is not as questionable as you think. And there are *worse* things than being a true German." She turned to Friedrich. "You *must* join the Hitler Youth. You would be with boys your own age from our neighborhood. There are meetings, and rallies, and outdoor competitions. It is such fun."

Friedrich touched his face. Had Elisabeth forgotten how boys his own age from their own neighborhood had treated him? And what about Hitler's plan to cleanse the population? Would Friedrich qualify as a true German? Was he pure enough? Softly, he said, "I don't think they would like the way I look."

"Oh, but you should ignore your pride, Friedrich. It's important that *all* Germans come together for the fatherland. For the good of the country and the common man."

It struck Friedrich that almost word for word, Elisabeth sounded like Anselm. Had they been to the same meetings?

"Friedrich will not be taking that chance," said Father.

"Father, you are stubborn and unreasonable. At least at Margarethe's I have support. *She* understands and shares my feelings, as do her parents."

"Her parents?" asked Father.

Elisabeth raised her chin. "They were the ones who suggested we go to our first meeting."

Father's face pinched as he slumped back in his chair. "Our own relatives . . . *This* is how you spend your time?"

"My League work is only Wednesday nights and Saturdays," said Elisabeth. "And it has given me a much higher standing with the doctors and nurses." She pushed her chair away from the table and stood up. "Father, I *love* it. We go hiking and on outings. We sing. I am involved in the community, helping people. They value me because of my medical training. I am already in the Youth Medical Service. And I am determined to become a leader. To set an example for the younger girls."

"You are starry-eyed," said Father.

Elisabeth ignored him. "I won't be home much

because as a potential Youth Leader, my extra time will be devoted to the League. Father, I need my baptism papers. And yours and Mother's. Or notices of marriage. And any of my grandparents', if by some miracle you have them. Oh, that would be *wonderful* if we had those records and I could prove my lineage that far back. Then I might be guaranteed a leadership position."

Leadership? His sister was going to train others to be followers of Hitler?

There was a knock at the front door.

"There's Uncle Gunter with his accordion, no doubt," said Elisabeth. "Maybe *he'll* be more excited for me." She hurried from the kitchen.

Father stood and muttered, "Uncle Gunter will *not* be more excited. I'm going to bed."

"Don't you want strudel?" said Friedrich. "And what about playing some music?"

As Father walked from the room he said, "I have a sour stomach."

A few moments later, Uncle Gunter came into the kitchen with an arm around Elisabeth. "At last, Friedrich! We're all together again."

Friedrich pulled a chair out at the table for Uncle Gunter. "Yes . . . all together, except for Father, who asks to be excused. His stomach."

"Ah, too bad. But all the more for me," he said, eyeing the dessert.

Elisabeth served the strudel and chatted away, her face animated, unconcerned about Father's absence or Friedrich's mood.

At first, Uncle Gunter was genial and asked questions about Elisabeth's work. Then, with each of her revelations, Friedrich watched him grow more and more quiet, set down the half-eaten dessert he loved, and excuse himself early. Feigning tiredness, he put on his coat and picked up his accordion.

Before he left, Uncle Gunter looked at Friedrich. His eyes filled with something Friedrich couldn't decipher—pity or fear or apprehension?

Was he worried for Elisabeth?

Or for Friedrich and Father?

Early the next morning, Friedrich found Father sitting in the parlor, slumped in a chair.

He looked small and withered, as if all of the air had been squeezed from his body. In his lap, he held a fabric-covered hatbox. Papers and photos were strewn around him, the box lid on the floor.

"Father, what's all this?"

"The papers Elisabeth asked for."

"Why? If you don't give them to her, she won't be able to become a leader and maybe . . . maybe she will come to her senses."

"Friedrich, they are all public records. If she does not get them from me, she might solicit copies through a lawyer. I can't help but think that she was unduly influenced . . ." Father shook his head. "Our own relatives!"

Father held up several documents. "Here are the baptism and marriage records she needs. I finally found them." He nodded to the round box. "I never looked inside. Always thought it held a hat. I haven't looked through any of these things since your mother . . ." Father looked down, rubbing his forehead with his fingers. "Too painful, I suppose."

"Where is Elisabeth?" asked Friedrich.

"Visiting next door with Mrs. von Gerber. She'll know more about Trossingen than we do by the time she returns. Put everything back in the box for me, will you? And take it to my room. I have a student coming soon. But I need a cup of tea first." Father headed to the kitchen.

Friedrich collected the photos. He stopped at a portrait of Father at about twelve years old, standing next to his cello. Friedrich was startled by their resemblance. He touched the photo. How would his life have been different if he had been born without a birthmark, like Father?

In another photo of a school orchestra, he found Father in the cello section, first chair. But his eyes settled on the young conductor, standing in front and holding his baton. Would that ever be him?

He put the photographs in his pocket to prop on his dresser later. Then he gathered the rest with the papers and stacked them in the hatbox. An envelope had been affixed to the underside of the lid. He pulled out a piece of paper. On it was an ink impression of an infant's footprints. At the bottom was his name, Friedrich Martin Schmidt. Below that, his birth date, followed by the words: *Cause of death, epilepsy.*

His heart skipped.

He read it again.

It was *his* name and *his* birth date. So they had to be *his* footprints. But he wasn't an epileptic. And he was very much alive! Who had written this? Why did it say he was dead? His hand shook as he studied the tiny impressions.

He hadn't heard the front door open, but Elisabeth was standing before him, taking off her scarf.

"As usual, Mrs. von Gerber knows everything about everybody so it was easy to catch up on the neighborhood in one sitting. She was excited about my assignment in Berlin. And happy to report that

Dr. Braun is extremely pleased one of his own patients is going into medicine, even if I can't intern with him. She said she's missed my quince jam. But I promised to make some soon and send it to her." Elisabeth put her hands on her hips and stared at Friedrich. "What's wrong? You look pallid."

He held out the paper.

As soon as she read it, her mouth opened, but no words came out. Finally, she said, "It must be a mistake."

"It's my birth date and my name," he said.

"Friedrich, there *must* be an explanation. Come."

In a daze, Friedrich followed her to the kitchen, where Father stood at the basin, filling the teakettle.

"Father?" asked Elisabeth. She held the paper out to him.

He studied it, confused at first, and then recognition came over him. "Where did you find this?"

"Friedrich found it."

Father nodded. "It's been so long, I'd forgotten."

"Why does it say I'm dead?" asked Friedrich.

Father looked from him to Elisabeth. "I can explain. Please . . . sit down."

9

Friedrich and Elisabeth sat across from Father, who rested the cold teakettle on the table, between his hands.

He took a deep breath. "Your mother went into labor in the middle of the night. Dr. Braun and his nurse came to the house. Immediately after you were born, you began to have seizures. Dr. Braun said they were so severe you wouldn't make it through the night. Before the nurse left, she made the ink prints, as a gesture of comfort, something your mother could keep. But then, you *did* make it through the night. And the next. And the one after that. A few months later, it was your mother . . . who began to fail." Father's eyes watered.

"Why have you never said anything?" asked Friedrich. "About the epilepsy?"

"From her hospital bed, your mother made me promise not to tell anyone. Each week, your birthmark had become more prominent, as did the gossip and superstitions. Mrs. von Gerber was convinced your mother spilled a glass of red wine on her stomach when she was pregnant and *that* caused the mark. The clerk at the bakery said your mother had a horrible fright before you were born and the shock made the stain on your face."

"I remember," said Elisabeth. "And a Gypsy on the street thought it was a sign of a blood secret, something in our family's history that was never brought to light."

"It was all nonsense," said Father. "Your mother did not drink wine. She feared nothing. Nor did she carry any unspeakable family knowledge. But she *was* worried for you, Friedrich. She had an aunt with the same type of birthmark, and knew that it would be burden enough. Adding the stigma of epilepsy would be too much."

Confused, Friedrich looked at Elisabeth. "Stigma?"

"More old wives' tales," she said. "Some people think the convulsions are caused by demons or insanity and that it's not a medical condition. But that's just ignorant conjecture."

"So you see why your mother begged me and Dr. Braun to keep the seizures a secret. And we promised. To be quite honest, I had forgotten about them. You never had another seizure after you were a year old."

Friedrich had seen an epileptic fit once, when he was in kindergarten. He'd been painting at an easel when the boy next to him dropped to the ground. The brush the boy had been holding flew across the room. He made gagging sounds and his entire body contorted and shook. His hands clenched into fists and turned inward toward his body. And he howled like an animal. For a few seconds, the boy did look insane, as if he'd been possessed by demons. But it all stopped as quickly as it started. The teacher had ordered all the children outside. When they came back into the classroom, the boy was gone. Friedrich never saw him again.

Could Friedrich have a seizure when he least expected it?

What if he had one during his audition? Would the conservatory want him if they knew? Was he insane? He rubbed his temples.

Father held the teakettle out to him. "We could all use some tea."

Friedrich took the kettle, carried it to the stove, and lit the fire.

Elisabeth frowned. "The seizures were probably febrile, from a fever. But even so, I'm sure Dr. Braun wrote everything down in a chart. It's standard procedure." She pushed away from the table, stood, and began to pace, her brow furrowed in concentration.

Father shook his head. "What does it matter? Dr. Braun promised he would never say a word and he hasn't."

"Father, regardless, there would still be a *record*. Don't you see?" said Elisabeth. "Friedrich has a birthmark that is a physical deformity we now know runs in the family. You said yourself Mother had an aunt with the same affliction. And now there is a record of epilepsy, which is also considered hereditary. The new law is specific."

"Which new law?" Friedrich asked.

Elisabeth looked at Father. "You haven't told him? Father, I wrote you about it months ago."

The teakettle sputtered.

"I've read it. He's *not* a candidate," said Father.

"He was *always* a candidate with the birthmark alone," said Elisabeth. "And now with epilepsy, it is certain. I've been briefed about the law at length at the hospital, and . . ."

Friedrich slammed his hand on the counter. "Stop talking about me as if I'm not here! I'm not a baby anymore. What law? Candidate for what?"

Elisabeth crossed her arms. "The Law for the Prevention of Genetically Diseased Offspring. It passed in July. Doctors have until January to report patients with physical deformities or hereditary conditions. Most will need an operation to prevent them from ever having children, so as not to pass along the undesirable traits."

Friedrich looked at Father. "Surgery?"

"You will *not* have this surgery!" said Father.

Elisabeth looked at Father as if he were a small child. "He won't have a choice. Every doctor has been *ordered* to report all of their patients with physical deformities, alcoholism, mental illnesses, blindness, deafness, epilepsy—there's a list of transgressions."

"Friedrich committed no crime."

"The conditions, should they be passed on," said Elisabeth, "would be transgressions against future German citizens. That's why there is this new law—to prevent them from happening ever again."

Friedrich had an unnatural sensation in his stomach, the way he used to feel immediately before someone was about to punch him on the playground. Questions swam in his mind: Was his face a crime? Wasn't there more to him than his birthmark and an illness he no longer had? What would happen to him if he was too dreadful for the Nazis?

"You endorse this new law?" asked Father.

"I *understand* it," said Elisabeth. "Dr. Braun will be required to report Friedrich. And me too, since the epilepsy and birthmark have shown in my family. I'll volunteer for the surgery. It's the least I can do for my country. And I'll be congratulated for it. Friedrich should do the same."

Friedrich stared at Elisabeth. Was she really turning the surgery into an opportunity to prove her patriotism? And she wanted him to have it, too?

Father's face reddened and he choked out his words. "There is already speculation about how many will actually survive this surgery. Who is to say they won't just kill people the Nazis think are undesirable, to create Hitler's so-called pure race?"

Friedrich felt the blood drain from his face. "Father . . . ?"

"Do not worry, son. I will make an appointment and talk to Dr. Braun myself."

"That's a good idea." Elisabeth gripped the back of her chair. "And when I'm around, Father, I request that you speak favorably of Hitler, or say nothing. I need to believe that you might join the party, so that when I am questioned about my family by my superiors—*and I will be questioned*—I can say that I have no reason to suspect you of opposition. If I have to admit that you are not a follower, it might not bode well."

"What?" Friedrich couldn't believe what he had heard. "You would report your own father?"

Elisabeth raised her chin. "The party rewards those who are forthright. If there were dissenters in my family, and I didn't reveal it when I was questioned, it would affect my position within the League. And that could affect my work at the hospital. My career would be over. It would be the ruination of me."

"The ruination of *you*?" said Friedrich. "What about Father? They're putting people who don't agree with Hitler in prison, where they work them to death. What about me? They could kill me under anesthesia because I'm not perfect." He tasted bile in the back of his throat.

"Friedrich, not another word," said Father.

What? Had Father lost his mind?

Father ran both of his hands through his hair. He stood and squared his shoulders. He studied Elisabeth, then locked eyes with Friedrich, his stare intense. "Listen carefully, Friedrich. Elisabeth is right. We will be loyal Germans."

"But—"

"Not another word goes against Hitler or the Nazis in this house," said Father. "I won't allow it."

Friedrich gasped. "Father, you cannot agree—"

Father's voice shook with anger. "Not! Another! Word! Do you understand?"

In his entire life, Friedrich couldn't remember Father ever yelling at him like that. He whispered, "Yes."

Father picked up a stack of papers from one end of the table and slapped them in front of Elisabeth. "Everything you need is there: your baptism papers, mine and Mother's, and your grandparents' marriage notices. You may rest assured that you are one-hundred-percent German. Now, I have a student coming soon. I must prepare." Father stormed out of the kitchen.

Seconds later, the parlor door slammed.

Elisabeth gathered the papers and left the room, humming.

Friedrich stared at the kitchen doorway long after she disappeared.

The teakettle screamed.

10

Upstairs in his room, Friedrich's mind grappled with all that had just happened.

He busied himself to calm his thoughts. He spread a tea towel at one end of his desk and laid out the tools he would need to clean the harmonica. With a tiny screwdriver, he removed the posts that held the cover plates and lifted them off.

From downstairs, the familiar sounds of the cello thrummed as Father's student began the lesson. Soon, Friedrich heard the prelude from Bach's Cello Suite no. 1. He raised his head to listen to the arpeggios.

In the broken chords, he heard the rhythm of Father and Elisabeth's argument. The alternating notes—their banter back and forth—rose and fell. The music was as precise as their conversation had been brittle. As the piece progressed, he felt the gathering tension wind tighter and tighter, like unspoken anxiety. After the movement, a sadness lingered, unresolved.

Friedrich returned to the harmonica, inspecting the pear-wood body and the reed plates. He separated them and lined them up on the towel. He dipped a soft cloth in rubbing alcohol and wiped down the parts. With a small, soft brush, he cleaned the comb. When the reed plates were dry, he screwed them back onto the body. Lifting the harmonica to his mouth, he blew into the holes, making the sequential notes of the scale.

Friedrich repeated the scale, took the harmonica from his lips, and studied it.

"The third and the eighth," said Elisabeth, standing in his doorway.

"I agree." Friedrich looked up. "They're flat. You still have a good ear."

"Years of Father insisting on piano whether I liked it or not. May I come in?"

He shrugged.

She entered, sat on the end of his bed, and looked around. "Everything is the same."

Friedrich scanned the room. She was right. The bed was covered with the quilt he'd had since he was a small boy. The dresser was stacked with sheet music. A framed photo of his mother and father on their wedding day sat on his desk. "I like it this way."

"Of course you do. You were never one for change." Her voice was soft and kind.

Did she think she could act as if nothing had happened?

Friedrich heard Father's muffled voice directing his student downstairs. Then the prelude began again. He took a tiny, sharp tool and made small scrapes on the copper reeds. He blew and scraped a little more. When he was satisfied the harmonica was in tune, he set the cover plates, one at a time, and tightened the screws.

He blew into the harmonica again, running the octave.

Elisabeth tilted her head. "It doesn't sound like other harmonicas."

Friedrich agreed. It had a warm and ethereal tone. "Too bad it's unacceptable . . . like me."

Elisabeth tensed. "Why can't you understand? I *believe* in Hitler and what he stands for. He is our benevolent father, who is going to lead our country out of the darkness of poverty and a watered-down population into greatness and wealth."

Again she sounded like she was reading from the same script as Anselm.

"I intend to concentrate all of my efforts on the League," she said. "They appreciate me. For my knowledge as a nurse, for my moral character and exemplary behavior. I'm . . . I'm *somebody* to them."

"You're somebody to us, too. And you don't have to go along with everything they say. You used to have your own feelings and think your own thoughts."

"These *are* my feelings now. Besides, the girls are the sisters I never had. We're a family."

"You already *have* a family."

"This is different. Bigger. The League is a community and I love being a part of it." Elisabeth stared at the quilt on his bed as if the design were the most interesting she'd ever seen. "Friedrich, have you ever thought about what my childhood was like?"

"The same as mine," said Friedrich.

"No, not exactly. I was only six when Mother died. She and I were so close and I felt lost without her. Father had already quit the orchestra and was working at the factory. A nurse came during the day to care for you. But Father and I took over in the evenings. And when you got older, I walked you to school and picked you up afterward. I also took care of the house and prepared the meals. All the things a mother would do. But I *wasn't* a mother. I was just a girl. On weekends, Father taught lessons, so I watched you again. There were no opportunities for me to go on outings, or to a play, or to a school event that was not during school hours. And invitations? There were none. Try being the sister of . . ." Elisabeth bit her lip.

"Monster Boy?" said Friedrich.

"I'm sorry. I don't mean to hurt you."

Anger and sadness choked Friedrich. His words came out stilted. "Then why do you say it? Is this your way of being forthright? Because you won't be rewarded for it here. What is wrong with you, Elisabeth? Don't you see? You *have* hurt Father. And me. It's like you're someone we've never met before!"

She stood, went to the window, and gazed out, her eyes transfixed on something Friedrich could not see. She turned to him. "I *am* a different person, with a different life. Is that so wrong?"

When he didn't answer, she shook her head and sighed. "I'm going to a League activity this afternoon, if you'd like to come. We're planting crops for a nearby farmer. You see, Friedrich, we do good deeds in the community for the sake of our fatherland."

Friedrich looked at her, dumbfounded, and shook his head.

She walked from the room, closing the door behind her.

He raised the harmonica and began to play, trying to replicate the Bach he had heard coming from Father's student downstairs. The unusual instrument sounded as if it carried the pain he felt—startling revelation, disappointment, and overpowering sadness. And yet, at the same time, the smooth and elegant tone seemed to swaddle him.

He'd been oblivious to Elisabeth's childhood.

His face had been her burden, too.

How was it that he'd never known?

He lowered the harmonica and walked to the mirror above his dresser. He stared at the stain blooming on his right cheek. A fury unfolded inside him.

He threw the harmonica across the room. He swept his arms across the dresser, the stacks of sheet music flying.

Why had he been born this way?

11

Sunday, the house was hushed, except for the ticking cuckoo clock and its spurts of birdcalls.

Uncle Gunter had made a polite excuse to stay at home. Father read in the parlor. Friedrich stayed in his room.

Elisabeth was preoccupied with becoming someone else. She changed her tailored clothes to an old-fashioned dirndl skirt and peasant blouse. She wove her hair into long, thick braids. Even her room changed. Her bed was still covered in the crocheted blanket that their mother had made, but the oil painting of a field of flowers that had always hung above it was replaced by a large poster of an angelic-looking girl and boy in uniforms. They gazed upward, a swastika radiating light upon their golden hair and perfect faces.

That evening, Elisabeth made Friedrich and Father's favorite stew with wurst for dinner. As they sat around the table, there was no talk of politics. No arguing. Father and Elisabeth tripped over the niceties of civil conversation. But she hadn't said another word to Friedrich, nor he to her. Elisabeth was pensive. Father picked at his food. Friedrich couldn't eat, either. After only a few bites, he pushed away from the table and went upstairs.

Later, after everyone had gone to bed, Friedrich heard Father pad down the hall and quietly open the door to Elisabeth's room. A moment later, he opened Friedrich's and then headed back to his own room.

Friedrich heard the click of a lamp, the scrape of a chair against the wood floor as it was scooted forward, and a few short warm-up strums of the bow across the cello. He felt his heart ache as Father began Brahms' Lullaby.

When he and Elisabeth were little and couldn't sleep, they would rush into Father's bedroom to beg for a good-night concert. Father always pretended to be too tired, but after they showered him with kisses, he agreed. Shooing them back to their rooms, Father told them to say farewell to their troubles because they were about to fly away on the wings of the music.

"Farewell! Farewell!" they always squealed, running back to their beds and leaving the doors wide open for the performance.

Tonight, Friedrich wished it were possible— that the heaviness that pressed on his heart and mind might take flight.

The song took him back to when Elisabeth had been a constant, always there, whispering in his ear. *Don't listen to others. They're not your family. Your family tells you the truth.*

All those years, had *she* been telling the truth?

Father repeated the song three times, each version slower and softer and more melancholy.

Friedrich pulled the quilt over his head.

All those years, had she loved him as he'd loved her?

The last phrase Father played seemed to mourn the family's unraveling.

The final note trembled.

Friedrich's eyes filled with tears.

And he wept.

12

Elisabeth left early the next morning without saying good-bye.

Friedrich had been asleep, but even so, she hadn't called out a farewell, or written a note, or asked Father to pass along a message. Had she really disappeared from their lives without a word?

"She won't be coming back, will she?" Friedrich asked Father after dinner as he set up his cello in the parlor for his weekly lesson.

"No, son. At least, not soon. Maybe someday. I fear it's all my fault. I always expected so much from her because she was so capable. I didn't consider her needs as I might have, being wrapped up in my own grief after your mother . . . I'd always hoped that when I retired, I'd have more time to spend with her. But now, it seems I'm too late. She's caught up in that . . . that *fanatic's* idealism."

Friedrich tightened and rosined his bow. "I

thought you didn't want to hear another word against Hitler in this house."

"Friedrich, surely you know I only said that for Elisabeth's sake. It's important she thinks we're followers. For the safety of all of us. I would do anything to protect you and Elisabeth, even join the Nazi Party, if it ever came to that. As much as I hate to admit it, she is right about one thing. If we oppose Hitler, we must keep our thoughts to ourselves. Do you understand? Look and listen. That should be our policy. Trust no one. Be especially careful around the neighbors and at work. Except with your uncle, of course."

Friedrich shook his head. "Father, *I* am not the one . . ."

Father raised a hand. "I know. I know. I'm far too outspoken and excitable. But I am vowing to hold my tongue and keep my opinions to myself. I said it was time to be prudent, not close my mind altogether."

Friedrich swept his hand toward a candy dish overflowing with anise lozenges. "But you continue to shop at the Jewish grocery, don't you?"

Father sighed. "Yes, Friedrich. You know it is the only place I can get my lozenges. And that it belongs to the family of one of my students. Besides, this morning, the storm troopers painted a sloppy yellow star on the door and hung a sign: The Jews Are Germany's Misfortune. I watched three customers walk up, reconsider, and turn away. It is not right."

"Didn't you just say . . . ?"

"I said I would keep my *opinions* to myself, Friedrich. And I did. I didn't say one word in that store. I only bought some much-needed groceries. They cannot arrest me for that. At least, not yet."

Father walked to the piano and played the A.

Friedrich drew the bow across the A string, back and forth, adjusting the pegs. Before he began his exercises, he looked up. "Why do you carry on, Father, for the Jews? Wouldn't it be safer for us to go along with the boycotts?"

Father walked to him and put a hand on his shoulder. "I don't carry on just for the Jews, Friedrich. I carry on for you, too. Any injustice the Nazis impose on the Jews, they will impose on you, or anyone else they deem undesirable. It is unconscionable!"

"Will . . . will I have to have that surgery?" asked Friedrich.

"I already made an appointment with Dr. Braun. A week from Friday, we will discuss it. For our safety, let us both promise that from now on . . ." Father put his thumb and forefinger on one corner of his mouth and pretended to zipper it. He smiled, closemouthed.

Friedrich nodded. "I promise."

But he doubted Father could keep his word.

13

Two Fridays later, Friedrich waited at the factory gates after work, pacing in the cold October air.

He clapped his arms to stay warm and to tame his anxiety about Father's meeting with Dr. Braun. Father had promised to meet Friedrich afterward so they could walk home together, but he was late.

Anselm exited the factory grounds and quickly cornered Friedrich. "What luck! I was hoping to talk to you."

Couldn't Anselm leave him alone?

"I'm going to a Hitler Youth meeting next Wednesday," said Anselm. "I'm a leader and I get honored if I bring a guest."

"Thank you, I am not interested," said Friedrich, avoiding his eyes.

"Your sister is a good friend of my sister, and she asked . . ."

So this was Elisabeth's doing? "It's not for me." Friedrich took a few steps to the side.

Anselm followed. "You'll join sooner or later, Friedrich. And it would mean ever so much to me, and make me look good to my superiors. Come. See how you like it."

Friedrich knew how he'd like it. But he remembered his promise to Father and said nothing.

"Another time, then," said Anselm, poking his finger into Friedrich's shoulder a little too hard. "That is my vow, Friedrich. To get you to a meeting." He turned and walked away, whistling.

Friedrich clenched his hands. Would Anselm never give up? And Elisabeth? Hadn't he made it clear to her that he didn't want to join? He'd have to dream up some excuses to give Anselm next week.

His thoughts were interrupted by two students, a girl and a boy, walking toward him, toting instrument cases. Friedrich knew they must be heading home from the conservatory. As they passed, he heard them talking about "the Beethoven piece." Which was it? A symphony or a concerto? He wanted to shout at them, "I know Beethoven's works, too!" Instead, he watched them walk away. If he was accepted at the conservatory in January, would they become his friends? Would they mind the way he looked? Or ridicule him? For the hundredth time, he wanted and feared all at once.

Where was Father? While Friedrich waited, he pulled out the harmonica, which he always kept in his chest pocket, and played a passage from Beethoven's Ninth, the fourth movement. With his hands covering part of his face, he was inconspicuous in the dark, just a boy making joyous music on the street. He didn't even mind when people looked his way, because they didn't seem to be looking at his birthmark. Instead, they smiled and nodded, as if Friedrich had something to say with the harmonica in a language they all understood.

Was it the same when others performed? The music was what mattered and the performer's countenance was secondary? If he was accomplished enough as a musician, could people look beyond his face to his ability? Would the conservatory judges? And maybe, one day, an audience?

The rich sound of the harmonica pervaded his thoughts with an undeniable brightness, as if he were looking at the world through a clear lens. Hope burned like a tiny ember. When he finished, he lowered the harmonica, feeling a satisfied stillness.

A man approached and gave him a coin. "That was extraordinary," he said before continuing on his way.

Friedrich laughed. He hadn't been playing for money!

"Friedrich!"

He turned to see Father striding toward him, and his joy melted. Even from a distance, Friedrich could tell he was troubled.

"Sorry I'm late," said Father when he reached him. "The meeting with Dr. Braun ran long."

Friedrich's voice tightened. "How did it resolve?"

Father took a deep breath. "We talked at length. But unfortunately, his hands are tied. In January, he will be obligated to report what is in your file. He doesn't make the final decision, though. There is something called the Genetic Health Court, which will review every case. They decide. And Dr. Braun says your birthmark and the epilepsy match the criteria for the law."

"Father . . . does that mean . . . ?"

Father ran his hands through his hair. "I told him my fears about the surgery. And about your promising future if you're accepted at the conservatory—he's known of your talent since you were small. He said if you're admitted, we can ask a conservatory representative to write a letter on your behalf—a dispensation letter. Apparently, Hitler and the Nazis make concessions for 'loyal and true Germans of great aptitude.' Your musical ability could be your saving grace."

Friedrich took Father's arm, holding on to him as he grasped the possibility that his musicianship might save him. They began to slowly walk home. "And if I'm not accepted to the conservatory, I must have the surgery?"

Father nodded. "The government will insist with force, if necessary. But in that event, son, be reassured I will go to the authorities myself."

What would happen if Father made a scene

with the authorities? Friedrich shook his head. "You cannot pound on someone's desk as you did when I was little, Father. This is a *law*. They are putting people in prison for speaking out against the government." Friedrich tried to keep his voice low as they walked. "Father, if I do not get accepted, you must promise me that you will not . . ."

"Friedrich, I could never stand by and let this happen." Tension was building in Father's voice. "You are brilliant and kind and responsible and talented and . . . and now this . . . this . . . law! Why can't people just accept you and look on the inside of you? I couldn't live with myself if they . . ." Father's face crumbled. "There must be something I can do . . ."

Friedrich put an arm around Father and pretended to be calm. "You can coach me. And oversee my practice. Let's look at scores tonight so that I might start considering pieces for the audition. Yes?"

Father nodded. "But that might not be enough. There must be something more I can do . . ." His words trailed off into the darkness.

All his life, Father had protected him, defended him, opened doors for him. But now, something bigger and uncontrollable had shaken Father's strength and resolve.

An unfamiliar fear gripped Friedrich: He was falling.

If Father wasn't below to catch him, could he catch himself?

14

"No . . . no . . . no . . ." said Friedrich.

Every evening for the past two weeks, he'd sat at one end of the kitchen table and sorted through stacks of music for a piece he might perform for his audition.

Father usually did the same, but tonight, he sat across from him, writing yet another letter to Elisabeth.

Friedrich tapped the top of the stack. "How about this one? Haydn. The Concerto no. 2?"

Father looked up, nodding. "It's complex enough. Put it with the others we're considering. And remember what I always tell you and all my students: Whichever music you choose, you must perform in such a way that the audience has no choice but to listen with its heart."

Friedrich set it on a short stack and pushed back from the table. He needed a break. He pulled the harmonica from his pocket and played Brahms' Lullaby.

When he finished, Father gazed at him, shaking his head with admiration. "That is exactly what I mean, son. That was ... radiant. I felt it"—Father put a hand on his heart—"here. And that harmonica! Such a remarkable tone. It's as if you are playing three instruments, not one."

Friedrich puzzled. "It's true. I hear it as well. Every song I play sounds as if it is in harmony with ... something inside of me."

Father nodded. "Some instruments have a quality that cannot be explained. Maybe you've found the Stradivarius of harmonicas."

Friedrich studied it. "If only it was as revered as the Stradivarius violins. Too bad I can't audition with it."

Father chuckled. "With the current sentiment about the harmonica, I can only imagine the upheaval that would cause at the conservatory."

Father folded the letter, put it in an envelope, and addressed it. He held it out to Friedrich.

"Would you drop this at the post office for me on your way to work tomorrow?"

Friedrich took the envelope and set it aside. "She's been gone for a month now. Why do you continue to write to her every week when you've heard nothing in return? Isn't it clear she has made her choice?"

Father put down his pen. "I know you're angry with her. But I'm her father. I continue because I love her, and I want her to remember the sound of my voice."

Friedrich nodded toward the envelope. "Did you tell her that our own dentist has closed his doors because of yet another law prohibiting Jews to practice medicine? Did you ask her if she attends the bonfires in Berlin where they burn books that don't glorify Hitler's ideals? Or about all the Germans who are fleeing the country because they are opponents of Hitler?"

Father looked at him soberly. "Be careful, Friedrich. Your voice has an edge to it. I fear you are beginning to sound far too much like me. And no, as a matter of course, I never mention politics to Elisabeth. I write to her about the two of you and some of my fondest memories of your childhoods. I tell her how proud I am of her nursing accomplishments. I tell her what we had for dinner. Don't you see? I am not giving up the hope that she might someday be my daughter and your sister again. Just as I would never, ever give up on you. There's so little I can do for her now. Except to let her know I am here. And to let her be. You might consider doing the same."

Friedrich frowned and crossed his arms on his chest.

"I know it is hard for you to understand right now," said Father. "But someday . . . if I am not around, or your uncle Gunter isn't around, you might need her. You might need *each other.*"

What was Father talking about? "I won't need her, Father, unless her feelings have changed."

"Son, there might come a time . . ."

"Father, stop!" He swept the letter from the table and it flew to the floor. Friedrich stood and stormed from the room, calling over his shoulder, "You and Uncle Gunter aren't going anywhere!"

15

When Friedrich came home from work the following Thursday evening, the furniture in the parlor had been moved toward the walls, and four kitchen chairs and music stands were positioned in a half circle in the center of the room.

A small table was set with tea, shortbread, and a bowl of anise lozenges.

"Father, what's all this?"

Father clapped his hands together. "Something fortuitous has happened, Friedrich. I called a few friends to see if they'd join me to play some impromptu chamber music tonight and they've agreed." He nodded to the table. "I bought a few things. To make everything nice. I have a violinist and a violist coming. I can be the other violinist, unpracticed as I am. Would you indulge me and play cello, if only for tonight?"

Friedrich took off his knit cap, wool scarf, and coat. "I don't know, Father . . ." He hesitated.

"It's Rudolph and Josef. You've met them both so you need not feel uncomfortable."

Rudolph's daughter had taken cello lessons from Father, so he'd been to the house many times. And Josef was one of Father's oldest friends. They'd played in the Berlin Philharmonic together. Now he was a music professor at the university in Stuttgart. Whenever he visited, Josef always took a special interest in Friedrich, listening to him perform and giving him advice on how to improve.

"There are good reasons for you to play with us, not the least of which is to make a favorable impression."

"A favorable impression?"

Father was beaming. "I've discovered that Rudolph sits on the *directors' board* at the conservatory. So you see, it's advantageous that you two become better acquainted. And Josef attended the conservatory so he's quite familiar with the auditions. I've asked him to look through our music selections and make a recommendation about what you might play for the jury."

Friedrich put his hands on his hips and raised his eyebrows. "Please tell me that you are not trying to manipulate . . ."

Father raised his hands to stop him. "I assure you, Friedrich, it was all a lucky coincidence. I didn't find out until after I asked Rudolph to come that he was affiliated with the conservatory. And the only reason I called Josef in the first place was because . . . I know he needs this. He lost his job." Father muttered, "Hitler's new Law for the Restoration of the Professional Civil Service."

"The what?" asked Friedrich.

"It forbids Jews from working as teachers or professors. He's Jewish *and* a professor. And brilliant. The best viola player I've ever known. When I called him, he told me that a few weeks ago in the middle of the night, he packed up his wife and children and sent them away to relatives because he could no longer pay his rent. He has stayed behind to care for his father, who is not well enough to travel. I encouraged him to come and play tonight because music is the best medicine for the soul."

"Father, that was kind of you."

"I'd love for you to start the evening by playing that harmonica. The same piece you played for me last week, the Brahms. I think our guests will be delighted by your prowess and its unusual sound." Father's eyes twinkled.

Friedrich hadn't seen him so animated since the day before Elisabeth came home. How could he refuse him? Friedrich nodded.

"Now quickly, into the kitchen with you and eat your dinner and then upstairs to change. They'll be here soon. And don't forget the harmonica."

Friedrich patted his chest pocket. He wouldn't forget it. Maybe Father was right. Tonight would bring good luck.

16

Friedrich had just come downstairs when there was a knock on the door.

Rudolph, tall and lumbering, entered, toting his violin. A few moments later, Josef arrived, carrying the viola. He pulled black-framed eyeglasses from his pocket and put them on.

After the brief introductions, the two men were soon unpacking their instruments and rosining their bows.

"Before we talk about the repertoire," said Father, "Friedrich has agreed to play something for you at my bidding."

Friedrich smiled self-consciously. He turned his birthmark away from the men and pulled the harmonica from his pocket. He blew a few chords. His pulse raced. How could he feel so nervous in his own parlor?

He closed his eyes and began the Brahms. Swept away and soothed by the familiar voice of the harmonica, he repeated the refrain. When he finished, he turned to face the men. If he impressed anyone, he hoped it would be Rudolph, since he'd be judging him soon.

But it was Josef who said, "That was lovely. It did not sound so much like a harmonica as it did a clarinet, and at times, a piccolo."

"It has a unique sound," said Father, looking at Rudolph, who pursed his lips. "Did you not like the piece?"

"Martin, it's a toy, not an instrument," said Rudolph. "And it's not authorized by the government. It's considered vulgar."

Friedrich saw Father bristle.

"Yes . . . well . . ." Father frowned.

Friedrich cleared his throat and quickly said, "We should talk about the repertoire."

Rudolph spoke up. "I suggest Beethoven or Bruckner. Possibly Bach. They are sanctioned by the Nazi Party."

Friedrich caught Father's startled look. Rudolph was a Hitlerite. And Father hadn't known. Did Rudolph know that Josef was Jewish?

Josef shifted in his chair, looking uncomfortable. "I . . . I have no problem playing any of those composers."

"It's settled, then," said Rudolph. He nodded to Josef, his eyes searching his face. "We've met before, haven't we? You used to play in the orchestra with Martin. Or am I mistaken?"

Josef laid his viola in his lap. "You are correct."

"Are you still with the Berlin Philharmonic?"

"No, I've been for some years teaching music at the university in Stuttgart," said Josef. "Until recently."

A sliver of recognition crossed Rudolph's face. "Your family is from Trossingen, though. Your father and uncle have a tailor shop. Cohen Brothers. Isn't that right? But it was closed due to current . . . tensions and sentiment."

"That's right," said Josef.

Rudolph turned to Father. "I cannot play with a Jew."

Father stood and held out his hands, pleading. "Rudolph, can't we put such feelings aside for the sake of our art since we are performing for ourselves in my parlor? Josef is a musician, the best viola player I know. *You* are a musician . . . We all have that love in common."

Rudolph stood and pointed his bow at Father, his voice sharp. "For heaven's sake, Martin, my brother is the new regional commandant for the Nazi police. Don't you understand? I cannot risk being thought a sympathizer. I cannot even be in the same house with a Jew. If anyone thought I was colluding . . ." His eyes darted toward the windows. "My brother's son, my own nephew, Anselm, works at the factory with Friedrich. If Friedrich were to mention to him that I was here . . ."

Friedrich winced. Anselm was the son of the commandant for the Nazi police? No wonder he acted as he did. "Sir, I will *never* mention it."

Rudolph put his violin and bow back in the case. "Jewish sympathizers are *not* taken lightly by the Nazis."

Father blurted, "You and I have discussed politics many times. You've never been a supporter of the new regime! Surely, you do not endorse the outrageous laws: We must *play* the music Hitler wishes! We must *read* only what Hitler approves! We must *look* as Hitler wants us to look!"

Friedrich wanted to scream at Father. Had he forgotten he was no longer allowed to be a free-thinker? Had he forgotten his promise to keep his opinions to himself? Had he forgotten that Friedrich should make a favorable impression?

"Things have changed," said Rudolph, snapping his case shut. "I *abide* by the new laws, for Germany's sake and the future of my family." He waved his hand toward Friedrich. "Have you looked at your own son, Martin? Maybe the new laws are for good reason."

Friedrich's face stung as if he'd been smacked. Was this what people now thought when they saw his birthmark? Thank goodness for the new laws?

"I should leave," said Josef, standing.

"No!" said Father. And then more softly, "You are my guest."

Rudolph gathered his coat. "You've chosen sides, Martin. I hope you understand that I am obligated to discuss this with my brother." He shook his head. "I'm disappointed in you, as will my brother be. What were you thinking?" He left, slamming the front door behind him.

Father slumped in his chair, muttering, "I was thinking we would make music." He looked from Josef to Friedrich. "I had no idea things would deteriorate so. I supposed that everyone would get along. We're all musicians . . ."

Josef put a hand on Father's shoulder. "You are naive, my friend, to speak on my behalf. It won't be looked upon favorably. And there's nothing I can do to help."

"It is *I* who should be helping *you*," said Father.

Josef began packing up his viola. "I need to leave, too. You know how people talk. One piece of advice to you, Friedrich. When you audition for the conservatory, avoid the Jewish composers. Play Wagner. Hitler *loves* Wagner, and so his followers must love Wagner, too. And no matter the politics, Wagner is a worthy composer.

Good-bye, my friends." He grabbed his coat and hurried out.

Friedrich turned to Father. "What will happen now?"

Father took a deep breath. "I'll be questioned, to be sure. After that, I don't know. I should have kept quiet . . ." His body caved inward and he looked very small. "Rudolph and I have been friends for over twenty years. I taught his daughter the cello. We've gone to concerts together . . . Friedrich, nothing makes sense anymore. Neighbors reporting neighbors. Friends reporting friends . . . Everyone afraid. What horror is next?"

Friedrich helped Father to the sofa. He walked to the table, poured a cup of tea, and carried it to him. "Stay right here, Father. I'm going for Uncle Gunter."

17

Uncle Gunter paced the room as Friedrich and Father recounted all that had happened earlier that evening.

Afterward, he pulled one of the kitchen chairs directly in front of the sofa where Father and Friedrich sat. He looked from one to the other.

"Do you understand what must be done?"

Father nodded. "We must leave."

"Leave Trossingen?" asked Friedrich. "But we'll be back as soon as all this is sorted out, right? In time for my audition in January?"

Father's face crumbled. "I am so sorry."

Uncle Gunter shook his head, his eyes solemn. "I don't think you understand, Friedrich. We must not only leave *Trossingen*. We must leave *Germany*."

"Son, if there was any other way to guarantee our safety . . ."

"They will be watching all of us now," said Uncle Gunter.

Friedrich slumped back against the sofa. Leave Germany? Leave the only home he'd ever known? Father's and his uncle's voices spun around him.

Must be soon . . . tomorrow . . . Friedrich and I will go to work as usual . . . go to the bank and take out money, but not enough to arouse suspicion . . . luggage packed and ready . . . must have a pretense . . . to see Elisabeth in Berlin . . . meet at Gunter's . . . walk by night and sleep in fields by day . . . south . . . Berne, Switzerland . . .

Friedrich shifted his eyes from Father to Uncle Gunter. Was this real? Was this happening?

He left them in the parlor and slowly walked upstairs to his room, their quiet murmurings a constant hum as they continued to make plans.

Friedrich sat on the edge of his bed, despondent. All his hopes and dreams and the world he knew to be safe were gone. How could his life have changed so quickly?

He reached out and touched the cello that sat propped next to the bed. They would take the instruments to Uncle Gunter's apartment tomorrow night. He had a storage room that could be locked for safekeeping. But how long would they languish there? Months? Years? Forever?

He reached in his pocket for the harmonica. He began to play the familiar "Jesu, Joy of Man's Desiring," the final chorale in Bach's Cantata no. 147, and was immediately transported to when he first heard it.

He was a kindergartner, walking with Father into the music store to buy bow rosin. A gramophone sat in the center of the store in a carved wooden case as high as a podium. A recording of the chorale movement was playing. Friedrich was mesmerized. When it finished, he begged the store owner to begin it again, and he obliged. That night, Friedrich had stood in front of Father with a hair comb as a baton and hummed the music, as if reciting a story, note by note. It was his first memory of conducting, and he could still see the surprise and delight in Father's and Elisabeth's faces as they clapped for him.

He lay down on his pillow and stared into the darkness.

Was there a conservatory in Berne? Or anything as wonderful as his life in Trossingen with Father and Uncle Gunter and his factory family?

From the hall below, he heard the tiny door click open on the clock, the steadfast bird sliding forward and cuckooing the hour. But instead of its usual cheerful twitter, it sounded like a warning.

18

The next morning on the way to work, Friedrich was shadowed by worry and exhaustion; he'd hardly slept, and when he had, it was fitful.

He was almost to the factory when he heard Anselm's voice.

"Friedrich, wait!"

He couldn't be bothered with Anselm today. He kept walking, pretending not to hear him.

He felt someone grab his arm and spin him around.

"I asked you to wait for me!" At first, Anselm looked angry, but then his face broke into a smile. "I promised to take you to a Hitler Youth meeting, remember? There's one tonight. It's time you saw what fun it is. I'll pick you up at your house at seven o'clock."

Why couldn't Anselm leave him alone? Friedrich pulled his arm from his hand. "I've told you, I'm not interested." He tried to keep his voice steady. He hunched forward and walked faster toward the factory gates.

Anselm kept up with him. "It doesn't matter if you're interested, Friedrich. You will be after you attend a meeting. You see, *your* sister made *my* sister promise that I'd get you to a meeting for your own good, and the good of your family. And I mean to live up to the request. It's too late for your father, Friedrich. But not for you."

Friedrich stopped, his body tensed, and his hands clutched in fists.

"That's right, Friedrich. Late last night, my uncle told my father all about Martin Schmidt and his Jew friend. From what I hear, things aren't going to go well for your father." He put his hand on Friedrich's shoulder and squeezed. "But there is still hope for you. Tonight, then? For your salvation and for Germany."

Friedrich stepped away from Anselm's grasp. "I can't tonight. I have plans."

"What plans, Friedrich? What is more important?"

"I . . . I won't be home!"

"Where will you be, then? Tell me!"

Why was Anselm badgering him? He wanted
to yell at him to mind his own concerns, but
Friedrich knew he wouldn't give up. He blurted,
"We're visiting my sister in Berlin this weekend. A
family matter."

Anselm tilted his head, staring at him. "Is that
so?" Then, as if something had dawned on him,
he nodded and broke into a grin. He turned and
jogged away, calling over his shoulder, "Whatever
you say, Friedrich."

Why had Anselm suddenly backed off? And
why was he jogging toward town, instead of to the
factory?

When Friedrich arrived home from work, the
luggage and the cellos sat packed and waiting by
the door. Had Father remembered everything?

He and Father ate dinner quietly and slowly;
it was still too early to leave for Uncle Gunter's.
After, Father washed the dishes and handed them
to Friedrich, who dried and stacked each piece, his

hands going through the motions but his mind elsewhere.

A rude knocking startled him. Friedrich locked eyes with Father. "Are you expecting anyone?"

Father shook his head. He walked to the parlor and peered through the curtains. "It's the authorities. Friedrich, listen to me. Say nothing. No matter what their accusations."

"Father . . ." Friedrich felt a sinking in his stomach.

Father turned and grabbed him, hugging him close. "I'm sorry, Friedrich. I was the one who brought this upon us. No matter what happens, don't say a word." Father released him and opened the door.

Two storm troopers in brown shirts stared at them. One was short and stout, the other at least a foot taller than his companion.

"Mr. Schmidt," said the tall one. "I am Captain Eiffel and this"—he nodded to his companion— "is Captain Faber. May we come in?" Before Father could answer, they stepped into the hallway.

Eiffel nodded to the bags Father had packed. "You are going on a trip?"

"Yes, to Berlin to see my daughter."

The two soldiers walked into the parlor and looked around. Father followed with Friedrich close at his side. No one sat.

"You see, Mr. Schmidt, *that* is the problem," said Faber. "We received word that you were heading to Berlin to see your daughter. The problem is that your daughter is not *in* Berlin. She's with the commandant's daughter preparing for a rally in Munich and will be there all weekend."

"We . . . we have other family to visit," said Father.

"They will be in Munich at the rally as well," said Eiffel. "Going to Berlin is a charade, isn't it?"

Friedrich felt light-headed as he put the pieces together. That was why Anselm had stopped harassing him so suddenly this morning. He'd known about the rally in Munich and that Elisabeth would be there with Margarethe. He'd caught Friedrich in a lie and told his father, the commandant. Now Father had been caught in a lie, too.

"I'm afraid you will have to postpone your travels since you have no official reason to go to Berlin," said Faber.

"And we need you to accompany us to the regional headquarters. For questioning," said Eiffel.

"For what purpose?" said Father.

"That will all be explained. You will join us?" Faber swept an arm toward the door.

"Of course." Father turned to Friedrich. "I'm sure this will not take long."

Eiffel walked to Friedrich, stopping a few inches from his face.

Friedrich backed away.

"The boy. He is deformed. Is he also affected?" Eiffel spoke as if Friedrich weren't standing close enough to smell his breath.

"He is not deformed or affected. He is brilliant," said Father. "It is only a birthmark."

"It is ugly and offensive," said Eiffel. "Does he have someone to look after him?"

"Yes," said Father. "Me. I'll be back in a few hours, isn't that correct?"

The two men exchanged a glance.

Faber raised an eyebrow. "Does he have someone, *other* than you, who might look after him if
this takes more than a few hours? Otherwise, there
is a place we can send him. You've heard of the
Home for Unfortunates?"

The asylum? Friedrich reached for Father as he
had when he was a small boy.

"That won't be necessary." Father took
Friedrich's hand and looked at him. "Don't worry,
son. I am sure this is a misunderstanding. In the
meantime, please go to Uncle Gunter's."

Faber turned to Friedrich. "Your uncle. Does
he share your father's politics? Family members
usually do. Is he, by chance, a Jew-lover, too? We'll
need his name."

Wide-eyed, Friedrich looked from the guard
to Father, who gave him the subtlest shake of
his head.

"No matter. We'll find out from your father."

"Leave the boy, and let's get on with this," said
Eiffel.

Father squeezed Friedrich's hand and then
let go.

Faber stood at attention and announced, "Based on Article One of the Decree of the Reich President for the Protection of People and State of 28 February 1933, you are taken into protective custody in the interest of public security and order, on suspicion of activities dangerous to the State."

The storm troopers flanked Father and escorted him out the front door and into a large black car.

Friedrich waited until it pulled away, then grabbed his coat and ran.

19

Friedrich didn't remember how he arrived at Uncle Gunter's building.

By the time he stood in the hallway in front of the apartment, Friedrich's chest ached and he gasped for air. He pounded on the door.

When Uncle Gunter opened it, Friedrich plunged into the room.

The color drained from Uncle Gunter's face. "So they have come already."

Friedrich nodded, trying to catch his breath.

Uncle Gunter shut the door, ushering Friedrich into the kitchen, where they sat. "Tell me exactly what they said."

The words swam in Friedrich's head, but he tried to repeat them as best he could.

"Were they wearing the brown shirts of the storm troopers? Or the local police uniform?"

"Brown shirts."

Uncle Gunter rubbed his forehead. "This is worse than we expected. The local guard is more sympathetic . . ."

"Father said he would be home in a few hours," said Friedrich, standing. "I need to go back to the house to wait for him."

Uncle Gunter shook his head. "No, Friedrich. He will not be back in a few hours. And you can't stay there. They will be back to search."

"For what?" asked Friedrich.

"Information. Evidence. Anything valuable. If they find books or music that are not approved, they will confiscate and burn them."

Friedrich put his hands on his head. "This is all my fault. I told Anselm we were leaving to meet Elisabeth in Berlin. How was I to know she wasn't in Berlin and that she was with the commandant's daughter, Anselm's *sister*, in Munich?"

"Nephew, none of us could have known. This is not your fault. But right now, we don't have time to debate. We must move quickly and go back and get your things."

The familiar and comforting streets of Trossingen suddenly felt dangerous. Were they being watched? Would someone report them? How long until Uncle Gunter might be questioned, too?

Once inside the house, Friedrich quickly gathered the photo of Father and Mother from his dresser, some sheet music, and his cello. He patted his pocket to make sure the harmonica was still there.

Uncle Gunter picked up Father's cello and grabbed the still-waiting luggage. He turned out all the lights and locked the door.

As they hurried away, Friedrich looked back at his house, now a black cavity between the lamp-lit others.

Uncle Gunter urged him to walk faster, even as they struggled with the instruments and luggage. Fear pressed on Friedrich's chest. What would happen if the Nazis saw them? Would they be mistaken for Jews who hadn't paid their rent? Was this what it was like for Josef's family when they were forced to leave their home? Would he and Father ever return to theirs?

★　　★　　★

Later, as Friedrich lay on the cot Uncle Gunter had set up for him in front of the hearth, he looked around the small two-room apartment, now crowded with his and Father's bags and the cellos.

He clutched the harmonica to his chest and cried into his pillow. He could have sworn he heard music . . . the Brahms . . . first as a child's lullaby, then a mournful lament, and finally, a staccato march, accompanied by the ominous sound of jackboots.

Was it his imagination? Or a premonition?

20

Friedrich passed the weekend in a state of numbness and anxiety.

He and Uncle Gunter had hoped Father would be questioned and released the next day or the following. When he wasn't, they mulled the same questions over and over: Was Father being detained in town? Or had he been taken far away? Would he be released? Or held indefinitely? Was he safe? Or . . .

Early Monday morning, before work, Friedrich and Uncle Gunter went to check the house. Friedrich couldn't help but wish they'd find Father, sitting in the kitchen, sorting sheet music.

Mrs. von Gerber was sweeping her front steps when they arrived. She nodded to them. "Friedrich, I saw soldiers take your father the other night. Is there any news?"

Friedrich shook his head. He wished he knew for certain if Mrs. von Gerber was concerned or just fishing for gossip.

"It's unfortunate that the government thinks Mr. Schmidt is their enemy," said Uncle Gunter. "He's just a temperamental musician."

"He's always been that way," said Mrs. von Gerber. "Prone to emotional outbursts. Elisabeth is certainly a credit to the family and the new government." She raised her chin toward the Nazi flag in her window. "I intend to follow her example. I don't want any trouble." Her eyes darted up and down the street. She gave one final push of her broom and disappeared inside her house.

Friedrich gazed at the flag. "Mrs. von Gerber?"

Uncle Gunter tugged on Friedrich's arm. "Do not believe everything you see. Come. Let's check inside."

When Friedrich and Uncle Gunter reached the door, they noticed the jamb was splintered. They exchanged a worried look before they slowly entered. Photographs that had hung on the wall were askew, and coats and hats lay in a heap on the floor beneath the hall tree. The cuckoo held court, unscathed.

"Maybe it isn't so bad," said Friedrich.

Uncle Gunter stood in the doorway to the parlor, his face telling another story.

Friedrich stepped forward and his eyes widened. The room was in shambles. Furniture had been tipped. Old cello bows had been cracked in half. Sheet music was scattered. Books lay strewn on the floor. Only *Mein Kampf* by Adolf Hitler was left standing face out on a shelf.

Friedrich and Uncle Gunter walked through the house. Every room had been searched and turned upside down; every drawer and closet had been pillaged. Except Elisabeth's room. The poster of the Nazi girl and boy in their uniforms had been left untouched.

"Friedrich, I want you to go on to work. Tell Ernst I wasn't feeling well but will be back tomorrow. Say nothing about the break-in. Do you understand?"

"I want to stay with you," said Friedrich.

Uncle Gunter shook his head. "I'm going to get answers if I can, but in secret. I have a friend I can trust who works with the local police. He owes me a favor. I'll ask him to inquire at the commandant's headquarters on our behalf. I need you to go to the factory and act as if all is well. I'll meet you at home tonight."

News of Father's arrest had traveled fast.

When Friedrich walked onto the factory floor, he felt more self-conscious than he ever had from his birthmark. It seemed everyone's eyes searched him out: eyes full of worry, or piercing gazes of superiority that said Father should have known better, and the all-too-familiar looks of pity that were, this time, for something other than his face.

He kept his head down, hurried to his station, and set to work. When Ernst made his rounds, Friedrich told him that Uncle Gunter wasn't feeling well but would be back tomorrow.

Ernst nodded. "I was deeply sorry, Friedrich, to

hear about Martin." His voice was so sincere that Friedrich couldn't look up for fear he'd cry.

When Anselm came by to deliver harmonicas, he was as puffed up as a rooster. "Guess you'll think twice the next time you turn me down for a meeting, right, Friedrich?"

Friedrich refused to meet his gaze and kept working.

Anselm leaned in. "There's another Youth Rally next month for Winter Solstice. You'll come with me this time. We don't want the same thing to happen to your uncle that happened to your father, do we, Friedrich?" He sauntered away, whistling.

Anselm's threat burned inside him. Friedrich gritted his teeth to keep from saying something he'd regret.

21

After work, Friedrich found Uncle Gunter waiting for him at the kitchen table in the apartment.

Friedrich pulled out a chair and sat next to him, searching his troubled face. "The news is not good, is it?"

Uncle Gunter shook his head. "He was taken to Dachau on a train with a group of other political prisoners. He's confined there."

Dachau. WORK WILL SET YOU FREE. Friedrich shuddered. "The hard-labor prison?"

"Yes," said Uncle Gunter.

"For how long?" whispered Friedrich.

"I don't know. I went to see some friends who have a family member there. People have been given sentences of as little as a month, and as much as several years. It depends on how long the Nazis think it will take to reeducate the prisoner to the Nazi way of thinking."

Friedrich swiped at his tears. "But can't a prisoner just *say* he's reeducated?"

"They have ways of knowing if the person is sincere," said Uncle Gunter. "Nazis put spies inside the camp, posing as other prisoners. They read their mail and watch their families, hoping to round up more dissenters."

"Will they try and round you up?"

Uncle Gunter put a hand on his arm. "Maybe. But let's worry about your father right now. There's a way we might shorten his sentence."

Friedrich leaned forward. "How?"

Uncle Gunter looked around as if someone might be listening. "Once a prisoner has been there a month, a family member may bring a sizable ransom to the commandant at Dachau. Then the prisoner will be released on probation."

"A ransom?" Friedrich brightened. "I have money from my earnings. I was going to use it for books at the conservatory, but . . ." He shrugged. Would he ever go to the conservatory now, anyway? And for Father, he'd do anything. "It's as much as three months' worth of my regular pay."

"I have double your amount I can add," said Uncle Gunter. "But it is still not enough. What about . . . Elisabeth?"

"Elisabeth? No," said Friedrich. It would be just what she'd want to hear. That Father hadn't listened to her advice and was now in trouble. And wouldn't she delight in lecturing Friedrich?

"Friedrich, please reconsider," said Uncle Gunter. "You could write her and tell her what she wants to hear. That Martin and I are eager to join the Nazi Party. That you will join the Hitler Youth. And that you need help for your father's sake, to bring him back into Germany's arms. Part of it would be a ruse. But what difference would it make if it saves Martin's life? And if *she* were the one to deliver the money—the family's shining example— they would surely let him go."

"Couldn't we ask Margarethe's parents?"

Uncle Gunter shook his head. "Your father has never trusted them. And this ransom is not exactly . . . officially permitted."

"It's illegal?" Friedrich shook his head. "Then Elisabeth will want nothing to do with it."

"Don't be so sure. He's her father, too. She has a right to know where he is and what he's facing," said Uncle Gunter. "And you won't be asking for a ransom. You'll be asking for assistance with a re-education stipend. Besides, there is no one else who might help. If you won't write to her, I'll do it myself. But it would be better coming from you. What will it hurt to ask?"

Friedrich took a deep breath, closing his eyes for a moment. He knew the answer. "Only my pride."

"It has worked for others. And the sooner we get him out, the better. They work them until . . . I . . . I can't let that happen to my brother." Uncle Gunter rubbed at his damp eyes. "Friedrich, until we can get your father away from there, we must appear loyal. Tomorrow, I will register for the party and get two Nazi flags, one for your house and one for mine. That should keep me from an interview any time soon."

Friedrich sighed. "And tonight, I will write to Elisabeth, the loyal Hitlerite."

22

Trossingen prepared for the holidays, but Friedrich's heart was joyless and sick with worry.

Father had been in Dachau for over a month, and still Friedrich hadn't heard from Elisabeth. Nor had Father answered one of Friedrich's or Uncle Gunter's letters. Was he ill? Was he warm enough? Had he enough to eat? Was he . . . alive?

Uncle Gunter nodded to the dinner. "You barely sleep, you pick at your food, your work at the factory has slowed. I haven't heard a sound from your harmonica in weeks. Eat, Friedrich. You need to stay strong."

Just as Friedrich raised his fork, there was a series of quick knocks at the door. His heart sped up. Was it storm troopers again? He followed Uncle Gunter to the door, clutching his arm.

But this time, it was Mrs. von Gerber in a long wool coat, holding a shopping basket.

166

"Please come in," said Uncle Gunter.

She stepped inside. "I won't stay. I am delivering a package to Friedrich. It came to my house inside a box addressed to me. That dear Elisabeth remembered to send me several jars of quince jam. And she had it hand-delivered by a friend. Her note said she didn't want to send it through the post because the jars are fragile. And she asked if I could give this to you without delay." From beneath her groceries, Mrs. von Gerber pulled a fat, square package wrapped in brown paper and tied with string. She handed it to Friedrich. "She asked for my discretion in the matter."

"Thank you," said Friedrich.

She nodded to Uncle Gunter and lowered her voice. "They canvass the house every day. Soldiers came again yesterday and questioned the neighbors. They asked about you, your dispositions, your feelings about Jews. I told them I only knew you as Elisabeth and Friedrich's kindly uncle. Nothing more. After they left, they stood on my step, smoking. I couldn't help but hear. One said, 'Question him on Wednesday with the others, and if he's not believable, put him with his brother.'"

Uncle Gunter took Mrs. von Gerber's hand. "You're very kind . . ."

She pulled away. "I'll be going. I must visit a friend on the next floor. She's my excuse for being in the building." She quickly slipped out the door and was gone.

Uncle Gunter locked the door behind her and pulled the shades.

"Uncle, they are going to question you . . ."

"It is nothing we didn't suspect. Besides, I'll be believable. I know what to say to please them. Now, let's see what Elisabeth has sent." He nodded toward the package.

Friedrich sat down at the table. With a knife, he carefully cut the string and unwrapped the brown paper. An envelope lay on the lid of a square tin. He took a deep breath before he opened it, unfolded the letter, and began to read.

Dear Friedrich,

Thank you for your recent correspondence. I wish you a Happy Winter Solstice, instead of a Merry Christmas. Even if you still celebrate Christmas, it is recommended that people not put stars on top of their trees. A six-pointed star is a Jewish symbol and a five-pointed star is a Communist symbol, both of which do not align with Nazi ideology. Stars of any type are not appropriate.

My work goes well . . .

He scanned the rest. It was all about her League work and her hope that Friedrich would join the Hitler Youth. He opened the box and unfolded the paper. "Cookies shaped like swastikas! Is it all she can think about?"

He shoved his chair backward, stood, tossed the letter on the table, and began to pace around the kitchen.

"I wrote her that Father is in *Dachau*! I asked her to help me and all she talks about are stars! She didn't even *ask* about him!" Tears welled in his eyes.

Uncle Gunter picked up the letter and began to read it.

"Friedrich, what does the postscript mean? 'I hope you enjoy the cookies. I made them myself, especially for you and Uncle. Don't eat them all at once as you tried to do before, especially since I won't be there to hide them from you.'"

Friedrich threw his hands in the air, trying to remember. "When I was little . . . I ate an entire plate of cookies. She was so angry she hid the next batch in the bread box, under the crumb tray."

Uncle Gunter raised his eyebrows. He leaned over the tin. Carefully, he lifted the cookies out one at a time, layer by layer. When the box was empty, he picked up the knife, put the point beneath the base, and pried.

A false bottom popped up.

Friedrich sucked in his breath.

Underneath were stacks of Reichsmarks. Wide-eyed, Friedrich carefully picked them up, fanned them out, then laid them on the table. "Is it enough?"

Uncle Gunter nodded. "It is plenty. And it was a great risk for her to send them. If Mrs. von Gerber hadn't been trustworthy, Elisabeth could be the one questioned next. I think we can assume she won't be our emissary. We should carry the money in the box, as she sent it. It's a good ploy. And patriotic, too. We still need to figure out how to deliver it. Let us sleep on it and talk again in the morning." Uncle Gunter smiled. "Elisabeth may not be the Nazi she seems. Nor Mrs. von Gerber, for that matter."

After Uncle Gunter went to bed, Friedrich sat in the small kitchen looking at the Reichsmarks. He pulled the harmonica from his pocket and began to play "O Tannenbaum," "O Christmas Tree."

He closed his eyes and was swept back in time. Elisabeth was at the piano in the parlor, playing and singing. She was twelve years old. Her fingers danced over the keys and her head swayed with the music.

Friedrich could still remember feeling transfixed.

When she noticed him, she stopped and patted the bench so that he might climb next to her. She began again, and together they sang.

O Christmas Tree, O Christmas Tree,
How lovely are thy branches.
They're green when summer days are bright,

They're green when winter snow is white.
O Christmas Tree, O Christmas Tree,
How lovely are thy branches.

When they had finished singing, they turned to each other and laughed. And Elisabeth impulsively took his face in her hands and kissed his cheeks. No matter what she had said in recent months, she *had* loved him once. Did she still?

He laid the harmonica on the table next to all the Reichsmarks.

Then he gathered paper and pen and wrote to Elisabeth, thanking her for the information about the stars. He thanked her, too, for the cookies, and said they would go far in making their holiday more rewarding. He wrote about the smallest of his daily tasks and what he and Uncle Gunter had had for dinner. And he reminded her of the time she put a mustard poultice on his face to try to make his birthmark disappear.

He wished her well. And addressed the envelope with the endearment 'lisbeth Schmidt, so she wouldn't forget the sound of his voice.

23

An hour before first light, Friedrich suddenly awoke and sat up on the cot.

From the next room, he heard Uncle Gunter's gentle snoring.

Even before he'd fallen asleep last night, an idea had begun to knit in his mind. Now the prospect was fully formed. He lay down again and went over all that would need to happen and in which order. And he found his hands in the air, conducting.

He threw off his blanket. He needed to convince Uncle Gunter.

"I don't like it, Friedrich. I don't like it at all."

Uncle Gunter sat on the edge of his bed in his overalls and pulled on his work boots. "Let's eat a piece of bread and get to the factory." He headed into the kitchen.

Friedrich followed and tried to reason with him. "Uncle, even if Elisabeth had offered to be our messenger, which she did not, she's in Berlin in the north, twelve or more hours by train. Dachau is only half the time from here, and it is east. It makes *sense* for it to be me. Besides, they are watching you. You *must* leave. Just as we planned before Father was taken."

"I promised your father I would not—"

"If you are arrested, you will have to leave me anyway. You heard Mrs. von Gerber. They will question you on Wednesday. How many people do they question and just let go? They'll take you. And then what will become of me?"

"Friedrich, if I just disappear before they come to question me, it will take only one telephone call to block any attempts on your part to release your father from Dachau."

"Not if I've already gone there." Friedrich took a deep breath. "I have a plan. Today is Friday. When we get to work, you must think of something to tell Ernst as to why you will not be in on Monday. Then, tonight after dark, you will leave for Berne.

That will give you three days to reach there, walking the back roads at night and sleeping during the day, just like we'd originally planned before Father was taken. It's the weekend. No one will be the wiser. I'll go to work on Monday and leave at lunchtime, making an excuse to Mr. Eichmann about not reading to him that day. Then I'll take the afternoon train. And deliver the ransom first thing Tuesday morning."

Uncle Gunter raised his eyebrows. "And when you and I don't show up for work on Tuesday morning?"

"They'll send someone here eventually," said Friedrich, sweeping his hand around the room. "I have that worked out, too. When they arrive, they'll presume to know what happened to us. But they'll be wrong."

Uncle Gunter sliced a piece of bread for both of them as Friedrich continued explaining.

Uncle Gunter blew out a deep breath and rubbed his chin. "It's clever."

"You must leave tonight."

Uncle Gunter went to the tiny window over

the basin and stared out. "But think of all that could go wrong. We don't know Martin's condition. What if he's not well enough to travel?" He held up a finger. "Wait. I have a friend we can trust who is a doctor in Munich. If your father needs medical help, you can go to him."

Friedrich smiled. "You can give me his information."

"Yes . . . yes . . . that is a possibility." He turned to Friedrich. "You can take nothing of sentiment or value or it will be confiscated by the Nazis, except for the Reichsmarks, of course. It's good that it's the holidays. Many people will be traveling and will be preoccupied. I suspect the commandant at Dachau will feel more amenable right before Christmas, too."

Uncle Gunter looked at him. The seriousness and risk of what they were about to do filled the room.

"Friedrich, you understand that once we leave, there's no coming back."

"Yes, Uncle, I understand."

"Nephew . . . from where have you found your conviction?"

"From Father, and you. And even from Elisabeth. If she can jeopardize everything important in her life to save Father, shouldn't I?"

Uncle Gunter nodded. "Well then, here is what I will tell Ernst when I get to work this morning: I've been nursing a toothache for days. I called a dentist but the first appointment I can get is Monday and I suspect it needs to be pulled so I'll have to miss a day of work."

Friedrich smiled. "And I will tell Mr. Eichmann I can't read to him on Monday afternoon because I need to help you home from the dentist."

Uncle Gunter took a deep breath, his face wrenched with worry.

Friedrich instinctively patted the pocket that held his harmonica. "We can do it, Uncle. One foot in front of the other."

24

That evening after dark had settled, Uncle Gunter stood near his door, bundled for a night in the cold.

He wrapped a heavy wool scarf around his neck and pulled on a knit cap. He put on gloves, his eyes sweeping the small apartment. "Make it look as if it really happened."

Friedrich nodded. "I will."

"And remember all we've discussed."

"Uncle, we went over it a dozen times."

"I know. I'm proud of you, Friedrich. And so will your father be." He pulled Friedrich close one last time and hugged him. "Don't forget who is your real uncle. Who taught you to ride a bicycle?"

"You."

"And to play the harmonica?"

Friedrich laughed, fighting back tears. "You. I won't forget."

"With luck, I'll see you in a week. Be safe."

Uncle Gunter picked up his bag, stepped out the door, and pulled it shut behind him.

"I'll try," whispered Friedrich.

Friedrich woke on Saturday morning, shivering.

He built the fire, pulled the cot closer to the hearth, and watched the flames leap. He realized that for the first time in his life, he was alone. Not only that, he held the fate of his family in his hands. If he could not complete this undertaking, what might happen to them all?

The reality of what he was soon to do came crashing down upon him. He'd have to buy tickets, take trains, and sit across from strangers. He'd have to suffer the stares of clerks, porters, conductors, and people he'd never met.

He held his hands out toward the hearth to warm them, his mind reviewing what he and Uncle Gunter had discussed. He would take the train to Stuttgart and transfer to Munich. But he mustn't draw undue attention to himself.

The money was a concern. He couldn't lose it or let it fall into the wrong hands. When he reached

Munich, he would walk to Dachau. Before the main gate, he would find the administration building and ask to speak to the commandant about his father, Martin Schmidt.

He must be humble and polite. And appear sincere. He must not take anything with him that was of sentiment or value because his bag would be searched and anything desirable would be confiscated. If the guards or the commandant asked about the birthmark, he would tell them he was volunteering to have the surgery to prove his loyalty to the fatherland.

He would lie.

He practiced what he would say when he delivered the ransom. "My family is ready to receive my father back into the world of Hitler's Germany to embrace the Nazi ideals. And as a sign of good faith and respect, I have brought a package of delicacies for the commandant."

The words rolled around in his mouth like marbles, hard and slick, making him wish he could spit them out.

But he repeated them again. And again.

25

On Sunday evening, Friedrich packed a small satchel and put it by the door.

He set the dinner table for two, filling both plates and eating off both of them. Then he strewed a stack of newspapers around the room. He opened cupboards, took out plates, and broke them, muffling the sound beneath tea towels. Silently and methodically—so as not to alert the neighbors yet—he tipped over lamps and chairs, rifled through old mail, and tossed clothing from drawers. He left the remnants of dinner on the table as if he and Uncle Gunter had been interrupted mid-meal. After dark, he took a screwdriver and, from the hallway, quietly splintered the doorjamb. Then he did his mathematics homework.

When the stage was set, he sat on the cot, lifted the harmonica, and played a good-night concert, soothed by the beauty of the music and the lyrics in his mind.

Lullaby, and good night, with pink roses bedight . . .

He swayed, as if cradling Trossingen and its half-timbered houses. He played for the tall stone building, the conservatory, and the notes that sprinkled down in a shower, washing his face clean. He played for the factory with its cobblestone square, the huddled buildings and the fat water tower that had kept him safe. He bid his greedy lunch mates adieu, along with the graveyard room where most men wouldn't dare to go alone. And the A-frame ladder with the perch from where he imagined directing a percussive symphony of machinery. He said good night to Mrs. Steinweg, Mr. Karl, Mr. Eichmann, and to Mr. Adler and Mr. Engel, who were still arguing about which of them was the most suited to teach him Secondary History.

He played for his house, the kitchen with the walnut hutch, his mother's collection of plates, the tin canisters that sat in descending order, the green shutters, the parlor that smelled of bow rosin and Father's anise lozenges, his bedroom that still looked the same, the way he liked it, and Elisabeth's room, the oil painting of a field of flowers above her bed, back where it belonged.

> *With lilies o'er spread, is my baby's wee bed.*
> *Lay thee down now and rest, may thy slumber*
>   *be blessed . . .*

He played for the cuckoo, resting and waiting behind its tiny door for the quarter hour.

> *. . . may thy slumber be blessed.*

He lay down, fully dressed, on the cot he would upturn in the morning, and pulled a blanket over himself.

"Good night," he whispered.

26

At the factory, Friedrich tried to act as if it was any other Monday morning.

He pretended that carrying a satchel with his coat draped over it was usual. And that hiding the satchel in the cupboard at his work space, knowing that hundreds of Reichsmarks were inches from his feet, was an everyday occurrence. He was nonchalant as he sent an apprentice to tell Mr. Eichmann that he couldn't read to him that afternoon because Uncle Gunter needed his help getting home from the dentist. When Mr. Karl came by, Friedrich handed over his mathematics homework but begged off reviewing it with him until tomorrow for the same reason—he had to leave early today.

He kept his head down, inspecting and polishing, until he caught sight of Anselm, coming toward him with a box of harmonicas.

"Friedrich, the Winter Solstice Rally is Thursday. We can go together from work at two o'clock. I'd hate for you to decline again . . ."

"I'll go," said Friedrich, forcing a smile.

"Of course you will! You won't be disappointed. And I'll have fulfilled my promise to your sister. I am sure, when she hears, she'll be surprised that I was able to convince you. But I can be persuasive, right?"

Friedrich nodded and turned back to his work. "Right."

For the rest of the morning, he watched the clock.

Finally, he pulled the harmonica from his pocket and spent far more time polishing it than needed. He had meant to send it with Uncle Gunter, but with his mind consumed by the plan, he'd forgotten. Now Uncle Gunter's words played in his head: *You can take nothing of sentiment or value or it will be confiscated by the Nazis.* Friedrich looked around to see if anyone was watching, and then one last time he blew into the harmonica that had filled him with such confidence and determination. The

chord sounded . . . hopeful. He massaged the red
𝒜 on the side, tucked it into a box, and felt a
pang as he put on the lid. He nestled the box in
a slim case with a dozen others that would soon be
packed into a crate, carted to an electric train,
pulled by a steam engine to a cargo ship, and fer-
ried from Germany across the ocean and out into
the world.

"*Gute Reise*, old friend," Friedrich whispered,
wondering who might play it next and whether it
would bring that person as much joy and comfort
as it had brought him.

The lunch whistle blew. Friedrich let most of
the men flood off the factory floor before he
grabbed the satchel from the cupboard, draped it
with his coat again, and walked from the building.

A light snow fell and when Friedrich exhaled,
the cold air made cloudy puffs in front of him.
Once beyond the factory gates, he stopped to put
on his coat. His hands shook. Was he nervous or
cold? He pulled a knit cap below his ears and
wrapped a wool scarf around his neck so that only

a sliver of his face was exposed. He picked up the satchel and hurried to the train station.

He purchased a ticket. There were few passengers waiting this time of day. He sat on a bench beneath an overhang, watching the snow fall. He heard the swish of a broom as a clerk pushed snow from the platform, the giggling of two young women on the next bench over, the clacking of a cart the porter pushed over the wooden planks. Friedrich stuffed his hands under his legs to keep from conducting.

The train arrived on schedule and stopped in a blast of steam.

He climbed aboard and sat pressed to a window.

From the car ahead, two soldiers emerged. "Papers! This is an inspection. All passengers present your papers!"

Friedrich's heart pounded. He recognized the voices! They belonged to the same soldiers who had come to his house and taken Father. The same soldiers who thought Friedrich ugly and offensive.

Had they been the ones who ransacked his house, too? Would they make trouble for him now?

Passenger by passenger, Eiffel and Faber worked their way down the aisle until Faber stood next to him.

"Your papers!"

Friedrich's hands trembled as he pulled his identification from his pocket and handed it to him.

"Your purpose for travel?"

"To see relatives for the holiday."

Faber glanced at his papers and handed them back. "You are cleared." He moved on.

Relief flooded through Friedrich.

Until Eiffel stopped in front of him. "Wait!"

Faber turned back.

Eiffel leaned across the seat and pulled Friedrich's cap and scarf from his face.

"Well, well, well," said Eiffel. "*Who* do we have here? It's the ugly son of a Jew-lover. I always say, like father, like son."

Friedrich hugged the satchel tighter. His eyes darted from one man to the other, fear rising in his throat.

Faber stood straighter. "Friedrich Schmidt, hand over your bag and step into the aisle for inspection in the name of Adolf Hitler and the Third Reich."

Friedrich's breathing became quick and shallow. Was his journey ending before it had even begun?

The steam engine started chuffing.

He inched slowly across his seat and stood in the aisle.

A burst of wind hit the train and a snow flurry descended. All eyes shifted to the outside. Enormous snowflakes swirled, pirouetting like dancers in Tchaikovsky's ballet.

Friedrich heard the *Sleeping Beauty* waltz played by a symphony orchestra—strings, winds, brass, percussion—a hundred instruments strong. And in that moment, something mysterious took hold of him—whether it was an instinct to delay or the impulse to distract the soldiers or something else, Friedrich could not say—but he was unable to control his hands. He dropped the satchel and began to conduct.

Faber gave him a disgusted look, grabbed the satchel, and rummaged through it.

"Stop that nonsense," yelled Eiffel as he struggled to search Friedrich's pockets. "You will soon see the inside of a cell, you lunatic!"

Even as Eiffel and Faber grabbed him by the scruff of the neck and marched him toward the train door, Friedrich imagined only snowy ballerinas—tiny, pure-white stars—twirling and leaping to the hypnotic music.

One, two, three. One, two, three. One, two, three . . .

TWO

JUNE 1935

PHILADELPHIA COUNTY, PENNSYLVANIA

U.S.A.

America the Beautiful

music by Samuel A. Ward
lyrics by Katharine Lee Bates

6   6   5   5   6   6   -4   -4
O beau-ti-ful for spa-cious skies,

5   -5   6   -6   -7   6
For am-ber waves of grain,

6   6   5   5   6   6 -4 -4
For pur-ple moun-tain maj-es-ties

-8   -8   -8   8   -6   -8
A-bove the fruit-ed plain.

6   8   8 -8   7   7 -7 -7
A-mer-i-ca! A-mer-i-ca!

7   -8   -7   -6   6   7
God shed His grace on thee,

7   7   -6   -6   7   7   6   6
And crown thy good with broth-er-hood

6   -6   7   6   -8   6
From sea to shin-ing sea.

I

After a night of wrestling the heat in the Upper Boys' dormitory, Mike Flannery nuzzled into his pillow, savoring the cool air that finally drifted through the open windows at The Bishop's Home for Friendless and Destitute Children.

A mourning dove cooed. Sink faucets dripped. Bedsprings creaked as the lads shifted and settled in their narrow cots.

Through a cobweb of dreams, Mike heard Frankie's distinctive whistle—the last six notes of "America the Beautiful," their signal for emergencies.

He propped himself on one elbow, rubbed his eyes, and hoped he'd imagined it. Mike heard it again and the lyrics played in his mind: ". . . from sea to shining sea." He flung off his sheet, tiptoed to the second-story window, and looked down.

His little brother, Frankie, stood next to a hydrangea bush, pointing to the oak that hugged the side of the brick building.

Mike hurried back to his cot, put on his knickers and shirt, and slipped into his suspenders, being careful not to wake the nineteen other boys still asleep in the room. He ran his fingers through what little hair he had left. Yesterday, a barber had donated his services, and Mike's hair was so short that the cowlick above his left eyebrow stood straight up like an exclamation point. It was bad enough to be almost six feet tall at eleven years old *and* have red hair. It was worse to draw attention to it. He pulled on his cap.

Barefooted, he tiptoed down the hall and past the door of Mrs. Godfrey, the floor warden. The snoring coming from inside reassured him that she wouldn't budge any time soon. He opened the stairwell door, closed it behind him, and took the steps two at a time to the landing between floors. At the window, he lifted the sash and stuck out his head.

Frankie had already scaled to the tree's saddle where the limbs forked. He waved and began to climb upward.

Mike couldn't watch. Heights frightened him and looking straight down made him dizzy. He took a step back and waited, shifting his eyes to the Pennsylvania countryside. Bishop's was only a few hours from Philadelphia by automobile, but it might as well be in the middle of nowhere for all the cornfields surrounding it.

Frankie was across from him now, steadying himself with one hand on an overhead branch and walking tightrope fashion across a limb toward the window. The kid was fearless. Mike held his breath until Frankie swung his leg over the sill and tumbled into the stairwell.

Mike helped him stand. "What are you doing up so early? If Mrs. Delancey finds out you left your building before morning bell, she'll tell Pennyweather and you'll get detention in the cellar again." He brushed twigs from Frankie's hair. He'd seen the barber yesterday, too, but he had the younger boys' bowl cut. "I hate it when you come up the tree."

"It's a 'mergency," whispered Frankie, his large eyes sincere and insistent. "And I *had* to climb up. The side doors are still locked and if you let me in the front door, it'll make too much noise."

"What happened?" asked Mike, herding him toward the stairs. Frankie sat on one step and Mike sat two below so he wouldn't tower over the kid.

There was no mistaking they were brothers. Frankie was a younger version of Mike by four years. His hair wasn't as red, though; it was a far more acceptable auburn. They were both fair with freckles, but Frankie had fewer. Although they were tall for their ages, Mike leaned toward gangly, clumsy, and quiet; Frankie was wiry, athletic, and talkative.

"Last night, Mrs. Delancey was trying to get us to settle in bed," said Frankie. "Me and some of the boys were acting out and playing hide-and-seek. She found me and jerked my arm and told me she can't wait to get rid of me. She said Pennyweather told her you and me are being called up on Friday. That's *tomorrow*. Some families are coming to get boys."

Mike sucked in his breath. "We're getting fostered out?"

"If they like us. What if Pennyweather tries to separate us again?"

"I've told you before," said Mike. "We're not supposed to be separated. Remember? You and me, we stick together." Mike held up a fist.

Frankie did the same, tapping Mike's. "Yeah. You and me, we stick together."

Mike helped him up. "You better go before Mrs. Delancey wakes up. How're you getting back into your building?"

"My buddy James is waiting at a window for me."

Mike lifted Frankie to the sill so he could climb down. He looked across at the Lowers' building, which housed the boys who were five to nine years old. It was a replica of the Uppers', a mammoth brick fortress with intricate herringbone borders around each door and window. Some might consider them handsome buildings. But Mike couldn't say much nice about a place that felt more like a kennel than a home.

They had been at Bishop's a little over five months, which was nothing compared to how long most of the boys had been there. Weekdays, they were supposed to go to school. But since the first of May, schooling had gone by the wayside for working on neighboring farms. Mike would rather have been in class. And Frankie needed more teaching. He could barely read.

Mike paced in the stairwell until he heard the whistle that meant Frankie was safely on the ground. He hurried to the window and watched him dash across the walkway and knock on a ground-floor window. It opened and James helped Frankie inside. Mike shook his head, amazed. The kid already had more friends here than he could count.

Mike couldn't claim one. That was fine by him. None of the Uppers ever bothered him because of his size, but they didn't include him, either. He couldn't blame them. He wasn't good at sports, kept to himself, and as much as he tried, he couldn't help his seriousness.

He'd promised Granny he'd look out for Frankie and take care of him. That responsibility had become another layer of skin. Just when he thought he might shed a little, or breathe easy, or even laugh out loud, it tightened over him. In every situation, Mike wondered first, what could go wrong, and second, how he would protect Frankie if it did.

Mike quietly crept back into his dorm room. Mouse was sprawled across the space next to him. He was older and taller than Mike and didn't fit well on the cot. Mike carefully stepped around him and climbed onto his own thin mattress. In the gray light, he lay back and stared at the wrinkles of old paint on the ceiling.

Maybe the people coming tomorrow would be the answer to getting out of this place. Maybe they even had a piano. Mike rubbed his forehead. Much as it pained him to imagine it, he'd forgo the piano if they were decent folks and he and Frankie could stay together.

Then again, what if he and Frankie were fostered out to someone mean to the bone?

There was always so much that could go wrong.

2

Pennyweather sent for them on Friday afternoon at three o'clock.

Mike and Frankie waited in the Visitation Room connected to her office. The draperies had been pulled open wide so the sunlight streamed in, making everything look bright and cheerful. Centered in the room was a long table with benches on either side. A bowl of shiny apples and a vase of flowers had been positioned just so. Pennyweather always liked to put on a good show.

The office door was open and Mike could hear her talking on the phone.

"Musical instruments? Yes, we have a piano . . . There are several boys here who could . . . Of course I'd consider . . . Yes, you could hear it played. It's an upright. Very good quality. That would be fine. A week from today at one o'clock, and if you like what you hear, you can arrange to take . . . Yes, good-bye."

Mike winced. Pennyweather was selling the piano?

The broken-down upright in the dining hall was out of tune from years of boys pounding on it. One of the pedals was broken. Even so, it was still playable. His first day at Bishop's, Mike had wolfed his food at every meal and then scooted over to play. Pennyweather quickly put an end to that, saying she didn't need more noise during meals with the dishes rattling and all the boys yapping.

Mike had found a way around it. After the boys were excused from dinner, Pennyweather left. He hung back to scrape food off the plates and stack them for the cooks and whoever was on dish duty. If he was fast about it, he had a half hour or more at the keyboard before he had to be back in the dorm. Sometimes, Frankie stayed and played duets with him. At first, the boys in the kitchen threw bread scraps at them, until they heard Mike's and Frankie's talent. Now they made requests. Even in the piano's sorry condition, Mike hated to see it go. Then again, if they were fostered out, it wouldn't make any difference.

Pennyweather walked into the Visitation Room.

Frankie ran to Mike and clung to his arm.

She stood in front of them in her navy-blue, high-necked dress, looking pinched. Her gray hair had been pulled so tight into a topknot that her eyes squinted. Mike wondered if it hurt.

"Stand straight and don't fidget," she said. "Mr. and Mrs. Rutledge will be in here shortly. They're the last appointment of the day. Don't speak unless you're spoken to. And try to look pleasant. They want two boys, which, as you know, doesn't happen very often."

Mike's heart pounded. They wanted *two*?

He looked at Frankie, who smiled up at him. Mike wiped a smudge from Frankie's cheek. The kid's pants were torn and he had no socks. Mike's shirt was stained and threadbare. The clothes Granny had sent with them, that she'd washed and pressed and carefully folded, had disappeared into the general laundry at Bishop's, which left everything the same dingy gray.

"Do I look all right?" asked Frankie.

"Mouse told me the more raggedy you look,

the more likely you are to be fostered 'cause people feel sorry," whispered Mike. If that was the case, he and Frankie were on their way out of Bishop's.

The door opened and a couple stepped into the room. The man wore coveralls and a blue work shirt. He held a wide-brimmed hat in his hand. Farmers. But Mike wouldn't mind the labor as long as they were kind.

The woman, her hands in white gloves, and a pocketbook in the crook of her arm, fidgeted with the buttons on her calico shirtwaist.

"Mr. and Mrs. Rutledge," said Pennyweather, smiling. "Welcome to The Bishop's Home for—"

"Them the boys?" interrupted the man.

"Yes. Michael and Franklin Flannery."

"I know I mentioned I needed two, but I stopped at the state home on the way here and got me a couple strappin' boys can work a farm. Grown men want a paycheck, and all I got to offer is room and board. Hard times, you know. Still, Mother here has her heart set on a youngster for the house so I agreed."

The woman stepped forward. "Feeding the chickens, pulling weeds, fetch and carry."

The man walked over to Frankie and squished his upper arm as if to check his muscle. "He seems kinda puny."

Frankie jerked away.

"Oh, I assure you, Mr. Rutledge, he's stronger than he looks," said Pennyweather. "And if you would like another the same age as Franklin, you can have both for the same arrangement we discussed on the phone earlier."

"Now, that's a deal! That okay with you, Mother?"

The woman shrugged. "Sometimes two is easier than one, just like puppies."

Mike's heart pounded. They were going to take two Lowers and not him?

He put an arm around Frankie. "We're brothers. We stay together."

The man rubbed his chin and studied Mike. "You got any special skills? Roofing? Fencing? Drivin' a tractor?"

Mike stammered. "I . . . I play the piano."

"That doesn't do me no good. Nah. I already got me the two plow boys. Just the younger boys will do."

Pennyweather walked toward Mike and glared. "This is a good opportunity for Franklin . . ."

"No!" screamed Frankie, hugging Mike's leg.

"There now!" said the man. "We'll have none of that!" He reached out and grabbed Frankie's arm.

Mike shoved the man. "Leave my brother alone!"

Mr. Rutledge stumbled backward. "Now *just* a minute here! You keep your hands to yourself!"

Frankie lunged toward the man, grabbed his hand, pulled it to his mouth, and bit.

"Ahhh!" he yelled.

Pennyweather reached for Frankie and missed. "Franklin!"

He darted behind Mike.

"He's bleeding!" cried the woman.

Blood dots beaded up on the man's hand. He pulled a handkerchief from his pocket and bandaged it.

Frankie scrambled into Mike's arms, wrapping his legs around him and burying his face in his neck.

"It's no use, mister," said Mike, hugging Frankie to him. "First chance, he'll run away. He's no good to you without me."

"In all my days, I never seen such a thing," said the man. He turned to Pennyweather. "What're you raising here? Animals? C'mon, Mother." He held the door for his wife, gave the boys a disgusted look, and slammed the door behind him.

Mike put Frankie down and looked at Pennyweather. Her face was anger-stricken; her eyebrows nearly touched her hairline. She marched across the room, opened the door, and pointed to Frankie. "Wait outside!"

After slamming the door, she whipped around to confront Mike.

He felt his face grow warm and knew it would be pink and splotchy in seconds. At the slightest feelings of embarrassment or blame or anger, he lit up like a thermometer sensing a high fever. Granny had always said it was a consequence of being red-haired and fair-skinned.

"Your brother has been called up twice since you've been here. The first time, he spat on a woman's baby. And now this! There are places much worse than Bishop's for wild boys like him."

Mike talked fast. "He didn't mean it. He only acts out because he wants to stay with me. He gets along good with all the other boys. As long as we're together, he's just fine."

Pennyweather crossed her arms. "It's hard enough to get people to take *one* child, let alone two!"

Mike stood as tall as he could, his eyes pleading. "You *promised* our grandmother."

"I promised her I'd *try* to keep you together. It was by no means binding." Pennyweather's anger stayed in her eyes, but her face changed and she smiled. "It won't make a bit of difference soon. Hathaway House in Montgomery County is filled to overflowing with boys over fourteen. They are making it worth my while to create room for them here. Any of the Lowers left by September will go to the state home to free up beds for the Hathaway boys."

Mike felt as if someone had jerked a rug out from under him and he might topple at any minute. He steadied himself on the table. "Then I'll go with Frankie."

"Not if I put you out to hire."

"It's not legal till I'm fourteen! I'm not even twelve for another six months."

Pennyweather shook her head. "Who's going to believe you're not fourteen, tall as you are? All I have to say is you came with no birth certificate. It happens all the time. You could be on a farm fifty miles away in another county. You better hope a family comes along for Franklin before September and he behaves enough for them to want him, or he'll be in the state home and you'll be working who-knows-where. You two can mull that over long and hard in the cellar."

Since the day they'd arrived, Mike had worried about what might happen if he and Frankie were separated. It was a dark cloud on the horizon of his mind—always looming, always menacing. He'd thought he had time to figure things out.

Now, instead of two and a half years away, the storm was overhead.

3

The cellar was a large dungeon-like room below the kitchen.

At one time, the walls had been whitewashed, but the paint was spotty and the old bricks showed through. Above, a ground-level window let in a shaft of light. Cupboards lined the back. A narrow wooden table sat in the center of the room, its benches pushed against a side wall.

"Least it's cool down here," said Frankie.

Mike sat on a bench and leaned against the bricks.

Frankie sat next to him. "Sorry I bit him."

Mike tousled his hair. "I'm not."

Frankie stared at the padlocked cupboards. "What do you think's inside?"

"Probably everything she ever took from a boy," said Mike.

"Like the harmonicas Granny gave us?"

"Like the harmonicas," said Mike.

The first day they arrived, Pennyweather had confiscated them, saying if she let every boy have one, she'd be batty from all the noise. She dropped them into a box, never to be seen again.

Frankie lay down on the bench, put his hands behind his head, and stared at the ceiling. "Tell me the story again."

Mike didn't have to ask which one. There was only one story Frankie ever wanted.

"It's your turn to tell," said Mike, knowing full well that Frankie would do most of the talking anyway.

"Okay," said Frankie. "Our dad and mom lived in a town with a lumber mill."

"Allentown," said Mike.

"I'm telling, 'member?" said Frankie. "Allentown. When I was just a tiny baby, there was a accident at the mill and our dad died. Our mom brought us to Granny's 'cause we didn't have any money and the lords were going to turn us out on the street."

"*Land*lords," said Mike.

"Yeah. So our mom got a job at the diner and we all lived together at Granny's and it was crowded."

"And where was that?" asked Mike.

"Philly. That's what the lads call Philadelphia for short. Philly."

Mike nodded, remembering Granny's tiny third-floor apartment with its hand-printed sign propped in her front window: PIANO LESSONS. The upright was in the parlor, and while she taught, Mike had to stay in the bedroom and entertain Frankie. When it was warm enough and Frankie was napping, Mike took to the stoop outside, where he played the harmonica. Even then he could copy any song he heard on the radio.

"And our mom sang to us," said Frankie.

"Every night. 'Twinkle, Twinkle, Little Star' . . . 'Hush, Little Baby' . . . 'Are You Sleeping?' . . ."

"Then our mom started getting sick with 'sumption."

"*Con*sumption," said Mike.

"Yeah. And she coughed all the time and got skinny and one day she went to the hospital, and even the doctors couldn't fix her. It was sad 'cept I don't remember because I was only two, but you remember 'cause you were six."

"Yes, I do," whispered Mike.

Granny had been giving a piano lesson to Maribeth Flanagan from across the hall. When Maribeth finished her piece, "America the Beautiful," Granny shook her head and said, "Maribeth, I'd jump for joy if you'd learn that piece proper and put a little of your heart and soul into it. Practice this week and come back and make me proud."

At that moment, his mother walked in from work at the diner, looked from Granny to Maribeth Flanagan to Mike, and fainted. When she came to, Granny ran to get help. Then she took Mama to the hospital while Mrs. Flanagan sat with Mike and Frankie. Only Granny came home.

Day after day, Mike had stood at the front window, watching for his mother. Granny would gently pull him away but he'd wander back, like a homing pigeon rooted to one post. It seemed there'd been no minutes or hours. Just one long day of searching out that window and waiting—one long day that lasted two weeks, until Granny told him his mother hadn't been strong enough for this world.

What other world was there? And where was it?

After that, Granny tried to interest him in storybooks and games, but nothing worked until she sat him next to her at the piano. As she taught lesson after lesson, Mike stayed at her side, his new perch, watching other children's fingers on the keys and listening to the metronome tick.

One day between students, Granny had left him sitting on the piano bench. He reached out toward the keyboard, placing his fingers as he'd seen the others do, and pressed. But instead of a harmonious chord, it was a jarring and painful sound, as if his sadness had traveled from his fingers onto the keys, and the sounds repeated the awfulness he felt inside. With his fingers wide, he pounded on the keys, over and over, as the room filled with his grief.

When Granny came back into the room and saw his wrenched face and his wild hands hammering away, she sank into a chair, all the while crying herself.

That evening, she started teaching him proper. Each time he learned a song, it seemed that it mirrored his sorrow and anger and love. Granny said he had a God-given gift for music. Secretly, he thought his mother must have sent the gift so that she could hear him playing from the other world. Sometimes, he even imagined her humming along.

"Mike! Are you listening?" Frankie sat up on the bench in the cellar and shook his arm.

"Yeah. I'm listening."

"Granny took care of us and loved us."

"Yes, she did," said Mike. "We didn't have a lot but we always had her."

Things had been difficult the last few years they'd lived with Granny. So many people were out of work. Piano lessons became a luxury few could afford. Granny's students dwindled to a small handful. And even those families often paid with food or a used jacket for Mike or Frankie instead of money. Most months, Granny just squeaked by with the rent. Even so, weather permitting, every

Sunday afternoon she threw open her front window and she and Mike took turns playing the piano for the entire neighborhood. Brahms, Chopin, Mozart, Debussy. She said people on hard times deserved to have beauty in their lives as much as anyone else, whether or not they could pay their rent or were walking to a breadline. Granny said that just because someone was poor didn't mean they were poor of heart.

"Then when Granny got too old and delicate to take care of us anymore, she brought us to Bishop's 'cause it was the only place with a piano," said Frankie.

Mike closed his eyes. He could still see Granny standing in Pennyweather's office with a nurse at her side. Withered and trembling, she had hugged them one last time. Her voice had wavered. *Be my sweet boys and promise to take care of each other. The right person will come and want two fine boys. I know it in my soul.*

The cellar seemed to close in on Mike. "That's right, Frankie," he said, pushing tears from his cheek. "She chose Bishop's because it had a piano."

"And then Granny went to the old folks' home and she died," said Frankie. "I miss her."

Mike put his arm around him.

"And that's the end of the story," whispered Frankie.

"Nah. It's not the end," said Mike. "There's more. Remember? Someday we'll get away from Bishop's and go to . . . C'mon, you're telling the story."

"New York City," said Frankie, waving his arm in an arc. "The Big Apple. Granny went there to visit and *loved* it."

"We're going to live there," said Mike. "It's going to be our city."

"We're going to take the train. And get all fancied up and go to a concert at Carnegie Hall, just like Granny did," said Frankie.

"That's right," said Mike. "She always wanted to take us there."

"There will be a big, shiny, black piano, right?" said Frankie. "And a famous piano player and an orchestra."

"Right," said Mike. "The theater will be full, even the top balconies. Granny said the balconies are golden and the seats are red. And all the musicians are dressed in black. And at the end—"

"Let me say it!" said Frankie. "We will stand up and clap and yell, 'Bravo! Bravo!'"

Mike nodded. He didn't tell Frankie that when he imagined the scene at Carnegie Hall, he didn't see himself in one of those plush red seats. He saw himself onstage in a black tuxedo, standing next to the piano and bowing to the audience.

"And after the concert, you and me will go to dinner at a *restaurant* and order roasted beef and ice cream. It won't be like here, right, Mike?"

Mike looked down at Frankie in his tattered clothes. He could hear the kid's stomach grumbling for dinner.

"No. I promise. It won't be like here."

4

Dinner was long over when Pennyweather let them out of the cellar and sent Mike and Frankie to their dormitories.

Most of the boys on Mike's floor were huddled around the radio listening to *Buck Rogers in the 25th Century*. They must have behaved at dinner for Mrs. Godfrey to give them the privilege. Mike flopped down on his cot.

Mouse, who was reading the funnies in a weeks-old newspaper, sat up, pulled two apples and a hunk of bread from behind his pillow, and held them out. "You only missed creamed chicken, otherwise known as mystery gravy. I smuggled Frankie some food with his buddies. The little lads thought it was the most important mission of their lives."

"Hey, thanks," said Mike, taking the food and biting into an apple. Mouse was almost sixteen and one of the oldest at Bishop's. Most of the boys didn't like him because he was Pennyweather's pet, but Mike thought him decent enough. His name was Stephen, though no one ever called him that. With his milky skin, pale eyes, and white hair buzzed so close to his head that pink scalp showed through, Mouse couldn't complain one bit about his nickname.

"Danny Moriarty was in the nurse's office next to the Visitation Room today," said Mouse. "He heard what happened. You really punch a guy? And did Frankie bite him and draw blood?"

Mike nodded. "My punch was more of a push. But Frankie left a set of teeth marks."

"Heard Pennyweather's going to put you out to hire."

"I'm not even *close* to fourteen," said Mike.

Mouse shrugged. "Wise up. Bishop's is a work mill. You ain't been around this time of year before, but you'll see. Farmers are here first thing every morning taking us older boys for day work. If their farm is far away, they take us for weeks then bring us back when the plowing or picking or stacking is finished. Our measly stipend goes to Pennyweather for clothes and school supplies. You see any clothes or school supplies?"

"Why doesn't someone tell—"

"Ain't no one to tell," said Mouse. "Old man Bishop owns this place but lives in the city. Heard the cooks talking 'bout how Pennyweather only has to deliver a certain amount a money to him each month to keep him happy. She pockets the rest. None of them dare say a word with so many of their husbands skint and out of work. Can't afford to lose their jobs. Did Pennyweather really say she's gettin' rid of all the Lowers and filling Bishop's with Hathaway boys?"

Mike nodded.

"Uppers bring in the money. Lowers take up space. She's all business." Mouse chewed on his lip and nodded. "That's gonna make things difficult for me. I won't be one of the oldest anymore. Might be time . . ."

Mike frowned. "I thought you had it good. Aren't you Pennyweather's . . . ?" He caught himself and closed his mouth.

"Pet? I admit it. I'm as nice as pie to

Pennyweather so she gives me privileges. What's wrong with that? Speaking of which, tomorrow morning I'm taking the wagon to make a delivery to Four Corners 'cause the truck broke down. She told me to get someone to go with me. Want to come? Be back by noon. Beats working for Otis pulling weeds and rocks from his fields. One of the boys can let Frankie know."

Mike studied the apple core. He hadn't been away from Bishop's since the day they'd arrived. Plus, boys were never fostered out on weekends, so Frankie wouldn't be called up. And the kid liked working at Otis's because at the end of the day, Mr. Otis pressed a penny into each boy's hand. Mike nodded. "Yeah. I'll go."

Before dawn, Mike and Mouse rode in the flat-bed wagon down the long road leading away from Bishop's.

On either side, cornfields walled in their view of everything but the green stalks and the gray sky. The air was cool, the horse's clip-clopping hypnotic. For a while, neither boy spoke. The morning brightened. When the fields stopped, the world opened up on vast pastures.

"Sure is pretty," said Mouse, nudging Mike with his elbow.

"Anything is prettier than Bishop's." Mike nodded toward the back of the wagon bed. He and Mouse had carefully stacked a dozen boxes on top of an old quilt to pad the ride. "What's inside, anyway?"

"Supposed to be a secret. But one time, I came down to the cellar before Pennyweather had finished packing. The cupboards were open and filled to choking with canned peaches, plums, jams. You name it. Jars had labels on 'em that said *Methodist Women's Auxiliary*. You know those church ladies who show up at Bishop's every month?"

"The smiley ones with the covered baskets?" said Mike.

Mouse nodded. "They make pints of preserves for us poor orphans. Pennyweather changes the labels, sells 'em, and pockets the money. One day I noticed a jar was missing the sealing ring. So I asked if I could have it. Told her it wouldn't sell anyway and how I loved peaches. And that I always heard she was fair-minded. She let me eat the whole thing."

"So Pennyweather has a heart . . ."

Mouse nodded. "Everybody has a heart. Sometimes you gotta work hard to find it. One thing I learned is that if there's something you want or need to know from grown folks, you gotta step up and ask for it mannerly. Plead your case, that's what I say. More times than naught, you'll get exactly what you asked for. You know the saying, 'You catch more flies with honey than with vinegar'?"

If Granny had said it once, she'd said it a thousand times. "Means you get more by being nice and polite than being otherwise."

"That's right. Made my time at Bishop's more bearable, that's for sure. What do you want to do once you're outta there?"

Mike frowned. "I can't think past getting Frankie settled."

"You tell Frankie what Pennyweather's up to?"

Mike shook his head. "Didn't have it in me."

"Listen," said Mouse. "You gotta keep Frankie outta the state home. Ain't fit for a river rat. Kids have lice and fleas. Last year it was quarantined 'cause two boys died from a fever. *Dead.* Makes Bishop's look like the Biltmore Hotel. Next time he gets called up, you gotta make sure he goes. Pennyweather has to let you know where he is. It's a law. You can write him. Heard they even let brothers visit on holidays. Face it, you're confined to Bishop's till you're eighteen. But Frankie might have a chance to get out. Make a plan. You gotta have a plan."

They passed a sign that said, FOUR CORNERS, 2 MILES.

Before the intersection of two lanes, Mouse stopped the horse and handed Mike the reins. "Here's where I get off. I'm going on the lam."

"What? You're running away?" Mike's thoughts raced. "Hey! I don't want any trouble at Bishop's."

"Relax. Deliver the boxes to Four Corners, get the money, and take it to Pennyweather. Tell her I took off and you couldn't stop me. She'll report me, but I'll be long gone before a truant officer can catch up. Besides, all she cares about is some-one bringing back the dough." He jumped down from the seat.

"But . . . where will you go? What will you do?"

"Don't worry. Got a plan. When I turn eigh-teen I got two choices: the U.S. Army or the Tree Army."

"The what?"

"Civilian Conservation Corps. Lads call it the Tree Army. It's part of the president's New Deal to get the country outta the sad slump we're in. It's jobs for young men like yours truly. I can work any number of places, planting trees, stocking rivers with fish, building parks. Get paid thirty-five bucks a month, too. I figure I'll do that for a year or so until I've seen some of the U.S. of A. Then, I'll join the military and see the world. Know a guy in the marines told me there's always a war to fight somewhere in the world."

"What're you going to do until you turn eighteen?"

"I'm almost seventeen. I can get by for a year. I got a friend who works at the train station in

Philly can sneak me on without a ticket. Heading to New York City. I'll live on the streets. Done it before. I know the safe places to sleep, the soup kitchens. Even know how to sneak into Yankee games and theaters." Mouse grinned.

Mike felt a tug at his heart. New York City. That was supposed to be his plan, too. His and Frankie's.

Mouse climbed into the wagon bed and moved the boxes aside until he'd pulled the quilt from beneath them. He folded it like a jelly roll, tucked it under his arm, and jumped down. "If you get Frankie sorted out and want to join me, my friend at the station is McAllister. Tell him I sent you. He'll get you on a train and tell you my usual whereabouts."

Without looking back, Mouse walked away, whistling.

Mike sat in the wagon, watching him saunter down the road. He tried to imagine what it felt like to have no worries, to have nothing but a bedroll to carry and the wide world in front of you. There was something exciting about the idea of taking a train to the big city, sleeping who-knows-where, and sneaking into a theater. Mike *would* go with Mouse, if it weren't for Frankie. On his own, he could make do with little. It would be so easy . . .

Guilt squirmed into his thoughts.

Be my sweet boys and promise to take care of each other.

How could he even think of leaving Frankie? The kid loved Mike and Mike loved him. Mike shook his head, disgusted with himself. What kind of brother was he?

Mouse disappeared over a rise in the road.

Mike flicked the reins and the horse walked forward. Mouse was right. There was always a war somewhere in the world. And Mike had his own, fighting for Frankie. He made the delivery to Four Corners, collected the money, and drove back to Bishop's.

The entire way, he felt like a wild bird trapped in a house, swooping up and down and into walls, wings flapping against windows, trying to find a way out.

5

On Monday morning, Mike was startled from a nightmare about lice and fevers and fleas.

He bolted upright in his cot, his heart pounding. Before he could lie back down, he heard Frankie's whistle. It could only mean one thing.

As Mike scrambled from his cot, he heard Mouse's warning again. *You gotta keep Frankie out of the state home . . . You gotta have a plan.* If the kid was called up, how would Mike convince him he had to go?

By the time Mike reached the stairwell and opened the window, Frankie was already waiting on the tree limb to be let in.

Mike helped him inside, put his hands on Frankie's shoulders, and said, "Whatever happens, I'll figure out *something*. I promise. Okay?"

Frankie shrugged. "Okay . . . Look." He reached

into his waistband and pulled out a folded news-paper page. He dropped cross-legged onto the floor, opened it up, and smoothed the paper out flat. The headline ran across both pages: HOXIE'S HARMONICA WIZARDS.

"It's the biggest harmonica band you've ever seen. Sixty boys! Mrs. Delancey read the article to us and let us listen on the radio last night. When she put the paper in the bin, I snuck back and took this page before anyone else could. Mike, there's nothing like 'em anywhere. You'd swear by the sound it was every kind of instrument and not just harmonicas."

Mike sank to the floor and leaned against the wall, blowing out a long breath. He nodded toward the newspaper. "Frankie, *that* is the emergency? Remember we talked about using the signal only when it was very, very important?"

"Mike, *look* at them," said Frankie, tapping a photo that took up half a page. "Before he died, John Philip Sousa wrote 'em a special song called 'The Harmonica Wizard March.' And once he even directed the band in a concert. They've played in parades. And for *three* presidents!" Frankie held up his fingers and ticked them off. "Coolidge, Hoover, and our very own 'Happy Days Are Here Again' Franklin Delano Roosevelt. They even played for a *queen*. And that's no lie. Now people call 'em the Harmonica Wizards and—"

"Take a breath, Frankie. You sound just like a radio announcer."

Frankie looked down and chewed on his lip. "See, I can buy the official band harmonica if I have sixty-five cents, but I only saved up twenty-three."

Mike couldn't help but smile. "Frankie, last month you listened to a radio commercial for Wheaties and wanted the Lou Gehrig baseball card from the back of the box. Before that, it was a Buck Rogers planetary map."

"Except I couldn't get those," said Frankie, "because you needed to buy somethin' else first. To get the baseball card, you had to buy a box of Wheaties. And for the planetary map, you needed a label from a can of Cocomalt. But for the harmonica, you don't need to *get* something else first. You can just order it. See?"

"Frankie, what's so important about this that you had to whistle for me?"

Frankie barely took a breath. "At the end of summer, there's going to be a big contest with prizes. The top winners get a spot in the band. And if a boy gets into the band, he's on easy street. The director, Hoxie, he pays for *everything*: uniforms, new harmonicas, music lessons. You name it. They even have their own touring bus. And every summer, there's somethin' called Camp Harmonica, all expenses paid!" He pointed to the paper. "Ain't they swell? I bet *we* could get into the band."

Mike read the caption under the photograph. "'Philadelphia Harmonica Band led by Albert N. Hoxie for boys ages ten to fourteen.' Frankie, you're only seven."

Frankie pointed to a boy in the photo in the front row. "He looks younger than me."

Mike leaned closer. Frankie was right. The boy looked to be about five. "It lists him as a mascot performer. He's probably someone's little brother that plays decent and looks fine in a uniform."

"*You* could try out. If you got in, maybe they'd let me be a mascot."

Mike shook his head. "You think Pennyweather is going to let me audition for a band? And how do you plan to get anything delivered without her finding out? Plus, even if we got a harmonica, she isn't going to let us keep it. She took away our others first thing."

"I already got that figured," said Frankie. "Lowers do mail duty every day. We go in twos to the letter box at the end of the lane and then deliver the mail to her office. Someone will grab it for me and I'll hide it. You and me can take turns practicing when we're working in the fields, where Pennyweather can't hear."

Frankie tapped the paper. "It says here Hoxie even finds homes for kids who don't have families . . . if they're good enough for the band. See, we could run away and try out in August . . . before . . . before September gets here." He stared at the paper, frowning.

Mike felt a lump in his throat. He should have known Frankie would find out about Pennyweather's deadline. At Bishop's, news was like water passed in a bucket brigade. "So you heard about her gettin' rid of the Lowers to make room for Hathaway boys, and me bein' put out to hire?"

Frankie looked up at Mike, his eyes solemn, and nodded.

Mike put an arm around him. "This band . . . that's good thinkin', Frankie." He leaned over the paper and read the mail-in form next to the photograph. "'Hohner Harmonica. The official instrument of the Harmonica Wizards. You, too, can learn to be a musician. Instruction booklet included.'" He looked at Frankie. "I've only got about thirty cents. We'll have to wait till we save up."

Frankie handed the paper to Mike. "Can you keep this and my money for me? Eddie, two beds down, likes to steal." He pulled a handful of pennies and nickels from his pocket.

"Sure. I'll take good care of them." Mike helped him up.

When Frankie had one leg over the sill, he turned to Mike. "It *was* very, very important."

Mike nodded. "I know, kid. See you later." He watched Frankie climb out the window and waited until he heard the whistle that meant he was safely down.

Mike went back to his room and sat on the edge of his cot, studying the fine print on the order form for the harmonica.

Allow four to six weeks for delivery.

He covered his face with his hands, rubbing his forehead. By the time he and Frankie saved up the money, mailed away for the harmonica, and waited for it to arrive, it would be too late. Frankie would be in the state home.

Mike pulled a slim metal box from a slit in the seam of his mattress. He had found it one day, left by some boy who'd slept in the cot before him. Luckily, it had escaped all of Pennyweather's surprise inspections, where she confiscated anything the boys tried to keep safe. He slipped the newspaper and the coins inside, buried it again, and sighed. Why couldn't he and Frankie catch a break?

Mike's eyes drifted to Mouse's empty cot. Mouse was surely in New York City by now. Maybe Mike and Frankie should run away, too. They could find McAllister at the train station and meet up with Mouse. If Mike was smart about it, he could get them far enough away from Bishop's before Pennyweather reported them.

But how? And when?

6

For the rest of the week, Mike fretted about their escape.

Four Lowers had been fostered out within the last few days. Pennyweather was getting rid of the little lads like they were a grocer's special— two for the price of one. How much time did Mike have? How far could they travel before Pennyweather became suspicious and reported them? What would happen if a truant officer caught up to them?

The questions continued to weigh on Mike as he mopped the stairs on Friday afternoon.

Mrs. Godfrey appeared below him in the entry. "Michael, Mrs. Pennyweather wants you right quick in the dining hall. Your brother is already there."

Mike dropped the mop and clambered down the stairs.

Out of breath, he arrived in the dining hall to find a man in overalls packing up tools and Pennyweather wiping down the piano with lemon oil. Three chairs had been positioned nearby in a straight line.

Frankie sat on the piano bench, swinging his legs.

Pennyweather looked up. "Michael, please join your brother."

He did, and Frankie leaned over and whispered, "Pennyweather had the piano tuned. She wants us to play a song."

Mike sighed and tried to calm his racing heart. "Is that all?"

Frankie nodded. "That's what she said."

Frankie wasn't being fostered out? Mike couldn't decide if he was disappointed or relieved.

The man closed his toolbox. "All done, Mrs. Pennyweather. I fixed the pedals, too. She's got a beautiful sound. And you don't need to pay me. Anything for them orphan boys."

Pennyweather smiled. "I am so grateful for your kindness."

When he was gone, she put her hands on her hips and faced Mike and Frankie. "I have some men coming to look at the piano. They've asked if we have anyone here who is musical so they can determine the quality." She shook her head. "Don't know why they can't do that themselves. Regardless, you are the only ones who can play this noisemaker without pounding on it. The cooks told me you've been practicing some piece every night after dinner that makes them cry. Sentimental fools. So play that one. And make it sound just as good, or you'll both be back in the cellar." She turned and began polishing the lid.

Frankie tugged on Mike's sleeve and whispered, "But Granny picked here 'cause of the piano."

Mike leaned his head toward Frankie's. "Shhh. Better we keep Pennyweather happy."

Two men, wearing suits with vests, walked into the room. The taller, gray-haired man carried a briefcase. "Mrs. Pennyweather, I presume? I'm Mr. Golding, attorney-at-law, and this is my associate, Mr. Howard."

The younger man was the same height as Mike,

fair-headed and freckled. "I'm also a family friend of the client. I've been given the authority to make a decision in this matter."

They both removed their hats.

"Gentlemen," said Pennyweather, nodding. "Pardon me, but I'm confused. Why do we need lawyers for this matter?"

Mr. Golding frowned. "Certainly if we come to an agreement, Mrs. Pennyweather, everything needs to be legal."

Pennyweather shrugged and looked puzzled. "Well then, let's get on with it. Here are Michael and Franklin Flannery, our best musicians, like you asked."

"Wonderful," said Mr. Golding. "We'd like to hear them play."

"Of course," said Pennyweather, sweeping a hand toward the chairs. "Please. Sit down, gentlemen. Boys?"

Mike and Frankie slid around and faced the keyboard.

"'America the Beautiful,'" whispered Mike. "You come in after *amber waves of grain*, just like I taught you. But at first, nice and slow like a lullaby, until almost the end . . ."

"I know," said Frankie, "then like a storm, until the *sea to shining sea* part, and we make it all calm again." He poised his hands, ready.

Mike began to play. After a few bars, he nodded to Frankie, who came in on cue.

Mike couldn't believe this was the same piano. There were no sour notes. No avoiding a sharp because it wasn't. The man was right. The piano had a beautiful tone. Mike filled up on the sound, as if he were eating something delicious, each bite better than the last. For a few moments, there was nothing but the music. No worries. No Pennyweather. Just him and Frankie. Mike could almost believe that he was back in Granny's parlor, playing on a Sunday afternoon with the window open so everyone in the neighborhood could hear the music and have a little beauty in their lives.

Mike used the damper pedal, and the chords filled the room.

Before the last bars, he stopped playing altogether and let Frankie finish the song alone, simple and sweet.

Mike glanced around the room.

At the far end of the hall, the cooks had stepped from the kitchen and were dabbing at their eyes.

Uppers congregated at the windows and leaned on the sills.

Lowers crowded the doorways, peeking in.

Pennyweather furrowed her brow, as if she didn't believe what she was hearing.

Mr. Golding raised an eyebrow at Mr. Howard.

After Frankie played the last note, there was a long breath of silence. Then the lads began to clap and whistle until Pennyweather stood, spun around, and waved everyone out.

Mike and Frankie shifted around on the bench.

Mr. Howard leaned forward. "Michael? How old are you?"

"Eleven, sir."

"How did you learn to play the piano?" His voice was soft and kind.

"My . . ." He nodded to Frankie. "Our grand-mother. She was a piano teacher."

"Mike's the best player I know," said Frankie.

Mr. Howard smiled. "And how old are you, Franklin?"

"Everyone calls me Frankie. I'm seven, sir. Almost eight. I'm the second-best player I know, but Mike's a progeny."

Mr. Howard smiled at his misuse of the word *prodigy*. "You're right, Frankie. He's *very* good. And so are you." He looked at Mike. "You arranged that piece?"

"Yes, sir."

"That was . . . quite beautiful." He cleared his throat. "How long have you two been here?"

"Five months and a few weeks," said Mike. "We lived with Granny most of our lives, until . . . until we came here."

"Granny picked here because it was the only orph'nage with a piano," said Frankie. "We *gotta* have a piano."

Pennyweather clapped her hands to interrupt.

"Gentlemen, can we get back to business? Boys, you are dismissed."

"Actually, I'd like them to stay," said Mr. Howard.

Pennyweather pursed her lips. "I don't see any reason—"

Mr. Golding interrupted. "Mrs. Pennyweather, our firm represents Eunice Dow Sturbridge. She is the daughter of Thomas Dow. Are you familiar with the name?"

"Who in Pennsylvania isn't?" said Pennyweather. "Mr. Dow was a businessman. Tire company, wasn't it? I read in the newspaper he died last year." Pennyweather crossed her arms. "What does *he* have to do with any of this?"

"Now that Mr. Dow has passed, his daughter is without any family," said Mr. Howard. "She must . . . She'd like to adopt a child."

Mrs. Pennyweather's eyes darted from one man to the other. "I thought you were here to buy the piano."

"Oh, *heavens* no," said Mr. Golding. "And I apologize if our intention was misleading. We asked if you had a piano and if there was a child here who was musical who could play it for us. So we could determine the quality of the *musician*. You see, it must be a child who is musical."

Mr. Howard nodded. "Mrs. Sturbridge is a pianist of great talent. So you understand the desire for a child with the same inclination. We'd like to start adoption proceedings. Today."

7

Mike's thoughts played leapfrog.

They wanted to adopt a boy, *today?*

Mrs. Sturbridge was a rich woman. If she adopted Frankie, he'd have a home. He'd be safe. He'd have things. He'd probably go to a private school. And Mike would know where he was. This was Frankie's chance.

"The papers have been readied in accordance," said Mr. Golding, reaching for his briefcase and opening it on his lap. "And I can file them at the courthouse this afternoon. We're prepared to make a donation to the orphanage and give you a stipend for your personal attention to this matter."

A smile played on Pennyweather's lips. "I will gratefully accept . . . for the orphans." She gestured toward Mike and Frankie. "Now, as to who to adopt. My recommendation is that you take

Franklin. And don't worry about Michael. He'll be grateful for his brother's unusually good fortune." She shot Mike a smile, but he knew it was meant as a warning.

"I don't want to leave Mike," said Frankie.

Mike wrapped an arm around him.

"I'd like to talk to the boys in private," said Mr. Howard.

Pennyweather stood. "I'm afraid that's not allowed."

Mr. Howard stood, too, and Mr. Golding snapped his briefcase shut. "Then I suppose we'll be going to pay a visit at Hathaway House."

"Wait! Don't be hasty, gentlemen. I can make an exception." She stepped into her office and closed the door.

As soon as she was gone, Frankie blurted, "They're not *supposed* to separate us."

Mike looked from Mr. Golding to Mr. Howard. "Sirs, if you mean to take only one of us, it should be Frankie. He's one of the youngest here. Mrs. Pennyweather plans to put me out to hire soon. I'm not old enough, but I guess I'm big enough. It's why she's not too keen on me leaving. But if I'm out working for months at a time, I won't be able to look out for Frankie. And he's still little."

"No, Mike!" whimpered Frankie, his eyes tearing up. "We stick together, remember? And we're going to save our money for harmonicas and try out for Hoxie's band and *he'll* find us a home and . . ." Frankie cried harder.

Mike dropped to one knee and pulled him close. "Don't throw a fit this time. Don't you see? If you go today, I'll know where to find you and you won't end up in the state home." He swallowed hard, looked at Mr. Golding, and blinked back his own tears. "Could I write and come visit him?"

"Of course," said Mr. Golding. "I could even put a stipulation in the paperwork."

Frankie shook his head, sniffling. "No."

"And I bet there's a piano." Mike looked at Mr. Howard.

He nodded. "There's a piano that sorely needs playing."

Mike stroked Frankie's back. He knew this was the right thing. But he couldn't stand looking in the kid's eyes and seeing the hurt. "I knew it. There's a piano. And I'll visit regular. It will all be okay. I promise."

Mike looked at Mr. Howard for reassurance.

He turned away from Mike's gaze and walked to the window. A moment later, he came back, blinking, his eyes bright. He cleared his throat and said to Mr. Golding, "It doesn't seem like a promising place, does it?"

"No," said Mr. Golding. "And it has a dreadful standing. But, hard as it is, Mr. Howard, time is of the essence. This is the fifth orphanage we've visited in the last two weeks and there's not been one child who came close to either of these boys. They're polite, endearing, and from what I've heard, extremely talented. If one of them will do, then let's take care of business."

Mr. Howard paced back and forth with his hands on his hips.

The office door opened. Pennyweather came back into the room. "Gentlemen?"

"We understand that Michael is to be put out for hire soon?" said Mr. Howard.

"That's right," said Pennyweather.

"Making a child an indentured servant is against the law."

"It's called 'fostering' now, Mr. Howard. If a business owner or farmer comes here to 'foster' a child, it's none of my business what the child is expected to do to earn his keep. Call it what you like—indenturing, fostering, adopting—it's all the same to me."

Frankie looked up at Mike, tears streaming down his cheeks. "I don't want to leave you."

Mike forced a smile. "You'll be in a nice house. And when I visit, we'll play that piano together. I bet there's trees to climb, too, and a big yard, and good food. I bet they have Wheaties and Cocomalt. You'll go to school . . ."

"I don't care about Wheaties and Cocomalt. I want to stay with you!" Frankie sobbed into Mike's arm.

Mike's resolve crumbled. He knelt in front of Frankie and held him tight.

Mr. Howard ran both hands through his hair. He walked to Mr. Golding and whispered in his ear.

"You're the representative in this matter," said Mr. Golding. "You've made up your mind?"

"I have," said Mr. Howard.

"Very well," said Mr. Golding. He turned to Pennyweather. "I'd like to speak with you in your office and draw up the papers."

"I think you'll be very happy with Franklin," said Pennyweather, smiling. "And let's discuss that donation for the unfortunate orphans and my small stipend."

Mr. Golding smiled back. "Oh, Mrs. Pennyweather, I think you underestimate us. We don't do anything in a small way."

8

Mr. Golding idled the black Ford sedan on Amaryllis Drive, where the homes kept their distance from the neighbors and the street.

After they climbed out, Mr. Golding called, "Good luck to you, Mr. Howard. I'm headed to the courthouse now. I'm glad *I'm* not the one to tell her!" He honked the car horn and pulled away.

Frankie waved.

Mr. Howard shook his head, smiling, and pushed open the wrought iron gate.

At the end of a long walkway sat a caramel-colored house with white trim and red accents. An elevated porch with a wooden latticework skirt wrapped around two sides of the first level. A round two-story tower with a cone-shaped roof jutted from the left corner of the house and was topped with a weather vane. Steep gables pointed to the sky.

Frankie stopped, openmouthed, and stared.

"It's lovely, isn't it?" said Mr. Howard, taking his hand. "Queen Anne architecture. It needs some updating inside, but she's a beauty."

"How many people live here?" asked Frankie.

Mr. Howard laughed. "Just one woman. And now, you and Michael."

Mike's eyes swept across the wide lawns, the old elm in the side yard, and the manicured hedges.

"We're going to live here, Mike," said Frankie, grinning ear to ear. He let go of Mr. Howard's hand and skipped toward the house. "We're being 'dopted, *not* fostered."

Mike wanted to feel Frankie's joy, but some tiny intuition told him it had all been too easy. In only a matter of hours, they'd been gathered up with their few belongings and brought *here*. Fostering was one thing. But adoption was another. It meant being part of a family. Forever. But *no one* ever adopted children without meeting them first.

Granny always said if something seemed too good to be true, it was probably a swindle. At the market, she had once showed him how the shiny, waxed apples on top of the bushel often hid the bruised and rotten ones underneath. Was this house a shiny apple hiding something?

A dark-skinned man knelt by a flower bed near the porch. As they approached, he set his trowel aside and stood, his height and sturdiness now apparent.

Mr. Howard waved to him. "Hello, Mr. Potter. This is Michael and Franklin, Mrs. Sturbridge's new wards."

Mr. Potter looked from one to the other, wiped his hands on his green apron, and nodded. "Pleased to meet you."

Mr. Howard turned to Mike and Frankie. "Mr. Potter is the groundskeeper and Mrs. Sturbridge's driver. He keeps the Packard up and running. He is also married to *Mrs.* Potter, the housekeeper. Mr. Potter, would you like to come inside for the introductions?"

Mr. Potter shook his head. "I best get back to the geraniums. Seems safer. Mr. Howard, sir, you just stirred the pot real good." He winked at the boys.

"What pot?" asked Frankie.

Mr. Howard smiled. "He just means things will be different around here from now on."

Mike and Frankie followed Mr. Howard up the wide porch steps, where he rang the bell. "Here we go, boys."

A woman in a gray dress and white apron opened the door. A pleated maid's cap, like a crescent moon, perched on her head. Her brown skin was the same color as her sleeked-back hair, which was knotted in a bun at the nape of her neck.

"Hello, Mrs. Potter," said Mr. Howard. "Here we are. This is Michael. And this is Franklin. Boys, meet the woman who runs this house."

Mrs. Potter raised her eyebrows at Mr. Howard.

"Before you say anything," said Mr. Howard, "yes, they are boys. And there are two of them. Where is she?"

"In the library, sir. And might I say you are a brave man."

. . . I'm glad I'm not the one to tell her . . . seems safer . . . stirred the pot real good . . . brave man . . .

Why were they all talking in code? He and Frankie had been adopted. Wouldn't Mrs. Sturbridge be happy to see them?

They followed Mr. Howard inside and stood in

an entry hall the size of Granny's entire apartment. The floor was a checkerboard of black and white marble squares. A wide stairway with a dark wood banister hugged the left wall and curved toward the second story.

"Wow," whispered Frankie, craning his neck upward and pointing to the gilded chandelier dripping with three layers of giant teardrop crystals. "She must have lots of money."

"Shhh . . ." said Mike, even though that was exactly what he was thinking. So this was how rich folks lived. Mike had never felt poor. But he'd never known any different, either. When they'd lived with Granny, they'd had enough to eat and a safe place to sleep. And they had Granny, who loved them, so nothing else mattered. She used to say she never wanted for splendor as long as she could have a piano and her two boys. If she could have seen all this, she would have said that none of it made one bit of difference unless the owner's heart was as beautiful as the house.

"Michael, Franklin, wait here." Mr. Howard pointed to an upholstered bench. He walked through a set of double doors on the left and shut them partway behind him.

Mrs. Potter headed down the hallway, shaking her head. "There's a storm brewin', sure as I live."

Mike sat on the bench and watched Frankie walk halfway up the staircase.

"*Boys?*" yelled a woman's voice from behind the doors. "I send you for *one girl* and you come back with *two boys*? How *could* you?"

Mike felt his stomach twist. He checked to see if Frankie heard, but he was too preoccupied with sliding his hand along the stair banister.

"You appointed me your representative, so I made the decision," said Mr. Howard. "And it's the right one. The papers have been filed. They're brothers, and I couldn't bring myself to separate them. You'll understand that, I hope. And besides, two will be easier. They'll have each other. Now come and meet them. They're in the hall."

Her voice was shrill. "What have you done?"

"Only what was required," said Mr. Howard. "Something *you* left until the final hour."

"I never thought it would come to this. I'm *trying* to get things changed!"

"I'm afraid you're out of time," said Mr. Howard.

Mike heard something hit the wall, then glass breaking.

Frankie darted from the stairs to Mike's side.

"It's okay, Frankie," whispered Mike. At least, he hoped it was.

She had wanted a girl and Mr. Howard came back with them. If it had mattered so much, why hadn't she chosen a child herself? Something didn't feel right.

Mike pulled Frankie in front of him and looked him square in the eyes. "We need to watch our every step. And remember our manners. We don't want to get her angry. Understand?"

Before Frankie could answer, Mr. Howard stepped out of the library. He stood by the door, waiting. A woman appeared next to him, her mouth set in a grim line. Even though her face was red from anger or crying—Mike couldn't tell which—he could still see the brilliant yellow flecks in her hazel eyes. Her brown hair was a short bob of curls. Her black dress came past her knees. In her high-heeled shoes, she was as tall as Mike but thin as a willow. A powdery vanilla scent surrounded her. The way Frankie gazed up at her, Mike could see he was smitten.

"Michael. Franklin. This is Eunice Dow Sturbridge," said Mr. Howard.

Mike nodded. "Ma'am. Thank you for adopting us."

Frankie blurted, "Are *you* going to be our new mother? You are *much* prettier than we 'spected and you smell *lots* better than Mrs. Pennyweather."

Mrs. Sturbridge's eyes filled with tears as she looked them over and made a face as if she'd just seen a dead animal in the gutter. She turned and hurried up the stairs. At the top, she leaned over the railing and yelled, "Get them to Mrs. Potter, immediately!" She disappeared down the hallway. A few seconds later, a door slammed so hard that the chandelier tinkled.

"Believe it or not, boys," said Mr. Howard, "that went well."

9

A bar of soap floated on the steaming surface of the water in the claw-footed bathtub.

Mrs. Potter stood in front of Mike and Frankie with her arms crossed, appraising their cleanliness.

She did not seem pleased.

Mike had seen that look before, in Granny's eyes every Saturday when they had to take a bath whether they needed it or not.

"After I leave, you'll get undressed and take turns in the tub and scrub from head to toe. Put the clothes in the basket. Tomorrow I'll wash the rest of your things."

"We don't have more clothes," said Frankie.

Mike looked at the floor, his face turning red. "When we lived with our granny, we had more and nicer . . ."

"But they got lost at Bishop's," said Frankie.

"Then I'll be washing what you're wearing later tonight," said Mrs. Potter. "Thank goodness the missus has a newfangled clothing dryer for just this sort of emergency. They won't smell line-fresh, but they'll be clean. I'll go ask Mr. Howard to bring over some nightshirts for you. They'll be hanging on the other side of the door when you're done."

"Does Mr. Howard live nearby?" asked Mike.

"He does. Lives at the end of the street. His father was Mr. Dow's lawyer. Mr. Dow being the missus's father, but I suppose you know that already. And now Mr. Howard is the same for the missus. But he's more family than lawyer. He's known her since she was knee-high."

Frankie began unbuttoning his shirt. "Why do you call her the missus?"

"Mr. Potter and I have been here since the day she was born. We never called her anything other."

"Is she nice or mean?" asked Frankie.

Mrs. Potter handed them each a washcloth. "Since Mr. Dow, bless his heart, died a year past, she's not been herself. But that's to be expected, considering all she's been through. Even so, I'd say she's a kind and loving soul, underneath all the rest."

"She didn't like the way we looked. Do you think she will like us once we're scrubbed clean?" asked Frankie.

"That remains to be seen," said Mrs. Potter. "It appears there's lots of ifs and maybes to be sorted out."

Mike pulled Frankie closer and helped him unbutton his shirt. Ifs and maybes. *If* they were girls . . . *if* they didn't resemble something dragged from the street . . . *if* they weren't poor . . . *maybe* she'd like them?

"Mrs. Potter, do you live here?" asked Frankie.

She nodded. "Mr. Potter and I live in the cottage to the side of the garden."

"Do you have any boys my age?" asked Frankie.

She laughed. "No. We have a grown daughter living and working in Atlantic City. Grew up right alongside the missus. She's a teacher now. We see her most every chance we get."

"Does Mr. Potter like to play checkers?" asked Frankie.

"As a matter of fact, he does. And so does Mr. Howard. Now, are you going to wear me out with questions?"

"He's just excited," said Mike. "We never thought we'd be in a house nice as this. Or that we'd get to stay together."

Mrs. Potter's face softened. "It's been a day of surprises for all of us. Now into the tub. We have chicken and potatoes for dinner, but since you have nothing decent to wear to the table, I'll bring up your food on a tray."

"On a tray?" said Frankie. "I *never* had dinner on a tray."

Mrs. Potter tried not to smile. "I'll be back to show you to the tower room."

Frankie's eyes widened. "We get to sleep in a tower?"

"Get on with the bathing now." She pulled the door shut.

"She's nice," said Frankie.

Mike nodded. Mrs. Potter reminded him of Granny, all business and practicality, but at the same time mothering them like a hen.

★　　★　　★

That night, Mike leaned back against the pillows in the four-posted double bed.

The tower was the bedroom on the second floor beneath the cone-shaped roof. A mahogany dresser stood against one wall, woven rugs covered the hardwood floors, and needlepoint pillows sat propped in the window seat. It was a far cry from Bishop's.

The door opened. Frankie slipped inside, wearing one of Mr. Howard's nightshirts, the sleeves rolled up. He leaped onto the bed next to Mike.

"Did you brush your teeth?"

Frankie nodded, crawling under the sheet.

Mike turned off the lamp.

A cricket chirped.

"It's awful quiet," said Frankie.

"I was just thinking the same thing."

"Mike, I'm scared."

"Want me to keep the light on?"

"No. I'm not scared of the dark." Frankie scooted closer and put an arm across Mike's chest. "I'm scared if I close my eyes and go to sleep, I . . . I might wake up at Bishop's."

"I know," said Mike. "But I promise you'll wake up here."

Mike stared into the shadows. His mind couldn't settle with all that had happened or was said that day.

. . . She is a pianist of great talent . . . must adopt . . . only doing what's required . . . you're out of time . . . she's not been her usual self . . . all she's been through . . . ifs and maybes . . .

Mike heard Frankie's breathing change and knew he was already asleep. He gently lifted Frankie's hand and tucked the sheet around him. The kid smelled like soap and the chicken from dinner. And it hadn't been creamed chicken, either. It had been plump roasted drumsticks.

What if it *was* all a dream?

Just in case, Mike battled to keep his eyes open. But he lost.

IO

At first, Mike didn't know where he was.

He sat up, blinking and staring into the bed-room until the events of yesterday came back to him. Next to him, Frankie rolled over, still sleeping.

The clothes they'd worn when they arrived had been washed and folded and placed on a low bench at the end of the bed. Mike dressed and walked downstairs, where all was still quiet.

The double doors to the library were open. Mike stepped inside. It was dim and cave-like. Every window was covered with wooden shutters and closed tight. He studied the paneled walls, the fringed lampshades, and the large desk angled across a corner. His eyes drifted to the floor-to-ceiling bookcases filled with books and the sliding ladder that stretched to the topmost shelves. A collection of metronomes sat on a small round table.

Where was the piano?

Retracing his steps, he crossed the entry hall to another set of double doors. He opened one and sucked in his breath.

The morning sun streamed through the tall windows, illuminating tiny specks of dust in the air. Potted palms appointed each corner. In the middle of the room sat the most magnificent instrument Mike had ever seen—a concert grand.

It had to be nine feet from keyboard to end. Once, Granny had taken him to buy sheet music and the shop owner had a baby grand. He let Mike play it. The notes had seemed to leap from inside the instrument, the sound flying around the room. What power would an even larger piano hold?

Mike ran his hands over the shiny ebony wood. He raised the lid and pulled the prop into place. For a few moments, he gazed at the intricate insides: the tuning pins, the treble and bass strings, the soundboard and the hammers. Sliding onto the bench, he squeezed his hands into fists, released them, and spread his fingers wide. Hadn't Mr.

Howard said the piano sorely needed playing? Hadn't they been chosen from Bishop's because they were musical? If Mrs. Sturbridge heard someone playing, maybe she'd be pleased. Was that one of the *ifs and maybes?*

A music book stood on the stand. He flipped the pages until he came to the Chopin Nocturne no. 20. He positioned his hands, feeling the desire, like a magnet drawing his fingertips closer.

He played the opening chords. The room filled with the rich timbre of the piano and its full-bodied tone. It wasn't like any piano he'd ever heard before. The high notes sounded brighter, the low ones darker and more ominous.

He began several times. At first, his phrasing was stilted, unpracticed. Then he felt himself descend into the music. He remembered Granny teaching him the piece when he was nine. When he finished the first pass, he heard her voice: *Once more. But first, I'm going to open the window so the entire neighborhood can hear you play.*

Mike succumbed to the melancholy notes, the insinuations of a march, the delicate filigree, and the final runs, slower and slower . . . until the final haunting note. He could almost sense Granny next to him on the piano bench and hear his mother humming . . .

He was startled by a strange sound, a cross between a squeak and a gasp, and he looked up.

Mrs. Sturbridge stood in the doorway, her hand on her heart, looking as if she'd seen a ghost.

Before Mike could say a word, Mrs. Potter rushed into the room. "I'm sorry, missus, I didn't hear him come down." She took Mike's arm and led him to the kitchen. She sat him down at the table. "As much as your playing filled my heart, it pains me to say you must leave the piano be. It's *never* to be touched." Her eyes filled with regret. "It's a shame, beautiful instrument like that, just begging to be played. And to think of all the music that used to come from it."

"I don't understand," said Mike. "Mr. Howard said—"

Mrs. Potter held up a hand to interrupt. "Lots of things don't make sense around here. You'll get used to it. Now, go get your brother and come to the kitchen for breakfast. Mr. Howard will be over shortly to take you to town for new clothes."

"Is she coming with us?" If so, Mike could apologize about the piano and explain how he and Frankie used to look cleaner and nicer.

Mrs. Potter shook her head. "She has plans and won't be back till after dinner. And she's not inclined to being with you boys just yet. Go on now."

Mike headed upstairs to retrieve Frankie. Why had she adopted them if she didn't want to be with them?

How much more didn't make sense around here?

II

Mike held Frankie's hand as they hurried after Mr. Howard, who walked down Amaryllis Drive with brisk purpose, whistling all the while.

Striding past, he pointed out his house on the corner. Two enormous elms grew on either side of the center walkway, the branches almost touching in the middle. "It's the same age and style as Mrs. Sturbridge's, but I've had it all remodeled." He pulled his watch from his pocket. "Come on, boys, if we cut through the park and hurry, we can catch the next trolley."

Mike took longer strides to keep up. Two blocks down, Mr. Howard pointed to the park square where a gazebo sat in the center. They dashed through to the boulevard on the other side, just in time to catch the approaching trolley.

Within a few stops, the houses changed from older, stately homes to more modest bungalows.

Mile by mile, the buildings grew taller. When the trolley rattled to a stop in the bustle of downtown Philadelphia, they stepped off.

Even though it was hotter and more humid here within the narrow streets where a breeze couldn't find its way, Mike felt more at home. It reminded him of Granny's neighborhood: walk-up apartments, girls jumping rope across the sidewalk, boys playing pimple ball in the street, cars and trucks honking. He looked up, hoping to see a window with a hand-printed sign for piano lessons, knowing full well he wasn't anywhere near where he used to live.

When Mr. Howard led them through the revolving doors of Highlander's Department Store, the noise fell away. Inside, everything was shined and polished: the glass cases, the merchandise, the faces of the salesmen and salesladies. Even the air smelled expensive. All the customers wore what looked like their Sunday best. Mike ran his hands over his clothes, feeling all wrong.

"Boys, go on up to the third floor. The Young Gentlemen's Department," said Mr. Howard. "I'll meet you there. I need to take care of Mrs. Sturbridge's account in the office first."

Mike and Frankie slowly walked between cases topped with gloves and scarves, umbrellas, wallets, hats, and perfumery. Frankie stopped to gawk at a display of glass figurines. A saleslady rushed forward and frowned.

Mike pulled Frankie toward the elevator. "Third floor," he told the elevator operator.

The man looked at them and sniffed. He swept his fingers over the lapels of his blue suit, as if brushing away dirt. "Boys, you cannot run around ripshod through this establishment."

"We weren't running," said Frankie.

"Do you plan on purchasing something?" asked the man.

"Yes, sir," said Mike. "In the Young Gentlemen's Department."

The man's eyes inspected them. He signaled to a salesman, who hurried over. The two men whispered.

Mike heard only bits of what they said.

No money . . . one thing in mind . . . little thieves.

Mike felt his face grow hot and knew it was reddening.

The salesman signaled to several nearby clerks, then grabbed Frankie's arm. "Boys, let me escort you back outside. I think you are in the wrong place."

Frankie jerked his arm away and clung to Mike. "Leave us alone!"

The clerks hurried forward and spread their arms wide, surrounding them. The salesman grabbed the neck of Mike's shirt and twisted his right arm behind his back, marching him toward the door.

Mike panicked. "Let me go! What are you doing?" He hadn't ever been manhandled like this before. He tried to wriggle from the man's grip.

The salesman tightened his hold and whispered in his ear, "Find another store to pilfer."

Frankie began to scream, "Stop! Stop!" He lunged forward, pounding the man with his fists.

"Call the police!" yelled the elevator operator.

Mr. Howard's voice boomed. "Take your hands off those boys and step aside! Or *I'll* call the authorities. And I don't mean the police. I mean Mr. Highlander himself."

The salesman released Mike and backed away.

Mike's entire body shook. Tears stung his eyes. They had thought they were thieves? He'd never stolen a thing in his life.

Mr. Howard strode closer and put an arm around each of them. "You boys okay?"

"They wanted us to leave. They wanted to take Mike away!" whimpered Frankie. "For no reason."

"We'll see about that." Mr. Howard looked at one of the salesmen. "Call the store manager at once!"

Mr. Howard sat in an overstuffed chair in the Young Gentlemen's Department with Frankie on his lap and Mike at his side.

"My apologies, Mr. Howard," said the store manager, a short man with a skinny mustache. He paced in front of them. "It was a misunderstanding. We had no way of knowing these boys were with you."

Mr. Howard raised his eyebrows. "As I recall, over the years, my client, Mrs. Sturbridge, has spent a fair amount of money in this store and in this very department."

"Oh, *yes*, sir, she has, indeed."

"These boys are her wards," said Mr. Howard. "They are clean and polite. They're poorly dressed, yes. But does that make them shoplifters? No, it makes them in need of new clothes, which is *why* we're here. There's something very wrong about how they were treated, sir, when they were doing exactly what I told them. Do you think I need to mention this to Mr. Highlander?"

"Oh, n-n-o, Mr. Howard," stammered the store manager. He snapped his fingers and a young salesman stepped forward. "Charles will assist you. No reason ever to mention it again and you can be sure I'll talk to the employees. I'll call a special meeting. Count on it."

"Fine, then," said Mr. Howard. "I need a wardrobe for each of these young gentlemen: four shirts, three pair of trousers, stockings, romper togs for unders, suspenders, and a cap—wool or felt. Make one of the pants and shirts for dress. And throw in a vest and tie for each. Oh, and we'd better have shoes." He looked at their feet. "Two pair. Brown lace-up leathers for everyday and black oxfords for dress."

Frankie grinned at Mike.

Mike couldn't smile back. The embarrassment still smarted, and his face still pulsed from the humiliation. He looked down as Charles ushered them into a dressing room. Had Mrs. Sturbridge thought the same when she first saw them? Had she wondered if they were little thieves, too?

"I'll be sitting right here, boys, reading the paper," said Mr. Howard. "When you're ready, come out and show me your outfits."

Behind the curtain, Mike relaxed. He and Frankie spent an hour trying on clothes and darting back and forth to Mr. Howard for approval. When they were alone in the dressing room, they made goofy faces at each other in the mirror. Once fitted, they followed Mr. Howard, now laden with parcels, outside to the front of Highlander's.

"Thank you, Mr. Howard," said Mike. "For bringing us. We never had so much new or nice at one time. And thank you for standing up for us, too."

Mr. Howard smiled. "You have just as much right to be in that store as the next person. So, you're welcome. But it's Eunie you should thank for your clothes. She's your benefactor."

Mike nodded. "I will, sir. First chance I get."

"Eunie?" Frankie crinkled his nose.

"Her given name is Eunice," said Mr. Howard. "I started calling her Eunie when we were children."

"What should we call her?" asked Frankie. "She didn't like it when I asked her if she was going to be our mother."

"No . . . well . . . let's give her some time," said Mr. Howard. "For now, just ma'am or Mrs. Sturbridge will do."

As they headed down the street, Mike couldn't stop peeking at himself in store windows. Was it really him? He didn't look at all like something dragged from the gutter. He looked smart and new, as if he belonged with Mr. Howard.

Would Mrs. Sturbridge or ma'am, or whatever they called her, agree?

12

On the way back to the trolley stop, Frankie skipped ahead of Mike and Mr. Howard and stopped in front of a shop window.

He turned, wide-eyed, waving for them to hurry.

Mike jogged to him. "What is it, kid?"

"It's them!" he said, pointing to a large poster displayed in the window of Wilkenson's Music Emporium. "It's the Harmonica Wizards!" Frankie pressed his nose on the glass.

Mike looked up at the poster of over sixty boys in military-style uniforms, capes, and plumed hats.

A tiny man wearing a red apron stepped from the shop. His gray mustache had been waxed into an old-fashioned handlebar, curling up on both ends. "Good day, gentlemen." He nodded toward the poster. "Aren't they something? The famous

Philadelphia Harmonica Band. Are you boys going to enter the contest? Still plenty of time."

"Sir, what's all this?" asked Mr. Howard.

"Citywide competition in August. Thousands of children taking lessons all over Philadelphia. Lots of prizes, including musical instruments. It's an audition of sorts. Top five winners are invited to join the band and travel all over. They have their own Women's Auxiliary raising money for uniforms, finding homes for boys to board in, even sending them to college."

Frankie nodded as if he were an expert. "We *were* going to try out so we could get out of the orph'nage, but we don't have to now, 'cause we got 'dopted."

"Well, that's wonderful. Doesn't mean you still can't enter for the fun of it," said Mr. Wilkenson.

"But you gotta have the official harmonica and you gotta be ten years old, 'cept if you're a mascot. See." Frankie pointed to the young boy in the poster.

"That's right. The youngster is a novelty and only plays with the band when it's in town. Doesn't travel with them. Band's got all sorts of rules about such things. But he's sure a crowd-pleaser in that uniform." He winked at Frankie. "And you're right about the harmonica. Has to be the Hohner Marine Band in the key of C. I just received a shipment from the warehouse yesterday and they're going like hotcakes. Only sixty-five cents each." He pulled a striped handkerchief from his apron pocket and began blotting his forehead. "Speaking of hotcakes, this weather is a steamy kitchen. The heat has about got me beat."

Frankie looked up at Mr. Howard. "Mrs. Pennyweather took away the harmonicas Granny bought for us."

Mr. Howard smiled. "Mr. Wilkenson, I don't think we're interested in the contest, but two harmonicas might just be the ticket."

"Right this way," said Mr. Wilkenson. He opened the shop door and a bell on the frame jingled.

Mr. Howard and Frankie followed Mr. Wilkenson to the counter near the register.

"There are kittens underfoot so watch your step," said Mr. Wilkenson. "Three of 'em somewhere in the store."

Mike walked down the narrow center aisle, mindful of where he stepped and savoring the smell of bow rosin, leather cases, and wood polish. His eyes couldn't look fast enough at all the instruments that crowded every available space: trumpets in a glass case, cellos propped at attention, violins suspended from the ceiling, crash cymbals and snare drums, a bass drum on a pedestal. It reminded him of the shop where Granny used to take him to buy sheet music. *Isn't it wonderful!* she'd say. *Music is just waiting to escape from all these instruments.* He smiled, remembering how he'd always expected to see a string of black notes fleeing from the bell of a tuba or a trombone.

Frankie ran toward him, holding a calico kitten in one hand and a new harmonica in the other. "Look, Mike. It comes with an instruction booklet with songs. Listen." He ran his mouth over the harmonica. "Doesn't it sound grand? I took the last one by the register, but Mr. Wilkenson said for you to go to the back counter and get one from the carton he just opened." Frankie wandered back to where Mr. Howard and Mr. Wilkenson stood together, talking.

Mike worked his way to the back of the store until he reached a counter in front of a curtained storeroom. On top sat a big open carton filled with slim cases. Mike lifted one and opened it. Inside, twelve individual boxes lay in a row, each imprinted with a photo of the United States Marine Band.

The last box on the bottom caught his eye. The blue border seemed brighter than the rest, the red lettering bolder, the photograph of the Marine Band sharper. When he lifted the box, he could have sworn he heard a chord erupt, like a high-pitched chime. He glanced around. It must have been Mr. Wilkenson's cash register.

Mike opened the box, picked up the harmonica, and turned it over. He noticed a small red hand-painted *M* on one edge. He lifted the harmonica to his lips, ran the scale, and then played the last six notes of "America the Beautiful." During the pause

288

after the final note and before his next breath, all the instruments in the shop struck a long, echoing chord.

He spun around, his eyes darting to the motionless instruments. No one else was around. Everything was quiet.

It was stuffy in the shop and he felt light-headed. He swiped at his brow, now beaded with perspiration, and put the harmonica back in its box. He clutched it in his hand as he headed toward the front.

He was escorted by a chorus of sounds: the hoots of clarinets, the *swish-swish* of the snare drum, the plucking of violin strings, and the deep strum of the cello. When he passed the trumpets, a fanfare blasted.

He glanced over his shoulder. Everything looked the same. Had Granny been right? Was the music escaping? Or was this all some clever trick of Mr. Wilkenson's? A kitten followed him, pawing at his ankles. With each step, the space around him felt more crowded and the air thicker.

"I've already paid," said Mr. Howard when Mike reached him. "I see you chose a harmonica."

Mike nodded.

Mr. Wilkenson winked at him. "I always say the instrument chooses the musician instead of the other way around." He nodded to Mr. Howard. "Thank you for your business."

As they walked out and the door swung shut behind them, the bell on the frame fluttered like a giddy piccolo.

Outside, Mike rubbed his forehead.

Maybe the heat had him beat, too. Even the harmonica felt warm in his hand. He leaned toward Frankie. "You hear anything funny in there?"

"No, but guess what. Mr. Howard said Mr. Potter is the best harmonica player he's ever heard in his *entire life* and tomorrow's his day off and maybe he can teach us some songs!"

All the way to the trolley stop, Mike and Frankie played the harmonicas.

Mike's sounded different from Frankie's. His had a tone he couldn't explain . . . It seemed older and rounder somehow. As he played songs he already knew by heart, his steps became more buoyant, and his heart filled with something he had not felt for a long while. Was it happiness?

The trolley stopped, bell clanging.

Mr. Howard smiled and said, "C'mon, boys. Time to head home."

Frankie grabbed Mike's hand and squeezed it.

Mike looked at the kid's smiling face and squeezed in return.

Mr. Howard had said *home*.

Maybe this time, they could catch a break and everything would go right.

13

Mr. Potter could make the harmonica sound like a train on a track, a baby crying, or rain falling in the wind.

Sunday afternoon, Mike and Frankie sat on a bench under a shade tree next to the Potters' cottage, hypnotized by his playing.

Mike couldn't take his eyes from Mr. Potter's hands or his mouth, and the way his head swayed with the music. He recognized familiar melodies, but they were peppered with repeating rhythms. The sound seemed to transport him to another place and time. Someplace ancient and earthy. The beat started and stopped, questioned and answered. Mike had never heard anything like it before. When Mr. Potter paused, Mike asked, "What is that sound?"

Mr. Potter nodded and grinned. "Kinda catches you, doesn't it? Called *the blues*."

"Why?" asked Frankie.

"Ever heard someone say they're feeling blue?" asked Mr. Potter. "Means sad or they got the melancholies about life. So blues music is about all the trials and tribulations people got in their hearts from living. It's about what folks *want* but don't *have*. Blues is a song begging for its life."

"But the music doesn't sound sad all the time," said Mike.

"No, the songs are full of something else, too," said Mr. Potter. "That's the thing. No matter how much you don't have, there's always so much more of life to be had. So, no matter how much sadness is in a song, there's equal 'mount of maybe-things'll-get-better-someday-soon."

"Can you make any song the blues?" asked Mike.

"Not always. But you can make most sound blues-y."

Frankie laughed. "Blues-y. That's funny."

"Means you can give 'most any song the flavor of the blues." Mr. Potter put his harmonica to his lips and played "Twinkle, Twinkle, Little Star." It was the same melody their mom used to sing, but with repeating phrases. At the end, Mr. Potter seemed to goad the song into wailing.

"How did you do that?" asked Mike.

"Easy." Mr. Potter grinned. "You take the tune and break it up. Then do over some of the lines. Then sprinkle in some grit from your insides. You play the song like you're testifying to the feelings you hold in your heart: happy, sad, angry. Mike, you follow what I do." He played two chords.

Mike repeated them.

He played a note, bending it.

Mike copied him.

Mr. Potter made each phrase different from the last. Back and forth they went—first Mr. Potter and then Mike. Short notes, like words. Followed by longer phrases, like full sentences. Then, entire paragraphs of music, as if the two of them were having a conversation.

When they were done, Frankie clapped. "Now me!" he said.

Mr. Potter started over, making the phrases simpler.

After Frankie caught on, Mike joined in. In the shade of the tree, with the sounds of the three harmonicas talking to one another, and all that had happened to them in the last few days, Mike dared to let another sliver of happiness creep into his heart.

Mrs. Potter called to Frankie and Mike from the back door of the main house and waved them over.

Frankie ran ahead.

Mr. Potter pointed to Mike's harmonica. "That is somethin' special. Got a quality I never heard before."

Mike nodded. "I . . . I feel different when I play it."

Mr. Potter smiled. "Sometimes an instrument does that to a person. Makes the world seem brighter, with more possibilities."

Mike understood what he meant. He'd felt it. He held out the harmonica, pointing to the tiny scroll-like *M* on the pear-wood edge that he'd noticed yesterday. "What's this mean, Mr. Potter?"

"I don't know. Never saw such a thing. Frankie's have it?"

Mike shook his head. "No, I checked."

"Probably put there by its maker. That harmonica isn't the only thing special. You got a natural talent. Mrs. Potter told me about your piano playing. Now I know what she was going on about. Wait here."

Mr. Potter went into the cottage. A few minutes later, he came back and handed Mike a thick book of music with harmonica tabs. "You can borrow this awhile. It'll pique your interest just fine. You gonna come back tomorrow and jam with me some more?"

Mike nodded. "Thank you. Yes, sir."

Slowly, Mike made his way toward the house, playing the songs he'd just learned. When a movement caught his eye, he glanced up at a second-story window. Mrs. Sturbridge stood watching him. But before he could raise his hand to wave, she disappeared, and the draperies plunged closed.

He hadn't had an opportunity to apologize for

playing the piano yesterday. Was she still upset about that? Or was it something else?

Mrs. Sturbridge's strange behavior continued.

For two weeks, they hardly saw her.

Mrs. Potter kept them busy with a schedule of meals and playtime and chores. Mr. Potter let Frankie follow him around like a puppy. Mr. Howard came every few evenings and ate dinner with them, staying after to play catch on the lawn or a game of checkers on the porch. *He* took them to the park on weekends. *She* never joined them.

Mike tried to tell himself it didn't matter. That just being together was enough for him and Frankie. But he saw how the kid's eyes followed Mrs. Sturbridge when she whisked past them. He felt Frankie's longing to be part of a family again. And sometimes, in his heart of hearts, Mike even dared to wish the same for himself.

He took comfort in the blues. He practiced as much as he could with Mr. Potter, working through the music book and making each song blues-y.

Every time he played, he felt buoyed, lifted up, and full of possibility, as if he were riding on the shoulders of some unknown power. He could sense something optimistic in his heart, making his music shine from the inside out.

In the hours between playing, though, he felt confused and unsettled. Something about being on Amaryllis Drive was rotten.

The night before the Fourth of July, Mike sat on his side of the bed, flipping through the pages of the book Mr. Potter had given him and studying the music.

He started at the beginning with "Goodnight, Ladies," followed by "For He's a Jolly Good Fellow" and "Oh! Susanna."

Frankie came into the bedroom and climbed up next to him. "Play me a song, please."

Mike obliged, easing into "My Old Kentucky Home."

"That was good," said Frankie, his eyes already drooping. "Mike, do you think *tomorrow* . . ." His eyes closed and his forehead wrinkled as if he were wishing hard for something.

Mike didn't need Frankie to finish the question. Every night, he asked the same ones.

Do you think tomorrow she will spend time with us? Or maybe let us eat in the dining room with her 'stead of in the kitchen?

Mike reached over and smoothed Frankie's forehead.

"Do you think she'll take us to see the fireworks at the park 'cause of Fourth of July," Frankie murmured. "'Specially since Mr. Howard is out of town?"

"Sure, kid," whispered Mike. "Go to sleep now. Maybe tomorrow will be the day."

14

The Fourth of July came and went without mention.

The Saturday following, after breakfast, Mike sat in the bedroom playing the harmonica while he and Frankie waited for Mr. Howard to take them to the park.

Frankie got up from the floor where he'd been pencil-drawing and went to the mirror above the dresser. "Mike, do you think I need another haircut?"

Mike stopped playing and studied Frankie. "Maybe in a few weeks, but you look fine for now."

"Do you think I'm too noisy?"

"Frankie, no . . . Why?"

"'Cause everybody here likes us . . . 'cept her. I've been leaving nosegays from the garden by her bedroom door and making pictures and leaving them at her place at the dining table. But she doesn't ever talk to us. So, I was just thinking if Mr. Howard took me for a haircut, or if I was quieter . . . then maybe . . ." He shrugged.

"Listen, like I tell you every day, she's just getting used to us. She wasn't expecting boys. Or *two* of anything. And it takes some folks longer than others to warm up. At least we're not at Bishop's and we're together. Right?"

Frankie nodded. "Right."

"You know, sometimes I feel guilty we have so many nice things now, when so many other kids don't have anything," said Mike. "You ever feel that way?"

Frankie nodded. "I think about James and how he's still at Bishop's with shoes too small and I have new ones."

"Same here. I think about Mouse living on the streets and wonder what he's going to do when it gets cold, and here I have a bed full of blankets. I think about these things a lot—about how come it was us and not someone else got picked to come here. We're the lucky ones, kid."

Frankie gave him a wobbly smile.

Mike wished he believed his own words. But even though they had so much, too many things still didn't add up. And even though Mrs. Potter had said Mike would get used to things not making sense, after three weeks, he hadn't, and that worried him. There was something big gnawing at him—a question far more confounding than a piano in the music room that sorely needed playing.

Mrs. Potter appeared in the doorway. "Mr. Howard is here. Frankie, let's get you cleaned up a bit."

"Is she coming with us?" asked Frankie.

Mike looked at Mrs. Potter and caught the look of pity in her eyes and the almost imperceptible shake of her head.

She put on a smile. "Not today. But lots of vendors are still in the park, being it's just after the holiday. You'll enjoy it." She took Frankie's hand and led him from the room.

Mike heard voices from the open window. He stepped closer. Down below, Mrs. Sturbridge and Mr. Howard stood on the front walk. She was dressed for town in her usual black, carrying gloves and a handbag.

Mr. Howard had his hands on his hips. "You're going to see Golding *today*? Why don't you come with us?"

"I'm trying to undo what's been done."

"They're good boys, Eunie. And talented. You'd see that if you gave them a chance."

Whatever Mrs. Sturbridge said next was so quiet that Mike couldn't hear. But her gaze dropped to the ground.

Mr. Howard shook his head. "I know you've suffered, Eunie. But so have those boys. I'm sorry I put you in a situation that was far different from what you were expecting. I was doing my best, given that time was running out. You know . . . all your father ever wanted was for this house to be filled with children and music and for you to open your heart again."

She looked up at Mr. Howard. "What good has opening my heart ever done? Everyone who matters to me *leaves* me!"

"That's not true. *I* never left you. Not on the playground when you were a girl and lost your mother. Not when you married a man your father didn't approve of. I stayed at your side when little Henry . . . and your father . . ." He choked up and his voice cracked. "I never left through all of it. And I'm *still* here. But if this is your way of telling me that *I* don't matter to you, then maybe it's time I move on." He turned and walked into the house.

Her eyes followed him. She looked up and caught Mike watching her from the window.

He felt the blood rush to his face. Would she be angry he was eavesdropping? She didn't look mad. She looked as if she might cry. Before he could blink, she spun around and strode to the Packard, where Mr. Potter held the door open.

Mike watched the car pull away, more questions taunting him.

What did her dead father have to do with their adoption?

Who was Henry?

And what was she trying to undo?

15

As they walked toward the park, Mr. Howard didn't talk or whistle, and the spring in his step was gone.

When they passed his house, Frankie asked, "Have you ever climbed those trees?"

Mr. Howard shook his head. "Not since I was a boy. But you boys can climb them any time you like."

"Mike won't ever, 'cause he's afraid of heights."

"Is that true, Mike?"

Mike nodded.

"I'm afraid of spiders," said Frankie. "What are you afraid of, sir?"

"Frankie, these days I'm afraid of losing everything I ever cared about." He looked from Frankie to Mike. "And I'm afraid of losing the things I'm *beginning* to care about."

"Like us?" asked Frankie.

Mr. Howard smiled but looked sad, too.

Mike felt a pang in his heart.

"You see, I had hoped that one day Eunie and I might . . ." Mr. Howard frowned.

"Get married?" asked Frankie.

Mr. Howard blushed. Even his freckles looked brighter.

"You *love* her?" asked Frankie.

He flung out his hands. "It might not matter anymore. I have an opportunity with my firm to transfer to San Francisco at the end of the year. I haven't told them yes or no yet."

Frankie took his hand. "Please don't go."

"I can't promise to stay," he said. "It depends on what happens here."

Mike puzzled. What needed to happen for Mr. Howard to stay?

As they approached the park, Frankie ran ahead and joined some boys playing ball. Mike and Mr. Howard sat on a bench.

What would become of them if Mr. Howard left? There'd be no more Saturday outings, no more playing ball on the lawn, no more checkers after dinner. Without him around, the house would seem bigger, their lives emptier, especially since Mrs. Sturbridge barely spoke to them.

Mike took a deep breath, the big question burning in his stomach. He forced himself to ask it.

"Mr. Howard, sir, how come Mrs. Sturbridge adopted us? We've hardly seen her since we got here. Even though we look presentable now, she still doesn't seem to want us."

Mr. Howard took off his hat and stared at it as if it held all the answers. "I guess it must feel that way. I suppose you're old enough to understand and have a right to know. You see, Michael, you and Frankie are her father's final wish."

"You mean when he was dying?"

Mr. Howard leaned back. "Not exactly. You see . . . when Eunie was twenty, she married a violinist she met in New York at a symphony benefit. He performed abroad for months at a time, so she lived in the big house with her father. Her husband came and went. A few years later, they had a son. Henry. That house became a different place with him toddling and then running around, so full of life and laughter and joy. He became the light of Eunie's and her father's lives. She and Mr. Dow spoiled him a little too much."

"In the Young Gentlemen's Department," remembered Mike. "Where is Henry now?"

"Against her wishes, Eunie's husband took him to a nearby lake one day. Henry was only three and couldn't swim. Her husband wasn't watching—he'd met some friends there and had his eyes on other things—and there was an accident. And . . . Henry died."

Suddenly, everything became clear. Mike whispered, "That's why she didn't want to adopt a child . . . especially a boy."

Mr. Howard stared into the park. "She never forgave her husband. They stayed together for a few years, but he was rarely home and soon he was squandering her money. They finally divorced. Then Eunie shut out the world. She hardly ever left the house."

"She still had her father, though," said Mike.

"Yes. For five years. He was in a wheelchair by

then. Polio. Taking care of him gave her some purpose. But as Mr. Dow grew frailer, he worried that Eunie would never have a family. All he wanted was for her to feel joy and love again. Secretly, he changed his will so that she would inherit his wealth only if she started proceedings to adopt a child within one year of his death. Preferably a child who was musical. Otherwise, everything would go to charity, including the house. Eunie hadn't performed with an orchestra for years, so if she didn't oblige, she would have no income."

"Was she surprised?" asked Mike.

"That's putting it mildly. Angry, surprised, indignant, and sad that her father had died on top of it. At first, she said she wouldn't dishonor Henry's life by replacing him with another child. She tried to get the will changed, but her father was clever. It's almost ironclad. She put off adopting until the year deadline was only weeks away. That's when she sent me to choose a child for her so she'd be within the law . . . to buy her more time." Mr. Howard looked at Mike, apologetic.

"I thought our adoption was final."

"The papers have been filed. But they don't become legal until three months have passed. You were adopted the second week of June. The second week of September, it will be said and done."

Mike's stomach began to churn. So that's what she meant when she said, *I'm trying to undo what's been done.* That's why they'd hardly seen her. She *didn't* want to spend any time with them. She was trying to get rid of them.

"Mike, are you all right?"

Mike said slowly, "So we were brought here so the lawyers could have an extra three months to figure out how she can *un*-adopt us?"

Mr. Howard nervously rotated his hat around and around. "I'm sorry." He put an arm on Mike's shoulder.

Mike pulled away, choking out his words. "How soon is she going to send us back? Just tell me, Mr. Howard. I *have* to know."

"Legally, she's only required to adopt one child. I suppose she *could* send you both back and start proceedings on another child. As long as the adoption process is under way, she meets the criteria. But that's not likely to happen."

Mike felt as if he'd been scrambling up a cliff, but just as he reached the top, he slipped and fell to the bottom. "So she could just keep adopting a different boy every three months until the waiting period is up? And make him think he is going to live in a beautiful house, have good things to eat, and get nice clothes, and spend time with *you*? And then, when he gets his hopes up that something right is *finally* happening in his life, she will send him back to Bishop's?"

"Mike, I don't think it will ever come to that."

Mike's mind raced and his words tumbled. "I gotta look out for Frankie. Bishop's won't be taking any Lowers come September and he just can't go to the state home. Kids die there!" Mike clenched his fists. "Why did you choose us if you *knew*? Maybe another family would have come along! Maybe a family who *cared* about us would have . . ." He choked back a lump in his throat.

"Mike, listen to me. When I met you and

Frankie, I knew immediately there was something special about you boys. I lost my own brother in the war. And I'd give anything to have him back. I *couldn't* separate you. That day at Bishop's, it became apparent that Mrs. Pennyweather intended to do just that. I figured if I brought you here, you and Frankie would be safely together for at least the summer. And hopefully longer."

Mike dropped his head. "I knew it was too good to be true."

Mr. Howard said quietly, "It will all be good-and-true in the end. I'm hanging my hat on it." He blew out a long breath. "You know, Mike, she wasn't always closed off and distant. Grief did that to her. She was such a loving mother and when she was with Henry, her happiness just spilled over. She could be . . . *can* be . . . quite wonderful. And so talented. She was a concert pianist, you know. When she walked out onstage, my heart and the whole world stood still. I admit that bringing you and Frankie here was a risk. But I still think it was the right thing. Can't we hope for the best?"

How could Mike hope for the best when the worst seemed so much more probable? He didn't answer.

Mr. Howard sighed and patted Mike on the back. "I would adopt you myself if the law allowed a single man to do such a thing, but it doesn't." He stood and walked to a vendor with a pushcart and came back with three Good Humor bars. He called to Frankie and waved him over.

Frankie climbed up on the bench and grinned, his cheeks pink from playing. "Thank you, Mr. Howard." He licked the dribbles from his ice-cream bar as quickly as they melted. He looked up at Mike. "You're not eating. What's wrong?"

"Nothin', kid." Mike wasn't going to fill Frankie's mind with the prospect of the state home. Besides, it was *his* job to worry.

Frankie finished and begged Mr. Howard to push him on a swing.

Mike stayed on the bench, staring at the Good Humor bar, watching the chocolate slide from the vanilla center. He held it over the grass as it fell apart: first the shell and then the insides.

16

That night, Mike couldn't sleep.

The hours and his problems seemed never-ending. His mind was a fog. He watched patches of light crawl across the ceiling as the moon tried to peek through the branches of the elm in the side yard. He slid from the bed and paced, clenching and unclenching his hands, feeling as helpless as he had at Bishop's. He looked at Frankie, safe and fed and sound asleep, his mouth curled in a smile.

Mike picked up the harmonica and leaned on the windowsill, looking out. The North Star gleamed. Softly, he began a slow and simple rendition of "Home, Sweet Home." He missed Granny. He wished he could be little again, leaning against her on the piano bench while she gave lessons. What should he do now? She had said the right person would find them. But who? And where was the path he should take?

The second time through the song, he broke up the tune like Mr. Potter had taught him, sprinkling in the trials and tribulations in his heart. Mr. Potter's words played in his mind:

It's about what folks want but don't have. No matter how much you don't have, there's always so much more of life to be had . . . there's equal 'mount of maybe-things'll-get-better-someday-soon.

His clouded thoughts began to thin.

Frankie wanted a family. Mrs. Sturbridge needed to fulfill her father's final wish. One child would do that. One child was what she'd been expecting. Would she be more inclined to keep Frankie if Mike were out of the picture?

He filled up on the music and on an idea. He lowered the harmonica and turned it over in his hands. The moonlight caught it and it glowed. He traced a finger over the *M*.

He closed his eyes. Where could he go?

If he went back to Bishop's and was put out to

hire, or ran away, Frankie would be devastated. But if Mike did something else . . . like audition and join the harmonica band, the kid would be thrilled for him.

He slipped away from the windowsill and took his metal box from a drawer in the dresser. He pulled out the newspaper article from the *Inquirer* and ran his finger across the headline, HOXIE'S HARMONICA WIZARDS. Mike's eyes scanned the page, searching for the paragraph he needed.

The band has the support and philanthropy of their own Women's Auxiliary. In cases where children are itinerant and in need, Mr. Hoxie and the Women's Auxiliary have taken in exceptional players and placed them with patron families so they can experience the dynamic benefits of the band and its musical camaraderie while living in a home environment.

If Mike made the band, he wouldn't need to tell Frankie that he was planning to live with another family until later. By then, it would be

September and time for school to start. He'd make sure Frankie saw this as a big opportunity for Mike. He'd pretend it was what he'd always wanted. He'd promise to come home between tours. He'd tell his brother anything to keep him safe.

Convincing Frankie would be the easy part. The rest would only work if he was chosen by Hoxie. And if *she* could open her heart again.

What had Mouse said?

Everybody has a heart. Sometimes you gotta work hard to find it . . . if there's something you want or need to know from grown folks, you gotta step up and ask for it mannerly. Plead your case.

Mike went back to bed, put a protective arm around Frankie, and fell asleep with a familiar burden—wondering about all the things that could go wrong.

Mike was grateful to have a plan. But putting it in motion proved harder than he'd thought.

All week, he watched for Mrs. Sturbridge but saw her only in fleeting moments. When she was home, she stayed in her bedroom or in the library with the door closed and was not to be disturbed. If she was in the garden and Mike came out, she hurried in. It was only after Mike and Frankie went upstairs in the evening that she came down.

Each time he asked Mrs. Potter about her whereabouts, she shook her head and said, "Meetings with lawyers again."

By Saturday morning, Mike was tied up in knots with worry. It was already the middle of July. The summer was moving too fast. Time would soon run out.

Before Mr. Howard arrived to take them to the

park, Mike saw his chance. He took a deep breath and knocked on the library doors.

"Come in."

He stepped inside, where she sat at the desk with a pen in her hand.

"Yes?"

"Ma'am . . . I . . . I . . ." Mike's breath shortened. He patted his shirt pocket and felt a pulse of reassurance from the harmonica.

"What is it, Michael? I'm very busy. I'll be leaving for an appointment soon and I have things . . ."

Mike looked at the floor. His chest felt tight. He tried to unscramble the words in his head. "I know why you brought us here," he managed. "Mr. Howard told me about your father's will. And how you were forced to adopt us. And about your son. I guess that's why you didn't want boys."

She frowned and set the pen on the desk. "It wasn't Mr. Howard's place to say those things. I'll speak to him about that."

"It wasn't his fault. I asked him straight out why we were here. I knew there was something wrong. The way you act around us, well, it isn't hard to figure out that you don't want us." He took a deep breath. "I'd like to know if what Mrs. Potter and Mr. Howard said about you is true."

She raised an eyebrow. "And what, exactly, did they say?" She stood and walked to the window.

"Mrs. Potter said you were a kind and loving soul, underneath all the rest. I guess that means your heart's so sad that it's hard to get out from under the weight. When I was sad about my mother dying, Granny used to say grief is the heaviest thing to carry alone. So I know all about that."

She stood in profile, gazing into the yard, and frowned. Was she already unhappy with what he was saying?

Mouse's words urged him to keep going. *Plead your case.*

"Mr. Howard said you were a loving mother and that when you were with your son your happiness spilled over. He said you were talented, too, and that you can be wonderful. So, if all that is true, I was wondering . . . if you would consider keeping Frankie. You see, if you send us back to Bishop's, they'll put Frankie in the state home and it's not fit for river rats. I couldn't bear to think of what might happen to him there. He's little and he needs someone to look after him. See, I am the lucky one. I remember our mother . . ." Mike bit the inside of his cheek so he wouldn't cry. "But Frankie doesn't."

He took another deep breath and his voice cracked. "And Granny, well, she was the next best thing, but now she's gone, too. And Frankie needs a mother. I see the way he looks at you. He's just hoping you'll notice him and want him. That's why he's been drawing pictures for you and leaving flowers at your door and asking me every night if tomorrow you'll spend time with him."

She turned and faced him, slowly shaking her head.

His thoughts poured out. "I promise he wouldn't be trying to take the *place* of your son. And he wouldn't need to call you Mother, either. Maybe you could be like his aunt. We never had an aunt."

Mike didn't know where all his words were coming from. "Mr. Howard told me you only have to keep one child. I thought a lot on this. I could leave. I could try out for Hoxie's Harmonica Band. See, if you make the band and you don't have a home, the director, Hoxie, he finds you one. Mr. Potter says I'm as fine a player as he's ever heard, so maybe I have a chance. If I got in the band, I could live with a host family until I'm old enough to join the army. You wouldn't have to worry about me. The only one you'd have to look after is Frankie."

She whispered, "Is that what *you* want, Michael?"

"If it means Frankie can stay, then I guess it's what I want. And if I don't make the band, you could send me back to Bishop's, as long as I could visit Frankie now and again. I just have to see him sometimes . . . and he needs to see me." Mike swiped at his eyes. "If he was here with you, no matter if I was back at Bishop's or working on a farm somewhere or in the band, at least I'd have the peace of mind knowing he was safe and not being bullied."

Mrs. Sturbridge put a hand over her mouth.

Had his words made her feel queasy? Mike couldn't stop now. "Frankie likes Mr. and Mrs.

Potter real well. And Mr. Howard, he's the closest thing Frankie ever had to a father, that is, if he doesn't move to San Francisco. He doesn't want to move. One word from you and he'd stay right here forever. He . . . he loves you."

Tears welled in her eyes.

The doorbell rang.

"That's Mr. Howard, here to take us to the park," said Mike.

She nodded and whispered, "Then you better go along."

"Ma'am, this is the nicest place he'll ever find. It's the nicest place *anyone* would ever find. My granny said that finery and fancy houses don't make one bit of difference unless the person who owns them has a heart as beautiful. So if it's all true what they say about you being kind and loving and wonderful . . . could you keep Frankie?"

She turned back toward the window and stood as still as a statue. But Mike was sure he saw tears rolling down the side of her cheek.

If only he knew what they meant.

18

As they walked to the park, Mike couldn't shake the feeling that he'd forgotten something.

But what? He touched his head to make sure he'd remembered his cap and put his hand into his pocket to make sure the harmonica was still there. Had he forgotten to *say* something? He still couldn't tell if Mrs. Sturbridge was more inclined to keep Frankie, or if he had made matters worse. Should he have apologized for making her cry? Or for his boldness? Should he have, at least, told Mrs. Potter she was upset?

"Mr. Howard, sir, I'm going back to the house," said Mike. "I forgot to do something."

"Are you sure?" Mr. Howard asked.

Mike nodded, smiled to reassure him, and turned back. "I'll see you later," he called.

As Mike drew closer to the house, he noticed the Packard was still out front. Hadn't Mr. Potter left to take Mrs. Sturbridge to her appointment yet? He went around to the kitchen and quietly slipped inside.

Mr. Potter sat at the kitchen table, his head tilted to the side, gazing off, a small smile on his face. Mrs. Potter stood at the sink, motionless, her eyes wide and a hand over her heart.

Mike took a step closer to them.

When Mrs. Potter saw Mike, she quickly raised one finger over her mouth to tell him not to make a sound.

What was wrong? Why did he have to be . . .

Suddenly, he understood.

The piano.

Someone was playing the Chopin Nocturne no. 20, the same piece he had played his first morning there, except this . . . this was masterful. Was it *her*?

Mike felt himself drawn forward. He took a few careful steps into the hall.

One of the doors to the music room was halfway open. He stepped behind it and peeked through the crack of the doorjamb.

Mrs. Sturbridge sat at the keyboard, poised and elegant, her arms and head leaning into the music as it filled the room. Mike breathed it in, almost sighing with the emotion of it. Mr. Howard was right. The world seemed to stand still. Riveted, he felt his eyelids drop as he was swept into the piece.

Moments later, he was jarred from his trance by an angry clamor. He peered into the room again and saw Mrs. Sturbridge pounding on the keys. He felt a hauntingly familiar tremor in his bones.

In his mind's eye, he was back in Granny's parlor, hammering on the piano, sadness traveling from his heart to his fingers, filling the room with grief. He blinked back tears. He knew this pain.

Mrs. Sturbridge pushed away from the piano, stood, and swung her arm at the prop. The lid crashed in a deafening clap. She dropped to the piano bench and collapsed across the keyboard, burying her head in the crook of an elbow. She trembled from her sobbing, dissonant notes erupting with each heave of her body.

Mike pressed himself against the wall, his eyes stinging. As Mrs. Potter rushed past him, he stayed frozen. He still hadn't moved when she emerged with her arm around Mrs. Sturbridge, now a limp rag doll, and guided her upstairs.

Was all this his fault? Had he asked for too much?

19

For most of the week, Mrs. Potter shuttled from the kitchen to Mrs. Sturbridge's room, taking her meals on trays and shushing everyone because the missus needed to rest.

Mike dragged around his guilt. He still hadn't told anyone about his conversation with her. He wanted to apologize, but he couldn't see how or when.

The nosegays Frankie left by her door withered; his drawings collected by her place at the dining table. Mr. Howard came to visit but Mrs. Sturbridge refused to see him. He halfheartedly played catch on the lawn with Frankie, or sat on the porch and played checkers, letting the kid win every game.

By Thursday, Mrs. Potter said that if the missus didn't perk up soon, she would call the doctor. Mike was so distraught, thinking she might have to go to the hospital, he told Mr. Howard everything. Mr. Howard only patted him on the shoulder and said Mike had given her the best medicine possible. But Mike hadn't a clue what that meant.

Late that night, he finally heard talking coming from the library, and the voices sounded like Mrs. Sturbridge's and Mr. Howard's. The murmurings were low and somber, so he couldn't make out what they were saying. Had she come to a decision about him and Frankie? A knot in Mike's stomach tightened.

The next evening, as Mike and Frankie readied for bed, there was a knock on the bedroom door. Mike opened it, expecting Mrs. Potter, and was surprised to find Mrs. Sturbridge. She wore a dressing gown with a shawl wrapped around her and looked weary-eyed.

"Michael, a word with you, please."

He stepped from the room and closed the door. Before she could say anything, he blurted, "Ma'am, about the other day, I'm sorry if I upset—"

She held up a hand and shook her head. "You needn't apologize. I've thought about what you asked of me. I hadn't considered . . . your and Franklin's circumstances. I . . . I see now . . ." She frowned and fidgeted with the fringe on the end of the shawl. "I've come to tell you that if this arrangement is what you really want, then I will agree to it. But, I want you to know that no matter what happens with the band . . ."

The bedroom door swung open. Frankie stood before them, looking hopeful. "Do you want a word with me, too?"

Her eyes softened. "As a matter of fact, I wanted to thank you for all the lovely flowers and pictures." She caught Mike's eye and nodded.

No matter what happens . . .

She would still keep Frankie.

He whispered, "Thank you."

Saturday evening, Frankie rushed into the bedroom before dinner, his eyes wide.

"Mrs. Potter says for us to come down to the library in fifteen minutes. Mr. Howard is coming over for dinner. And guess what. *She's* feeling better and is going to eat with us *in the dining room.*

Mrs. Potter says it's about time for things to change around here. Oh, and we need to spruce up. That means put on a clean shirt and comb our hair and look smart."

Mike laughed and helped Frankie comb his hair. It seemed like things were looking up. And since his talk with Mrs. Sturbridge, he'd noticed other changes, too. Yesterday, Mr. Potter hung a rope swing in the elm in the side yard. The shutters in the library had been pulled aside so that light flooded the room. One of Frankie's drawings had been pinned up in the kitchen. And this morning, a piano tuner came.

As Mike shepherded Frankie downstairs and into the library, he couldn't help but be happy to see the kid grinning from ear to ear, knowing that he would be settled here. At the same time, he felt heavyhearted at the prospect of being on his own without his little brother. Did he need Frankie as much as Frankie needed him?

Mr. Howard rose from the sofa where he'd been sitting with Mrs. Sturbridge. She looked prettier and younger in a blue dress.

"Boys, we're happy to see you," said Mr. Howard.

She nodded. "Michael. Franklin. Come in and sit down for a few minutes before we go in to dinner."

She motioned to the two chairs opposite the sofa.

Mr. Howard held up a newspaper section so they could see the headline, HARMONICA CONTEST SET TO BEGIN. Beneath it was a photograph of Hoxie's band. "Remember when Mr. Wilkenson at the music shop told us about the harmonica competition? Well, I was pleasantly surprised when Eunie called me and told me she saw an article about it in the newspaper today," said Mr. Howard. "She thought it would be something for you to do this summer, Mike, if you're interested."

Frankie tripped over his words. "Ma'am . . . I mean, Mrs. Sturbridge. The harmonica band? Really? Mike could try out?"

She nodded. "Mr. Potter thinks he's more than talented. And it would occupy his time until . . . until September. And, Franklin, it would be fine if you and Michael call me Aunt Eunie."

Frankie turned to Mike. "It's fine if we call her *Aunt* Eunie."

Mike knew he probably wouldn't be calling her Aunt Eunie. And he wanted to be excited. The band sounded like a great adventure. But all he could think about were the words *until September* . . . when he'd be leaving.

Mr. Howard held up the paper. "Let's hear all about it." He cleared his throat and read. "'Since June, over five thousand boys and girls have enrolled in harmonica classes and are prepared to show their prowess at a competition that will begin in various greater Philadelphia churches, neighborhood houses, and YMCAs.'"

"Over *five thousand*." Mike's jaw dropped. He'd never suspected there'd be so many.

Frankie whistled at the number.

Mr. Howard continued. "'The first round of competitions will be held on August tenth in front of a jury. Each student will perform one set piece and one optional piece. The jury will choose the semifinalists.'"

"Where would I try out?" asked Mike.

"Let's see," said Mr. Howard. "There's a list here. It looks like the closest is the downtown YMCA."

"What happens after that?" Mike leaned forward.

Mr. Howard continued. "'A week later, the semifinalists will compete in the second round at the Baptist Temple. Twenty will be chosen to compete in the private reception room of the mayor's offices at City Hall. The day after the finals, Albert Hoxie and his famous Philadelphia Harmonica Band, which has played for dignitaries such as Charles Lindbergh and the queen of Romania, will perform in a community concert at said venue. The musical wizards never fail to entertain audiences of all ages. All finalists and their families will have preferred seating at this event.'"

"What's preferred seating?" asked Frankie.

"The best seats closest to the stage," said Mrs. Sturbridge.

Mr. Howard began again. "'A few days subsequent, allowing time for the judges to convene again and consider the skills of the finalists, winners of the competition will be notified by U.S. Post and bestowed with prizes including musical instruments, credits for clothing at local merchants, and the most anticipated commendation of all—an invitation to join the famous band, should they wish to consign.'"

Frankie turned to Mike. "Please say yes. If you're a finalist, we could be guests at the concert. If not, no harm done. We just won't have the best seats up front. But we could still see 'em." He moved his arm in an arc. "Hoxie's Harmonica Band of Wizards." Frankie held up both hands, fingers crossed, eyes hopeful.

Mrs. Sturbridge caught Mike's eye and nodded.

"Okay, Frankie. I'll do it," said Mike.

Frankie flung himself into Mike's arms. "Yippeee!"

"What is the set piece for the first round?" Mrs. Sturbridge asked.

Mr. Howard turned to another page. "'My Old Kentucky Home.'"

"Mike already knows that one frontwards and

backwards. It was in our instruction booklet," said Frankie.

"And for the optional piece?" she asked.

"I could play Brahms' Lullaby or maybe 'America the Beautiful,'" said Mike.

"'America the Beautiful' might be lovely," she said. "Patriotic pieces make people emotional. And Mr. Howard told me that when you and Franklin played it at the orphanage, everyone was quite moved by your rendition."

"The cooks were weeping into their tea towels," said Mr. Howard.

"I'm not sure how to make some of the phrasing work for the harmonica," said Mike.

"In the morning, we'll start working at the piano and figure out how to adapt it." Mrs. Sturbridge smiled. "I've already asked Mr. Potter for his assistance. He said he'd be honored to coach you. Now, I'm going to tell you a secret, Michael. To be successful in any competition, you must perform something that cannot be ignored. No matter how simple or complicated a piece, you must make it memorable. And to do that, you must practice.

But we'll talk more about all of this later. I can smell Mrs. Potter's roast and I'm famished. Shall we go in to dinner?" She stood.

Frankie rushed to her side, offering his arm.

Mr. Howard winked at Mike. "I told you to hope for the best. Miracles never cease."

But Mike knew it wasn't a miracle.

He and Mrs. Sturbridge had an agreement, and she was keeping her end of the bargain.

20

Morning after morning for the next three weeks, Mike sat next to Mrs. Sturbridge at the piano as she helped him adapt and practice "America the Beautiful."

She suggested that he start off with his own arrangement and then, for the next verse, merge into the blues, and finish as he'd once taught Frankie, simple and unfettered. She said it would be memorable.

Every afternoon, he practiced with Mr. Potter, who helped him with the blues section. Mike didn't have any trouble feeling melancholy in his heart. Or knowing what he wanted but didn't have. If the blues meant a song begging for its life, then Mike's middle section of "America the Beautiful" was a cry for a place to call home.

The day before the first audition, Mike came downstairs in the morning and, as usual, found Mrs. Sturbridge at the piano. He sat next to her and pulled his harmonica from his pocket.

She waved a finger at him. "No rehearsing for the contest this morning. You're more than ready. Today, you just play." She smiled at him as she swept one hand toward the keyboard and held sheet music in the other. "Brahms? Or Beethoven for my student?"

Mike blushed. Had she really said *my student?* He knew it didn't mean anything, but still . . . "Beethoven," he said.

She placed the music on the stand. "Do you know 'Für Elise'?"

He nodded. "I played it for a recital once. I haven't practiced it in a while. I'm not good at the middle part."

She patted his shoulder. "Just start and stop as you wish. We'll play it together."

Mike began, concentrating on the notes. She played the middle section and Mike finished.

"Now you the treble and I the bass," she said.

They started again, Mike playing the right hand and she playing the left. When they bungled it, she laughed. And he did, too. Out loud.

He didn't want to stop. "Now just you," said Mike.

Her fingers flew across the keyboard. When she finished, she put an arm around his shoulder and hugged him, laughing. It had been an impulse—a quick, spontaneous gesture. He knew that. But he liked the feeling of being under her wing and knowing she was watching out for him, at least for the time being.

21

The next day, Mike sailed through the first round at the YMCA.

A week later, after the semifinals at the Baptist Temple, he moved on to the finals.

Now, after yet another week had passed, he was walking down the long corridor at City Hall toward the mayor's reception room. He could hardly believe that he'd made it this far, or that the summer was almost over.

Aunt Eunie, Mr. Howard, and Frankie followed alongside until they all reached the door with a sign on it: WAITING ROOM FOR FINAL-ISTS ONLY.

"Why can't we go in, too?" asked Frankie.

"The finals are *closed* auditions," said Aunt Eunie. "We'll see Michael when it's over."

Frankie looked up at him. "Good luck, Mike."

Mike tousled Frankie's hair. "Thanks, kid."

Mr. Howard shook his hand, then stepped back. "I'll hope for the best."

Aunt Eunie put a hand on his arm. "I've heard what you can do and I think you're remarkable. And Mr. Potter couldn't be more proud." She smiled. "I should have said this before, Michael. Everything you asked me that day in the library . . . It has all been *resolved*. Do you understand?"

"Yes, ma'am," he said. "Thank you for keeping your promise about Frankie."

"It's not just the promise about Frankie. It's about you, too."

"I know," he said. He did understand. She'd kept her promise to him, making all this possible. Tomorrow was the concert, and next week he'd know by a letter in the mail if he'd made the band, and that would determine whether or not he'd be going back to Bishop's.

As Mike watched Aunt Eunie and Mr. Howard and Frankie walk away holding hands down the corridor, his heart ached. He took a deep breath and forced himself to stop wanting something he couldn't have. He had to focus on the competition.

Another boy rushed toward the door. "Hey," he said. "You're the redhead everyone's talking about. I saw you at the semifinals. Good luck today."

"Thanks. You too," said Mike, grabbing the door, holding it open, and following him inside.

Finalists crowded every corner. Harmonica chords, octave runs, and phrasing from "My Old Kentucky Home" filled the room. A volunteer wearing a Women's Auxiliary sash walked among them, passing out the day's schedule. Boys counseled one another.

"What time slot did you get? Later is best. They remember you more."

"Nah. Later is worse. More time to get nervous."

"My ma made me wear a Sunday shirt and a bow tie to make a good impression."

"You better play good, too."

Mike looked at the paper that had been shoved into his hand. He was last in the order.

The lady with the sash clapped her hands to get their attention. "We will proceed. Each of you will go into the adjoining reception room when your name is called. The jury is situated there. You will play the set piece followed by your optional piece. Then exit from the door on the other side of that room. Family members will meet you in the main hallway. The judges will not deliberate until Monday. The winners will be notified in the mail next week and the results will be in the *Inquirer* next Saturday."

She looked at her notes. "One more thing. The concert is tomorrow night. If you have any old harmonicas that you wish to donate to the collection box, bring them to the concert."

Mike found a seat and patted his chest pocket where the harmonica rested. By now it felt like an old friend. In an odd way, it had made his plan to save Frankie possible. And it had brought him closer, even for a little while, to Aunt Eunie. All that from one little instrument. By what miracle had Mike and this harmonica found each other? Maybe Mr. Wilkenson, who'd sold it to him, had been right. Maybe the harmonica had chosen him.

The door to the mayor's reception room opened. Another Women's Auxiliary volunteer smiled at them, then called the first name.

The room fell silent. The boy stood, crossed the threshold, and was swallowed inside.

The boys started talking again.

"What's the collection box?"

"They take used instruments and fix them up and send them to poor kids in California who don't got a penny to their name."

"Hoxie's always doing stuff like that. He's soft for any sad story."

"He's partial to orphans. Band is full of them. If you ain't got parents, it's practically a sure thing you'll get in. Just my luck I got a ma and pa."

"Don't say that," Mike blurted, surprising himself. Then more quietly he said, "You're lucky you've got a family."

Mike waited and watched as, one by one, each of the finalists was called in.

By the time the clerk called his name, he felt as if he might be sick.

22

Mike walked into a paneled room that reminded him of Aunt Eunie's library.

At the front, a seven-person jury sat behind a long table, each with a pencil and paper. The Women's Auxiliary volunteer introduced the judges: the director of the city orchestra, the director of the community chorus, the *Philadelphia Inquirer* music critic, a councilman, the owner of a local theater, the mayor of Philadelphia, and Albert N. Hoxie.

Hoxie was dressed in a band uniform. Stout and full-cheeked with wavy hair combed straight back, he looked like a model of kind authority. "You are Michael Flannery?"

"Yes, sir."

"Well then, son, we look forward to hearing what you can do. Good luck. You may begin whenever you're ready."

346

Mike raised the harmonica and began his set piece. He played it just as Aunt Eunie had taught him, with no improvising and as technically perfect as he could. When he finished, he paused for a moment, looked at each judge, and then began "America the Beautiful."

He played the first verse nice and slow, like a lullaby. The second verse was the blues version with trills and chords and bended notes. It wasn't hard for Mike to drop into the music and testify to the journey he'd been on. His eyes closed and he traveled back: arriving on Amaryllis Drive, riding in the wagon with Mouse, lying on his cot in the dormitory and staring at the wrinkled paint on the ceiling, standing at Granny's window, waiting, and listening to his mother sing to him and Frankie.

He played the third verse like he and Frankie used to play it, the refrain sounding like a storm crashing up to the *sea to shining sea* part, where he slowed down, the notes calm and simple, clear and sweet.

When he finally lowered the harmonica and looked up, the judges stared at him. Awkwardly,

Mike shifted from one foot to the other. Had he played poorly? Several of the judges cleared their throats. Then they all began to scribble on their pads.

Mr. Hoxie stood, came around the table, and shook Mike's hand. "Thank you, Michael. That was a very impressive performance. You can pick up your tickets for the concert tomorrow night on the way out. And you'll receive a letter with the results of the competition next week. Good luck to you. You are a *very* promising candidate."

Mike blushed, but this time with pride. "Thank you, sir."

When they arrived home, Mr. and Mrs. Potter were waiting for them in the kitchen with a cake.

"To celebrate," said Aunt Eunie.

"But we don't even know if Mike made it," said Frankie.

"When I was a girl," said Aunt Eunie, "my father insisted on cake after big auditions and *before* the results. He said cake should be as much for trying as for anything else."

Mr. Howard looked at her and smiled. "If cake is for trying, then you deserve it, too, Eunie."

She smiled back at him.

Mr. Howard rubbed his hands together. "You're in for a treat, boys. Mrs. Potter makes a delicious chocolate fudge layer."

"That she does," said Mr. Potter.

Mrs. Potter put a wedge in front of Frankie.

"Wow," he said. "What does Mike get if he makes the band?"

Mike blurted, "I get to start practicing again. Right, Auntie?"

Frankie giggled. "Auntie?"

They all laughed.

Mike felt his cheeks flush. The word had just slipped out. Had she minded? He glanced at her and she gave him a small smile and nodded, as if everything was as it should be.

Make the band or not, he'd be leaving them all soon. Mike concentrated on his cake, taking a big bite, so he could think about anything but his feelings.

He glanced at each of them. Mr. Howard reached over and brushed cake crumbs from Aunt Eunie's sleeve. She took a napkin and dabbed at Frankie's frosting-smudged cheek. Frankie looked at Mike and smiled with chocolate-coated teeth.

Mr. and Mrs. Potter laughed at Frankie's antics.

Mike took it all in: the kitchen, the laughter, the smell of chocolate cake that had been made for trying.

He closed his eyes, hoping to capture this moment so he'd always remember when and where he had once belonged.

23

As they dressed for the concert on Sunday afternoon, Frankie peppered Mike with questions.

"Do you think the band will wear their capes? How do they keep those tall hats on? What songs do you think they'll play? You're sure we get to sit right up front in the best seats?"

"Frankie," said Mike, "you are going to wear me out with questions, just like you do to Mrs. Potter. I can only concentrate on gettin' ready right now. Yes, we get to sit right up front. And remember, you can't ask me questions during. You gotta use best concert manners."

"I know. But, Mike, if you make it, you gonna join?"

"We already talked about this a dozen times. If I don't make it, no harm done, just like you said. If I do make it, I'll have to think about it."

"Aunt Eunie would probably let you, long as you weren't gone from home too much."

Mike avoided his eyes. "Yeah. She'd probably let me. But we won't know anything till the middle of the week when the letter comes."

Mrs. Potter came into the room, carrying two white shirts, starched and ironed. "It's time. The missus is waiting for you downstairs to knot your ties. Mr. Howard is already here. And Mr. Potter is bringing the car around front. You enjoy the concert, Michael. You deserve to sit and listen and enjoy somethin' after all the practicing you've done the last month."

"Thank you, Mrs. Potter."

When they were all heading down the front walk to the car, Aunt Eunie put her hand on her head. "I forgot my hat."

"I'll get it," Mike offered.

"Thank you. It's in the library on my desk. The felt cloche. But be careful of the hat pin."

Mike ran back. On Aunt Eunie's desk, he found the bell-shaped hat with the pearl-tipped pin woven through the crown. He carefully picked it up from the top of a stack of papers.

Beneath it was a letter from Mr. Golding's office. Mike couldn't help but see the words stamped across the top in large red letters.

APPEAL GRANTED

He read the first sentence.

Your appeal for the reversal of the adoptions of Michael Flannery and Franklin Flannery has been granted and will become final upon receipt and filing of the required notarized signature below, on or before the fifteenth of September, 1935.

She was un-adopting them? Mike felt like he'd been kicked in the stomach.

She'd lied to him?

He held on to the desk, his body shaking.

How could he not have seen it? Didn't they

have an agreement? Hadn't she said that every-thing was *resolved*? What about the lessons at the piano, the cake, the kind words? What about Frankie? She acted like she *cared* about him and was beginning to love him.

How could he have been so wrong about her?

What a fool he had been! It had all been a swin-dle. A three-month swindle so her lawyers could have more time. She never intended to keep *either* of them.

The car horn beeped.

Mrs. Potter stepped into the library. "Michael, you best hurry. They're waiting. Are you feeling well? You don't have a speck of color."

Without answering, he grabbed the cloche and hurried from the room. As he ran down the drive-way, his heart pounded. He was so dumbfounded that he just climbed into the backseat of the car and handed her the hat, as if nothing was wrong. He'd been careful of the hat pin, but he still felt a stabbing pain in his chest.

The car cruised down Amaryllis Drive. When they passed the park, Mike stared at the bench where Mr. Howard had asked him to hope for the best—where he said that everything would be good-and-true in the end, and that he didn't think it would ever come to this. But it *had* come to this. He stared out the window and felt light-headed.

"Mike? You're awfully quiet," said Mr. Howard.

Had he known, too?

"Just tired," Mike said, keeping his face turned away and trying to make sense of it all. If he made the band, he couldn't join because Frankie would have no place to go except the state home. If he didn't make the band, they'd be sent back to Bishop's. But Mike couldn't let that happen, either, for the same reason.

What could he do?

At first, the solution that popped into his mind seemed preposterous.

But as they walked into the theater at City Hall and were seated up front with the twenty finalists and their families, the idea took hold.

The doors opened in the back of the theater. The Philadelphia Harmonica Band marched down the center aisle two by two with elegant precision.

Everything about the band was majestic: their blue cadet-like uniforms with the shiny buttons, the hats, the shoes polished to a gleam. The band members strode past the audience toward the stage, arms swinging and harmonicas flashing in their left hands. When the regiment reached the front of the theater, the lines split, one line veered right, the other left. The musicians climbed the stairs of the stage from both sides and filled the risers.

Mr. Albert N. Hoxie came onto the stage. The applause was thunderous and the band hadn't yet played a note. He raised his baton. Their spectacular sound—like an entire orchestra with every kind of instrument—filled the theater with a rousing march, the one that John Philip Sousa wrote especially for them.

They were as stunning and talented as everyone had said. Mike listened with a mix of regret and determination, knowing he'd never have the chance to join them.

As the music swelled, so did his new plan.

24

In the middle of the night, Mike dressed and packed his and Frankie's clothes in a small suitcase.

He gathered a few books, the metal box he'd brought from Bishop's, and their harmonicas. He slipped his into his chest pocket. He looked at Frankie, sleeping peacefully across the room. Mike hated to take him from a place where he was so happy. But what choice did he have?

He waited until four thirty in the morning so Frankie could get some rest. It would be a long day and he didn't know when or where they'd be sleeping next. He gently shook his shoulder, whispering, "Wake up."

Without opening his eyes, Frankie mumbled, "I'm tired."

Mike gently pulled him into a sitting position. "I know it's early, Frankie, but you gotta get dressed. We have to leave."

Heavy-lidded, Frankie looked up at Mike. "Leave? Where? When are we coming back?"

"We're not coming back. We have to leave for good."

Frankie rubbed his eyes and sat straighter. "Why? I like it here. I don't want to leave."

"Shhh. I like it here, too," whispered Mike. "But it's no matter. Listen to me. Last night before the concert, I found some papers on Aunt Eunie's desk. She's sending us back to Bishop's."

Frankie shook his head. "No. She wouldn't . . ."

Mike put his arms around his brother. "I'm not lying to you."

"But . . . she likes us now," Frankie whimpered. "I can tell, Mike. She likes us real well."

Mike hugged Frankie. "I thought so, too. But she must not want any kids because the lawyer's paper says she's reversing our adoption."

"I don't *want* to go back to Bishop's."

"Don't worry. We are not going there because we're not supposed to be separated. Remember? We're getting out of here before she can send us back." He pulled Frankie's nightshirt up and over his head and handed him some clothes. "Come on now. Get dressed."

Frankie threw his arms around Mike's neck. "What about Mr. and Mrs. Potter and Mr. Howard?" He was crying now.

Mike rocked him, choking back his own tears. "I . . . I wrote a note, telling them we were leaving. And how it was the best summer of our lives. They'll have to understand. Maybe someday we can come back and visit. But right now, we gotta go. You and me, we stick together, remember?"

Frankie nodded into Mike's neck. Sniffling, he slid from the bed and began to dress. "Where . . . where we going?"

"On a train. You always wanted to go on a train, right?"

Frankie nodded, his eyes wide and watery. "To where?"

"New York City."

Frankie hiccupped and his voice shook. "Are

we going to Carnegie Hall and to eat roasted beef and ice cream?"

"Maybe," said Mike. He walked to the window at the side of their room. "We can't risk going downstairs. Too much noise unlatching and closing the doors." He pointed to the elm outside next to the window. "Think I could climb down?"

Frankie nodded. "It's an easy one."

Mike opened the window and studied the route down, his stomach squirming. He tossed their bag to the grass, then pulled back inside and nodded for Frankie to come.

Reluctantly, Frankie came forward. He climbed onto the sill, straddled it, and looked into the bedroom. "I liked our room." He reached up to hold on to an overhanging limb and climbed out. "It's sturdy. Watch how I go down." Frankie took a big step out onto another branch and sat on it, scooting on his bottom toward the main trunk, where he stood and began climbing down limb by limb.

Mike forced himself to watch. At the lowest

branch, Frankie wrapped his body around it, flipped to the underside, dangled his legs, and dropped to the grass.

Mike turned to look back one last time and whispered, "I liked our room, too, kid." He put a leg over the sill and grabbed the limb above him. Then he stepped out on the one below, just as Frankie had done, lowering himself to a sitting position and scooting slowly across. When he reached the trunk, he hugged it tight, eyes closed.

Frankie whispered, "Don't look at the ground. It'll make you dizzy. Just reach your leg to the next limb."

Mike took a deep breath and opened his eyes, staring at tree bark. His heart pounded. He stretched one leg, until he felt the limb below. He inched his arms down the trunk, reaching with his other leg. A breeze stirred the leaves. His leg flailed and he couldn't find the limb.

Without thinking, Mike looked down. He was much higher up than he'd thought. Dizzy, he tipped sideways, grabbing a nearby branch. The harmonica slid from his pocket and landed in the fork of a smaller branch. He thought he could reach it, so he righted himself and leaned out, stretching his fingers until he grabbed it. But he wobbled.

And fell.

In the seconds before his body and the earth collided, the wind blew a chord through the harmonica clutched in his hand.

The ground slapped the air from him.

Lying on his back during the interminable moments of breathlessness, he stared into the night. He could not rise. Or talk. He could only wait, and hope to inhale again.

Above him, the dark, gnarled branches of the elm reached toward the heavens like a witch's crooked fingers. And yet, even in this strange limbo, Mike saw stars above him, tiny dots of light bobbing in and out from behind the fluttering leaves.

His chest tightened.

Frankie appeared above him, wild-eyed and calling his name. But Frankie's voice faded behind the sound of someone playing Brahms' Lullaby on a cello.

And then that faded, too . . .

Until all Mike could hear was birdsong, a brook trickling over smooth stones, and the yodel of the wind through hollow logs.

THREE

DECEMBER 1942

SOUTHERN CALIFORNIA

U.S.A.

Auld Lang Syne

words by Robert Burns

6   7 7   7   8 -8 7 -8

Should auld ac-quain-tance be for-got,

8 7 7   8   9 -10

And nev-er brought to mind?

-10   9 8 8   7 -8 7 -8

Should auld ac-quain-tance be for-got,

8 7 -6 -6 6   7

And days of auld lang syne?

-10 9 8 8 7 -8   7 -8

For au-ld la-ng syne, my dear,

-10 9 8 8 9 -10

For au-ld la-ng syne,

-10 9 8 8 7 -8   7 -8

We'll take a cup o' kind-ness yet,

8 -8 7 -6 -6 6   7

Fo-r au-ld la-ng syne.

I

In La Colonia, a barrio of whitewashed bungalows on the outskirts of Fresno County, Ivy Maria
Lopez and her mother walked toward the post
office, hoping for a letter.

With one hand, Mama clutched to her neck
her heavy sweater, and with the other, she held
an empty laundry basket.

Ivy dawdled, playing the harmonica. She was
far enough away that Mama couldn't hear the music,
but she kept the notes low and muted anyway. Next
week she would be on the radio with her class. She
hadn't told Mama and Papa the surprise yet. Her
teacher, Miss Delgado, had chosen *her* to perform
a solo.

"Come, Ivy!" called Mama. "We need to get the
mail *and* the laundry before dark." She looked up.
"And before the rain."

Ivy hurried to keep up, her eyes following Mama's. Clouds the color of charcoal smudged the sky, brooding. She slipped the harmonica inside the jacket. *His* gray wool jacket with its hidden pocket that zipped so pennies could not escape.

"Mama, is it possible to be inside a song?"

"Ivy, what nonsense is this?"

"When I play the harmonica, I feel like I'm traveling on the notes. To faraway places."

In the distance, a truck horn beeped five times.

Mama groaned. "Oh, Ivy, there's no time for your silliness. The mail is just arriving. We will have to wait for the clerk to call names. You go to the post office and I will get the clothes."

"Can I meet Araceli after?" asked Ivy. "I promised her."

"Do you have schoolwork? You know how Papa feels about—"

Ivy shook her head. "Miss Delgado says our only assignment is to practice our songs for the performance next week." She opened both arms wide. "Presenting Miss Delgado's fifth-grade class on *The Colgate Family Hour.*"

Mama smiled, but it was halfhearted. "Yes, I know."

"Do you think everyone in La Colonia will listen? And even people farther away than Fresno will hear? Do you think the radio station will ask us back for more performances?"

Mama's brow furrowed. "Ivy, always with so many questions about frivolous things. This is why Papa says you have your head in the clouds. You must come down to earth." Her eyes drifted across the barrio in the direction of the post office. Ivy could see she was too preoccupied to indulge her.

Still, Mama's words stung. Ivy couldn't help asking questions. And playing harmonica on the radio wasn't any more frivolous than her older brother, Fernando, playing basketball in high school. Mama and Papa never said *that* was frivolous. They went to every game.

Ivy stuffed down her hurt feelings. She was sure when they heard her solo on the radio they would see what Miss Delgado already knew: There was something remarkable about Ivy, too.

"If there is mail, bring it to us *before* you meet Araceli."

"I will." Ivy stood on tiptoe to kiss Mama's cheek. As she watched Mama walk away, swaying toward the community clotheslines, the basket perched on a hip, she couldn't help but notice how much she and Fernando resembled her: tall, thin, and wide-eyed with thick dark hair. Papa was the opposite: short, round, bald, and, when he smiled, squinty-eyed. Ivy touched one of her long braids. Did Fernando look more like Papa now that his head was shaved?

Nearby, someone played "Silent Night" on a guitar. As she walked, Ivy raised her harmonica and accompanied the music. Christmas lights glowed in bungalow windows. Dark billows shifted overhead. A breeze lifted. Ivy's imagination filled with the blur of the colored lights, the tender song, and the whiff of rain-soaked earth on the wind. She closed her eyes and felt herself drift some-where in time. She was a vagabond in a jeweled

373

robe, following a caravan across the everlasting sand under a starlit sky.

. . . all is calm . . . all is bright . . .

When the song finished, she looked up to see her neighbors, Mrs. Perez and her daughter-in-law, listening and nodding. People paid attention when she played the harmonica. They took her seriously and appreciated her talent. When Mama and Papa heard her performance at the radio station, Ivy hoped they would, too.

Inside the post office, she wiggled through the crowd to the front counter and waited for the clerk to open the mail sack. Recruitment posters covered each wall: JOIN THE ARMY NURSE CORPS! ARMY AIRBORNE ALL THE WAY! MAN THE GUNS, JOIN THE NAVY! ALWAYS ADVANCE WITH THE MARINES! It seemed the United States military wanted everyone over eighteen for something. Although Fernando hadn't needed a poster to convince *him*.

As the clerk called out names, Ivy watched the hungry eyes of mothers and young wives. "Alberto Moreno. Martina Alvarado. Maria Peña. José Hernandez. Elena Guzman. Victor Lopez . . ."

Ivy's heart jumped. "Here!" She raised her hand and reached for the large, fat envelope addressed to Papa, with a row of three-cent stamps affixed to it. She studied the return address and felt a pinch of disappointment. It was not from Fernando. It had been well over a month since they last heard from him, and each day, Mama and Papa grew more tense.

She waited until the clerk shook out the bag and said, "That is all for now, my friends. If not today, maybe tomorrow."

Ivy hurried back to the bungalow, where she found Papa sitting at the kitchen table. His eyes lit up when he saw the envelope. "A letter?"

Ivy laid it on the table. "Sorry, Papa. It is not from Nando." She headed toward the door.

"Wait. Where are you going in such a hurry? It is almost dark."

She turned. "To meet Araceli. Mama said I could."

"Come back very soon." He waved, opened the envelope, and began to read.

Before Ivy reached the front door, she heard Papa calling Mama's name. "Luz! Luz!"

Mama rushed from the bedroom. "Victor, what is it?"

Ivy paused, her hand on the doorknob.

"It is from my cousin Guillermo. It is the miracle we have been waiting for! A farm in Orange County, near Los Angeles. Guillermo made the arrangements and has sent the papers."

Ivy's heart pounded and she whispered, "No."

Papa's voice carried. "The owner needs someone who knows about supervising *and* irrigation. That is me! There is a letter for you, too. From his wife, Bertina. And the papers to register Ivy for school. And all the instructions from the owner. Ivy Maria! We have news!"

Ivy didn't wait to hear more.

She pulled open the door and ran.

2

Where was Araceli?

Ivy paced beneath the pepper trees where they always met, the winter limbs now naked with balled fists. Icy sprinkles stung her face. She whispered, "Hurry . . ."

Araceli was her first best friend. It had been hard to make friends of any sort when she had lived so many places: Buttonwillow, Modesto, Selma, Shafter, and other towns whose names she'd long forgotten. All that had changed when they moved to Fresno. For the first time ever, Papa had worked in one place for a year. An *entire* year.

She and Araceli had both arrived at La Colonia the same week. Even though Araceli was a year older in school, the two girls looked so much alike, with their black lashes, long brown braids, and wide smiles, that people thought they were sisters.

They quickly discovered that they had even more in common. Araceli had lived all over central California, too, even in some of the same places as Ivy, but at different times. They both loved to read, play jacks, and could jump rope a hundred times double Dutch without missing.

Ivy breathed into the harmonica, creating a lonely wail.

"Ivy!"

She whirled around.

Araceli rushed toward her, wearing a purple crocheted hat pulled down over her ears. She kissed Ivy on the cheek, keeping one arm behind her back. "Sorry I am late. I had to go to the store for my mother."

Ivy tried to sound happy. "New hat?"

"My mother made it. And . . ." She smiled and revealed what was behind her back. "I asked her to make a matching one for you."

She held out an identical purple crocheted hat.

Ivy pulled it on. "How do I look?"

"The same as me!" Araceli giggled. "Now no one can tell us apart."

Ivy laughed, too, but her happiness became all mixed up with her sadness and she began to cry.

"What's wrong?"

"I . . . I am leaving."

Araceli's face crimped with disbelief. "No . . . When? To where?"

"Soon, I think. Somewhere near Los Angeles." Ivy looked down. Brittle leaves scampered across her shoes, whispering their good-byes. She kicked at the stragglers.

Araceli hugged her. "Don't cry. We will always be friends. Besides, if not you, it would probably be me and my family leaving. My father says everyone moves from La Colonia sooner or later, if they want to get ahead in this world."

Ivy sniffled and tried to smile. Why did it have to be sooner rather than later?

"Let's promise to write to each other every week," said Araceli. "Twice a week. Three times!" Her eyes drooped. "You won't forget me, will you?"

Ivy shook her head. "Never."

Fat raindrops splattered the dirt as the sky opened.

"Run!" yelled Araceli.

Squealing, they darted beneath the eaves of a corner bungalow where they needed to go their separate ways. They faced each other and held hands. But Ivy could not make herself jump up and down or laugh like they usually did.

Araceli leaned in and kissed Ivy's cheek. "See you tomorrow!" Then she darted across the road to her home, opened the door, and stood on the threshold, backlit by the light inside.

Ivy tried to etch the image into her mind: her best friend, wearing a matching purple hat, waving, and blowing kisses to her. She blew kisses in return and pretended they were not the beginning of good-bye.

As she dashed back to her bungalow, the rain pelted her.

Ivy slammed the door on the downpour.

Her hands and feet ached, changing from ice-cold to warm. She pulled off her hat and jacket and heard Papa talking to Mama in the kitchen.

"What about Nando?" said Mama.

"I will write to him tonight," said Papa. "When this war is finished, he will return to a *real* home. A house. *Finally!* A house, Luz. We cannot dismiss the opportunity. I am sorry we must leave at once."

Ivy frowned and stepped into the kitchen. "When?"

Mama looked at Ivy, her eyes apologizing. "In the morning."

Ivy stiffened. "The morning? But . . . what about my friends and Miss Delgado?" Disappointment slapped her as the news sank in. She blurted her secret: "And the performance on the radio! I am playing a solo! It was a surprise for you!"

Papa rubbed both hands over his head. "Ivy, this is a once-in-a-lifetime opportunity for our family. There will be other chances for you to perform, maybe at your new school." He held out his arms to her as if pleading for her to understand.

Ivy's eyes smarted and she blinked back tears. She was sure if Fernando were here and *he* had a basketball game, Papa would wait until after to leave. As much as Ivy wanted to speak her mind, she held back. Mama would think it improper to use Fernando as an example when he was away fighting a war. And Papa was Papa. When he said it was time to leave, they left. He wasn't going to change his mind unless she thought of a practical reason.

"I need to tell Miss Delgado I can't perform the solo. She is counting on me. And Araceli thinks we're meeting tomorrow."

Mama's eyes filled with regret, but her voice was firm. "It cannot be helped. Guillermo and Bertina had to leave the farm. All of Bertina's brothers are at war, and her father took ill. They had to move to Texas to help her family. We cannot leave the property unattended much longer. So you understand the urgency.

"You can write Miss Delgado and Araceli notes, and we can drop them at the post office on our way out."

Ivy whimpered. "It's not the *same* as in person. Araceli is my best friend. And Miss Delgado is my favorite teacher. The best teacher I've ever had."

"I know," said Mama, putting an arm around Ivy. "But there will be other teachers and other friends. And we will have a house and a yard where we can plant flowers and a garden. There is a washing machine. Can you imagine? We will not have to haul clothes across camp anymore. I will take over Bertina's job helping a neighbor with laundry. It is all arranged."

"And I will be in charge of sixty acres," said Papa. He held up the envelope. "We are fortunate that Guillermo recommended me. Very fortunate."

Ivy stared at Papa, feeling numb.

"Ivy, there is a possibility this situation will be *permanent*," said Papa. "It is what we've always wanted. You will go to a new school—a better school, with fine teachers! And the weather cannot be compared. I promise you, everything will be better."

"I was going to play a solo! I've been practicing and practicing!"

Papa threw out his arms. "Ivy! There are far more serious matters at hand than this . . . this indulgence of yours."

Papa's words stabbed her. Why did he think so little of her harmonica playing? And why, for once, couldn't he change his mind? Ivy stared at the floor and bit her lip to keep from crying.

In La Colonia, she'd finally belonged—to Araceli, to Miss Delgado, to her neighbors. None of them thought her frivolous or indulgent. Now all that mattering was being cast aside, like rubbish on the road. And for what? Would this move really be different from the rest?

Papa sighed. "Ivy, do you expect us to stay here for six more days when there are trees to be watered and a house waiting for us and the chance at a permanent situation, just so you can play a two-minute song on the harmonica?"

Her thoughts swirled. She knew how she wanted to answer, but then she remembered the promise she'd made to Fernando to be a good little soldier and help Mama and Papa while he was away. Did that mean doing anything to make Mama and Papa happy, even if it made her unhappy?

"No," she whispered.

"Mama and I need to talk to my bosses and say some good-byes. We'll be back in one hour to pack our things." He patted her shoulder before they left.

Ivy went to the bedroom she had shared with Fernando before he left. Several empty boxes already sat on one bed. Her suitcase was lying open on the other. She flung clothes at it. At the end of next week, Christmas vacation started. Other parents waited until their children were out of school, but not Papa. They had to leave *at once*. Ivy sank to her bed, letting the tears come.

Better. Papa was always looking for a place called Better. Once, this place, Fresno, had been better. Now it was nothing more than the last place she'd lived.

She knew how it would be after they left. For a

few days, the news would burn on everyone's lips like the oil of serrano chilies. Then, in a few weeks, the memory of Ivy Maria Lopez would fade away as if she had never lived there . . . as if she'd never belonged somewhere for an entire year.

3

The morning was gray and yawning when Papa crowded his belly behind the wheel of the truck. Mama sat next to him in the middle, and Ivy leaned against the passenger window.

They stopped in front of the post office.

Ivy tried not to cry as she climbed out of the cab and slipped the letters for Miss Delgado and Araceli into the mail slot. A few tears spilled out anyway. Before climbing back in, she took one last look at La Colonia, now a soft blur in the dense fog.

Papa inched the truck toward Highway 99, squinting at what little road he could see in front of him. "One year ago in December we came to Fresno. It was foggy then. It is foggy now. Nothing has changed."

Ivy stared ahead. Even though Papa was talking about the weather, how could he say such a thing? Everything had changed, including her. She could even point a finger at the exact day three months ago when her life had become different.

September eighth had started like so many other first days of school: a new teacher, a new classroom, and a nervous stomach.

As always, Fernando insisted on walking her to school, holding her hand as they headed down the county road, grape fields on one side, almond trees on the other. "I want everyone to see that you have a protective older brother," he said. "Besides, I need to tell you something. Can you keep a secret?"

Ivy nodded. "I love secrets."

"Today is an important day. Do you know why?"

"Because it is your birthday. *And* my first day of fifth grade."

"There is something more. Do you remember what happened last December on the day after we arrived in Fresno?"

"No one can forget," she said. "Pearl Harbor." It was Sunday and they had just stepped from Our

Lady of Miracles Church when a man ran toward them, waving his arms and yelling. The United States had been attacked by Japanese bombs in Hawaii. Papa had hurried the family home. All afternoon they'd huddled around the radio.

Fernando squeezed her hand. "Do you remember how President Roosevelt declared war the next day, and I said I wanted to enlist?"

She nodded. He and Papa had listened to the news night after night. Even then Fernando had that look in his eyes: eagerness, frustration, and wanting to *do* something. "Yes. But Mama said the war would be over before you were old enough to . . ." As she realized what it all meant, she stopped and looked up at him. Today was his *eighteenth* birthday. "Nando?"

He knelt in front of her and held her arms, looking straight into her eyes. "I am going with two of my buddies this afternoon to join the army. But I need your help. I don't know how long it will take and I don't want Mama and Papa to worry. If they ask where I am this afternoon, can you tell them I took someone to the train? It is not a lie.

We are dropping someone at the station on the way. And tell them I'll be home in time for dinner. Can you do that?"

Ivy didn't like this secret. It tasted sour. But she nodded. "How long before you go away?"

"About three weeks, I think." He hugged her and they continued walking. "I will tell them tonight. So not *a word* until then."

The rest of the walk to school, Ivy was quiet, trying to make sense of what this would mean for their family. Hadn't Fernando and his buddies said they knew people who tried to enlist but were refused because they weren't fit for the military? Maybe the same thing would happen to Fernando. After all, war was something for men—for *soldiers*—not for a boy who teased and pulled her braids and played hide-and-seek. Fernando was quiet and gentle. He took things apart and reassembled them to see how they worked. He fixed broken things, often asking Ivy to be his assistant and hand him the tools. He was a *tinkerer*, not a *fighter*. She was sure the army would realize soon enough that he was not suited for war.

Even so, the secret pestered her all day.

Her new teacher, Miss Delgado, was round-faced and rosy-cheeked with short curly hair. As she assigned desks, went over classroom rules, and taught lessons, Ivy worried how Mama and Papa would react to Fernando's news. Would they be angry? Disappointed? Could they forbid him from going?

An hour before the final bell, Ivy gazed out the window, watching three squirrels scamper up and down the tree next to their classroom, her mind still on Fernando. Miss Delgado clapped her hands to get everyone's attention and called them to sit on the floor.

Miss Delgado cradled a box on her lap. "I have a surprise for you. Our local radio station is doing a promotion to raise money for the war effort *and* to help our school." She held up a stamp booklet. "When we save enough war stamps to fill this book, our class will be invited to perform *on the radio*."

Everyone's eyes grew wide.

"You can buy ten-cent war stamps at many stores," Miss Delgado explained. "Once the booklet is filled with a little over eighteen dollars' worth, it can be turned in for a savings bond, which in ten years will be worth twenty-five dollars for our school."

"What will we sing?" someone asked.

Miss Delgado shook her head. "Other classes will sing. Our class will do something extra-special." She reached inside the box and took out a shiny harmonica. "These were donated to me. They've been restored like new, and there is one for each of you to keep. I'm going to teach you how to play. I am hoping we can make beautiful music together."

Everyone clapped and cheered.

One by one, Miss Delgado called names so each student could choose a harmonica from the box. When it was her turn, Ivy looked inside. The afternoon sun streamed through the windows and glinted off one of the harmonicas, making it shine brighter. The intricate carvings on the cover plate looked more distinct than the others, more deeply carved and, somehow, fancier. Ivy wrapped her fingers around it.

Returning to her seat, she examined the harmonica and traced her finger over the tiny red *M* painted on one edge. Did the other harmonicas have letters on them? Had the person who owned this one before her had a name that started with M?

Miss Delgado taught them to breathe in and out of the harmonica to make sounds for the different notes. She gave them each a booklet, *Harmonica Playing Made Easy*, and taught them to follow the harmonica tablature for "Twinkle, Twinkle, Little Star." Soon the room filled with confusing noise. Miss Delgado tapped her chalkboard pointer to quiet them. "Let's try it together."

Ivy concentrated, following the notations above the words. From the first phrase, her harmonica sang above the others . . . *up above the world so high* . . . clear and resonant, the tone haunting and silky . . . *like a diamond in the sky* . . . She closed her eyes and felt herself float in the blackest night among shimmering crystals . . . One by one, each child stopped playing to listen, until Ivy was the only one making music. She opened her eyes.

When she realized that the entire class was staring at her, she stopped.

"Ivy, do you play a musical instrument?" asked Miss Delgado.

She shook her head, embarrassed.

"That was *lovely*. You have a gift, a real talent for music. I imagine you could learn almost any instrument if you tried."

Ivy felt her cheeks blush with pride.

Miss Delgado turned to the class. "I want everyone to practice at home. And to start saving your pennies for war stamps."

But Ivy could only hear her earlier words, playing over in her mind: *You have a gift, a real talent for music.*

Miss Delgado might not have known it, but she had planted a seed that wouldn't stop growing. Mama had a talent for sewing and gardening. Papa had a talent for irrigation and supervising. Fernando had a talent for knowing how things worked and fixing them. Now Ivy had one, too. Had it been inside her all along, just waiting to be discovered?

After school, she was grateful she had the harmonica to show Mama and Papa, and the radio
program and stamp books to discuss, to keep her
mind off Fernando's secret while Mama prepared
his birthday dinner.

When at last he came home, he seemed to
have grown taller as he announced, "I enlisted in
the army. I want to protect our country against
Germany and Italy and Japan. It is my *duty* as an
American."

Papa had clapped him on the back, looking proud and resigned. Mama wept. Even after
Fernando hugged and reassured her, she couldn't
stop. So he'd asked Ivy to play the song she'd learned
on the harmonica to lighten the mood. Again, the
warm, pure sound seemed to startle all of them. It
had even stopped Mama's tears.

For the next three weeks, Fernando begged for
songs every night.

"Please, Ivy? I'll pay a penny for a concert and I
won't pull your braids."

Ivy was happy to oblige, surprising even herself

with how quickly she learned. She hardly needed to look at the booklet. At every spare moment, she practiced. The more she played, the more the harmonica seemed to fill her with a bravado and a worthiness she'd never felt before.

Those were happy evenings filled with sweet memories—all of them around the dinner table, Fernando reveling in the music and singing along; Mama and Papa lingering with their coffee, laughing, and sometimes clapping and singing, too; all of them clinging to their togetherness.

The night before Fernando and his two friends left for basic training, he brought Ivy the jacket. "You can wear it until I return."

"But, Nando, it is eighty degrees outside."

He draped it over her shoulders. "You'll thank me in winter when you are freezing to the bone. Remember what you do when it's cold and your blankets slip off at night?"

She nodded. "I always call for you. And you always get up from your bed and put the blankets back on me."

"Well, I won't be around to do that anymore. So I'll have to keep you warm with my jacket. If you wear it to bed, it can't slip off."

She giggled. "I might wear it. But not to bed."

Fernando put an arm around her. "Regardless, I want you to know that I'm still looking out for you and keeping you warm and safe, even from far away."

The weight of his leaving settled on them.

"Who will fix things while you are gone?" she asked.

"*You* will have to be the one to fix things now. Ivy, when I'm gone, you need to be a good little soldier for Mama and Papa."

"But I don't know how to fix things. I don't have tools."

"There are other ways to fix things. When I'm away, our family is going to be a little bit broken. I'm counting on you to hold it together. You're smart. Keep doing well in school. It will be one less thing Mama and Papa have to worry about with me away at war. You're talented. You *do* have a gift.

You saw how your harmonica playing brought joy to us these past few weeks. Keep playing. More than ever, Mama and Papa are going to need a little joy in their lives. You're caring. And Mama and Papa are going to need that kind of support, too, especially if my letters are slow to arrive. Or if something happens to me. So you see, you do have the tools. You'll do that for me, yes? Fix things while I'm gone and hold our family together?" He held out his little finger for her to seal the promise.

She locked her little finger with his. "But nothing is going to happen to you, right?"

"Not if I can help it." Fernando opened his other hand and offered her a penny. "One more song before I leave?"

She took the penny, put it in the zippered pocket of the jacket, and began the tune to the lyrics, *Over hill, over dale, as we hit the dusty trail. And those caissons go rolling along.* In her mind, she saw a dark forest where Fernando ran through briars and brambles, lonely and afraid, struggling to find a way out. A menacing shadow crept after him.

Fear made her breath quicken. She dropped the harmonica and it clattered to the step. "Be careful, Nando," she said, burying her head in his arms.

After basic training, Fernando's friends came home for leave, their heads shaved, arms muscled, and faces weathered. Their families besieged them with home cooking and affection. But Fernando never came home. Instead, he went straight to advanced training. The army thought him perfectly suited for war, after all.

Ivy and her family learned to live like so many others—letter to letter.

Her class had filled the stamp book and was invited to perform on *The Colgate Family Hour*. Together, they would play "Auld Lang Syne." After, there would be a solo of "America the Beautiful." When Miss Delgado chose Ivy for the solo, she had cried from the excitement of it all and immediately wrote to Fernando to tell him.

For over three hours, the truck crawled on Highway 99 behind the hazy red taillights of the cars in front of them, the fog still a thick soup.

Papa downshifted the gears, and the motor groaned as the truck began the slow grade up the mountain.

"How much longer?" asked Ivy.

"Another few hours. First, we must get over the ridge and through Los Angeles. We'll stop soon to stretch."

The truck climbed. The fog thinned and the world brightened.

In one magical instant—as if someone had snatched a gray veil from their heads—a blue sky startled them and the noses of mountains jutted forward, radiant and dewy in the glare of the sun.

Papa was right about one thing.

The weather was better.

"Look, Ivy. That must be your new school," said Mama.

It was late afternoon and Papa had finally turned off the highway and down a long road that stretched toward the horizon, orange trees on one side, lemon on the other. Papa slowed the truck through the small town and idled in front of a one-story white stucco building with a sign that read, LINCOLN SCHOOL.

A cluster of palm trees anchored the front corners of the property. Manicured lawns surrounded the building. Geraniums filled the flower beds beneath the windows, and rosebushes, some of them blooming, lined the walkway to the front steps.

"It is more green and pretty here, yes?" said Papa, rolling down his window and leaning his elbow out. A citrusy smell perfumed the cab. "Not so brown and gray like the valley in winter. A land of sunshine and flowers, even in December."

Ivy couldn't argue about that.

She read the sign taped across two classroom windows: FIFTH AND SIXTH GRADES JOIN THE LINCOLN ORCHESTRA. STARTS IN JANUARY!

"Orchestra?" said Ivy. None of her other schools had one. Even the word, like the school, felt beautiful and well kept. She imagined that most of the students who joined had already been taking music lessons and owned an instrument. Still, an orchestra!

As Papa drove on, Ivy craned her head to look back at the playground: a blacktop area painted with four-square grids, hopscotches, and a basketball hoop. Beyond was a grassy field with backstops for baseball and kickball.

"Are you *sure* this is my school?"

Papa reached forward and patted the large envelope on the dashboard. "Guillermo and Bertina sent the papers for Lincoln School, and that is what the sign says." He nudged her, grinning.

Ivy could not help but smile, too.

Papa drove a few more miles and turned down a long dirt drive through the middle of an orange grove. "There!"

He pointed ahead to an area cleared of trees where a wood-plank house sat in the center. It had a front porch just wide enough for the two old rocking chairs waiting to be occupied. The barn doors on the garage did not quite meet in the middle. And the house and garage both needed a new coat of paint, but they were bigger and more welcoming than their bungalow in Fresno.

They climbed from the truck, stretched, and walked around the property. The backyard was fenced with old pickets that could not make up their minds about which way to lean. In a swath of sun on the side of the house, two large T-shaped poles faced each other, with clotheslines strung between them. Iris plants, the leaves yellowed and brown, choked the flower beds.

Papa took a handmade map from the envelope and studied it. Looking up, he pointed through the rows of orange trees on the same side of the road.

"Through the grove, you can just see the owner's house in the distance."

"Does he have children?" asked Ivy.

"A boy a little older than Fernando, who is in the marines. And two girls close to your age. But they are not here right now . . ."

Ivy felt her heart leap. At least there were girls her age. She hoped they could be friends. She knew she'd never be friends with anyone like she was with Araceli, but at least she'd have someone. "Will they be back soon, Papa? Are they on vacation? Will we go to school together?"

Papa glanced at Mama but didn't answer. He busied himself untying Ivy's suitcase. As he handed it to her, she could sense there was something he wasn't telling her. But what?

Before she could ask another question, Mama took her hand and led her to the house. They stepped inside a screened-in back porch. A washer with a round tub sat in a corner. An electrical cord dangled from its side, and attached above it, the wringer, like two giant rolling pins one on top of the other, waited to be fed wet laundry. Mama smiled. "We will not have to scrub the clothes in a metal tub. What a luxury!"

They walked into the house, from room to room. "It has what we need: table and chairs, beds, a sofa in the living room," said Mama. "And we have the rest in the truck. It is simple, but clean. It feels like a home."

It was true. And Ivy couldn't help but notice the lilt in Mama's voice. Maybe coming here would make Mama happy and she wouldn't worry so much about Fernando. As they continued to walk through the house, peeking into every room, Ivy felt her own spirits lift.

They reached the smallest of the three bedrooms, which held a metal twin bed frame and mattress. The walls were covered with faded wallpaper of trailing green vines and tiny rose-colored buds.

Mama said, "And this is your bedroom."

Ivy looked at Mama. "*My own?*" She had always had to share with Fernando. She tried to imagine a room all to herself, without two twin beds crammed side by side, or a dresser crowded with

Fernando's basketball trophies, or having to share the drawers and the closet. "But, Mama, don't you need a room for your sewing?"

Mama smiled. "I will set up my machine in Fernando's bedroom until he comes home from the war. I think I will enjoy sewing next to all of his things."

Papa appeared, carrying the small three-drawer dresser. He positioned it against a wall and patted her on the shoulder. Before he left to unload, he grinned and said, "Didn't I tell you everything would be better?"

Ivy walked around the room. She bounced on the mattress, checked inside the closet, and gazed out the bedroom window at the rows upon rows of orange trees that surrounded the house. She thought about her new school. She was tempted to believe Papa, especially with Mama humming in the kitchen and Papa whistling as he carried in boxes, sounding happier than they had in months. Ivy let a tiny bit of happiness creep into her heart, too. She'd never once, in all the places they'd lived, had a room of her own.

She pulled the harmonica from her pocket and played the tune to the lyrics, *Sailing, sailing, over the bounding main* . . . And in her mind, she traveled to her own little island, surrounded by a green, waxy-leafed ocean, with golden, round-bellied fish bobbing in the waves.

5

Ivy had already unpacked her clothes, hung Fernando's jacket in the closet, and placed the harmonica on the dresser alongside the instruction booklet when there was a knock on the front door.

Had the owner's daughters returned home?

Ivy ran to the door and opened it as Mama appeared behind her.

A woman and a girl stood on the steps. The woman wore a Sunday dress, even though it was Thursday, a hat that looked like an upside-down rowboat, and a tweed coat. She held a stack of black fabric in her arms. The girl looked to be Ivy's age! She wore a matching blue coat and dress, and her hair was swept to the side and caught up in a blue bow. With her black hair, pale skin, and eyes the color of dark-green leaves, she looked like a porcelain doll from a toy-shop window.

Behind them, a large Buick was parked in the drive. A burly man with short, sandy hair stood next to the driver's door. His hands were behind his back, elbows out, and his feet planted apart, like a soldier might stand.

"Hello," said Mama.

"Good afternoon. I'm Joyce Ward," said the woman. "And this is my daughter, Susan. Are you"—she looked at a piece of paper in her hand— "Mrs. Lopez?"

"Yes, I am Luz Lopez," said Mama.

"Bertina said you'd be arriving soon. We were just driving by on our way home from town and saw your truck so we stopped. Did she write to you? About the laundry and ironing?"

"Oh, yes," said Mama. "Wednesdays I pick up the clothes and bring them back here. Fridays I bring them to your house and finish with the ironing."

"That's right. And you are willing?" said Mrs. Ward.

Mama nodded. "Of course. The address?"

"We're just down the road and around the

corner on Blanchard Lane. It's the tall white house with the green roof. Our back fields connect, but it will be easier for you to drive around. I'm so relieved. I've been lost without Bertina. You see, I have arthritis and it's hard for me to lift an iron. And the clothes are piling up."

"I can stop by and pick up a few things before Wednesday if you like."

"Could you?" said Mrs. Ward. "That would be a help."

Mama smiled. "Yes, of course. Tomorrow afternoon—"

Ivy cleared her throat.

Mama put a hand on Ivy's shoulder. "This is my daughter, Ivy. Our son, Fernando, is in the army."

Ivy noticed Mrs. Ward's face grow tight. "We will pray for his safety."

"Thank you," said Mama. "I have a question. Ivy will go to the Lincoln School, fifth grade. I need to turn in her papers tomorrow before she can start. Do you know where she will meet the bus?"

"At the end of your drive," said Mrs. Ward. "Susan gets picked up at eight o'clock and you would be the next stop. If you turn in her papers at the main office tomorrow, I imagine she can start on Monday. There's only one more week of school before Christmas vacation, but at least she can settle in. You probably saw the school on your way here."

Susan took a step closer to Ivy and smiled. "I'm in the fifth grade, too. We'll see each other every day."

Ivy smiled in return and nodded, relieved to have a familiar face on her first day. She'd never started a new school without Fernando by her side.

"I'll save you a seat on the bus," said Susan.

Mrs. Ward passed the stack of black fabric to Mama. "These are for you. My husband is retired military and is the chairman of the county CSO, the Civilian Safety Organization. They're blackout curtains for your windows. Everyone must use them after dark."

"So the Japanese can't see the west coast of America, to bomb us," said Susan. "One speck of light and their planes can see California."

Ivy reached for Mama's hand and squeezed it. Were they in danger?

Susan must have sensed her nervousness. "Oh, don't worry," she said. "My dad says we're perfectly safe as long as everyone uses the curtains."

"If you are interested," said Mrs. Ward, "I volunteer for the Red Cross on Sunday afternoons, making bandages and wound dressings for the troops. We are always looking for volunteers."

Mama nodded. "I think that is something I would like very much."

Mrs. Ward glanced back at the car and lowered her voice. "And you are welcome to bring Ivy with you whenever you come to the house. It would be company for Susan."

Susan's eyes grew larger. "Promise to come tomorrow with your mom?"

Ivy nodded. "Okay."

Mrs. Ward glanced back again. Mr. Ward had begun to pace near the car. Why hadn't he come to the door to introduce himself?

Mrs. Ward took Susan's hand. "We better go."

Ivy watched them walk down the drive.

Mr. Ward walked around the front of the car to open the passenger door for his wife, then the back door for Susan. After they were inside, he shut the doors, put his hands on his hips, and gave one curt nod toward Mama and Ivy, frowning.

As the car pulled away, Ivy said, "Mama, Mr. Ward does not look very friendly."

"No," Mama agreed. "He looks the opposite. But you cannot trust appearances. When someone wears a face like that, it is often hiding a reason we cannot see."

Ivy watched the car disappear. What could Mr. Ward be hiding?

6

"Why couldn't I go with Mama to the school?" Ivy asked Papa the next morning as they walked through the orange grove.

"Ivy Maria, we have been over this," said Papa.

"But *why* must I go with you to the owner's house? You said the daughters are not even there for me to meet. Isn't it more important I meet my new teacher?"

"Mama is only leaving your papers at the office and confirming you may start on Monday. The students and teachers are in class. And after, Mama has errands and we don't know how long that will take. I wanted you with me so I could explain some things . . ."

Ivy took the harmonica from Fernando's jacket and began to play "My Country, 'Tis of Thee." Before she finished, she lowered it and said, "Papa, do you think my new teacher will be as lovely as

Miss Delgado? Miss Delgado was like a queen who lived in a castle. We were her subjects and every day she opened a treasure box and gave us jewels . . ."

Papa frowned at her. "Ivy, enough with your pretending. You are getting too old for it. And you interrupted me. Did you not hear me say I needed to explain some things to you? Now put away your toy."

Ivy felt the sting of his words as she slipped the harmonica back into a pocket. "Sorry, Papa. What did you want to explain?"

Papa kept walking until they emerged from the trees, and then he swept his arm toward a dilapidated house. The lawn had turned brown from lack of water. The plants in the flower beds had shriveled and the ground was thick with weeds. Lumber had been nailed across the front door and all the windows. The wood porch and railing that wrapped around the front and one side of the house were caked with dust and dirt.

"Papa, what happened?"

"Do you remember last spring when all of the Japanese children left your school in Fresno?"

Ivy nodded. "Miss Delgado said they had to live in a special camp because we are at war with Japan." One day her classroom was full and every desk taken. The next, the class was half its size.

"That is what happened to the owner and his family," said Papa. "The Yamamotos are Japanese. The government calls them 'enemies of the United States.' There are hundreds of farms such as this in California where the owners have been confined in a camp. If the bills are not paid each month, the owners will lose everything. That is why I am here."

"You are here to save their farm?" asked Ivy.

Papa nodded. "I will run it for Mr. Yamamoto while he is away. I will take care of the bills, pay myself a salary, and save the profits for him. In return, when the war is over, he will keep me on as supervisor and deed me the house and the small piece of land it sits on. *To own.*" Papa said the words as if he were praying.

Own. That meant *staying* and not leaving, even after a year. And there were things to stay for: a school with an orchestra, her own room, Fernando coming home to a house, maybe even friends.

"In a few weeks, Mr. Yamamoto's son, Kenneth, will be allowed to bring me the legal papers," said Papa. "If he likes me and how I am caring for the property, we will sign an agreement that guarantees hope for both of our families. So you see, our future is tied to their future."

"If the son can come here from the Japanese camp, why can't they all come?"

Papa shook his head. "Kenneth is not in the camp. He is an officer in the United States Marines. A translator. He will have only a short leave, to take care of his father's business."

"His parents and sisters are enemies, but he is not?"

Papa shook his head. "I do not see how any of them could be enemies. The farm has been in the family for forty years. Mr. Yamamoto fought for the United States in World War I."

"Then why were they sent away?"

"Those are good questions, Ivy, but for some

questions there are no good answers." He walked toward the backyard.

Ivy followed, her mind filling with more questions. "What if the other Japanese farmers can't find someone like you to run their farms?"

"The bank will sell them for much less than they are worth. And there are many people who want to buy up the land. Mr. Ward, the neighbor, is one of the eager ones. He has bought three farms in the area already. He made an offer to Mr. Yamamoto but was refused."

Was that what Mr. Ward was hiding? That he wanted the Yamamoto farm but couldn't have it? Was he angry at Papa for coming to save it?

They wandered to the side of the house where there had once been a large vegetable garden. Wire trellises held up withered tomato vines with rotted fruit. Behind the garden sat a wooden shed with a window.

From his inside jacket pocket, Papa pulled the envelope Guillermo had sent, tilting it so a large ring with a dozen keys slid into his hand, along with two smaller rings, each with a single key. "Duplicates for the shed and house." He tried different keys in the padlock on the shed until the right one unlocked it. When he pulled it open, one of the hinges fell off. "I'll fix it tomorrow," said Papa.

Ivy looked inside as Papa took inventory of the shovels, rakes, and hoes. Large wide-brimmed straw hats hung from nails. A wood box held packets of seeds. But it was the child-sized wheelbarrow that tugged at Ivy's heart. It was filled with little trowels and sun hats and tiny clay pots, each one nesting inside another. She imagined the two girls following their father, planting seedlings in the garden. Plants they might never see grow.

When Papa finished surveying the tools, he shut the shed as best he could and they headed toward the house. Ivy gasped when they reached the back door. Someone had painted the words:

JAPS! YELLOW ENEMIES!

"Papa, that's awful!"

Papa sucked air through gritted teeth. "I do not like these words."

"Papa, the son's feelings will be hurt if he sees this. He wouldn't be pleased. We should paint over it."

"I'm glad you feel that way. That's exactly what we should do. We need to look inside the house, too, but it will take some time to go through their things. Maybe Mama can do it next week."

"Look for what?"

"When a house is closed for a long time it's always a good idea to check for water leaks or rodent nests, and to make sure all the windows are shut tight so squirrels or birds can't get in." Papa shook his head at what had been done to the door.

Ivy reached up and touched the angry words. "Papa, who would do such a thing?"

"I think there are many. I read in the newspaper that someone set fire to the building that was the Japanese church. And someone broke all the windows of the Japanese laundry. It is a matter of record that those buildings are still owned by Japanese. The same as this farm. People know Mr. Yamamoto did not sell."

Ivy worried. "Is it safe for you, Papa? Will people be upset with you for working here?"

"I don't think so. Farmers are in short supply. Do you know what the government calls us now?" Papa stood a little taller. "Food soldiers. Not only must we grow food for the country, but for the soldiers, too. That is why the government wants families to plant war gardens. To lessen the burden on the farmers. During the war, every American is a soldier of one kind or another. The government even has the Japanese Americans in the camps farming the surrounding fields."

"But, Papa, couldn't the Yamamotos have been food soldiers in their own fields?"

He sighed but didn't answer. Instead, he pulled a photograph from the envelope and studied it.

Ivy leaned closer to get a better look. It was a picture of Mr. and Mrs. Yamamoto and their family. They were standing in front of a church. He wore dark-rimmed glasses. She wore a dress with a white lace collar. Kenneth already stood a little taller than his father. The two girls, their hair in short pageboy cuts with straight bangs, wore Sunday dresses and Mary Jane shoes. The younger one tilted her head toward her sister, smiling and holding a well-loved doll. Ivy was not sure what enemies looked like, but she could not imagine that they looked like this family.

She pointed to the doll. "Do you think they let her take it with her?"

Papa nodded. "Probably. They could take what they could hold in their arms, but nothing more. Now it is our job to protect what they left behind, until they return."

Suddenly, Ivy felt guilty for complaining about packing up to leave Fresno so suddenly. At least she got to come here—to a house they might one day own—when the Yamamoto girls were in a camp with only what they could carry.

Ivy followed Papa back the way they had come and stopped in front of one section of the house that was covered, ground to eaves, with a wooden lattice that had been nailed over sheets of wood. Green vines climbed upward in overgrown confusion, runners dangling from the sides.

Ivy frowned. "It needs pruning, Papa."

He studied the latticework. "I agree. But Mr. Yamamoto asked in his letter that I let it grow and fill in. He is particular, to be sure. But I can tell that he loves his farm. I will do as he asks."

"With the windows all boarded, the house looks embarrassed and sad, Papa. Like a dog when it has been shamed."

"Yes," said Papa. "The house is very sad."

They walked down the drive toward a three-sided wood structure near the road. A rickety bench leaned against the back wall and a warped table sat in front.

"Is this a bus stop?" asked Ivy.

Papa shook his head. "It is Mrs. Yamamoto's stand. She sold oranges in the spring and vegetables in the summer."

While Papa inspected it, Ivy took the harmonica from her pocket and played "Skip to My Lou." She looked back at the house and, in her mind, saw a different place in a different time: a freshly painted home with lace curtains in the windows. A tidy green lawn where a picnic was laid out on an old quilt. And the Yamamoto girls, holding hands and dancing in a circle with the doll. *Skip, skip, skip to my Lou. Skip to my Lou, my darling.* They danced until they grew dizzy and collapsed on the grass, giddy and giggling.

Ivy lowered the harmonica, knowing the Yamamoto girls would have been her friends . . . if they hadn't been sent away.

7

The Ward house looked as if it belonged in a story-book instead of an orange grove.

It was large and white with a steep-pitched roof and it stretched two stories high. Green lattice-work wrapped the porch, and gingerbread trim hung from the eaves and windows. Prim and clean, the home sat in a grassy yard where the flower beds had been raked and planted with geraniums. Unlike the Yamamotos', there wasn't a dead leaf, weed, or withered blossom sullying the yard. Two small flags hung side by side in the front window. Both had a white field, red border, and a star in the center; one with a blue star, the other, gold.

"Mama, the house . . . it's beautiful," said Ivy as they climbed from the truck that afternoon to pick up the ironing.

"It is lovely, isn't it?" said Mama.

They walked up the front path to the door. Ivy whispered, "What if Mr. Ward is here?"

"Just be polite. And remember. Not everything is as it seems. I'm sure he's not as unfriendly on the inside as he appears on the outside."

Ivy rang the bell.

They heard chimes and then pounding footsteps. The door flung open and Susan stood before them, grinning. Her hair was braided, and she wore a green sweater over a white blouse with a lace-trimmed collar. Ivy ran her hands over Fernando's jacket and her dungarees and felt as if she should have worn something nicer.

"Come in!" said Susan. "My mother said to tell you she will be right back. She's in the garage. Ivy, look at my hair. I did it just like yours."

Ivy tried not to gawk at the splendor as she followed Mama inside the front hall. An oak staircase led to the second story. To the left was a parlor with burgundy, claw-footed couches. A Christmas tree touched the ceiling and was decorated with glass ornaments and topped with a golden-haired angel.

Ivy had never seen such luxury. Susan had everything: a fancy house, beautiful clothes, and a pretty face.

"Want to see my room?" she asked Ivy.

Ivy looked up at Mama and nodded.

"Maybe it is better if you stay with me," said Mama.

"It's okay, Mrs. Lopez," said Susan. "Bertina's daughter always came to my room and she was only five years old."

Mama relented. "For just a few minutes."

Ivy followed Susan up the stairs into a bedroom three times the size of hers. There was a white dresser and vanity, matching nightstand, and a canopied bed with a white chenille spread. One of the double closet doors was open, revealing a row of dresses. The room looked like a picture from the Sears catalog, the one Ivy and Fernando used to huddle over, dreaming of what they would purchase if they had the money. Suddenly, Ivy's excitement about her own new bedroom began to wither.

Did Susan *know* how lucky she was? It didn't seem fair, somehow, after seeing the Yamamotos' house that morning, and thinking of her own small room with the faded wallpaper, that Susan had so much.

Susan pointed to the harmonica poking from Ivy's jacket pocket. "Can you play something?"

Swallowing her jealousy, Ivy said, "Sure." She pulled it out and played "Jingle Bells."

Susan clapped when she finished. "That was great!"

"Thanks. I was going to be on the radio and perform a solo before we had to come here." Ivy felt a stab of regret.

"The radio! Wow! You should join the orchestra," said Susan. "Anybody in fifth or sixth who wants to can. There's an orientation meeting next Thursday after school and then lessons start in January after vacation. I bet you'd be good at flute. That's what I'm going to play."

"I wish I could. I don't have a flute. And I've never had any lessons."

"You don't need a flute," said Susan. "Mr. Daniels, the orchestra director, loans you one and teaches you how to play. We take lessons for three months and then practice all together as an orchestra after that. There's a recital in June and everything. I know because my brothers played clarinet." Susan grinned. "If you join, we could be together every Thursday after school."

Miss Delgado had said she could learn almost any instrument if she tried. And Ivy wanted to try. "I'll ask my parents."

"If they say yes, my mom can give you a ride home on Thursday after the meeting since we have to stay later than the bus." Susan nodded toward Ivy's harmonica. "I never played one before. Is it hard?"

"If you have one, I can teach you."

"In my brothers' room. Come on." She motioned for Ivy to follow.

Down the hall, they entered an even larger bedroom. All the furniture, the twin beds, dressers, and desks, were made of knotty pine. A large framed photograph of a uniformed soldier sat on each dresser, one of them draped with medals.

Susan rummaged through the top drawer of one of the desks. She nodded to the photos. "Those are my brothers, Donald and Tom. Tom is in the army and drives a tank, and Donald . . ." Frowning, she closed the drawer and opened the next one down. She held up a harmonica. "I *knew* there was one in here somewhere."

Ivy smiled. "I have a booklet at home that tells you how to play, step-by-step. I can bring it to you . . ."

Mama's and Mrs. Ward's voices floated up from downstairs.

"I better go," said Ivy.

"Want to meet tomorrow between the groves? You just walk all the way through the one behind your house to the division road. There's an old wagon there." She held up her harmonica. "You can give me my first lesson. Two o'clock?"

Ivy nodded. "Okay."

"Promise?" said Susan, sounding as if she didn't believe Ivy.

"Promise." Ivy hurried downstairs.

Susan followed and never stopped waving from the porch as Ivy and Mama climbed into the truck and backed slowly down the long drive.

"Susan seems nice," said Mama.

"Mama, you should see her room! It looks like a princess sleeps there. Her closet is filled with dresses. I wish I had just half of her dresses. She has *everything*,"

"Ivy, I don't like to hear you sounding so envious. Yes, she has things. But they are just that. *Things*. She is a girl like you. And it is nice for you to know someone your age who lives nearby."

"I don't know why she wants to be my friend. She must have dozens. Of course, she couldn't ever be my *best* friend because of Araceli."

"Maybe she wants to be your friend because she *needs* one," said Mama. "And, Ivy, you can have more than one best friend."

"Oh, no, Mama. That is Araceli's place in my heart."

Mama smiled. "Your heart is bigger than you think."

Ivy watched Susan and the house with the flags in the front window grow smaller. "Mama, what are those flags for?"

"Each star is for a soldier, for one of their sons in the war."

"We should have one for our house," said Ivy. "For Fernando. But maybe a gold one. They're prettier."

"Ivy Maria, do not *ever* say such a thing." Mama kept one hand on the steering wheel, and with the other, made the sign of the cross.

"Why not?" asked Ivy.

"The gold star is for a soldier who has died."

8

Even though the sun bloomed warm and bright on Saturday afternoon, Ivy still wore Fernando's jacket and the purple hat from Araceli.

She had written to both of them last night, telling all about the house and her own room, the Yamamotos and the Wards.

When she reached the dirt road that divided the two properties, Ivy saw Susan waving from the long wooden wagon nestled between two rows of trees across the way.

She raced over. "Hi," she said, climbing up and sitting on the bench across from Susan. "What's this wagon for?"

"A long time ago, my grandpa used to hitch horses to it and haul stuff around the farm. But now, it's just for playing. My dad built the benches."

Ivy pointed to three names carved into the inside planks of the wagon:

Donald   Tom   Kenny

"Did your brothers carve those?"

Susan nodded. "They used to carry orange crates up here and build forts, and when they played hide-and-seek in the grove, the wagon was home base."

"Who's Kenny?"

"Kenneth Yamamoto," said Susan. "We always called him Kenny." She stood and pointed across the fields to the yellow house in the distance. "From here, you can see the roofs of all three houses: yours, mine, and the Yamamotos'. It's a triangle. Kenny was Donald's best friend his whole entire life. He's the one who talked Donald into joining the marines. My dad didn't like that *one bit* because he is U.S. Army through and through, and he wanted his sons to choose army. Then Donald . . . He died in the bombs at Pearl Harbor."

Ivy felt her stomach sink. She ran her finger over his name in the wood. "That's why you have the flag with the gold star in your window?"

434

Susan nodded. "My mom and some other ladies sew them on their sewing machines. For remembering. My mom is making one for your house for your brother. I hope . . . I hope he doesn't die."

Ivy shuddered. Even though it wasn't cold and she was wearing Fernando's jacket, she felt goose bumps on her arms. She knew when Fernando went to war that it was dangerous. But the danger seemed so far away. "I hope he doesn't die, too." She took a deep breath. "Did Kenny Yamamoto get hurt in the bombs?"

Susan leaned closer. "No. And my dad says it's no miracle he escaped because he probably knew about the bombing in advance. He thinks Kenny should be locked up with the rest of the Japanese. He says if Donald hadn't listened to that Jap spy, he'd be alive today."

Ivy felt her body stiffen. "Spy?"

Susan's eyes widened and she nodded. "My dad says that, for all he knows, Kenny is just *pretending* to be a loyal American so he can get information and give it back to the Japanese. The *whole family* could be spies. He thinks the Yamamotos are hiding something. And if they are, and he can prove it, they'll be sent to prison, and their farm will be taken by the bank and sold."

"How would he prove it?"

"By inspecting their house inside and out."

Ivy's feelings tangled. She didn't even know the Yamamotos, but after being at their sad house and seeing their neglected yard and knowing where they were now, she felt protective of them. Besides, weren't they already in a kind of prison?

She sat up straighter. "My dad wouldn't work for spies so I'm sure they're not. And he doesn't like the word *Jap*. Someone wrote that on their house but we're going to paint over it."

Susan went on. "My dad knows these things because he used to be in Army Intelligence and now he's in charge of the CSO. They're always having meetings. He says every American must keep an eye out for suspicious activity and report it to the police. Even children. It's our *duty*. Have you seen anything suspicious over there?"

"Suspicious like what?"

"I don't know. Secret documents. Anything that could help the Japs, I mean the Japanese, win the war."

Ivy shrugged. "I haven't been in the house. Only the shed, but it was just gardening things."

"If you do go inside the house, be careful because it might be booby-trapped or rigged with bombs to protect their spy stuff. There could even be secret passageways. My dad says their type is .capable of anything."

Ivy shook her head and raised her eyebrows. Did Susan believe all the things she was saying?

Susan shrugged. "It *might* be true." Her shoulders dropped a little and she chewed on her lip. "I used to play with Kenny's sisters, Karen and Annie, all the time." She gazed in the direction of the Yamamoto house. "Their mom was my piano teacher. But that all ended after Donald . . ." Her eyes shifted to the harmonica in her hand. "Can you teach me?"

Ivy was more than happy to leave the spy talk behind. She didn't like worrying about what might become of the Yamamotos if they were sent to prison, or what would become of her family if the bank sold their farm. It was enough to worry about Fernando.

She went through the first pages of *Harmonica Playing Made Easy*, just as Miss Delgado had done, explaining the tabs to Susan. "It's simple. There are ten holes on the harmonica. Starting with the lowest note, each hole matches a number between one and ten. You look at the words of the song and the numbers above them. A regular number means blow into the hole for that note. A minus sign in front of a number means draw your breath, or inhale, for that note." She taught Susan "Twinkle, Twinkle, Little Star" and listened to her play it all the way through on her own. "You catch on really fast. You're good at music."

Susan gave Ivy a weak smile. "At least I'm good at something." She lay back on the bench and gazed up at the sky.

"I know what you mean," said Ivy, doing the same. "My brother, Fernando, is good at *every-thing*. He can take apart anything and put it back together again, even a sewing machine. Now he's finishing his training and will be sent to the fighting. It's *all* Mama and Papa talk about."

"It's all *anyone* talks about," said Susan. "Hey, why do you wear that jacket and that hat all the time?"

"The jacket is Fernando's. He loaned it to me while he's in the war. He wants me to know that he's still looking out for me—you know, keeping me warm and safe—even from far away. The hat is from my best friend, Araceli. Her mother made us matching ones. We look so much alike, people think . . . thought we were sisters." Ivy's words just kept coming, and Susan seemed so eager to listen that Ivy found herself telling all about Miss Delgado and the radio show and how sad she'd been to leave Fresno and how far ahead she was in the reading and math books.

"I used to be ahead in my class, too," said Susan. "But I got behind. I don't know why. Before . . . my parents always helped me with my homework. Now they're just too tired all the time . . . and sad."

Ivy tried to imagine her own family's life without Fernando and how it would take them apart. If the worst happened, she wasn't sure she'd be able to keep her promise to him and hold them together. Her heart felt heavy just imagining it. "I'll help you with your homework."

Susan sat up and looked at her with disbelief. "You will?"

"Sure," said Ivy. "We'll be doing the same assignments, right? You don't even have to tell anyone. It can be our secret."

Susan's eyes welled up and she swiped at them. "Thanks, Ivy. You know, I'm glad you moved here. I don't really have . . . friends."

Ivy rolled on her side, propping her head up with her hand. It was hard to believe that Susan, who had so much, didn't have friends. "Why?"

"I'm not allowed. I can't invite anyone over, and I can never, *ever* go to someone else's house unless my mom is with me. It's okay for you to come to my house because your mom works for us. If my dad asked what you were doing there, my mom would say Mrs. Lopez didn't have anyone to watch you while she worked. My mom . . . She makes it so it's okay."

Ivy was puzzled. "But we're together right now."

"I'm still on our property at arm's length. I play here all the time by myself. See, my mom says my dad is worried sick about losing another child, especially with Tom fighting somewhere in Europe. I don't know what would happen to us if Tom didn't come home safely, especially after Donald." She whispered, "Sometimes my dad still cries about Donald."

Ivy didn't know what to say. It was all so sad. And yet, she couldn't imagine the stone-faced Mr. Ward crying.

Susan looked down at her harmonica and frowned. "It was a telegram, you know. That's how we found out about Donald."

Ivy sat up, reached over, and squeezed Susan's hand. They stayed that way for a few moments, lost in their own thoughts, the only sounds the birds chirping from nearby trees.

In the distance, a clanging interrupted the quiet.

"That's my mom, ringing the back porch bell. I have to get right home." Susan climbed down from the wagon. "I'll see you on Monday morning. The bus picks me up first. Remember, I'll save you a seat if you want me to."

Ivy nodded. "Yes, please."

Susan kept talking as she inched backward toward the grove. "Want to start meeting here on Saturdays? I can't next Saturday because I'm going to my grandma's for Christmas. But I can after I get back. It could be *our* place now, instead of belonging to the boys."

"Sure," said Ivy.

"Cross your heart?"

Ivy smiled and wrinkled her forehead. "Why do you always make me promise?"

Susan shrugged. "I guess . . . because sometimes people say you'll see them again . . . and then you don't."

Ivy looked at the names carved in the wagon and understood. She made an X over her chest with her finger. "Cross my heart."

9

While Papa fixed the shed door on Sunday, Ivy painted over the words on the back door of the Yamamotos' house and tried not to think about spies.

Papa had said the Yamamotos' future was tied to their family's future. So, if someone proved the Yamamotos *were* spies, Papa would be out of work and they would have to move again, maybe to someplace not nearly as bright with possibilities like being in an orchestra or owning a house.

Later, as she laid out her clothes for school, spies kept popping into her mind. What did spies wear? Black clothes? Or did they dress like regular people during the day and save their spy clothes for nighttime when they did their spy work? Would black clothes be evidence?

Ivy slept fitfully and woke much too early on Monday morning. But she wasn't nearly as nervous as she was on other first days of school. At least she wouldn't have to worry about finding her way around or where to sit at lunch or who she might play with at recess. Susan would be there.

Mama walked with Ivy to the end of the drive and waited until the school bus wheezed to a stop.

Ivy kissed her good-bye and climbed up the steps.

Susan stood, grinning, and waved her over to her seat. Ivy scooted down the aisle and slid in next to her.

"Hi," said Susan, squeezing Ivy's hand. "Are you nervous?"

"Excited," she said, "and glad we're together."

As the bus rumbled down the back roads, picking up more students, Ivy and Susan talked about how they would turn the wagon into a clubhouse instead of a fort. Finally, the bus stopped in front of Lincoln Elementary. Some of the students stood to get off, but Ivy noticed that others stayed seated. She stood as Susan scooted past her down the aisle. Ivy followed.

At the front of the bus, the driver allowed Susan to pass, then put his arm in front of Ivy. "Young lady, where are you going?"

Susan spun around and looked at Ivy, her eyes big with surprise. And then a seed of understanding bloomed on her face.

She turned to the bus driver. "Oh, she's just moving to the front of the bus. Right, Ivy?" She tilted her head toward the front seat, indicating where Ivy should sit. "Save me a place on the way home, okay? The bus picks up at *your school* first so you'll get on before me." Susan hurried down the steps, waving and casting a worried glance back at Ivy.

Your school? What was Susan saying?

The bus driver shut the doors.

"Wait!" called Ivy, turning to him. "I'm in fifth grade at Lincoln."

The bus driver picked up a clipboard and studied it. "Ivy Lopez?"

"Yes."

"This is Lincoln Main. You go to Lincoln Annex, the Americanization school. Next stop."

Americanization? What did that mean? Ivy was already American. The driver put the bus in gear, and it lurched forward.

Ivy stumbled into the front seat.

As the bus pulled away, a group of boys on the steps of Lincoln Main waved and sang, *"Old MacDonald had a farm, ee-ii-ee-ii-ohhhh."*

Ivy felt her chest grow tight. This had to be a mistake. She turned to look at the other leftover students. They didn't seem concerned one bit that the bus was leaving. They talked and laughed with one another as if nothing odd had happened.

Several miles later, the driver stopped the bus and opened the doors. He called, "Lincoln Annex!"

Out the window, Ivy saw a long, squat building with a tin corrugated roof in the middle of a dirt field. There were no flower beds. No geraniums or roses. No palm trees. This was her school? It looked like a warehouse for farm equipment. That's when Ivy finally noticed that all the students on the bus and milling in front of the school looked the same: brown-eyed, dark-haired, and olive-skinned, like her.

A boy from the back of the bus stopped next to Ivy and motioned toward the door, smiling.

Without a word, Ivy slid from her seat and climbed down.

She stood on the walkway, staring at the school, as students and parents flooded around her.

The boy came up beside her. "I'm Ignacio. First day? From where?"

"Fresno," said Ivy, still confused.

"So, you didn't know there were two schools?"

She shook her head and looked down, feeling her face flush with embarrassment.

"What grade are you in?"

"Fifth," said Ivy.

"I'm in sixth. You'll like your teacher, Miss Carmelo. I was in her class last year. That is, you'll like her if you're a good student."

Ivy stood a little taller. "I had the best grades in my entire class at my other school."

Ignacio puffed his chest. "And I'm the fastest

runner in three counties. I hold the school track record. I have medals and everything."

Ivy crossed her arms. "I was going to perform on the radio!"

He laughed. "Come on, radio star, I'll show you your room. And in case you are wondering, yes, it's as bad as it looks. But we can go to Lincoln Main after school, if we're in sports or music."

She followed him inside. "But . . . I'm already American and I already speak English."

"Me too."

"But then . . . why are we here?"

He shrugged and pointed to the end of the hall. "Room sixteen. See you around."

Ivy glanced into each classroom until she came to her own. Miss Carmelo, a wisp of a woman with a black bun on her head, greeted Ivy and found a desk for her next to the windows.

Ignacio was right. She was nice. But she didn't let students work ahead. All morning, in every subject, Ivy finished before the others and sat with her hands folded on the desk, gazing out onto the empty field. Why hadn't Susan told her about the two schools? She'd acted as if they would be in the same class. Hadn't she? She'd said they'd see each other every day. Had she meant only on the bus?

At the outside lunch tables, Ivy sat by herself, looking onto what they called the playground, a weedy acre with a chain-link fence around it. There was no blacktop area painted with four-square courts and hopscotches. No grass. No backstops for baseball and kickball. Beyond the "playground" was an egg farm. Chickens pecked and clucked beneath row upon row of elevated coops. Chicken feathers littered both properties. No wonder the boys at Lincoln Main sang "Old MacDonald."

Ivy pulled the harmonica from her pocket, hoping to play and remind herself she was someone. She blew a chord and felt a speck of determination, a tiny spark of courage . . . until the wind shifted. The smell from the egg farm made her stomach turn and she thought she might gag. She put away the harmonica.

All afternoon Miss Carmelo reviewed English for those who didn't speak it well. Ivy thought she might fall asleep from boredom. But she answered every question correctly when she was called upon, and finished the work sheets within minutes.

At the end of the day, Miss Carmelo called Ivy to her desk. "Dear, you speak English very well. I don't think you need this review every afternoon."

"No, Miss Carmelo. I was born in the United States. I speak English perfectly."

"Yes. I see that. I think you would be better served elsewhere."

Relief flooded over Ivy and she gushed, "Thank you, Miss Carmelo. I *knew* there was a mistake and I was in the wrong place."

Miss Carmelo nodded. "How would you like to go down to the third-grade class and help with the younger children each afternoon? Miss Alapisco is in desperate need of a translator."

Ivy frowned. "A translator? I thought you were sending me to Lincoln Main."

"Oh, heavens no, dear. That's just not possible. You would help teach the little ones English. You'd be a teacher's assistant. Would you like that? It seems redundant for you here. You could start tomorrow after lunch."

Feeling her face redden, Ivy nodded and went back to her seat. She felt the tremble of angry tears trying to rise and pushed them down.

She stared out the windows again, wondering about all the things she might be doing in the afternoons if she went to Lincoln Main—all that she was missing. She didn't know what those things were. But she was sure they were far more interesting than helping in the third-grade class.

After school, as Ivy walked from the building, someone handed her a *Join the Orchestra* flyer with information about the orientation meeting on Thursday. She stuffed it into her pocket.

In line for the bus, she watched a young man ride by on a bicycle, pedaling fast. His white shirtsleeves were rolled up, and his blue pants were tied at the ankles with string so as not to get caught in the spokes. He wore a blue cap with some sort of emblem, and a leather pouch was slung across his chest. If only *she* had a bicycle she could ride to and from school so she wouldn't have to suffer the humiliation of the bus and hear the taunts of the Lincoln Main students.

When she boarded, a small girl, maybe a kindergartner, sat next to her. Ivy didn't even try to save the spot for Susan. At Lincoln Main, the students filed on, holding the same flyers. Ivy caught Susan's worried eyes searching for her, but she just nodded to her seatmate and shrugged.

The entire way home, Ivy stared out the window. Why hadn't someone—Susan, Mrs. Ward, Bertina, Guillermo—told Ivy or Mama or Papa about the two schools? Didn't they know things were different in other parts of California? Didn't they *know* this was humiliating? Again she fought back tears.

When Ivy walked down the aisle to get off the bus, Susan said, "'Bye, Ivy. See you tomorrow."

"'Bye," she said without meeting her eyes, too embarrassed to see Susan feeling sorry for her.

She climbed down the steps to the road. She'd

never been more grateful for a door closing behind her, or the sound of the bus pulling away.

The moment she saw Mama standing halfway down the drive, smiling with her arms open to welcome her home, all of Ivy's pent-up emotions brimmed. And she burst.

10

That evening at dinner, as Ivy listened to Papa's ranting, she felt as if she'd been fed through the wringers on the washing machine.

"My family has lived here for over one hundred years. My great-grandfather worked on a *rancho* when this very land belonged to Mexico and was not yet California! You, Ivy, are already an American just as Mama and I are. And our parents before us. And their parents before them, may they all rest in peace. Luz, they said nothing about two schools when you registered her?"

"Nothing," said Mama. "They took the papers. They told me thank you. They said she could start today and the bus would pick her up. Bertina did not mention it in her letter. Mrs. Ward said nothing when I asked her about the bus. Everyone here behaves as if this is the accepted way."

454

"And your friend said nothing?" said Papa, looking at Ivy.

Ivy shook her head.

All through dinner, Papa would be silent for a few minutes, then erupt again. "Why are things different here? In Fresno, many children went to school together: Japanese, Filipino, Mexican, Anglo. Are we not in the same state of California?"

He served himself spoonfuls of Mama's *albondigas* soup and continued talking, a meatball balanced on his spoon. "So it is fine if we join them for music and sports? But only *after* school! It is fine if we join them in a *war*. My own son is fighting for *our country*! What nonsense is this?" Papa slurped and chewed. "I will talk to the principals of both schools and have you transferred."

Ivy stared into her bowl, pushing the meatballs around. Something told her that Papa was not going to let this go. She was grateful for his defense but at the same time she worried. Would he make a scene with the principals? What if Papa was successful and she was transferred? Would the teachers treat her the same as the other students? Would the parents from Lincoln Annex complain and cause problems? And what if Papa *wasn't* successful? Would she be teased even more by the boys who sang "Old MacDonald"? Would the students at Lincoln Annex say Ivy held her nose in the air, thinking herself too good for them? Her head spun.

"I will call in the morning to make the appointments," said Papa. "Until then, you will stay home!"

A little voice in her head whispered *orchestra*.

Ivy panicked. "Papa, I don't want to miss the meeting about the orchestra on Thursday. Please?"

"Ivy, this is about your *education*, not about extra activities that serve no purpose."

She sat a little taller. "But it serves a purpose for me. Music is important to me. And Fernando told me to keep playing. He said it brought joy to our family."

Mama must have seen the desperation on Ivy's face, because she told Papa, "Victor, you will not make a problem. For Ivy's sake."

"I will not make a problem," said Papa. "I will make a *solution*!"

When Papa came home Wednesday evening, he walked straight to the living room and sank into a chair.

Ivy and Mama followed, sitting across from him on the sofa.

"What happened, Papa?" asked Ivy.

Papa just shook his head, looking defeated.

"Victor?" Mama pressed.

He cleared his throat. "The principals both said the same thing. That this was 'district policy.' They agreed it did not make sense. But their hands are tied." He looked at Ivy. "I am so sorry."

Ivy had never heard him sound so full of regret. She could tell he thought he had failed her. "Papa, it's all right."

"No, it is not. If things stay the same, it will never be all right."

He looked at Mama, perplexed. "He told me that the Mexican children are separated because of language and health issues."

"Health issues?" asked Mama.

"Like what, Papa? I'm not sick," said Ivy.

457

Papa frowned. "The principal at Lincoln Main looked me right in my eyes and said that many of the Mexican children are dirty and need baths. And that they have head lice and carry illnesses."

"Dirty? But that is not reasonable!" said Mama. "And all children have the same illnesses."

Now Papa's voice grew tight with frustration and anger. "Luz, there was no reasoning with him. I told him that Ivy speaks perfect English and that she is ahead of her grade in all subjects. And he said that while it might be true, he could not admit her to the school because then it would not be fair to other Mexican children. He also told me that it is illegal for me to keep her home from school if she is not sick. Illegal!"

"What about the principal at Lincoln Annex?" asked Ivy.

Papa sighed. "He agrees that you should not be spending every afternoon helping the third-grade teacher. They will test you for sixth grade after the vacation. He also told me that parents from all over Orange County are forming a group and they are inviting a lawyer to counsel them. There will be a meeting soon."

"Victor, maybe this is not the right place for us after all. Maybe we should go back to Fresno. Couldn't you get your job back?"

Stunned, Ivy looked at Mama. She was willing to give up all of this for her?

"Mama, the house and your garden and the washing machine."

"At what price, Ivy? You cannot even attend the regular public school. Papa is always saying education is everything."

Papa rose from the chair and paced the room. "That is a possibility. I am sure I could get my job back." He looked out the front window into the grove. But he wasn't nodding in agreement. He was shaking his head as if to say he didn't want to leave all this.

If they left, he would never get to fulfill this once-in-a-lifetime opportunity. As much as she missed Araceli and Miss Delgado, Ivy knew in her heart that if they returned to Fresno, it would be a step backward. It was just as Araceli's father had said. Everyone moves from La Colonia sooner or later, if they want to get ahead in this world. Ivy didn't want to risk all the things they had always wanted. Besides, Fernando was counting on her.

Before Papa could decide, Ivy blurted, "I think we should stay. I can make the best of Lincoln Annex. My teacher is kind. And . . . and I can ask for permission to work ahead, or go into sixth grade like you said. Besides, I already wrote Fernando all about our new house and how much he will love it here. I can live in two worlds. I will go to Lincoln Annex during the day and Lincoln Main after school."

Papa looked at Ivy as if he had never seen her before. Finally, he gave her a little smile and nodded. "I agree, Ivy. It is wiser to stay where there are more opportunities for all of us, and to fight for what is right. I promise I will do that. I am going to that meeting to see what can be done about this situation."

"But it will take time for things to change," said Mama, putting her hand on Ivy's arm.

"Yes," said Papa. "It will take time. The school district is not going to change their mind soon."

Ivy knew what they were saying. The change might not come in time for her benefit. She might have to go to Lincoln Annex for the next two years, even though it was wrong. She thought of the Yamamotos, also misplaced, and how their humiliation had to be ten times—a hundred times—worse.

"I understand. May I please go to the orchestra meeting tomorrow?"

Papa blew out a long breath. "Yes, if it is of such importance."

Ivy ran to Papa and gave him a hug. "It is, Papa. You will see."

Later, she lay on her bed and stared into the dark, second-guessing whether staying would be worth it. She didn't want to feel singled out or less than anyone else. She wanted to belong and to be someone who mattered. Even if she joined the orchestra at Lincoln Main, she would never really belong there. Not the way Susan or the others did.

Even though she'd taken a bath earlier, Ivy suddenly felt dirty. And even though she was healthy, she felt sick. She had never had head lice, but now, as she reached up and touched her hair, it felt as if tiny insects crawled on her scalp and nibbled at her skin.

Hot tears rolled down her cheeks. She slipped from her bed, took Fernando's jacket from the closet, and put it on. For the first time since he'd given it to her, she wore it to bed.

How would she keep her family together when she was the one who was a little bit broken?

11

When Ivy stepped aboard the bus Thursday morning, she could see Susan holding a protective arm across her seat.

Ivy slid in next to her.

"Are you okay? You missed two days of school."

"I wasn't feeling well," Ivy said, and it wasn't really a lie.

"Today is the orchestra meeting. My mom talked to your mom about giving you a ride home after."

Ivy nodded. "She told me."

"I didn't get to sit next to you Monday after school. You can always save seats. The bus driver allows it. How was your first day?" Susan seemed genuinely concerned about Ivy, so Ivy wasn't sure why she still felt betrayed.

"Okay," said Ivy, trying to sound cheerful. "My teacher is nice. I'm way ahead of everyone else, though. I might go into sixth grade."

Susan groaned. "We had a test in math. I'm so far behind." She looked desperate and sounded overwhelmed.

Ivy felt sorry for her all over again. "I can help you if you'd like. Remember, I said I would?"

The bus stopped at Lincoln Main. "That would be great!" Susan said, hugging her before she got up and headed down the aisle.

As the bus pulled away, Ivy heard the boys singing, *"And on that farm he had a pig . . ."*

She bit the inside of her lip a little too hard to keep from crying and tasted blood.

After school, Ivy was the only one to get off the bus at Lincoln Main for orchestra.

Why didn't any other students from Lincoln Annex come? Did they know something Ivy didn't?

The music room was the size of two classrooms. Several long tables stretched across the front, displaying assorted instruments in their cases: horns, flutes, violins, an oboe, a cello. Against the side wall, a piano and what looked like a drum set hid under padded covers.

About twenty students sat in front of Mr. Daniels, a stocky man with a gray beard and mustache.

Susan waved and pointed to the chair next to her in the front row. Ivy walked over and sat down.

Mr. Daniels pressed his hands together. "If you are here today, you are interested in embarking on an incredible adventure in the orchestra."

All heads nodded.

Mr. Daniels handed out information sheets and the schedule for practices. "Your parents will have to sign a permission slip and you will be responsible for your precious instrument. The government has issued a ban on making new ones because the manufacturers are now obligated to make products for the war effort. Unfortunately, we do not know how long it will last."

One of the girls raised her hand. "My mom said there might not even be an orchestra next year. Is that true?"

Mr. Daniels cleared his throat. "Some of the parents are questioning why the school district is paying for a music teacher during a war. Well! I think the opportunity to make music is a gift everyone should receive at least once in their lifetime, whether they unwrap it all the way or not. For many of you, this might be your only musical experience. If that is the case, I want to make it magnificent. Besides, everyone needs the beauty and light of music, *especially* during the worst of times. So! All the more reason to perform majestically this year and bring a little brightness to a dark world. In this way, we might convince our opponents that the music program is worthy enough to continue. I hope you agree."

Ivy liked Mr. Daniels already.

"Now let's get to know one another. As we work our way around the room, introduce yourself and tell me which instrument you'd like to learn, or if you already play an instrument."

Ivy listened as the students shared their preferences and Mr. Daniels recorded them on his clipboard. Some had taken piano. One boy had played the cello for four years. Another, the drums.

When it was her turn, she said, "My name is Ivy Maria Lopez."

Behind her, she heard one of the boys whisper, "*Ee-ii-ee-ii-oh . . .*"

And then giggling.

Her stomach did a somersault. She looked down at the floor. Was this why more students from Lincoln Annex hadn't come for orchestra?

Mr. Daniels clapped his hands three times. "That's enough! I expect concert manners in this class. And that means being respectful of every musician. Everyone in this room is welcome here. Go on, Ivy. Your friend Susan told me you would be joining us from the other school. Is it true you were going to play a solo on the radio?"

Susan had told him about her? She looked up and nodded. "When I lived in Fresno. I'm not sure which instrument I am interested in learning. Maybe the flute. So far, I only play harmonica."

More laughing erupted. Someone snickered. "That's not an instrument."

Mr. Daniels crossed his arms. "Some of you might be surprised to know that there is a classical harmonica player, Larry Adler, who performs with symphony orchestras all over the world. I

467

heard him play *Rhapsody in Blue* on the radio and it was sublime. Ivy, do you have your harmonica with you?"

Ivy nodded.

"Could you play us a little something?"

As she stood up and took the harmonica from her pocket, she looked around. Some of the students were hiding smirks with their hands. What if she didn't play well? They'd laugh even more.

She blew a warm-up chord and, in her head, heard Miss Delgado and Fernando telling her she had a gift. And in that moment, she knew she had just as much right to be there as the Lincoln Main students. She began "When Johnny Comes Marching Home."

> *When Johnny comes marching home again,*
> *Hurrah! Hurrah!*
> *We'll give him a hearty welcome then,*
> *Hurrah! Hurrah!*

She closed her eyes and let herself be carried away on the emotions of the song. She knew the heartache of missing someone long gone, and she imagined the joyousness of their reunion. She played the first verse like a march, rousing and purposeful. The second, she drew out slow and melancholy. The room had been designed for music and the sounds amplified. She played to the ceiling so the notes would travel upward and bounce back.

When she reached the last verse, she infused it with as much gumption and longing as she could pull from her heart. After the final note, there was a moment of silent expectation, the only sound the shuffling of feet. Ivy braced herself for laughter, but instead heard clapping.

"Ivy, thank you!" said Mr. Daniels. "That was unquestionably brilliant. You have *promise*. And I have a feeling"—he shook a finger at her and smiled—"that you are going to fall in love with the flute."

She beamed at Mr. Daniels and sat down. Still flushed from the playing, Ivy wished Fernando could have heard her. He would have given more than a penny for that concert!

"Now, if there are no other remarks about Ivy or the harmonica, and I see there are *none*, then let's talk about the schedule. I will teach strings on Mondays, percussion on Tuesdays, horns on Wednesdays, and winds on Thursdays. I'll hand out the instruments the week after you return from vacation. The week of January eleventh we will begin in earnest!"

Ivy sat rapt with attention. Mr. Daniels's words—*incredible adventure, beauty and light, unquestionably brilliant, begin in earnest*—fueled her with optimism.

"You did really good today," said Susan as they waited on the front steps of the school for Mrs. Ward.

Ivy polished the harmonica with the hem of her dress. "Thanks for telling Mr. Daniels I'd be coming from the other school. That was nice."

Susan whispered, "I'm sorry, Ivy. I thought you *knew* about the two schools. I felt so bad that you didn't. After my mom talked to your mom, she felt horrible, too. She said it never occurred to her to mention it. And she said it must have been quite a shock for all of you."

"I've never been separated before. *Ever.*"

"It's just what they do here," said Susan.

"But the Filipinos go to your school. And the Japanese went here before they were sent away. So why not the Mexicans?"

"I don't know. It's been like this since I can remember."

"They call Lincoln Annex the Old-MacDonald-Had-a-Farm School."

Susan looked down. "I know."

"My father talked to the principals yesterday, but . . ." She felt her eyes brimming.

"Yeah," said Susan. "Every year one of the Mexican families tries to get their child changed . . ." Her sentence trailed off.

Ivy knew what came next . . . *but it never does any good.* "My mom was so upset about the whole thing she said we should move back to Fresno."

Susan's face wrinkled. "You aren't going to, are you?"

Ivy saw the panic in her eyes. "No. We're

staying and fighting. And I'm going to stay in orchestra."

Susan let out a sigh. "I'm so glad."

"Me too," said Ivy.

"Tomorrow we're going to my grandma's for the holidays," said Susan. "My dad is coming back right after Christmas, but my mom and I are staying until New Year's Day. Want to meet at the wagon the day after I get home? Same time?" She held up crossed fingers, looking hopeful.

Susan seemed to have everything, except a friend. And she wanted so desperately to be Ivy's. Maybe Ivy wouldn't matter to the other students at Lincoln Main, but she mattered to Susan. How could Ivy turn her down?

She nodded. "I promise."

12

Christmas Eve didn't feel the same without Fernando, who had always insisted they drink hot chocolate and eat cookies and stay up until midnight to open presents.

Ivy sat between Mama and Papa on the sofa, the three of them indulging his tradition, yet feeling his absence.

Papa held up his cup of cocoa. "Merry Christmas."

Mama and Ivy raised theirs and repeated, "Merry Christmas."

Mama reached over and adjusted his high school photograph a tiny bit to the left. And back to the right. "And to Nando," she said. "We miss you."

"He is with us in spirit," said Papa. "And . . . I have a surprise for both of you." He pulled two envelopes from behind his back.

"Letters?" asked Ivy.

"They came this morning," said Papa. "I happened to be out front when the mailman arrived. I saved them as a surprise."

Ivy took the letter addressed to her.

Mama clutched the other to her chest. Even in the dim light, Ivy could see Mama's eyes glistening as she opened it and smoothed out the paper. She held the letter close to the lamp and read aloud.

Dear Mama and Papa,

I'm sorry I haven't written for so long. In advanced training we have not been able to send mail, only receive it. I guess they don't want any of our radio secrets to leak out. Loose Lips Sink Ships. That means if we talk without censoring our words, the information could fall into the enemy's hands and make things dangerous for other soldiers. I received Papa's letter yesterday. A house in Orange County! Well, that is something. It sounds like a good deal all around. It will be nice to come home, once and for all. I want to put down roots. Here is my news. I am now a certified field radio operator. I can take apart a radio and put it back together faster than anyone in my unit and I get reception when others cannot. My new

nickname is "Mars" Lopez. My buddies tease that I can
reach another planet on the radio if I set my mind to it.

Papa laughed. "Mars Lopez. That is fitting!"

The other news is that I have finally received my
orders. I will be going over soon on a military air
transport.

"Going over . . . to where?" asked Ivy.

"He is not allowed to say," said Papa. "Go
on, Luz."

You know those planes with the big bellies? I will be
inside one of them. I do not know the exact day. Only
that it will be within a few weeks. The talk here is that
this war cannot last too much longer. Even the officers
say so.

Mama looked up from the letter. "Even *the offi-*
cers say the war will be over soon."

Papa smiled and squeezed her hand as she continued reading.

*They show us newsreels every week and we see
how Americans all over the country are doing their
part, big and small, for the war. I feel proud to be
doing mine.*

With much love, your son, Fernando

"If the war ends soon, then next Christmas he
will be with us," said Mama.

Papa cleared his throat. "Yes. I predict that the
New Year will be even better. In two weeks, Mr.
Yamamoto's son will come to sign the papers. I will
attend the meetings to see what might be done
about Ivy's school. By the time this war is over,
we will have"—Papa's voice cracked—"our own
house for Fernando to come home to. Yes, next year
will be promising."

While Mama and Papa huddled together and
reread the letter, Ivy opened hers and read silently.

Dear Ivy,

*I just received your letter. I am sorry you had to miss
your performance on the radio. I hope you will play the*

solo for me when I come home. But it sounds like good things are coming for all of us once this war is over.

Every battalion has a motto: Brave in Difficulties. Our Utmost Forever. Ready in Peace and War. My battalion's motto is Forward to Defend the Truth. Let's do that in our family, too. I am counting on you to be a good little soldier and march forward.

I hope you are still playing harmonica. What I wouldn't give for one of your concerts now! Over. In radio lingo that means I'm finished talking and I'm waiting to hear what the person on the other end has to say. And that is you!

Love, Nando

P.S. Remember how you were saving war stamps in Fresno? My sergeant said a ten-cent war stamp will buy five bullets and each bullet will stop a Nazi. The truth is, the sooner we stop them, the sooner the war will be over and I'll be home.

At the bottom of the piece of paper, Fernando had taped a penny. Ivy held up the letter to show Mama and Papa and smiled. "For a concert."

It was just after midnight. She kissed Mama and Papa good night and left the letter with them so they could read it, too.

She went to her room and stood at the window, gazing into the shadows in the orange grove.

She raised the harmonica and played "The Battle Hymn of the Republic" for Fernando, the lyrics resounding with his pride and love and dedication.

Glory, glory, hallelujah!
Glory, glory, hallelujah!
Glory, glory, hallelujah!
His truth is marching on.

"Okay, Nando," she whispered. "Forward to Defend the Truth."

She sat on her bed and wrote him a letter. She told him about Lincoln Main and Lincoln Annex, their decision to stay in Orange County instead of going back to Fresno, the orchestra, Mr. Daniels, and flute lessons, and how she hoped everything worked out so that he could come home and put down roots. She assured him she was being a good little soldier and that he could keep counting on her.

She signed her letter without mentioning the two obstacles to her family's future: One was that Kenny Yamamoto and Papa still had to sign the papers. If Kenny Yamamoto wasn't pleased with what he saw when he came home, he might not sign.

That was something Ivy could fix.

The other obstacle was like a sliver in her finger that never stopped throbbing. If the Yamamotos were spies, they would go to prison and their farm would be sold. In that case, what would happen to her own family?

Susan had said the only way to prove the Yamamotos weren't spies was to inspect their house. Hadn't Papa mentioned they needed to do that very thing anyway? If Ivy could get inside and confirm there was nothing suspicious, she could tell Susan, who could tell her father. And that would be the end of all the spy talk.

But how and when could she get inside?

13

The day after Christmas, Ivy realized she had the perfect opportunity.

She and Mama were kneeling side by side on a folded blanket in front of an overgrown flower bed, prying up iris bottoms. With a trowel, Ivy dug up a dirt-encrusted clump and tossed it into a pile on a piece of burlap. "What color are they?"

Mama considered one. "They will have to bloom for us to know. I am hoping for purple with yellow tongues. Those are my favorite."

"What will you do with the ones we take out?" asked Ivy.

"They are easy to transplant. I will keep some for the side of the house, and I will give some to Mrs. Ward. The rest, I am not sure."

"Mama, I want to plant some at the owner's house. Everything there looks so drab."

"Ivy, what a good idea. I wish I had thought the same. Maybe by the time they take root and flower, the family will be back to enjoy them."

"We can take these over and store them in the shed until I can plant them." And then nonchalantly, Ivy added, "Oh, and Papa said we needed to check inside the house. We could do it while we are there."

"Yes," said Mama. "I promised Papa I'd do that but have not had the chance. Since he's gone to town buying supplies this afternoon, we might as well go over." She stood and brushed off her apron. "I will get the keys to the shed and the house."

Before they started through the grove, Mama grabbed a handful of clothespins from the line. "To pin up the blackout curtains and let in some light. The electricity is not on."

Ivy heard Susan's warnings. *If you do go inside, be careful because it might be booby-trapped or rigged with bombs to protect their spy stuff.*

Ivy didn't believe it and was ready to prove the Yamamotos were not spies. But still, should she tell Mama what Susan had said, just in case?

By the time Ivy had bundled the iris bottoms in the burlap, Mama was halfway through the grove. Ivy hurried after her to the Yamamotos' yard. When she caught up, Mama had opened the shed and was heading toward the back door. She laid the bundle on the dirt floor of the shed and quickly made her way to the house, deciding to warn Mama about the booby traps. But she wasn't fast enough. Mama had already unlocked the back door and now stood in a perfectly ordinary kitchen that did not look one bit like it belonged to spies. Ivy took a deep breath, relieved.

"Now," said Mama, pinning up a corner of the blackout curtain on the kitchen window, "we need to look inside every closet and cupboard."

"For mouse droppings or leaking water or bird and squirrel nests," said Ivy. "Papa told me."

Mama put her hands on her hips. "It is sad, no? The last time Kenneth Yamamoto left this house, his family was here." She shook her head. "Imagine how difficult it will be for him to come back to this."

The kitchen table looked stark and lonely without a bowl of fruit at its center and the chairs tucked tight to the edges. Had Mr. and Mrs. Yamamoto sat at each end with their children between them? Which seats were Karen's and Annie's?

Ivy helped Mama clip up the curtains in the living room. Boarded from the outside, the windows allowed in only slats of light. Furniture had been pushed to the center and covered with sheets, the mountainous shapes erupting like icebergs. The air smelled stale.

"Why do they still have blackout curtains if there's no electricity?" asked Ivy.

"The curtains were probably required before they were sent away. They were being good Americans. Now, at least if someone pries off the boards on the outside, they will not be able to see inside. When houses are abandoned, people do strange things. They think it is an invitation to steal."

Mama inspected each window and moved to the bedrooms. The first had been stripped bare, except for the double-bed frame and mattress. Mama opened a closet door. Adult clothing crowded the pole. On the floor, a radio was pushed into the corner, surrounded by tidy rows of cardboard boxes with words written on the front: *sheets, pillowcases, tablecloths.* A row of work boots lined the threshold. It must have been Mr. and Mrs. Yamamoto's room.

Mama pulled out a few boxes and carefully looked inside.

The next bedroom was much the same, with boxes lining the closet floor, but the shelf held baseball bats and deflated balls that probably belonged to Kenny. In the third bedroom, there were two beds where Karen and Annie must have slept. Ivy imagined them there, giggling and whispering secrets in the dark before they fell asleep, the younger one clutching her doll.

Mama opened the closet and a box with no lid toppled. Photos slid across the floor.

"Oh, what a mess!"

"I'll get them, Mama," said Ivy, curious to look at the photos.

"Thank you. I'll look through the kitchen cup-boards." The sound of Mama's footsteps faded as she walked away.

One by one, Ivy stacked the pictures back in the box. There was one of the Lincoln School orchestra with the Yamamoto girls performing a duet on flutes. They played flute, too! Ivy turned the photo over. Their names had been written on the back in perfect script. Another picture showed the two sisters in matching dresses, sitting at a piano. There were lots of baby pictures. A young Kenny, playing the violin, with the words *Lincoln Spring Concert* written in the white border. Mr. and Mrs. Yamamoto standing on the front steps of the house, holding an infant. Kenny and Donald and Tom, arms around one another, holding baseball bats and gloves, grinning. Kenny and Donald in their Marine Corps uniforms, shaking hands. Kenny must have been so sad when his best friend died in the bombs.

With each photo, Ivy felt pulled into the Yamamotos' lives, and heavyhearted for all they had lost. She lifted the box back into the closet.

She looked for the lid, pushing aside the hanging clothes.

That's when she saw a door at the back of the closet. Why would there be a door in a closet? Ivy's imagination raced. Was it an entrance to a secret passageway? Was this the evidence Susan's father was hoping to find? *Were* the Yamamotos hiding something?

Ivy looked up. At the top of the door, a flip latch was padlocked. She shoved some of the clothing farther aside, scooted boxes forward, and found another latch and padlock near the bottom of the door.

She took a deep breath. It was probably a storage room, she reasoned. For special things they would not risk leaving out in the house, breakable or precious things. Didn't Japanese people have fancy kimonos? It would make sense to lock them up. After all, Papa said they could take to the camp only what they could hold in their arms. And Mama said that people steal from abandoned houses. It made sense to lock up valuables.

Ivy suddenly felt heavy with the burden of responsibility—of knowing about this hidden closet. Should she tell Mama and Papa?

She thought she heard a chord, like a long exhale. She put her hand on the pocket of her dungarees and felt the harmonica. Had it played on its own? Or had Ivy let out a sigh? Or was she imagining things like Papa always said?

Her thoughts skipped. Her family and the Yamamotos were linked. If there was anything suspicious in the closet and it was discovered, both families would be in jeopardy. Ivy was probably the only one outside the Yamamoto family who knew the door was there. And she was good at keeping secrets. She didn't have to tell.

It would be her way of helping, of giving her family the chance to march forward together.

Ivy rearranged the hanging clothes and stacked the boxes in place.

"Ivy . . ." called Mama, "unclip the curtains as you come through the house and pull the back door tight. I will lock the shed and meet you out front."

"Okay, Mama!" Ivy shut the closet door and left the house, acting as though nothing unusual had happened.

But as she rounded the corner of the ramshackle garden, she stopped and froze.

Mr. Ward's Buick idled on the street at the end of the Yamamotos' drive. Ivy could see Mr. Ward crouching from the driver's seat and peering out the passenger window, as if he'd been watching and waiting.

Ivy's heart thudded. He couldn't have known what she had just discovered. Or could he? She tried to act innocent and casual as she walked down the drive and waved.

But Mr. Ward gunned the motor and sped away.

14

The next day, Ivy set out to conquer one of the obstacles standing in the way of her family's future.

"I want to go back to the Yamamotos'," she told Mama.

All morning she had thought of what to say, and when, so Mama would allow it. They had finished lunch and Mama was putting on her jacket to go make bandages with the Red Cross ladies. "We were just there yesterday."

"Yes, but I want to plant the irises and rake the flower beds and also fix the vegetable garden for when Kenny Yamamoto comes. I've helped you before. I know what to do. Papa said if Kenny Yamamoto likes how he is caring for the property, then he will sign the agreement. And you said it would be sad for him to come home to his house the way it is. Also, I was thinking that when the oranges and vegetables are ripe, I could sell them at Mrs. Yamamoto's stand and buy war stamps with the money. Maybe Susan could help me. Fernando says the sooner we stop the Nazis, the sooner the war will be over. I can tell Kenny Yamamoto I plan to exchange the stamps for war bonds and give them to his father when the war is over."

Mama looked at Ivy with awe. "What a generous and sensible idea. Since we arrived here, Ivy, I grow more and more proud of you. You are becoming such a mature, responsible girl, with your feet on the ground.

"Papa is working in the grove on the north of the house this afternoon if you need him. The extra key to the shed is in the drawer by the back door. Don't stay too late, and take your jacket."

Excited and relieved, Ivy stuffed the extra key to the shed in the pocket of her dungarees and ran to the Yamamotos'.

She gathered a trowel, a small rake, and some packets of seeds from the shed. She weeded the flower beds in front of the house and dug small holes for the iris bottoms, dropping them in and leaving just the tips to peek from the ground. She smoothed the dirt around them for their long nap in the earth.

As she worked, she found herself looking up at the house and wondering about the closet. She tried to push away her curiosity.

She walked to the garden, removing the wire trellises and setting them aside. She pulled up the old tomato plants and hoed the dirt into two long furrows. In one row, she planted carrot seeds. In another, radishes. The rest of the garden would have to wait for warmer weather.

In the shed, Ivy lined up the little clay pots beneath the window and planted sweet pea seeds, sprinkling them with water from a tiny watering can.

As she walked back to the front yard, she looked toward the road and saw the boy on the bicycle, the one she'd seen while waiting for the bus at school. He was hunched over the handlebars, pedaling as fast as he could down the road. Ivy waved, but he didn't wave back. Where was he going? Why was he always in such a hurry?

Ivy was glad she wasn't in a hurry. She slowly swept the front porch and then sat on the steps, satisfied with her work. There was something comforting about being at the foot of the sleeping house, smelling the freshly turned earth and looking at the snug beds of irises, waiting to rise.

Ivy lifted the harmonica and played "Angels We Have Heard on High." She closed her eyes. When she reached the refrain, she imagined a field of angels who had been sleeping in a faraway and ancient place—purple angels with yellow tongues, bursting through the topsoil, singing, *"Gloria . . . in excelsis Deo."*

The song filled her with contentment and a sense that everything might, once and for all, be better.

15

On Saturday, Ivy was so excited to meet Susan and tell her everything that had happened—almost everything—that she was much too early.

She sat in the old wagon, playing "Auld Lang Syne" on the harmonica, the song her class would have played on *The Colgate Family Hour.* Last night on the radio she'd heard Guy Lombardo's orchestra play it and people singing. She couldn't remember all the words, except that it kept asking the question, *Should old acquaintance be forgot?*

It had been over three weeks since she had moved, and Ivy had written to Araceli four times. But she hadn't received one letter in return. Mama said mail was slow during the holidays. Papa said Araceli's family could have moved from La Colonia, too. If that was the case, why hadn't she sent a new address? Had Araceli forgotten her?

Ivy was happy to have her thoughts interrupted by Susan, who ran through the grove, carrying papers and calling her name. She climbed into the wagon and sat next to Ivy. "Happy New Year!"

"And to you, too!"

They hugged and filled each other in on their Christmas presents and how they'd spent their vacation.

Ivy explained about fixing up the Yamamotos' yard and planting the war garden. "Kenny Yamamoto is coming home next weekend. If he likes Papa and how he is caring for the house and farm, they will both sign papers that say we can stay here forever."

"You mean you might have to *leave* if Kenny Yamamoto doesn't like how your father is doing things?"

Ivy nodded. "That's why I'm making everything look nice. And—" She grinned. "I'm going to sell oranges and vegetables at Mrs. Yamamoto's stand and buy war bonds with the money. Do you want to join me? We'll be helping America."

"Oh, I *want* to. And I don't want you to ever leave! But I'm not sure if my parents would let me . . . you know, because it's the Yamamotos' property."

"Don't worry," said Ivy. "You can tell your father that my mother and I inspected the entire inside of the house. I didn't see any secret documents or anything that could help Japan win the war." It wasn't a lie, but the hidden closet still nagged at her.

Susan chewed on her lip, thinking. "If it's for the war and our soldiers . . . maybe they'll say yes." She smiled. "Our very own stand! But first . . ." She held up the papers. "Work sheets. I need to catch up in math or my mom won't let me do *any* extra activities, even orchestra."

The air warmed. Ivy took off Fernando's jacket, spread it out in the wagon, and sat on it. She let Susan wear the purple hat as they huddled over Susan's homework.

Afterward, Ivy pulled out her harmonica and played "Auld Lang Syne."

"I wish I knew what the words mean," she said when she finished.

"My dad told me it means 'Times Gone By.' He said it's about good memories with old friends. And that even if you're separated for a really, really long time, or never see them again, you can still think about them with love and good feeling."

Ivy tilted her head. Mr. Ward had said that? It didn't seem as if he wanted anyone in his family to remember the Yamamotos that way. Had the war squashed all the good memories from his heart?

The bell clanged in the distance.

Susan gathered her things, handed Ivy the hat, and gave her a hug. "I'll tell my parents all about the orange-and-vegetable stand tonight. And that you inspected the house and the Yamamotos aren't spies so it's perfectly safe. Fingers crossed they say it's okay."

Ivy waved.

Before Susan disappeared among the trees, she turned and held a hand in the air, fingers crossed.

Ivy did the same.

16

"Do you think he will sign?" asked Ivy, as she followed Papa up and down row after row of orange trees.

He was marking each trunk with different-colored strips of cloth: yellow if they needed to be pruned, green if they needed to be treated for leaf curl, red if they should be removed altogether.

"We will find out one week from today, Sunday," said Papa. "He has only a three-day leave. First, he will travel to the camp in Arizona to meet with his father. Then he will take the bus here to meet with me. He will arrive in the morning, spend a few hours, and I will take him back to the bus in the afternoon."

Papa and Ivy got in the truck and drove to the outer groves, where Papa studied the irrigation pumps and the moats and pipes leading to the fields. He pulled oranges from trees, peeled them, and ate a bite, then handed the rest to Ivy to sample while he made notes about their sweetness or juiciness. "They will be ready to harvest in a few months or so."

"Then I can sell them!" She was excited to start and hoped Susan's parents had said she could help. Ivy looked around at the acres and acres of trees. "Who will help when it's time to pick?"

"That is a problem. I will talk with Kenneth about this. I know one farmer in San Bernardino who might loan me some workers. So many men are at war. So many women work in the factories that there are not enough people to harvest. The United States is begging for braceros from Mexico, because there are not enough 'strong arms' left in the United States."

"But if they had not put Mr. Yamamoto and all his Japanese workers in the camp . . ."

"Yes, Ivy. You are thinking the same as me. Then we would not be begging for braceros."

They climbed back into the truck and it rambled through the groves to the road. "Papa, can you

498

drop me at the Yamamotos' so I can water the garden? And I can show you the radishes. They are already up."

Papa turned the truck at the stand and headed down the drive. Closer to the house, he leaned forward, peering out the dusty windshield.

"What is it?" she asked.

He turned off the motor, reached for Ivy's hand, and helped her across the seat. "I'm not sure. Stay close to me."

They took a few steps toward the house, and Ivy sucked in her breath.

The front flower beds had been trampled, the irises pulled from the ground and thrown at the house, leaving splats of dirt. The porch was now littered with dirt clods and would-be irises. Ivy blinked, making sure it was real.

She pulled her hand from Papa's and ran to the side of the house. Someone had rampaged her war garden with a shovel. The radish sprouts had been chopped and scattered in clumps across the yard. The furrows had been flattened.

She felt her throat tighten. "Papa, all my work."

499

He came up behind her and put a hand on her shoulder. "Ivy Maria, I am so sorry."

She ran to the shed. The window was broken, the seedlings no longer on the sill. Papa unlocked the door. Inside, the clay pots lay shattered on the ground, among shards of glass.

Ivy felt as though someone had punched her in the stomach. All her hard work had been ruined.

As Papa herded her toward the truck, she saw what had been scrawled in red on the newly painted back door:

JAP SPIES
DON'T COME BACK!

Who would do such a thing? Mr. Ward?

"I don't want you coming here alone anymore," said Papa. "For your safety, Ivy Maria."

"But . . . I have to clean it all up. For Kenny." If he saw this destruction, surely he wouldn't sign the papers with Papa.

"No, Ivy. Not today. We will wait until right

before Kenneth Yamamoto arrives. So whoever did this does not have time to do it again."

"But . . . the seedlings . . . the radishes . . ."

"I know," said Papa. "I will explain everything to him."

Something big and fierce rose up inside Ivy. "What is wrong with people, Papa? Why is someone doing this? And why doesn't anyone stop them?"

"Their hearts hurt. People who used to be friends are no longer friends. Neighbors are not neighbors. During a war, people feel they must blame and take sides. Hearts grow smaller."

"Mama says hearts are bigger than we think!" Angry tears streamed down her cheeks.

Papa put his arm around her. "Ivy Maria, how did you get so wise so quickly? Where is that girl with her head in the clouds? I think I miss her a little." He squeezed her shoulder. "Can you play me something on the harmonica? That song you were going to play on the radio, perhaps? Your solo." He reached into his pocket, pulled out some coins, sorted through them, and handed her a penny.

She took the penny and hugged Papa. As they walked to the truck and all the way home, Ivy struggled to catch her breath, still choked by indignation, as she played a halting "America the Beautiful."

17

When Ivy answered the brisk knock at the door the next evening, she was surprised to find Mr. Ward standing in front of her.

He cleared his throat. "I'd like to speak to Mr. Lopez."

Papa came up behind Ivy. "How can we help you?"

"Could you step outside for a few minutes?"

Papa grabbed his jacket and pulled the door closed behind him.

Ivy watched them through the front window, frustrated that she couldn't hear. Papa leaned against the truck with his arms across his chest, listening. Mr. Ward stood in his usual stance, hands behind his back, elbows out.

After Mr. Ward walked to his car and drove away, Papa came inside, his brow furrowed.

"What is it, Victor?" asked Mama.

"He saw the vandalism at the Yamamoto house and he thinks he has a solution to end all of this. He would like to meet with Kenneth Yamamoto when he arrives. He wishes to buy the property. He said that the first time he made an offer, the Yamamotos were insulted because it was much too low. He realizes that now. I told him Mr. Yamamoto has written that he does not wish to sell under any circumstance, but . . ."

"But what?" asked Ivy.

"Mr. Ward said every man has his price. And he is right, Ivy. If the Yamamotos agree to sell, he said he would consider hiring me as field supervisor. But he made no guarantee. I said I would arrange the meeting because it is not my place to say no. It is Mr. Yamamoto's decision. Mr. Ward wants to inspect the property inside and out: the house, the shed, the garage. *Before* Kenneth Yamamoto arrives."

Ivy felt the blood rush to her face. What if he discovered the door in the back of the closet? Ivy tried to sound casual. "Why?"

"He says so he can prepare a worthy offer. He

will bring his lawyer with him, to advise. But I sense there is something more."

"I think I know, Papa. Susan told me Mr. Ward thinks the Yamamotos are spies for Japan."

"What?" said Mama. "Spies? Ivy, what nonsense is this?"

"I'm not making this up, Mama. Susan said her father thinks that inside the house there are maps and secret documents that helped Japan bomb Pearl Harbor, and if it can be proved, then the Yamamotos can be sent to prison. And they will lose the farm because the bank can sell it to anyone who has the money to buy it."

Mama looked at Papa. "Victor?"

Papa rubbed his chin. "It makes sense. If Mr. Yamamoto does not want to sell and Mr. Ward can prove something like this, it is another way to get the property. He asked me if I had been inside and what had been left behind. I told him that you and Ivy had opened every cupboard and door and saw nothing but the family's personal belongings."

"That is true," said Mama. "Right, Ivy?"

Ivy nodded. But she squirmed from her secret.

"He said, nevertheless, he would consider it a favor if he could take a look because he does not want to purchase if there is evidence that something un-American took place there. It would give the property a reputation, a problem that would make it difficult to sell again someday. I think what Susan told Ivy is right. Mr. Ward wants to find any evidence that can implicate the Yamamotos to get what he wants. And he is bringing his lawyer as a witness."

"Victor, you cannot be serious! Guillermo worked for Mr. Yamamoto for years. Surely he would have mentioned—"

"Luz. I am serious. Mr. Ward—I see it in his eyes," said Papa. "He believes that by purchasing the house and getting rid of the Yamamotos, he is protecting the neighborhood and his family. It is personal to him."

"He thinks Kenny is responsible for his son dying," said Ivy.

Mama's forehead wrinkled. "What? But how

could that be? Mrs. Ward told me her son died at Pearl Harbor."

"Mr. Ward didn't want Donald to join the marines, but Kenny talked him into it because they were best friends," said Ivy.

"But that is misguided. Oh, that poor, sad man," said Mama. "Victor, are you going to agree to let him in the house?"

"What am I to say? If I do not allow him in the house, and Mr. Ward somehow convinces the Yamamotos to sell, then he will hold it against me. You know what that will mean? He would never hire me and we would have to move again."

"I don't want to move," said Ivy.

"None of us want that," said Mama.

Papa cleared his throat. "Luz, he would like you and Ivy to be there, too, since you have already been in the house."

"When?" asked Mama.

"Friday afternoon at four o'clock."

Mama took a breath. "Let us be practical. We should not worry. There is no harm in them looking. Once they see there's nothing to find, it will all be settled."

Ivy went to her room and lay on her bed and worried. When they inspected the house, they would surely find the door in the back of the closet. What if there *was* something un-American behind it?

How could she find out?

One idea kept shoving its way into Ivy's thoughts. Even as she dismissed it as disobedient and dangerous, she remembered a question she had asked Fernando. *Who will fix things while you are gone?*

And his answer: *You will.*

She rubbed her forehead, knowing how she could do it. Today was Monday and she had until Friday afternoon. The bigger problem was *when.*

The thought that crossed her mind next was the most overwhelming. If she found something suspicious, what would she do with it?

18

When Ivy arrived home from school on Wednesday afternoon and found the house empty, she knew it was her chance.

Mama had left a note: She was working at the Wards' until five o'clock; Papa was at a meeting with the parents from Lincoln Annex and wouldn't be home until dinner.

Ivy rushed to the kitchen drawer by the back door, hoping Papa had left the big ring of keys. To her relief, he had. She slipped it into Fernando's jacket pocket and ran from the house. As she jogged through the grove, the keys bumped her side with each footfall.

At the back door of the Yamamoto house, Ivy looked over both shoulders to make sure no one was around. Then she quickly slipped inside, still catching her breath.

It felt strange to be in the house alone with

only the silence to keep her company. She went straight to the third bedroom, where she clothes-pinned the curtains to allow as much light as possible into the room. Heart pounding, she opened the closet. One by one, she scooted boxes into the room. When there were only two left, she pushed them closer to the door and stood on them to reach the top padlock.

Her hands trembled while she tried several keys. Finally, one clicked and she removed the lock.

She shoved the two boxes into the room so there was now a clear path to the door in the back of the closet. The bottom padlock sprang open with the first key she tried.

Her breathing quickened.

She eased open the hidden door.

Musty air and looming shadows accosted her. She took a step inside, blinking as her eyes adjusted to the dimness.

The larger figures in the room took shape. Incredulous, she walked farther into the room, not sure, at first, what she was seeing. And then she slowly began to understand what it all meant.

The back wall—the one that faced outside—was covered end to end by a Japanese screen, painted with delicate tree limbs and cherry blossoms. She peeked behind it and saw a wall with a set of double doors that met in the middle. The revelation of what was on the other side hit her: the wooden lattice and the climbing vines. *That's* why Mr. Yamamoto didn't want Papa to cut them back. Doing so would have revealed the doors.

Ivy ran her finger over a stack of papers on a table. Were they the documents that had helped Japan bomb Pearl Harbor? She glanced at a row of books. Was this the evidence that would send the Yamamotos to prison?

She looked around the room. How had they accomplished it? How had they maneuvered everything in here? Clearly, far more people than just the Yamamotos were involved. Had there been work parties and meetings? And secret late-night deliveries? It appeared so. They were all guilty of the same thing.

Ivy's eyes stung with tears. It was all so sad. It felt so wrong.

Mr. Ward had been right. The Yamamotos were hiding something. Something big.

She left everything as she found it, padlocked the room, and rearranged the closet as it had been.

Fernando had said that Americans all over the country were doing their part, big and small, for the war.

"I will do my part," she whispered.

On Friday afternoon, she would show Papa and Mama and the lawyer and Mr. Ward . . . the truth.

It was her duty as an American.

19

Mr. Ward stood on the front porch of the Yamamoto house Friday afternoon looking as though he were ready for battle.

He stood tall, arms crossed, and held a large flashlight in one hand. His lawyer stood at his side, holding a briefcase.

As Mama, Papa, and Ivy walked up the steps, Mr. Ward strode toward them and held out his free hand. "Mr. Lopez, this is my lawyer, Mr. Pauling."

Papa shook hands with both men. "This is my wife, Luz, and my daughter, Ivy."

Mr. Pauling nodded. "We appreciate your cooperation, Mr. Lopez. I want to point out that you do not have to allow us inside, legally, since you are not the owner of the property. And to confirm that as the caretaker, you are doing this as a favor to Mr. Ward, is that correct?"

"Yes," said Papa, sweeping a hand toward the boarded-up front door. "We must enter from the back of the house."

Mr. Ward gave Papa a curt nod. "I'll follow you."

Within a few minutes, they all stood in the Yamamoto kitchen.

Mama walked ahead of them and clipped up the curtains. Mr. Ward studied the kitchen like a prospective buyer, opening drawers, shining the flashlight into cupboards and under the sink, knocking on walls.

Mr. Pauling shadowed him.

"As you can see," said Papa, "everything is in good condition."

Mr. Ward said nothing and headed into the living room. He lifted the sheets and squinted at the furniture. He picked up a broom that had been left in a corner and tapped on the ceiling. He stomped on the wood floor. When he moved into the first bedroom, he opened the closet. "Have you searched these things?"

"We did not check inside the boxes. Ivy and I

checked only for rodents and water damage," said Mama. "And to be sure the windows were closed tight."

"I have to ask you, Mrs. Lopez," said Mr. Pauling. "Just as a matter of record, did you remove anything from the house?"

Mama shook her head. "I would never do such a thing."

Mr. Pauling looked at Ivy.

"No, sir. I haven't taken anything from the house."

"But you've spent quite some time here, working in the yard," said Mr. Ward.

Ivy nodded. "Yes. To make it nice for Kenny Yamamoto when he comes to visit on Sunday."

Mr. Ward knelt in front of Ivy. "Now, young lady, you do know that our country is at *war* with Japan and the Japanese?"

"Everybody knows," said Ivy. "Since Pearl Harbor."

Papa bristled. "Of course she knows. Our son, her brother, is fighting in the United States Army."

Mr. Ward stood up. "Mr. Lopez, do you understand that the Japanese who lived here are *confined* because of their threat to our security?"

"Threat?" asked Papa.

"When the Yamamotos lived here, there were always people coming and going from this house," said Mr. Ward. "Especially after the bombing at Pearl Harbor. And not just other Japanese farmers. Japanese carrying *briefcases*. And sometimes the lights were on very late at night. There were trucks arriving at all hours."

"But that does not mean . . ." said Papa.

"How do we know it wasn't ammunition? In times of war, we can't be too careful," said Mr. Ward. "There are Japanese sympathizers who watched our skies before Pearl Harbor. They wrote down descriptions of our planes that flew overhead and reported back to the Japanese government."

Papa shook his head. "I do not think the Yamamotos . . ."

Mr. Ward's face turned red. "I was *trained* in this type of work. If you do not allow me to inspect further, I will report my concerns to the police. Is that what you prefer?"

All the raised voices made Ivy anxious. She leaned against Mama.

Mr. Pauling put a hand on Mr. Ward's arm. "Let's calm down. You must have evidence before you go to the police."

Papa stared at Mr. Ward and Mr. Pauling. "I do not understand. I thought you were inspecting the house because you are interested in purchasing it."

Mr. Ward sniffed. "I have two concerns. Reporting threats to our safety and purchasing the house so the threats never return."

"Mr. Lopez, if you'll indulge him, we can get this over with," said Mr. Pauling.

Papa pointed to the closet.

Mr. Ward dragged box after box into the middle of the room, opening and inspecting each one.

He muttered, "Nothing but dishes and bed linens and tea towels."

Mr. Ward sniffed again, walked into the second bedroom, and repeated the same inspection. When he found only boxes of children's clothes, he knelt down in front of Ivy. "Now, Ivy, when you and your mother came into the house, did you see *anything* that seemed out of order? Have you seen anything in the shed or the garage or the house that didn't seem . . . usual?"

She looked from Mr. Ward, to Mr. Pauling, to Mama and Papa. Her heart exploded with anticipation. She took a deep breath and tried to appear calm.

"Ivy? Answer Mr. Ward, please," said Papa.

"Do you mean like a secret door?"

"I knew it!" said Mr. Ward.

Papa stepped forward. "Ivy! What are you talking about? This is not a time for pretending!"

Ivy shook her head. "I'm not, Papa! When we checked the house, a box of photographs spilled in the other bedroom. Remember, Mama? You left me to clean them up, and when I put the box on top of the others, I saw a door in the back of the closet, with locks on it. I can show you."

Mama's face went pale. "Why did you not tell me?"

"I'm sorry, Mama. I thought it was just another closet to store things." She hated deceiving Mama even for a few minutes, but it would soon be over.

"We should call the police!" said Mr. Ward.

Mr. Pauling held up a hand. "Let's make sure it's not just another closet first, shall we?"

"Ivy, show us," said Papa, holding out his hand.

She led him to the third bedroom.

Mama clothespinned the curtains to let in the light.

Ivy opened the closet door, pushed aside the clothing, and pointed to the hidden door.

She watched as Mr. Ward and Mr. Pauling pulled the boxes to the center of the room and moved the hanging clothes.

When the closet was clear, Papa tried different keys until both padlocks clicked. He opened the door.

Mr. Ward and Mr. Pauling followed the flashlight beam into the room, with Ivy, Mama, and Papa close behind.

The light illuminated the room and its contents. Every figure glowed.

"Oh!" Mama gasped.

"How?" asked Papa.

Ivy watched with satisfaction as Mr. Pauling stifled a smile and Mr. Ward's eyes darted from corner to corner.

Ivy walked around the room, unlatching and opening the cases.

Inside a space the size of a bedroom was not one but three pianos, one of them a grand. Assorted musical instruments lay about: four cellos, several basses, flutes, clarinets. Ivy opened at least a dozen violin cases, the instruments and bows resting in their velvet-lined beds.

Papa walked along the perimeter of the room. It didn't take him long to look behind the painted screen and see the doors, as Ivy had done yesterday. "Double doors. Outside, they are covered with vines and cannot be seen. It makes sense now, yes?" said Papa. "They could take so little with them to the camps. And Mr. Yamamoto was one of the few in the area who was able to keep his property. He is storing and protecting his friends' most prized possessions. The men you saw going and coming from the house with the briefcases . . ." Papa shrugged. "They were carrying instruments. They were musicians . . ." He looked at Ivy and smiled. "Like my daughter."

"I think we've seen enough," said Mr. Pauling, turning to leave.

"No, wait!" said Mr. Ward. Confused, he put his hands on his hips. "What about inside the piano benches? What about in the stacks of sheet music? There could be secret codes!"

Mr. Pauling raised his eyebrows and shook his head.

Papa lifted the lid of each piano bench and stood by while Mr. Ward rummaged through the Chopin and Beethoven and Brahms.

From the third piano bench, Papa took out the only thing inside: a flat box with an intricate pattern of inlaid woods, shiny with lacquer. He set it on the table.

Mr. Ward stepped forward.

Papa lifted the lid.

A letter lay on top of the contents. Papa unfolded it.

"What is it, Papa?" asked Ivy.

Papa turned and held out the paper, pointing to the letterhead. "This is the official seal of the President of the United States. The letter is a commendation for bravery." He pointed into the box. "And these are Mr. Yamamoto's medals for his service to the United States of America during World War I."

Mr. Pauling cleared his throat and turned to Mr. Ward. "I don't see any government documents, or diagrams of the California coastline, or pictures of airplanes and ships. Are you satisfied?"

Mr. Ward seemed puzzled as his eyes drifted around the room. He took a deep breath and stood straighter. "It is always better to be safe than sorry. Every man, woman, and child must be diligent . . ." His voice cracked and his eyes filled. "So many of our boys have died . . . so many of our boys . . . my boy . . ." Grief overtook him and his body shook.

Ivy walked to his side. He didn't seem unfriendly any longer. He looked like a father who had lost his son to war.

She looked up at him and took his hand.

Mama's eyes filled with tears as she appeared on his other side and gently held his arm.

And together, they led him from the house.

20

Papa repainted the back door of the Yamamoto house again.

While Mama repacked all the boxes that Mr. Ward had inspected yesterday afternoon, Ivy hosed the dirt from the front of the house and the porch.

They replanted the irises, raked the garden flat, and salvaged some of the seedlings from the clay pots in the shed.

Ivy's last gesture before Kenny Yamamoto came home was to hang a small flag with a red border and a white field on the boarded-up front window—one with a blue star.

The next morning, the kitchen filled with the smell of beef roasting in the oven and soup simmering on the stove.

Before Papa left for the bus station, he stood in the kitchen, put his hands on his hips, and said, "Luz, the entire Army of the United States of America could not eat all of this food."

Mama waved him off. "If Fernando was coming home and we were not here, I would want the mother of another soldier to cook for him."

"But Kenneth Yamamoto is only sharing one meal with us," said Papa, shaking his head.

She looked at Papa. "I will send him off with extra . . . for his trip. I have used many of our ration coupons, though."

Papa winked at Ivy and pointed to the cake on the counter. "It is good for us, yes?"

Ivy grinned and nodded.

When Kenny arrived in his khaki uniform, he placed his officer's cap on a table by the door.

His head was shaved and it made his ears look much too big for his head. He spoke quietly and politely, calling Papa "sir" and Mama "ma'am." He was far more serious than Ivy had expected, seeming much older than Fernando even though there were only two years between them.

At first, Ivy felt shy around him, but she found herself scooting her chair closer to his, listening to everything he said. He told about his time in Hawaii and how he had been reassigned to another ship.

"My brother said he is going over soon. In the belly of a big plane, but we don't know where," said Ivy.

"Can you keep a secret?"

Ivy smiled and nodded. "I love secrets . . . sometimes."

"'Going over' usually means the European Theater," said Kenny. "So he'll probably be in Italy or France or Germany. I'll be stationed in the same area, but on a ship."

As they lingered around the kitchen table, he and Papa did most of the talking. At first, the conversation was about the recent events on the farm, how Ivy had discovered the music room, and what had happened with Mr. Ward. Then it became about the war, where it was heading and how long it might last.

Serious talk. But when Papa got up to get more coffee and Mama was clearing dishes, Kenny reached over and pulled Ivy's braid, exactly as Fernando used to do. She didn't complain as she might have if it had been Fernando. Instead, she giggled.

After lunch, Kenny said, "I'd like to go see my house now. Want to cut through the grove with me, Ivy? Your father told me that you have big plans. You can show me."

Papa looked at his watch. "I will pull the truck over to the house and meet you and Ivy there in a half hour. Then I'm afraid it will already be time to take you back to the bus station."

Mama smiled. "I will make some sandwiches with the leftovers."

Kenny stood and put on his hat. "Good-bye, Mrs. Lopez. Thank you, for everything. I hope I will meet Fernando someday soon."

Mama became teary-eyed and opened her arms to hug him.

Kenny looked surprised, but he hugged her back.

Outside, as they walked through the orange grove, Kenny took a deep breath. "It's funny what you miss when you're away from home. I miss the smell of the orange trees, my mother's cooking, and my little sisters arguing over whose turn it is to be first for anything. And I miss wearing civilian clothes, like your jacket. Is that your brother's?"

"Fernando gave it to me until he comes home . . . so I would remember he is keeping me safe and warm, even from far away."

Kenny smiled. "I'm glad our families have decided to survive this war together, Ivy. I think we're more alike than different. Your father told me you signed up for orchestra. Did you know I was in the orchestra, too? And my sisters? They play flute. Mr. Daniels was our teacher. I played—"

"The violin!" said Ivy. "I know. I saw a picture in your house."

"Do you like Mr. Daniels?"

"He's my favorite teacher," said Ivy. "I like how he talks. He told us we have to play *majestically*."

Kenny laughed. "That sounds like Mr. Daniels."

Kenny was easy to talk to, and before she knew it, Ivy found herself telling him about the first day of orchestra and how the boys had laughed at her because she was from Lincoln Annex and how Mr. Daniels had put a stop to it. She told him about playing "When Johnny Comes Marching Home," how she hoped to play the flute, and wished she could go to Lincoln Main. "Some of the parents are asking why the school district is paying for a music teacher during a war. But Mr. Daniels says everyone needs a little beauty and light in their lives, especially during the worst of times."

Kenny nodded. "Mr. Daniels is right. Can you play the harmonica for me? I know you have it with you." He winked. "Your father told me you carry it everywhere and play beautifully."

Papa had said that? She blushed and pulled the harmonica from her pocket, but then hesitated.

Kenny prodded and teased her, like Fernando would have. "Just one song. Please? I don't want to have to pull your braids again." When he reached out and threatened, she laughed. Kenny didn't seem so grown-up now. He just seemed like someone's big brother.

Ivy played "Auld Lang Syne" and let herself fill up on the wondrous tone of her harmonica. Here within the trees, it seemed as though time stood still. She closed her eyes, riding the notes until she was inside the song.

She saw Kenny and Donald and Tom in the wagon, making a fort with crates, playing hide-and-seek and catch. And Susan taking piano lessons with Mrs. Yamamoto. Her mind drifted back to playing jacks with Araceli, jumping rope a hundred times double Dutch without missing, and seeing her in the doorway, wearing the purple hat and blowing kisses.

She trilled the last note, making it sound like a piccolo. When she opened her eyes, Kenny was nodding his approval. Ivy could tell by the far-away look in his eyes that he had remembered things, too.

"You have promise, Ivy. When I come home again, you will have learned the flute. Practice so I can come to a concert one day and sit in the audience while you perform onstage."

She smiled, warmed by his words. He made her feel like things were possible, just as Miss Delgado and Mr. Daniels had. She hoped that someday it would be true, that she'd be onstage in front of him. And that he'd be proud of her. Even though he was somebody else's brother, he felt like he belonged to her at least for this afternoon.

They came through the last row of trees to the Yamamotos' backyard. Ivy showed Kenny the shed and the seedlings and the war garden, and she told him her plans for the orange-and-vegetable stand. "Oranges for war bonds."

"I like that," he said.

When Kenny saw the flag with the blue star hanging on the boards over the front door, where Papa stood waiting, Ivy saw his lip quiver. He strode over to Papa and clasped his hand and said, "I thank you for everything. And my father thanks you."

They signed the papers, which would bind their families forever, right on the hood of the truck.

On the way to the bus station, they drove by Lincoln Main. Papa told him all about his efforts so Ivy could go there.

"Sir, I hope the lawyer can do some good," said Kenny.

"He is optimistic. There was a case near San Diego in 1931, *Roberto Alvarez v. the Lemon Grove School District*, with the same circumstances. The parents organized and they won, but only in a lower court. The lawyer says he can use this to plead the case. And the more parents who come forward to tell their children's stories, the better it will be for all children who follow. I am going to tell Ivy's story."

Kenny Yamamoto nodded. "That is good, sir. Everyone needs to fight for someone, on the battlefield or at home."

Papa pulled up to the bus terminal and turned off the motor.

Kenny turned to Papa. "Mr. Lopez, sir, I've been thinking about what I might send to my family that could be of some comfort to them in the internment camp, something that won't be too difficult to bring back home with them someday. Would you mind packaging and sending my sisters' flutes? They're in that music room you discovered and have their names on them."

"Of course," said Papa.

He looked at Ivy and winked. "Everyone needs a little beauty and light, especially during the worst of times, right?"

She smiled. "What about you?"

He shook his head. "I can't very well carry a violin on the battlefield."

Ivy pulled the harmonica from her pocket and turned it in her hands. Running her fingers over the shiny cover plate, with its beautiful engravings and the mysterious letter $\mathcal{M}$, she was overcome with a feeling of wanting to help Kenny. Impulsively, before he could climb down from the cab, Ivy grabbed his hand, pressed the harmonica into it, and closed his fingers around it.

He looked at it and then at her. "Are you sure?"

Ivy nodded.

"I promise I'll bring it back to you someday." Kenny slipped it into the chest pocket of his uniform, climbed down from the cab, and closed the truck door. Then he stepped forward, so he could see Ivy and Papa through the windshield, and saluted.

Ivy saluted back and whispered, "I know."

21

"I'm finished. What about you?" called Ivy.

Susan's head popped up from where she was working on a sign for Mrs. Yamamoto's stand.

All morning they had weeded around it, swept out spiderwebs, and each painted a piece of plywood to lean against either side of the stand so cars might see their message coming from either direction.

Since Papa signed the agreement with Kenny Yamamoto six weeks ago, a huge wave of relief seemed to have washed over all of them. Mama and Papa still clung to the belief that the war would end soon. Fernando's letters had been arriving in batches. They might not hear from him for two weeks, but then they would get four letters in one mail delivery, all filled with questions and excitement about the new home. Ivy received one letter from Araceli. She and her family were moving to another state. Ivy had written her back, but hadn't received another letter in return. Somehow, she knew she might not ever hear from Araceli again. Even so, if they were lucky enough to meet once more, Ivy knew they'd pick up where they'd left off, as best friends.

Orchestra had started in earnest and Mr. Daniels's prediction had come true. Ivy had fallen in love with the flute. He called Ivy his star pupil and said the only student who had ever come close to her ability was Karen Yamamoto. Ivy couldn't wait to meet her someday.

Ivy ran around to see Susan's sign. "It's perfect."

Coming soon
Oranges for War Bonds!
10 cents a bag or one war stamp
God Bless America!

"When do you think we can start selling?" asked Susan.

"Papa said the oranges are ready by the first of March. So next week! Later we'll do vegetables. I'm glad your dad said you can help."

"He said anything for the war effort that will bring our boys home sooner. He's even going to give us some of the vegetables from our garden. Zucchini for War Bonds!" said Susan.

"Green Beans for War Bonds!" giggled Ivy.

"Asparagus for . . ."

The boy on the bicycle rode past them, his white shirtsleeves rolled up, his blue pants tied at the ankles with string, as usual. He wore the same blue cap with an emblem and carried the same pouch slung across his chest.

Ivy waved, but he was pedaling quickly and didn't respond. "He never waves back," she complained to Susan.

But Susan didn't answer. And the color had drained from her face.

"Susan, what is it?"

"The boy . . ." Susan looked as if she might faint.

Ivy pulled her to the bench and sat down next to her.

"You know who he is?"

"Ivy, *everyone* knows who he is."

Susan's eyes were big pools of green. She looked down the road. "Did he turn at the crossroad? Or go straight?"

"Straight, I think. Why does it matter?" asked Ivy.

"Remember I told you how we found out that Donald was killed?"

"Yes. A telegram, right?"

Susan nodded. "It was brought to our house by a Western Union messenger . . . that boy on the bicycle." Susan's hands began to tremble. "Which way was he riding? Did he turn toward my house?"

"No," Ivy said. "He turned toward mine."

She shivered and grabbed Fernando's jacket from where she'd tossed it. Her head filled with a loud buzzing. Were there bees nearby? And then she heard music. "The Battle Hymn of the Republic."

Mine eyes have seen the glory
of the coming of the Lord;

Ivy stood. At first she walked up the Yamamotos' drive and then ran. She cut through the grove and wove around trees, oranges thudding to the ground as she knocked into them. Her feet and heart pounded. She could hear Susan behind her. "Ivy! Ivy!"

He is trampling out the vintage
where the grapes of wrath are stored;

Ivy ran so fast she felt dizzy. Still the music played on. When she reached the edge of the grove, she had to stop and bend over to catch her breath. She grabbed her side.

He hath loosed the fateful lightning
of His terrible swift sword:

Susan came up behind her and put an arm around Ivy's waist.

They took a few steps forward together, past the last of the trees, until Ivy's house came into view.

The bicycle leaned against the porch, and the boy stood at their door.

His truth is marching on.

FOUR

APRIL 1951

NEW YORK CITY, NEW YORK

U.S.A.

Some Enchanted Evening

music by Richard Rodgers
lyrics by Oscar Hammerstein II

7   -7   -8   7 7   -5

Some en-chant-ed eve-ning

7 -7   -8 7   7   8

You may see a stran-ger.

7   -7 -8 7   7   -9

You may see a stran-ger

-9 -9 -9 -8   -6   6

A-cross a crowd-ed room,

6   -6   7 -6   6

And some-how you know

6   -6   7 -6 -5

You know e-ven then

-8   8   -9   9   -9 8

That some-where you'll see him

-8   7 -6 6 -6

a-gain and a-gain.

I

On an evening embroidered with the thread of destiny, in a theater crowned with a halo of light, Friedrich Schmidt escorted Father and Uncle Gunter to the best-in-the-house seats.

Friedrich's eyes swept to the tiered boxes, dress circle, and upper balconies, their facades intricately carved with laurels and painted gold. He'd been told the concert was sold out, but he still couldn't imagine every seat filled with concertgoers. "You two don't mind waiting?"

In awe, Father waved his arm in an arc. "We will sit here and admire all this majesty."

"We *wanted* to be early," said Uncle Gunter. "To see the evening unfold, beginning to end. It is quite an honor to be seated by the conductor himself. It is a long road you have traveled, Friedrich."

"*We* have traveled, Uncle. *Together.* After all, who taught me to ride a bicycle and play the harmonica?"

Uncle Gunter laughed and winked. "I did. You're a sweet boy to remember."

"And who was my first and most accomplished teacher?" He squeezed Father's shoulder.

Father smiled at him. "Thank you, son."

Uncle Gunter tugged at his collar where the silk tie he wore was knotted. His suit was a far cry from their factory overalls. "You know I only wear a tie for a few occasions, but your concerts are always worth the trouble."

In recent years, Father and Uncle Gunter had attended many concerts where he had conducted, but tonight was a pinnacle debut. Friedrich perched on the arm of Father's seat, as impressed as they were with this moment and the miraculous journey that had taken them from Trossingen to Berne and ultimately here, to Carnegie Hall in New York City to conduct the Empire Philharmonic.

Tchaikovsky had conducted his own compositions on the hall's first opening night. *The* Tchaikovsky. Friedrich could hardly believe he'd stand on the same stage.

As if feeling his thoughts, Father said, "They

say that all the musicians who have performed here have left a wisp of their spirits behind."

Friedrich nodded. People talked about the undeniable energy in the building. How could he harness it? "Do you think Tchaikovsky was as nervous as I am?"

Father shook a finger at him. "Of course. And I would say the same thing to him. 'You have as much right to be on that stage as the next conductor. Just put one foot in front of the other. And look up!'"

Friedrich patted Father's shoulder and smiled. "I'll remember."

Onstage, the musicians' chairs sat empty in several large semicircles, waiting. A concert grand piano guarded the left of the stage.

Father put a hand on Friedrich's. "It is difficult to believe we are here. It seems like yesterday we were in Trossingen. I only wish . . ."

"I know, Father," whispered Friedrich. "I miss her, too."

Friedrich knew Father still held out hope that

he would one day see Elisabeth again. He'd never stopped writing to her so she wouldn't forget the sound of his voice. Not during the war when she had remained a devoted nurse, even caring for soldiers in a prisoner-of-war camp. Or in the years following, when she worked in a pediatric hospital in eastern Berlin.

Friedrich wrote, too, especially when the opportunity to move to America was arranged. He had begged her to join him and Father and Uncle Gunter for a chance at a new life in a new country. She refused, saying she'd found her true calling. Still, Friedrich couldn't help but continue to hope that he—like his brave imaginary friend Hansel—could one day lead his sister home to their father. And that someday they'd all be together once more.

Friedrich often wondered what might have happened to them if Elisabeth hadn't sent the Reichsmarks for Father's ransom. Father was right. It didn't feel like eighteen years had passed since that fateful day on the train heading to Dachau.

★   ★   ★

The engine had already started to chuff.

Friedrich had heard the music to Tchaikovsky's *Sleeping Beauty* waltz and pretended to conduct, infuriating the two officers, Eiffel and Faber. As they tried to march him off the train, calling Friedrich a lunatic and promising to lock him away, the whistle blew, long and insistent.

The train lurched forward and began to move. Eiffel and Faber shoved him aside, scrambled to the door, and leaped to the platform as the train tick-tick-ticked over the rails, leaving them far behind.

Uncle Gunter had been right about the holidays. More people were traveling. The trains were crowded. Everyone held packages and seemed more preoccupied with the season than with a self-conscious boy gripping his father's future on his way to Dachau.

After the commandant listened to Friedrich's appeal and examined the box of cookies, he accepted the package and sent for Father.

Friedrich tried not to look alarmed when he saw him. In a little over a month, Father had gone from energetic and strong to weak and frail. He dragged one leg. He seemed disoriented.

Friedrich helped him from the camp, walking and resting every few minutes until they reached the first farm, where Friedrich borrowed a goat cart and pulled Father to Munich to the home of Uncle Gunter's friend, the doctor.

It took weeks for Father to recuperate enough to begin their journey to Switzerland. Father refused to talk about what had happened to him at the camp, insisting that it was nothing compared to what was done to others, and becoming tearful and adamant that *he* was one of the fortunate. After a while, Friedrich stopped asking.

Uncle Gunter was waiting for them in Berne. He and Friedrich took jobs in a Swiss chocolate factory. Father gave cello lessons. Eventually, Friedrich applied to the Berne conservatory.

One path led to another.

It was strange how on such an auspicious occasion as tonight, in one of the most famous venues in the world, Friedrich's thoughts kept wandering back to his beginnings. He looked down at his father and uncle, who by some miracle were at his side, safe and healthy. And instead of the concert before him, Friedrich flashed back to his happiest childhood memories of Friday night get-togethers in the parlor with Elisabeth at the piano, Uncle Gunter on his accordion, Father on cello, and Friedrich on harmonica, their polkas accompanied by the occasional rally from the cuckoo clock in the hall.

Musicians began to appear on the grand stage.

Dressed in black, they took their chairs, adjusted their music stands, and opened the scores. The wind instruments ran the scale to warm the pipes. The violins mewled and purred.

Friedrich stood. "I should go." He smiled at Father and Uncle Gunter and headed toward the side stage door. Before he opened it, he glanced back at the house. Father and Uncle Gunter looked small amid the field of red velvet seats. Father sat straight and tall, studying his program. Friedrich could feel his pride even from a distance.

The ushers opened the lobby doors and people began to filter inside.

Friedrich fled backstage, stepping up to the wing and leaning against the wall. He closed his eyes and concentrated on the concert, A Portrait of Stage and Film. He smiled. Musicals and movies were such an American fondness and, he admitted, he liked them, too.

He replayed the program in his mind: the first half dedicated to George and Ira Gershwin, starting with *Porgy and Bess: A Symphonic Picture*, orchestration by Robert Russell Bennett, with the main songs from the opera. Friedrich loved the orchestral, classical composition. It would be followed by *Rhapsody in Blue* with a featured piano soloist. After intermission, he would conduct the *South Pacific* suite, music and lyrics by Rodgers and Hammerstein. It was the most popular musical in the city right now, and a coveted ticket on Broadway. The baritone, Robert Merrill, would perform selected songs from the musical, closing with "Some Enchanted Evening." There were rumors that the composer and librettist, Richard Rodgers and Oscar Hammerstein, friends of Robert Merrill, would be in the audience.

Friedrich closed his eyes, and his hands went through the motions of conducting the first overture. For a moment, he stopped and looked around before starting again, his memories so deeply set that he couldn't help but remember the school bench where he'd once been bullied for conducting an imaginary orchestra. But here, everyone was focused on becoming one voice. They all spoke the same language and had found their way to this night with their own stories of determination and practice and their love for music. Here he was safe.

The stage manager nodded to Friedrich. The musicians were in position.

The concertmaster stood and lifted his violin, playing the A. Onstage, the violins hummed in response. The cellos and basses moaned softly. Chords filled the room as the musicians checked the tuning of their instruments. The oboe sounded and the wind instruments matched it.

Friedrich searched out the new flutist. She'd seemed nervous in rehearsals, so he'd taken time to talk with her. She was one of the youngest players he'd ever encountered in a symphony orchestra, but supremely talented. There was something intense and purposeful about how she played, a feeling he couldn't quite pinpoint but, at the same time, understood. Her eagerness to embrace the music and surrender to it reminded him, somehow, of himself.

Bit by bit, the sounds dwindled. The hall hushed.

When the house lights dimmed, a smattering of clapping erupted.

The stage manager pointed at Friedrich.

Although he'd long come to terms with the birthmark on his face, and even refused the heavy stage makeup that some managers offered him, Friedrich still hesitated for a few seconds in the wing, wanting and dreading the walk onstage. Every performance in front of an audience was always a journey fraught with the unknown. He whispered the good-luck phrase he always said before he headed to the conductor's podium, the same words he'd whispered to his harmonica that day that he'd polished it and sent it out into the world. *"Gute Reise."* Safe travels.

He strode onstage and was met by a wave of applause.

Friedrich picked up his baton and raised his arms, poised to give a slight flick of the wrist to the percussionists.

Four long chimes, like stepping-stones to another world, rang out. Friedrich slipped into the opera's story, the music filling him with the emotion of Porgy's plight, much of it resonating in his own heart: a lonely man with a crippled body; a bully who thought he could rule the world; an ever-present evil; the loss of a loved one to something beyond his control; and what seemed an insurmountable challenge.

Friedrich moved the orchestra into the tender song "Summertime," and anticipated the rising emotion in the music. He imagined the lyrics . . . *hush . . . little baby, don't . . . you cry . . .*

The music was bigger than Friedrich, overpoweringly beautiful, euphoric, and true. He was swept inside it. The orchestra was *with* him and he with them.

This was what he had craved as a young boy when he imagined himself on the top rung of the A-frame ladder on the factory floor, two stories high, and directing an imaginary symphony—a magnificent sound from a union of many, a story that came alive through the playing.

He brought the orchestra to a crescendo and a final emphatic finish.

When the music stopped, Friedrich held his breath and waited.

There was always a moment after the last sounds and before the ovation—an elegant pause—that Friedrich cherished. It was a pure space filled with one question: Had the audience listened with its heart?

2

As the taxi pulled up to the corner of Fifty-Seventh Street and Seventh Avenue in New York City, Mike Flannery rushed from the lobby of the theater where he'd been waiting and pacing in his tuxedo.

The back door opened and Frankie jumped out, running to Mike and hugging him. "Look at you! Carnegie Hall! Just like we said. Are the balconies all gold and the seats all red?"

Mike laughed and patted Frankie on the back. "It's as if you're standing inside an ornate golden egg. And yes, the seats are just like Granny said they'd be." He held Frankie at arm's length, admiring his suit. "You don't look so bad yourself. Your first year of law school is agreeing with you."

"Top of the class, so far," he said, standing taller. "Guess what. We're going to eat roasted beef and ice cream after. For old times' sake. Or . . . for new times' sake. *Someone* made reservations at the Russian Tea Room." Frankie nodded toward the taxi, grinning.

Mr. Howard helped Aunt Eunie from the backseat. She looked elegant in her long black dress and gray fox stole.

"*I* made the reservations," she said, pulling Mike into a hug.

"Thank you, Auntie," said Mike, kissing her on the cheek. It had become his endearment for her, and she insisted it suited her far better than the much too formal Aunt Eunie.

"Mr. and Mrs. Potter send you their best," she said.

"How are they?" asked Mike.

"Happy as clams in Atlantic City with their daughter and grandchildren. As much as I miss them, retirement is agreeing with them."

After Mr. Howard paid for the taxi, he embraced Mike, too. "We're so proud of you, Mike. How have the rehearsals gone?"

"They've gone well, I think. I like the conductor, Friedrich Schmidt, very much. By the way, he is looking for a lawyer to help him finalize some paperwork for his father and uncle. I overheard him talking in the green room and I recommended your firm. He's interested in speaking with you. I can introduce you backstage after the concert."

"It will be my pleasure. And I'll offer him assistance pro bono."

Frankie leaned in. "That means without charge for the public good."

Mike rolled his eyes. "I know." He looked at Mr. Howard. "Is he becoming insufferable?"

"Only on occasion." He put his arms around Mike and Frankie, pulling them close. "Oh, it's so good to have all of us together again!"

Mike led them inside and handed them off to an usher. "I have to go now." He winked at Auntie. "I'm looking forward to the roasted beef and ice cream."

"And cake!" she said, smiling.

He kissed her cheek again. "Auntie, I'd never be here without you."

She straightened the lapel of his jacket. "We

helped each other, didn't we? But I think I received the best part of our arrangement. Two fine boys."

Mike blinked back tears. Granny had known it in her soul. The right person had found them.

Frankie leaned toward Mike and held out an upright fist. "You and me, we stick together."

Mike did the same, tapping Frankie's. "That's right, kid, you and me . . ."

In his dressing room, Mike waited for his call.

It was funny how Frankie's words could rekindle his childhood memories: Granny telling them all about Carnegie Hall, the cellar at Bishop's, and the night he and Frankie tried to run away.

It turned out that all those years ago, he'd been wrong about Auntie. She *had* wanted them.

Mike had been mistaken about the papers he'd seen on her desk. The appeal for the reversal of their adoptions had been approved and the papers sent to her. But they wouldn't become legal unless she signed them, which she never intended to do. When Mike had confronted her that day in the library, his love for Frankie had shined a light on her heart. She ceremoniously burned the papers in the fireplace the day after Mike's fall from the tree, when by some grace, nothing more than the wind was knocked out of him.

Mike, Frankie, Mr. and Mrs. Potter, Auntie and Mr. Howard—they never called him anything other than Mr. Howard, even after he and Auntie married—moved to his house on the corner. The best, not the worst, had happened to him and Frankie.

Mike was invited to join Hoxie's band and he did, for one year. Mr. Potter had been overjoyed and continued to be his coach. Then, as the piano consumed Mike's interest and time, he began to think about leaving the band. One day, a representative from the Women's Auxiliary gave an impassioned plea for old instruments that could be sent to poor children who might otherwise never have a chance at music.

Mike felt strangely compelled, as if he *should* pass his harmonica along, as if someone were waiting for it. So he gave it up, sending it on a journey to another child who needed the world to seem brighter with more possibilities, and wanted to testify to feelings in his or her heart, just as Mike had.

By the time Frankie was old enough to join, the famous Philadelphia Harmonica Band of Wizards had dissolved due to lack of funds. Frankie didn't mind because by then he hoped to be a cowboy and was saving Ralston-Purina cereal box tops for a series of Tom Mix comic books.

After high school, Mike was admitted to Juilliard School of Music in New York City. Before he could enter, the U.S. government lowered the draft age to eighteen. America was at war and Mike entered the U.S. Army. After his tour of duty, he finally went to Juilliard and then auditioned for the Philadelphia Philharmonic. A few years later, he moved to New York City, the place he always dreamed he would belong.

There was a knock on the private dressing room door. A voice from the other side said, "Mr. Flannery. Five minutes, sir."

"Thank you!" called Mike, taking a deep breath.

He headed toward the stage, catching the eye of the stage manager, who waved him over to the wing.

"About three minutes until your solo."

Mike heard the last lines of the *Porgy and Bess* suite. And the thunderous applause that followed.

Friedrich Schmidt walked off the stage to the wing, where Mike stood waiting. "Ready?" he asked, smiling.

Mike nodded. "Ready."

Friedrich waited until the orchestra had regrouped and turned the pages of their music before walking back onstage.

Mike followed and sat at the piano.

Friedrich raised his baton.

Mike heard the clarinet glissando that opened *Rhapsody in Blue*. He waited for the horns and strings and the rest of the orchestra to fan out around him. He stretched his fingers and held them over the keys as he had once done in Granny's parlor, and in the music room on Amaryllis Drive, feeling the all-too-familiar attraction to play and perform.

He waited for the crescendo, and began.

While he played, he thought about how Gershwin had composed much of the piece on a train, with the rattling and jiggling and clacking over the rails. Gershwin heard music in the midst of noise, and saw the piece as an array of all that was American: a composition of people of every color, rich and poor, quiet and loud, a mishmash of humanity.

Mike played it as if he were in Granny's neighborhood, with girls playing hopscotch and boys playing pimple ball and cars and trucks honking and mothers hollering out their windows for their children. At the tender interval before the finale, he heard his mother humming, and saw Granny throwing open the window so the entire neighborhood could hear the beauty of his playing.

The music sauntered through Central Park, strolled through boroughs, tiptoed across bridges, waltzed in ballrooms . . . ran.

The Big Apple. His city. The place he'd always wanted to be. The place Granny had loved and always wanted to take him. Was he really here on this stage?

He pounded out the rhythms of sledgehammers and the staccato riveters as the city grew upward, scraping the sky. He followed the music, but his heart was following his journey to this very spot in time: from Allentown to Philly to Bishop's and his and Frankie's promises to stick together. From Bishop's to Amaryllis Drive and learning to hope for the best and that no matter how much sadness there is in life, there are equal amounts of maybe-things'll-get-better-someday-soon. From Hoxie's Philadelphia Harmonica Band to the U.S. Army to Juilliard to this piano bench in Carnegie Hall where, for one moment, with any luck, the audience's heart and the world would stand still.

The conductor wrapped the orchestra around him. And together, they brought the audience to their feet.

Mike slid from the piano bench, took a breath, and bowed, as the applause embraced him.

Above all the cheers, he heard Frankie calling out, "Bravo! Bravo!"

3

Backstage, during intermission in the green room, Ivy looked in the mirror and smiled at herself with relief. She had made it through the first half of her concert debut with this orchestra. If only Fernando could have been here to walk her to the theater like the many times he had walked her to her first day of school, she might not have been so nervous.

Beforehand, she'd straightened her dress a dozen times, and worried so much about her hair that she'd finally pulled it back, straight and sleek, and tied it with a black ribbon at the nape of her neck so it wouldn't interfere with her playing. Even though she was only a fourth chair flutist, she was still the youngest member of the symphony orchestra. Everyone had been kind and supportive, and the conductor himself had taken her under his wing.

She wished Mama and Papa could be here tonight. With the travel time by train, though, it was too long for Papa to leave the farm. And Fernando needed Mama right now. They all sent Ivy flowers and their love.

As much as Papa had come around to appreciating Ivy's gift for the flute, it had still taken Fernando to convince him to let Ivy pursue a career in music. Papa couldn't figure out how Ivy might support herself. But Fernando had persisted. He said it was a great honor to have a musician in the family. He said that when Ivy played, it made people happy and helped them forget their troubles for a short time. He told Papa that without music, it would be a sad world. And he would have given anything to hear something as beautiful as an orchestra playing when he lay on the battlefield, not knowing whether he would live or die or ever see his family again.

All those years ago, the boy on the bicycle stood at their door and delivered a telegram. Fernando had been wounded in action while rescuing a fellow soldier in a minefield, and lost two fingers in the explosions. He was discharged from the army with honors for his bravery.

He came home to Orange County to put down roots and married Irma Alapisco, the third-grade teacher at Lincoln Annex, which, in 1945, due to the hard work and perseverance of parents, had been combined into one school with Lincoln Main. Fernando and Irma were due to have their first baby any day. Ivy smiled thinking about her family and friends in Orange County and the different paths all of their lives had taken.

She had come to the Empire Philharmonic in New York on an exchange program with the Los Angeles Philharmonic. Her best friend, Susan Ward, had become a legal secretary. Tom, Susan's brother, had been the only one of the boys from the three families to come through the war without injury, and now managed his father's farms. The Yamamotos came home and resumed their lives, tending to their farm with the same loving care they had before the war.

Over time, Karen and Annie also became Ivy's best friends. And, thankfully, Kenny had survived the war, too . . . just barely.

He was on furlough now, before his next tour of duty in South Korea, and was in the audience tonight. All those years ago, she had promised him a concert someday. Neither of them could have imagined it would be here, in New York City, at Carnegie Hall.

Before intermission, Ivy had been too nervous to search the audience for him. But now, as she walked back onstage and settled in her chair, she let her eyes scan the house before the lights went down. Kenny was easy to spot in his blue dress uniform. He was studying his program, then glanced up, caught her eye, and grinned.

She blushed and her heart swelled when she thought of all the things he had done for her and her family: deeding Papa the land and house after the war, finding her a master flute teacher, helping Fernando find a job as an electrician.

She picked up her new flute, a recent gift from Kenny. She had argued it was too grand a gift.

But he'd insisted it was long overdue. First, because he'd promised that day at the train station to someday return the harmonica to her and never did. He now kept it, and his Purple Heart, in the box with his father's World War I war medals. And second, because she'd saved his life. That wasn't *exactly* true. But she supposed if she'd never given him the harmonica, he might not be alive today.

Everyone said it was a miracle. Some called it an act of God. Others said the stars had aligned in his favor and it just wasn't his time to die. Even those who thought it was nothing more than a lucky coincidence were impressed and wanted to shake Kenny's hand so that some of his good fortune would rub off on them.

By now, Ivy had heard the story so many times, she could recite it. Oddly, she never tired of hearing the mysterious tale.

Since the day she had put it into his hand, Ivy's harmonica had become Kenny's own personal good-luck charm. He carried it in his left chest pocket, much in the way other soldiers carried a rabbit's foot or a religious medal. It was as much a part of his uniform as the dog tags he was required to wear around his neck.

Kenny had been on a routine patrol in a heavily wooded area when his unit was ambushed. The zipping and zinging of bullets rang in his ears. He felt the sting in his leg and blood trickling down into his boot. But it was his chest he gripped before he collapsed to the ground. He looked up into the pines above him. The world went white. And then black.

He woke in an old warehouse, converted to a German prisoner-of-war camp, in the hospital wing, his leg worse than he imagined. Three young women fussed over him as he drifted in and out of delirium. His fever soared and they mopped his brow. During moments of lucidity, he watched them straighten his sheets and sit at his side, leaning toward him, expectant. And he heard them whispering, "Live. You must live."

As he languished, they read him stories from an ancient book. Stories about castles and banished babies, a witch, an exceptional boy, orphans, and a girl running through an orange grove. In his darkest hour, when it looked as if he might die, they sang to him.

Their voices were beautiful and otherworldly, and they filled him with joy and determination. Their songs seemed to plead with him to carry on, as if they were begging for their own lives, as well as for his.

One night he took a turn for the better. His fever broke and he woke hungry. Moonlight streamed through the open yet barred window next to his bed, spilling slats of light on the floor. He smiled at the three women, who had never left his side. They smiled in return, nodded in unison, and held hands. But before he could utter a word, they swirled from the room, into the night, disappearing into another time and place.

In the morning, he asked his German nurse, Elisabeth, about the three women. He'd like to tell them thank you. Where had they gone? Had they been volunteers? Would they be back?

She insisted he'd had no visitors. She told him the medicine he'd been taking could cause hallucinations. Soldiers saw all sorts of strange things in the hospital. Hadn't he mentioned a mother and two sisters back home? Perhaps he had been dreaming of them. She patted his hand and said it had all been in his mind. She encouraged him to talk about his real family in the United States.

He found himself telling her how he used to play the violin, about his sisters who played the flute, and the story of the room behind the closet where his father had hidden three pianos and dozens of other musical instruments.

Elisabeth told him that her father had once played cello with the Berlin Philharmonic and that her little brother was an accomplished musician—the finest she'd ever heard—who would have auditioned for the conservatory in Germany had circumstances been different. Kenny had smiled. He thought it sweet that she was so proud of her brother.

During his stay in the hospital wing, Kenny became a celebrity. Prisoners, mostly French and American, and even the German guards, came to his bedside and asked to see the talisman that had saved his life.

Kenny always obliged, taking it from his pocket. He cradled it in the palm of his hand and held it out for all to see.

No matter how many times he showed it, he was still amazed by the miracle of the mangled harmonica that had trapped the deadly bullet meant for his heart.

Ivy adjusted the pages of her music. Although she had enjoyed the *Porgy and Bess* suite and *Rhapsody in Blue*, it was the Rodgers and Hammerstein *South Pacific* music she had waited for all night. She'd already seen the musical twice. Once, when she'd first moved to New York City a year ago, and last night, with Kenny.

The conductor, Friedrich Schmidt, walked onstage, followed by the pianist, Michael Flannery, who would join the orchestra for the second half with a solo in the finale. Next came the baritone from the Metropolitan Opera, Robert Merrill, also in black tuxedo and tails, who bowed and took a seat near the conductor. The audience applauded with anticipation.

The sweeping *South Pacific* overture began. Ivy felt the story speak to her all over again, taking her on its journey. It was a brave production, about discrimination and injustice—a woman in love with a man who had mixed-race children and her struggle to accept them; a soldier in love with a beautiful Tonkinese woman and his conflict over what his family back home might think if he were to marry her. It was a story framed by intolerance and war, themes all too familiar to her.

The overture was followed by Robert Merrill singing "My Girl Back Home," "Younger Than Springtime," "You've Got to Be Carefully Taught," and "This Nearly Was Mine." After each song, the audience was jubilant. An undeniable energy was building in the hall.

Friedrich Schmidt raised his baton again. Robert Merrill stood poised to sing. On the downbeat, Michael Flannery began a piano prelude, his own piano solo arrangement of "Some Enchanted Evening." At first, he played slowly like a lullaby, then louder like a storm, until the end of the verse when he made it calm again.

The conductor cued the orchestra.

Robert Merrill began to sing "Some Enchanted Evening."

Ivy breathed into her flute and surrendered to the song, its tender, heartrending proclamation of love bringing tears to her eyes.

Some enchanted evening
When you find your true love,
When you feel her call you
Across a crowded room,
Then fly to her side,
And make her your own
Or all through your life you
May dream all alone.

Ivy felt as if she'd been touched by magic. Her eyes caught the glances of other musicians. And it was clear they felt it, too.

Who can explain it?
Who can tell you why?
Fools give you reasons,
Wise men never try.
Some enchanted evening . . .

Tonight, there was a brilliance in the hall, a communion of spirits, as if Ivy and the conductor and the pianist and the orchestra and everyone in the audience were one, breathing in and out to the same tempo, feeling one another's strength and vision, filling with beauty and light, glowing beneath the same stars . . .

. . . and connected by the same silken thread.

TEN YEARS AFTER HE WAS LOST IN A DARK forest and found in a pear orchard, Otto married Mathilde. After all, she had always believed in him.

It took many years, but finally they had a baby named Annaliese, who was born crippled. When it became clear she would never walk without difficulty, the local doctor recommended that Otto and Mathilde confine her in an asylum with other unfortunates. But they could not bear the idea! They tried every potion and poultice, and sought out one doctor after another. Soon, Otto was in debt.

He was forced to sell their small cottage in the country and move his family into an apartment in the village. He took a job as a tuner in a shop where musical instruments were made. Over the years, he had somehow acquired the ability to detect perfect pitch, and customers began to ask for only him. Soon, his employer became jealous of his talent and notoriety and dismissed Otto from the shop. With no job, a sick daughter, and a wife who deserved better, Otto became despondent, often wandering the streets of the village before dawn, worrying.

One morning, he saw a notice in a shop window. The great harmonica factory in Trossingen was seeking craftsmen who could produce high-quality mouth harps. Makers could submit a sample for consideration on a given day. Could this be his chance? Was he even capable? He had to try.

Otto worked day and night at the kitchen table making a model: sanding the pear-wood comb, stamping the reed plate, and meticulously tuning the instrument to match the sound of the harmonica he so loved—the one that Eins, Zwei, and Drei had baptized with their breath all those years ago.

A week later, he wrapped the instrument in a tea towel, put it in his pocket, and left by horse and wagon for the factory town. When he arrived, men from all over the region had already lined up with their harmonicas. Otto felt his stomach sink. How would he be judged against so many able craftsmen?

The owner of the harmonica factory was particular. And Otto watched with dismay as most of the instruments were refused and the makers turned away. More than once, he noticed men blotting tears because their work had not measured up to the owner's standards. He prepared his heart for disappointment.

But when the owner examined and played Otto's harmonica, not only was he astounded by the quality and the tone, he placed a special order. "I need thirteen, one for each of the managers of my departments so they, too, might hear and appreciate this excellence. If you can deliver all of them within the month, and your harmonicas are as superior as I've seen and heard today, I would like to set up a shop for you in your village."

Otto was overjoyed! He would be able to honor his debts. He might buy back his cottage. But most of all, he and Mathilde would be able to care for their precious Annaliese. Otto rode home, happy and determined.

The evening before Otto was to deliver the order, he sat at the kitchen table, assembling the last of the instruments. The house was quiet and the hour was late. His wife had retired long ago. His beautiful daughter slept on a cot next to him. The dog snored at his feet. After he polished the cover plate, he sank into an exhausted sleep, slumping over his work space and knocking the instrument to the floor.

In the morning, he was preparing for his departure when he realized he could not find the thirteenth harmonica. He called to his wife for help.

Together, they searched the house. Minutes later, she stood before him, holding a chewed and ruined instrument. "The dog . . ."

Otto was seized with desperation. "I *must* deliver thirteen. There is no time to make another." He paced and fretted until his eyes landed on the harmonica Eins, Zwei, and Drei had once played, the one against which he measured the look and sound of all others. Could he part with it?

He picked it up and turned it in his hand. He imagined the three sisters within the tree circle, opening the book each time the sun rose to see if more of their story had been written. At that moment, as if echoing Otto's memory, the sun rose outside his window. The harmonica glimmered in his hand. Morning church bells pealed. Was it all a sign?

Otto looked at his wife, who now held his daughter.

Annaliese wriggled from her mother's arms and limped toward him. "Papa, can you play me a song, please?"

Otto's heart swelled with love for his family and gratitude for the promising future that spread before him.

He played the harmonica one last time, hearing birdsong, a brook trickling over smooth stones, and the yodel of the wind through hollow logs. He thought about the others in front of him, the people he would never meet, who needed the harmonica, and the one whose life must someday be saved.

He imagined Eins, Zwei, and Drei's reunion with their mother and brother somewhere in time. And he knew that what they'd once told him was true. The three sisters, Otto, and all the players who would one day breathe in and out of this unusual instrument were joined by the silken thread of destiny.

It was time to pass the mouth harp to another.

With a tiny brush, he tilted the harmonica and drew a small red *M* on one side of the pear wood.

M for messenger.

AT THE PRECARIOUS INSTANT WHEN *Kenny Yamamoto lived instead of died, the witch's spell broke and doubt was eclipsed by enchantment once more.*

The three sisters found themselves with the midwife at the tumbledown cottage deep in the forest, where everything from table to teacup had reappeared. Except for the witch, who was never seen again.

With the midwife leading the way, the three sisters fled the dark forest, like the little birds that so easily took wing, each in turn carrying the book that had finally been written, The Thirteenth Harmonica of Otto Messenger.

Forever after, Arabella, Roswitha, and Wilhelminia

lived in a safe and cozy castle with their family, who loved them and called them by name.

When their happiness overflowed, as it often did, they sang, their voices blending so magically that people in the kingdom often stopped to listen and marvel at their gifts.

And every night as they lay in their beds, wondering what joy tomorrow might bring, yet knowing how precarious life can be, they repeated the words:

"YOUR FATE IS NOT YET SEALED.

EVEN IN THE DARKEST NIGHT, A STAR WILL SHINE,

A BELL WILL CHIME, A PATH WILL BE REVEALED."

*A*CKNOWLEDGMENTS

With deepest gratitude to the following people:

First and always, my editor, Tracy Mack, the unquestionable star who shined on this book's path; Emellia Zamani and Kait Feldmann, who assisted; copyeditor Monique Vescia; and art director Marijka Kostiw. And to the rest of my extended publishing family at Scholastic for their professional expertise and personal friendship: Ellie Berger, Lori Benton, Jazan Higgins, Lizette Serrano, Rachel Coun, Tracy van Straaten, Charisse Meloto, Antonio Gonzalez, Krista Kucheman, Emily Heddleson, Rachael Hicks, Karyn Browne, Janelle DeLuise, Caite Panzer, Alan Smagler and Annette Hughes (and their stellar sales team), Alan Boyko and Judy Newman (and their amazing school market teams, especially Robin Hoffman and Jana Haussmann), and Scholastic president Dick Robinson.

Helen Ofield, president of the Lemon Grove Historical Society, who first showed me photographs of an elementary school harmonica band.

Robert Alvarez, Jr., professor of ethnic studies at University of California, San Diego, and John Valdez, professor of multicultural studies at Palomar College, for sharing their families' stories surrounding Mexican American school segregation in California in the 1930s, especially the court case *Roberto Alvarez v. the Board of Trustees of the Lemon Grove School District.*

The Hohner harmonica company and the historian of the German Harmonica and Accordion Museum in Trossingen for the tour of the factory and continued assistance with my research of the history and craft of harmonica making. It was there in a glass case that I discovered the letters from thankful family members of soldiers whose lives were once saved by Hohner harmonicas, and the mutilated instruments, some with bullets still embedded, that had protected them.

Russell Holland for his generous hospitality and support on my trip to Germany.

Michael Bowman for sharing his consummate research on Albert N. Hoxie and the Philadelphia Harmonica Band.

Calvin College, Grand Rapids, Michigan, and the German Propaganda Archive.

The musicians and early readers: Sally Husch Dean, Artistic Director, San Diego North Coast Singers; Ann Chase, soprano; David Chase, conductor, La Jolla Symphony and Chorus.

David Serlin, professor of communication at University of California, San Diego, for his thoughtful review and attention to the historical details in the manuscript.

John R. Whiteman, collector, for his expertise about the Marine Band harmonica and the gift of two pre–World War II instruments, each with the six-pointed star.

My agent, Kendra Marcus, at BookStop Literary Agency.

And, as ever, my family, for their patience and love.

TO MY SONS-IN-LAW,
JASON RETZLAFF AND CAMERON ABEL,
FOR LOVING THEM

Text copyright © 2015 by Pam Muñoz Ryan
Illustrations copyright © 2015 by Dinara Mirtalipova

"Some Enchanted Evening" by Richard Rodgers and Oscar Hammerstein II Copyright © 1949 by Williamson Music (ASCAP), an Imagem Company, owner of publication and allied rights throughout the World Copyright Renewed. International Copyright Secured. All Rights Reserved. Used by Permission.

All rights reserved. Published by Scholastic Press, an imprint of Scholastic Inc., *Publishers since 1920.* SCHOLASTIC, SCHOLASTIC PRESS, and associated logos are trademarks and/or registered trademarks of Scholastic Inc.

No part of this publication may be reproduced, stored in a retrieval system, or transmitted in any form or by any means, electronic, mechanical, photocopying, recording, or otherwise, without written permission of the publisher. For information regarding permission, write to Scholastic Inc., Attention: Permissions Department, 557 Broadway, New York, NY 10012.

LIBRARY OF CONGRESS CATALOGING-IN-PUBLICATION DATA
Ryan, Pam Muñoz, author. ★ Echo / by Pam Muñoz Ryan.—First edition. pages cm
★ Summary: Lost in the forest, Otto meets three mysterious sisters and finds himself entwined in a prophecy, a promise, and a harmonica—and decades later three children, Friedrich in Germany, Mike in Pennsylvania, and Ivy in California find themselves caught up in the same thread of destiny in the darkest days of the twentieth century, struggling to keep their families intact, and tied together by the music of the same harmonica. ★ ISBN 978-0-439-87402-1 ★ 1. Harmonica—Juvenile fiction. 2. Music—Juvenile fiction. 3. Fate and fatalism—Juvenile fiction. 4. Families—Juvenile fiction. 5. Germany—History—1933-1945—Juvenile fiction. 6. Pennsylvania—History—20th century—Juvenile fiction. 7. California—History—20th century—Juvenile fiction. [1. Harmonica—Fiction. 2. Music—Fiction. 3. Fate and fatalism—Fiction. 4. Family life—Fiction. 5. Germany—History—1933-1945—Fiction. 6. Pennsylvania—History—20th century—Fiction. 7. California—History—20th century—Fiction.] I. Title. ★ PZ7.R9553Ec 2015 813.54—dc23 2014021482 ★ 10 9 8 7 6 5 4 3 2 1 15 16 17 18 19
Printed in the U.S.A. 23 ★ First edition, March 2015

The text of this

book was set in 12 point Hoefler.

Named after Jonathan Hoefler (1970 – present),

this typeface was designed for Apple Computer, Inc.,

in 1991 to demonstrate advanced type technologies.

Hoefler is a contemporary serif Antiqua font, but draws

from a range of classic fonts, such as Garamond and Janson.

The hand-lettered jacket title, jacket art, and decorative

elements were painted with gouache and digitally

retouched by Dinara Mirtalipova.

The book was printed and bound by RR Donnelley.

It was designed by Marijka Kostiw, and

manufacturing was supervised

by Francine O'Bum.

OKANAGAN REGIONAL LIBRARY
3 3132 03742 4076